Kate Welsh is an author, critic and journalist. Her work has appeared in everything from the *Times Literary Supplement* to *Cosmopolitan* and she covers LGBT issues for the *Daily Telegraph*. Her short fiction, featuring roller derby, Greek myths and ghosts, has been published in several anthologies and she guest lectures on Creative Writing at universities around the UK.

She lives in Edinburgh with her wife, three cats and a lot of books.

Praise for *The Wages of Sin*:

'An enthrallingly gothic murder mystery' *The Herald*

'This powerful novel combines a disturbing look at late Victorian attitudes towards women and morality with a satisfying murder mystery' *Sunday Express*

'A gripping story, a great central character and full of riotous, beautifully drawn period detail' Kate Hamer

'Edinburgh is the superb gothic setting for this nail-biting debut' *Fabulous* Magazine

'A gripping story of murder, medicine and misogyny in Victorian Britain' *Emerald Street*

'A tremendous debut' *Daily Record*

'The first book in what will, one hopes, be a long-running series, featuring a new kind of historical leading lady, Welsh's debut is an inspiring feminist tale perfect for the modern age' *Library Journal*, Debut of the Month

KAITE WELSH

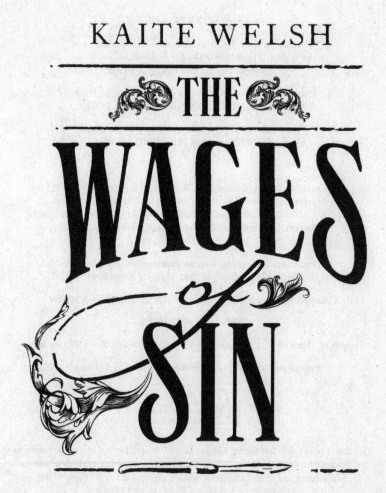

THE
WAGES
of
SIN

TINDER
PRESS

First published in Great Britain in 2017 by Tinder Press
An imprint of HEADLINE PUBLISHING GROUP

First published in paperback in 2018 by Tinder Press
An imprint of HEADLINE PUBLISHING GROUP

1

Cataloguing in Publication Data is available from the British Library

ISBN 978 1 4722 3982 2

Typeset in Aldine 401 BT by Avon DataSet Ltd, Bidford-on-Avon, Warwickshire

Printed and bound in Great Britain by Clays Ltd, St Ives plc

Headline's policy is to use papers that are natural, renewable and recyclable products
and made from wood grown in well-managed forests and other controlled sources.
The logging and manufacturing processes are expected to conform to the
environmental regulations of the country of origin.

HEADLINE PUBLISHING GROUP
An Hachette UK Company
Carmelite House
50 Victoria Embankment
London EC4Y 0DZ

www.tinderpress.co.uk
www.headline.co.uk
www.hachette.co.uk

Dedicated to the memory of my mother, Helen Welsh.
Everything that follows is because of you.

Chapter 1

The corpse on the table smelt rancid, and I pressed my handkerchief to my mouth. The scent of rose water mingled with embalming fluid as I tried not to gag – if I vomited, there was no hope for me. I had been waiting for this for so long; I could not lose my nerve now.

My specimen was a sorry spectacle and doubtless had been so even before he died, with his scrofulous neck, broken veins, and legs that bore all the hallmarks of rickets. He was thirty-five but looked older, and it was a miracle he had survived this long. It seemed cruel that he was to suffer this further indignity, and crueller still that I was happy to benefit from it. The smell hadn't been pleasant when he had been rolled in from the cool air of the university mortuary, and in the stifling atmosphere of the cramped room that doubled as a lecture theatre, he stank to high heaven. His eyes were sewn shut, his eyeballs no doubt in a jar of formaldehyde somewhere in the building awaiting dissection away from their former owner, and his head was poorly shaved so that only androgynous patches of dark hair covered it. He was naked to the waist, with a sheet of dubious cleanliness covering his lower extremities for the sake of those of us who lacked his gentlemanly attributes.

Professor Williamson looked flushed and hot, clearly resenting the room full of ladies in front of whom modesty forbade him from removing his tie, loosening his collar and allowing himself to cool down a little. I lacked even that option, encased in my whalebone corset, copious layers of underlinen turned damp with sweat, my hair heavy in its knot at the nape of my neck. I knew that when we were finished, we would be exposed once again to the freezing November air and the constant rain that characterised a Scottish winter – or any other season in this blasted country for that matter. I longed for the temperate climate of the university library, or even the blustery winds of the crags above the city. I could hardly think in this stuffy, overcrowded room.

As I stood there, trying not to inhale, I heard the sound of slow handclaps behind me, and my chest tightened. I gripped the table, my nails sinking into the wood, willing myself not to tremble.

'Are you unwell, Miss Gilchrist?' Professor Williamson's unflinching gaze bore into me, and I shook my head weakly. I could not help noticing that he had done nothing to silence the mocking applause. 'Good. The operating theatre is no place for ladies. If you must abandon both your upbringing and God's plan for you, kindly do the same with your delicate maidenly sensibilities. Once you walk through these doors, you are a doctor – nothing else. Understand?'

'Yes, sir,' I managed, feeling my face redden in embarrassment. Someone giggled suspiciously close to where Julia Latymer was sitting.

'In your own time, Miss Gilchrist,' Professor Williamson said behind me coldly, his tone implying that if I didn't pick up the knife right now, he would, and it might not be the corpse in front of us that he'd be dissecting. I pulled off my gloves, crumpling up the damp fabric and looking for somewhere to stow them. William McVeigh, the monosyllabic assistant-cum-porter, deliberately avoided my eye, looking faintly disgusted at the prospect of touching a lady's personal items, and the professor sighed audibly, tapping his foot. I swallowed my dignity and tossed my gloves onto the front bench, wiping my palms on my skirt.

I felt a dozen pairs of eyes on me as I picked up the knife and, willing my hand not to shake, made the first cut – a strong, neat incision down the abdomen, deep enough that the skin and muscle could be retracted to expose the peritoneal membrane. I sliced through the tough, fibrous tissue and fumbled around with sweating, shaky hands for the retractors on the tray next to me. I paused as McVeigh took up his place opposite me. His demeanour was sullen, and though he smirked as he caught my gaze, even that didn't reach his eyes. I placed the two flat blades of the cold metal instrument against the sides of the incision and cleared my throat awkwardly.

'Mr McVeigh, could you please pull on the retractors?'

He gave a mumbled 'aye', and took hold of the handles, taking especial care for his clammy hands to linger over mine. Shuddering, I turned my attention to the contents of the abdomen. I described to Professor Williamson what I saw, starting with the liver, the enlarged organ the colour of burnt sienna courtesy of a decade of cirrhosis.

After I had described everything immediately visible, I reached into the cavity to scoop out the intestines. The soft, ropy viscera were wickedly slippery. I bit my lip to stop myself from swearing. Everyone knew that O'Neill had cursed up a blue storm in one of the men's lectures the previous week and received nothing but laughter and scattered applause in response, but I had little doubt that one oath would be all it took for the professor to ban me from his operating rooms.

'Try both hands, Miss Gilchrist. They are rather on the small side, after all. Suitable for sewing, perhaps, but not much use for surgery.' Bastard. I heard him chuckle, and plunged both my hands into the cavity with renewed vigour. My fingers slithered, trying to find purchase on the slick twists of flesh, until finally they closed around my prize. I ran the guts through my fingers like strands of pearls, feeling for any abnormalities. Sure enough, the intestines were studded with small pouches, and I ran my thumb over one, feeling the soft protrusions give beneath it.

'There's considerable evidence of diverticula,' I told him, fascinated by the yards of slimy grey tube. 'But there's no sign of inflammation. Would you like me to continue?' My pulse was racing again, but my earlier anxiety was forgotten. This, I thought, up to my elbows in human viscera, was what I had abandoned my mother's plans of marriage, motherhood and good social standing for. Not that, in the end, I had been given a great deal of choice.

Professor Williamson waved me away. 'No, no. You've proven that you're perfectly adequate. It's time to close the poor bugg— ah, the poor gentleman up. Miss Latymer, if you will?'

Dismissed, I looked around for my abandoned gloves. They were gone, but Edith Menzies' pockets were bulging suspiciously, and she smirked at me as I returned to my seat. My glow of triumph dimmed as Julia swept past me, clearly furious to be left with the easy task. I ignored her, mentally calculating how much of my saved allowance I would have to dip into in order to replace my gloves without Aunt Emily noticing. I took my place in the cramped row of seats next to one of the stone-faced chaperones, an elderly former teacher at a local school who appeared unfazed by the mass of human innards on the table in front of her. It wasn't even a real lecture theatre, I thought bitterly, merely one of the smaller rooms normally given over to the faculty for their private use. Our number meant that we were all too frequently shuffled out of sight if the proper lecture halls were required by the 'real' medical students – in other words, the gentlemen. Whilst the first-year students numbered well over a hundred, only a dozen of us were female. A dozen too many, if our critics were to be believed.

If you were to ask the man on the proverbial Clapham omnibus what a female medical student looked like, he would probably describe a greying spinster with her bespectacled face buried in a textbook – that being the closest thing to the male anatomy she was likely to get – and the kind of dried, desiccated look about her that could only have been brought on by a bout of intensive education. The truth was, not one of us was over thirty, and there wasn't a wart or a moustache between us. If you had seen us taking tea, you would have assumed we were serious-minded but perfectly normal young ladies – New Women, perhaps, of the kind that had sprung up in the past decade, who fancied themselves equal to men in terms of intellect, but nothing that a good dose of marriage and motherhood wouldn't cure.

We were but two months into our studies, and whilst we had adjusted to the long hours, bad smells and frigid rooms, the rest of the university had yet to accept us. From Buccleuch Street to the South Bridge, 'undergraduettes' had infiltrated the higher echelons of learning in every department of one of Scotland's most elite establishments, much to the horror of their male fellows, but none were regarded with such disdain or suspicion as the immoral witches bent on a career in medicine.

The sudden influx of women into such a male institution had thrown up a whole set of problems for the faculty, not least that of propriety. The prospect of young, unmarried women being allowed to mingle with young, unmarried men was horrifying, and to prevent undesirable assignations, most universities employed chaperones to keep an eye on us. They were older women, God-fearing enough to be considered respectable, but sympathetic enough to our cause that they could be trusted not to order us home with every breath to our fathers, brothers and husbands. The women were silent, following us from room to room and sitting primly in the back row so they could keep their beady eyes on us. Some were silent from disapproval, some from an unwillingness to address those of us they deemed their betters. They were not the stern schoolmistresses of our childhood, nor the relatives sent to escort us at balls; neither they nor we knew how we should interact with them. Their job was simple and, for once, unvarnished. They were there to protect our virginity. Our reputations might have been irrevocably damaged, our innocence stripped away, but these widows and spinsters and suffragists could still safeguard that one remaining barrier, that tiny scrap of forbidding flesh that separated us from the wretched creatures that haunted the city's slums. We were ladies in theory, at least. Of course, if there was one thing we were all learning in these hallowed halls, it was that theory and reality could differ wildly.

Concluding the lecture, Professor Williamson twitched the sheet back across the waist of the dead man with a prudishness I doubted he displayed in front of the male students. He treated corpses the way our grandmothers had treated the legs of their pianofortes, covering all but the essential parts to avoid embarrassment, seeing spectres of sex everywhere, and painfully unaware that by doing so, they were calling attention to what they so doggedly concealed.

Williamson was a popular lecturer, and when he pronounced

the session over, he was met with the whoops and foot-stamping that marked the end of every class the students enjoyed. Even though his attitude towards us was repressive at best, the women applauded him with a gusto that would have been unthinkable in our previous existences. Bred to be decorous and reserved, we hollered like the rowdiest of men, encouraged rather than intimidated by his black scowl. We withdrew from the makeshift lecture hall as though from a dinner party, leaving Professor Williamson and his assistant to their embalmed body instead of port and cigars.

I trailed behind the others to join the throng of jostling students all heading home for the weekend. What began as a demure single file that would have put a governess and her charges to shame soon turned to a surge of bodies, all eager for a few days of relative freedom. Convention dictated that the male students let us out first, but as we had defied convention in entering these hallowed halls of learning, so they defied it by obstructing our exit.

I steeled myself to follow the others into the corridor, shrinking inwardly from the pressure of close to a hundred students – mostly male – shoving and laughing as they forced their way to the fresh air and space outside. Pressing in against us, their clammy hands pushed and nudged, taking liberties they would never have been granted elsewhere. Our chaperones finally intervened by means of pointedly cleared throats, and in one case a well-placed jab from a walking stick. Granting us safe passage through the throng – a feat the paternalistic Professor Williamson had not even thought of attempting – they marched ahead like generals and we followed in their wake, humbled at the display of a nerve we only feigned.

By the time I stumbled out into the open courtyard, I was dizzy and trembling. I breathed in deeply, less bothered by the sting of formaldehyde than by the smoke and sweat of the men. The peculiarly male odours were yet another reminder of how out of place we were, how outnumbered and at their mercy. I would not be one of those fragile flowers who had to resort to smelling salts at the slightest hint of impropriety. If I showed even a moment of weakness, our detractors would have won. I stood to the side, gulping in lungfuls of icy autumn air, whilst the others talked lazily about a supper party they were attending that evening.

Alison Thornhill glanced over at me, a half-question forming on her lips. A look from Julia quelled any overture of friendship she would have offered.

'Oh leave her, Alison,' Julia snapped. 'I'm sure she has gentlemen to flirt with.'

I felt my cheeks flame, and kept my gaze averted so that she wouldn't see how much her words stung.

Like me, Julia Latymer was from London, although being among the only Englishwomen in a group of Scots hardly endeared me to her. We had never moved in the same circles – the Latymers were far too liberal for my parents' liking – but I knew her well enough to nod a greeting at public lectures and women's suffrage meetings. We had enough acquaintances in common that by the time I had quit London and my old life, she believed she knew my character intimately – and did not like it one bit.

It didn't help that my uncle's profession was a source of considerable disgust. Julia and some of our cohort had signed the pledge abstaining from all forms of liquor, and the only spirits they came into contact with were preserving body parts. It was no secret that she and the rest of her wretched Temperance League thought that I lived a life of alcoholic decadence when I came home from lectures, despite the fact that no one but the servants would even consider drinking the ale my uncle's company brewed.

Buchanan Breweries was omnipresent in the city, from the brewer's drays that delivered casks to almost every public house in Edinburgh, to the very air itself. Although the smell was considerably less foul than when I had arrived in the middle of August, the fug of fermenting hops hung over the city year-round, and I had come to associate it inextricably with Uncle Hugh. At home, he was a shadowy presence confined to his study or his club, but in the city, his influence was everywhere. Even in the courtyard of the medical school, where I would eventually win my independence, I was not free of him.

As if summoned by my thoughts, the carriage drew up nearby. The driver was late – I knew my uncle believed I could not be trusted to spend a moment unchaperoned. If he could have ordered Calhoun to drive me from the lecture halls to the library he would have done so, and any tardiness on my part was invariably reported back.

Calhoun offered nothing by way of a greeting as I settled against the soft green leather of the seat and arranged a blanket over myself to ward off the November chill. He had clearly decided at the beginning of term that discretion was the better part of valour where the subject of my education was concerned, and as for my nightly activities – well, I doubted that he could have phrased his objections in a manner suited to the ears of a lady. Then again, if the servants gossiped as much as I suspected they did, he would have realised long ago that his employer's niece was no lady.

Despite the driver's dour countenance and gimlet eyes that missed nothing, I wasn't sad to leave Julia's mockery, or the reminder of yet another gathering to which I would not be invited. Let them have their cocoa and petty gossip. I had a much more interesting evening planned.

I gazed out of the window into the dying light, watching as

the genteel environs of the university were quickly replaced by
the shabbier tenements of the slums that crowded the city.
Centuries ago, entire wynds had been bricked off, inhabitants
still within, in an effort to contain the plague that had
ravaged the city. The intervening years had done little to
improve life for the remaining communities, and even those
who had survived the cholera epidemic of a decade ago no
doubt wished they had not.

At Greyfriars Kirk, we began the steep descent leading us
into poverty that, until a few months ago, I had never seen
outside a penny dreadful. As the horses made their tentative
way over cobblestones slick with remnants of sewage and late-
afternoon rain, I glanced out of my window at the rapidly
disappearing sky and shivered. Although I could not see it,
several feet above us lay the graveyard where my predecessors,
the Williams Burke and Hare, had dug up bodies by candlelight
and sold them to the university for a tidy profit – until they
grew greedy and hit upon a bloody scheme for providing
much fresher corpses. The proximity made my skin crawl,
and for once I was thankful as the carriage swung into the
Cowgate, plunging us into darkness.

Chapter 2

The gas lamps that had begun to illuminate the streets above were nowhere to be seen, the only light spilling out from the windows in dirty yellow puddles. The whole place stank of refuse, urine and the beer my uncle's brewery so kindly supplied to the local publicans. I heard Calhoun curse under his breath as he forced the carriage through the dark, narrow passage, past drunkards and doxies too intoxicated to notice our vehicle or simply beyond caring.

The building we drew up outside was indistinguishable from the rest save that it was marginally cleaner. The same sorry individuals congregated outside, loitering without any obvious intention of entering. Every so often, a woman pushed through the rowdy, ragged band, ignoring their jeers and catcalls or adding some of her own. Gathering my courage, I opened the carriage door and raised my skirts as far as modesty allowed, stepping into the filthy street below. To my silent relief, although they eyed me suspiciously, and one muttered something indistinguishable but probably obscene, they let me pass unchallenged. The subtle insignia on the carriage doors might have had something to do with that – they wouldn't think twice about abusing those members of the 'quality' who

ventured into their territory intent on philanthropy, but risking
the flow of ale to their local haunts warned them off.

Unlike its dingy, malodorous surroundings, the interior of
St Giles' Infirmary for Women and Children was both well lit
and clean to the point of reeking with carbolic. The waiting
room, however, was filled with the same unfortunates as the
streets outside – children in torn, dirty scraps of fabric that
passed as clothing, and women whose discoloured skin bulged
out at unnatural angles around the chin and mouth. *Phosphorus
necrosis* was one of the most common ailments the doctors
treated here – or at least attempted to. These women were all
employed at the match factories, where the white phosphorus
with which they worked corroded their jaws and left painful
open abscesses from which stinking pus escaped. Those
who showed no sign of phossy jaw were either accompanied
by listless children with whooping cough or rickets, or were
marked out for a very different profession by the cheap,
gaudy fabric of their dresses, beneath which disease invariably
lurked.

The clinic occupied a cramped, labyrinthine building that
had once housed an abattoir. It seemed to teeter permanently
on the edge of bankruptcy, for whilst there were countless
philanthropists and ladies bountiful eager to help Edinburgh's
unfortunates, they were less willing to help the women who
ran it. Prostitutes, it seemed, could be reformed; women
who had taken a medical degree were beyond help. It was
sustained primarily through the indefatigable energies of
Fiona Leadbetter, the clinic's founder and administrator, who
had somehow inveigled her way into a philanthropic dinner
and caught the eye of my uncle, a wealthy gentleman who
required some charitable work for a niece with an interest in
medicine he hoped to extinguish.

My role involved little more than holding surgical

instruments, winding bandages and assisting with basic routine examinations under Dr Leadbetter's stern but approving gaze, but I soaked up whatever knowledge I could. Fiona was the closest thing I had to an ally in this unwelcoming city, and whilst I was loath to trespass on her kindness more than I had to, the knowledge that I was not considered *persona non grata* everywhere reassured me.

With her dark hair neatly pinned back and a lively gaze that belied the fact that she had been on her feet for the best part of ten hours, Fiona exuded a cheerful authority. Heavy circles beneath her bright eyes suggested the toll the work took on her, but although her colleagues spoke in hushed tones of periodic bouts of depression, I had never seen her defeated.

'There you are, Sarah! Here, take these and go to the small examining room.' Rummaging in her pockets, she handed me a roll of bandages and pushed me towards the flimsy partition that offered the patients a modicum of privacy.

The patient, though docile at present, had clearly resisted treatment if the overturned tray of instruments and shattered glass on the floor was anything to go by. And from the reek of her breath, I suspected that gin rather than subservience was the cause of her present calmness. The wound on her leg was ugly, a few weeks old, and would probably turn septic even with medical attention. Next to her lay a bundle of filthy, pus-stained rags that had probably worsened the infection rather than helped it heal.

She eyed me warily. 'Wha's she daein'?' she slurred. 'I'll no' have a glaikit bitch like her pokin' away at me.'

'I've just come to replace your dirty bandages with clean ones,' I told her soothingly, hoping that my apprehension didn't show. She attempted a disdainful sniff, which turned into a heave, and I moved back hastily. The nurse, who had been trying to disinfect a fresh cut on the woman's cheek, was less fortunate. Both patient and nurse were hauled off to the sluice, leaving me to clean up.

As I knelt to scrub the last of the human effulgence from the floor, I mused that these were not quite the good works my relatives had had in mind when they informed me of their expectations regarding my conduct under their roof. Still, even my aunt had to admit that it was in many ways an ideal occupation. Thanks to the clinic's strict regulations, I would not come into contact with any member of the opposite sex over the age of ten who was not a clergyman, and the grim realities of the medical profession were doubtless enough to send me rushing for the smelling salts and vowing never to wield a scalpel again. Most importantly of all, I would be faced with constant reminders of my fate should I stray from the path of righteousness they had laid out for me.

A noise jolted me out of my reverie. Such a reminder was standing before me, the tracks of tears long since dried outlined in the powder on her face.

'One of Ruby McAllister's,' Fiona said in a low voice as she ushered the girl in. The whorehouse was one of a handful that entrusted the care of their wretched workforce into our care. I had been surprised, in my early days at the infirmary, to realise how many brothel-owners preferred their girls to be seen by male doctors. Fiona had explained, with an angry grimace, that those doctors were often happy to exchange their services for those of their patients. Most of the unfortunates who darkened our doors plied their trade in the streets and were grateful for whatever help they could get, but the few coins with which they could recompense us made barely a dent in the infirmary's mounting expenses. Ruby McAllister was one of the few abbesses to permit her girls to see us.

Had I been aware that my first and only meeting with Lucy took place only hours before she died, I might have softened the blow. As it was, I was tired and bad-tempered, my petticoats stiff with dried blood and my stomach reminding me loudly that I hadn't eaten anything since a slice of burnt toast at luncheon. A few months ago, I would have been shocked. A year ago, I would have been appalled. But she wasn't the first drab I'd seen all day, and doubtless she wouldn't be the last to cross the infirmary threshold tonight.

She certainly wasn't the first to be diagnosed with an unwanted pregnancy.

'My monthly's late,' she informed me starkly before shedding her gaudy, threadbare cape. From her dress – a vivid green garment that bore a passing resemblance to silk if one squinted – and the red hair that didn't match her over-plucked dark eyebrows, I knew that asking whether she had had intimate relations with a man was redundant, so I merely indicated the examination table and requested she remove her bloomers whilst we waited for Dr Leadbetter to wash her hands. Hitching up her skirt, she lay staring at the ceiling, and I wondered how many times she had adopted that pose. Probably more than she could count, assuming she could count at all.

She didn't flinch when Fiona began her examination, and something in me stirred at her lack of innocence. She couldn't have been more than twenty under the thick layers of powder and paint, and I knew women decades older who would die before allowing a man to touch anything other than their hand. Propriety was just one more luxury that she could not afford.

'You can sit up now,' I said softly, moving to the sink to wash the instruments with boiling water and a sliver of carbolic soap. I squinted dispiritedly at my reflection in the tiny looking glass. I had slept little the previous night, and it showed in the bruised blue shadows beneath my eyes.

I turned back to see her eyeing the two-day-old newspaper we kept to soak up whatever bodily fluids our patients spilt, and with a jolt of surprise I realised that she was reading it. The print was small, small enough that studying it by candlelight tended to give me a headache, but her keen eyes devoured each line. Some of the working girls could read, but few of them with the ease and curiosity of this one. Literacy was the key to a better life than one spent on an infested mattress whilst a stranger wheezed and grunted on top of them.

'Would you like to take it?' I asked, still as nervous of the clinic's patients as I was of my professors. Her eyes lit up for the briefest of seconds, but then her face hardened, and she snorted contemptuously.

'What am I gonnae do? Read whilst some poor bugger is going at it?' I shrugged helplessly – she had a point.

'I'm afraid you won't have time for reading in a few months, Miss Collins,' Fiona informed her crisply. 'I'd say your baby was due next May.'

I was used, by now, to the salty language of our patients. Still, Lucy's response to the news made even my eyes widen. Dr Leadbetter reminded her sternly that blasphemy was a sin, but I was secretly impressed by the originality of her cursing.

'You'll help me though, aye?' Her eyes widened, and suddenly she looked like the child she was, begging for a way out of an impossible situation. 'You wouldnae leave me in this condition?'

'You know I can't do that,' Fiona warned. She should have told her it was murder, a wicked thing to even be considering, but I doubted that committing one more sin would imperil Lucy's immortal soul any further.

'I cannae afford a bairn, miss! I can barely afford to feed myself most days. And who's going to want to shag a knocked-up tart?'

Tears pricked at the corners of her eyes, and her voice thickened with emotion. It was an impossible situation, but there was nothing I could do. Besides, abortionists were ten a penny in an area as heavily populated with brothels as the Cowgate. If she really wanted to rid herself of the unwanted burden, she'd find a way.

'Lucy,' Fiona explained firmly, 'you're asking me to perform an illegal operation. I can't risk my job – my life – by helping you. I wish I could, really. But there must be someone you can turn to for assistance. A family member, perhaps?'

'My brother helps me out sometimes.' Lucy sniffled into a grubby handkerchief. 'But he'll kill me for this, I swear he will.'

'It's only for a few months,' I said. 'And there's no reason that you can't . . . work for most of them. Then perhaps an orphanage – I could get you an address if you—'

'Bitch,' she hissed, a fleck of spittle hitting my cheek. 'Sanctimonious English cow. Just because no man would ever touch you if you paid him, never mind the other way around, you think you can pass judgement on me?'

If I flinched, Fiona took no notice.

'Miss Gilchrist is not the one sitting in judgement,' Fiona pointed out coldly. 'Nor is she the one carrying a child. I suggest you go home and reconsider your decision – not to mention your occupation.'

'If you won't help me, there's plenty of others who will,' snarled the girl, yanking on her drawers. 'I dinnae care if it kills me to do it, I'm no' getting stuck with a bairn.'

She flounced down the corridor, head held high as though that would disguise the tears that streaked her rouge.

'Wait here,' Fiona instructed. 'She can't go wandering the streets hysterical, not in her condition. Silly, silly girl.'

Anger flared white hot in my belly. Lucy wasn't a silly

girl; she was a desperate woman making a living the only way she could, and I was in no position to judge her. But I let Fiona go, and before the door slammed shut behind her I was already lost in memories, with little care for anyone's troubles but my own.

Chapter 3

After the foul, dank air of the Cowgate, it was a relief to be back in the warmth of my aunt's house. I wondered if I would ever come to think of it as home, or if that word would be forever associated in my mind with the rambling building in Kensington where it had been made painfully clear I was no longer welcome. Regardless of what I called it, the house had acquired a comforting sense of familiarity in the months since my arrival, and I was looking forward to a few hours' peace and quiet in my room before succumbing to sleep.

I needed a bath before letting anyone stand downwind of me – my cape reeked of cigar smoke, gin and cheap perfume, and I had a horrid suspicion that my hair was the same. If my aunt found me smelling like a dockside whore, I doubted I would be allowed to visit the clinic – or anywhere else – ever again.

I closed the front door as quietly as possible, hoping to sneak upstairs before Aunt Emily registered my arrival. Unluckily for me, the woman had the ears of a bat. The drawing room door creaked open and she stood there with that omnipresent frown on her face. I pulled my cloak a little tighter around me in an effort to disguise the state of my clothes and my conspicuously absent gloves, and breathed a sigh of relief that I had at least fixed my hair in the carriage.

'You missed dinner. You'll have to prevail on Cook's good graces if you want something to eat.' She glared at me. 'You know how I feel about punctuality, Sarah.'

'I came as soon as I could, Aunt Emily. My work at the infirmary detained me unexpectedly.' Telling her I had just come from dealing with a prostitute in a delicate condition wasn't likely to endear me to her, but I was ready to spin a tale of unfortunate but virtuous patients whose poverty and ill-health were matched only by their devout faith. Luckily she accepted my explanation, and waved me upstairs.

'Make yourself decent and I'll have a word with Cook about supper.' She sniffed the air, and shuddered. 'And ask Agnes to run you a bath. You smell of . . . well, I don't even know.'

I smelt of the vomit a fourteen-year-old prostitute had deposited on my boots after the cabbie who had knocked her down dragged her into our waiting room before making himself scarce. Had he waited, he would have realised that the fault wasn't his. The girl reeked of cheap gin, and it was mere coincidence that it took a hansom cab to knock her over – a stiff breeze would have done the job equally well. Judging it safest not to enlighten Aunt Emily, I headed to my room and rang the bell for Agnes as I stripped off my soiled, stinking clothing.

Not for the first time, I wondered what on earth had possessed me to study medicine. Life as the spouse of some titled gentleman might be dull, but at least it would be clean. I forced the fantasy out of my head – that might have been the world I grew up in, but I could no longer call it home. My mother had been very clear on that matter. Kicking off my boots with a viciousness they didn't deserve, I was glad when the arrival of Agnes offered me respite from my dark musings.

'A hot bath please, Agnes.' I offered her a conspiratorial smile that she failed to return. I'd be lucky if I got stale bread and a pitcher of water. For all I was niece to the lady of the house, the servants had no more respect for me than my aunt did. I was here on sufferance only, and they knew that perfectly well. The silent housemaid – I was beginning to suspect she was mute, since I hadn't heard a peep out of her in the few months I had been living under my aunt and uncle's roof – gave the briefest of nods and quitted the room, leaving me to rifle through my wardrobe in search of a half-decent gown to make me look something approaching the lady I was supposed to be. I sighed in relief when Agnes reappeared with the between-stairs maid, carrying the hot water for my bath. Once alone, I sank into it, warming my chilled body and easing away the cares of the day.

Cleaner – and considerably less malodorous – I took my place by the fire, overjoyed to see that supper was a generous plate of toasted crumpets with a small dish of honey. Aunt Emily disliked my clothes, my morals and most certainly my choice of profession, but even she wouldn't see her own sister's child starve. But as with all my aunt's gifts, this one came with a price.

Settling into her customary chair by the window – all the better to hear any scandal that might take place on the street outside – she picked something up from the table. Wonderful. Reading to me after dinner had become one of her favourite pastimes. Occasionally Biblical, but more usually a tract out of one of her blasted conduct books, there was always a dreary message aimed explicitly at me regarding repentance and submission. When I first arrived, she read Coventry Patmore's *The Angel in the House* in its entirety. It took weeks. Tonight, though, my luck had really run out. The latest edition of *Cornhill* magazine – always addressed to my uncle, despite the fact that he preferred hunting to high culture – contained, to Aunt Emily's delight, a scathing profile on the New Woman. There was nothing to do but smile demurely down at the sampler I was embroidering. The stitches were tiny and perfect; the one ladylike accomplishment I had managed to acquire in my twenty-seven years, and one that would stand me in good stead as a surgeon if I survived the gruelling pace of my studies. As if sensing my thoughts, she glared at me over her lorgnette and settled down to read aloud.

'The spirit of the majority of women serves more to strengthen their madness than their reason,' she began.

I suppressed a groan and focused on my handiwork, whilst she and *Cornhill* demolished everything I held dear in biting prose. At least my needlework was beyond reproach. I feigned interest without actually having to absorb any of the tosh the writer had penned. I didn't need to pay attention to guess at the ridiculous claims they would spout.

Setting down the journal, Aunt Emily waited for my response. I judged it prudent to stay silent rather than unleashing a stream of invective about the author's knowledge of women, men and society in general.

She grimaced, suspecting my inattention. 'Sarah, even you must see that this fad for the advancement of women is doomed to failure. Your uncle and I indulge you because . . . well, to be blunt, you must earn a living now that your inheritance has been . . . is no longer . . .' She started again. 'You have no money, my dear. And your chance of making a halfway decent match is not improved by this foolish notion of becoming a doctor. As if any patient would consent to be treated by a mere girl! You must work, I see that, but there are professions suited for a gentlewoman of impoverished means. The more you bury yourself in books, the more you risk losing those few female qualities you do possess – not to mention your looks. You're looking positively sallow these days, and you're far too thin. It's most unattractive, my dear.'

I couldn't help noticing that Aunt Emily only ever called me 'my dear' when she had just finished insulting me.

'This is where I'm needed, Aunt. I'm doing good work at the infirmary.' That, at least, was something she couldn't argue with. But whilst Aunt Emily firmly believed in helping those less fortunate, she also felt that one should do it from a distance.

'You hardly need to be a doctor for that.'

'I want to be a physician! If the professors at the medical school accept it, why can't you?' It was only a partial lie – some of our tutors were sympathetic to our cause, it was true, and some even encouraged us. But the majority felt as my aunt did – that women had no place in a university, and even less in a hospital.

I escaped to bed after an hour by pleading a headache. Changing into my nightgown, with a shawl wrapped tightly around me, I snuggled down under the blankets on my bed with a copy of *The Lancet* purloined from the university library. If only Aunt Emily would consent to reading this aloud, I thought with a smile. I yawned into my hot milk. Every part of my body ached, but I felt exhilarated. I thought back to my life in London, an endless parade of visits and dinner parties and balls, cinched into a variety of uncomfortable but fashionable dresses and introduced to countless eligible young bachelors – and some not-so-young ones too, provided they were rich enough. I had thought, in those carefree days, that I knew what it was like to be exhausted.

Gertie would be preparing for her first season by now, I realised. The thought of my shy younger sister making her entrance into society without me to hold her hand brought a lump to my throat. Gertie, I knew, was the real reason I had been sent away. My mother was convinced that my continued presence would lead her astray, and that my behaviour had already damaged her chances of making a good match. She was forbidden to write to me, and although I had written to her regularly since I had arrived in Edinburgh, she had never replied. I suspected that my fortnightly letters were thrown into the fire unopened. Without me at her side to tease her and whisper wicked comments in her ear, she would have only Mother to guide her.

I had crumpled up the page I was holding, rendering it illegible. I cursed silently, and furiously blinked back the tears that threatened to fall. In one of my lonelier moments, I had written to Mother begging her to send Gertie to Scotland – after all, if the supervision offered by my relatives was deemed strict enough for a lost cause like me, surely they would have no trouble with my impressionable mouse of a sister.

I didn't envy Gertie, not really. I'd been bored rigid ever since making my debut into society, longing for the intellectual stimulation of school and hiding myself away in the library of every house we visited. My throat constricted as I thought about the treasure trove in Lord and Lady Beresford's London town house; how I had made myself scarce during a ball and spent the evening lost in Euclid. And then Paul Beresford had walked in, and altered the course of my life irrevocably.

I could still feel his hand in mine, the warm pressure of his lips against my skin and my delight as he expressed an interest in what I was reading instead of staring at me like an exotic animal in a zoo – a woman who dared to have a brain and exercise it. In a way, I owed my life in Edinburgh to him. And yet I wished passionately that I had never met him.

Chapter 4

The body swayed high above the courtyard, its skirts lifting in the breeze to the delight of the jeering throng below. It cast a long shadow in the weak morning sun, and I shivered as I looked up.

I wondered which one of the smirking onlookers had put it there, and how they'd managed to climb up. More likely whoever had rigged up the anatomist's model – clad in an ill-fitting cap and gown and petticoats that looked as though they had been purloined from someone's Great-Aunt Muriel – had got inside the building and somehow managed it through a window. Meaning that one of the porters, or even a professor, had turned a blind eye, if not helped directly.

'Charming,' said a voice behind me. 'It really makes one feel welcome, don't you think?'

Julia Latymer was glaring daggers at the crowd. If looks could kill, not even their combined medical expertise could have saved the culprit.

'It's just a jape,' said one of them – a pockmarked second-year by the name of James Ross. 'If you ladies can't take a joke, you won't last a day inside a hospital ward.'

'Some of us,' she snapped, 'are here to study, not act the

fool. And if I were spending my free time lynching dummies, then I'd probably be ploughing my exams as well.'

Some of the onlookers cheered, relishing the sight of Ross, hardly the most modest of gentlemen, being bested by a woman, and even his friends elbowed him in the ribs.

'Oh go back to your embroidery,' he muttered, red-faced.

To the men's delight and my horror, Julia lunged forward, looking for all the world as though she was ready to fight him right there.

A voice roared from the echoing corridors within the building.

'For the love of God, would someone tell me what the bloody hell is going on out here? I thought this was a place of scientific study, not a music hall!'

Professor Gregory Merchiston strode into the courtyard. He looked like a crow with his black frock coat fluttering about him in the autumn breeze. He followed our collective gaze, spat out a curse and whirled around to face the assembled crowd.

'Who is responsible for this? Speak up now and I might not have you thrashed for sheer insolence.'

Silence. Merchiston was barely more than a decade older than his students, but what he lacked in seniority he made up for in temper. No one wanted to face his wrath, and certainly no one would own up to a vicious prank of this magnitude. But that wasn't all that was stilling the tongue of whoever was behind it. Out of the shadows and into the cold grey morning light, Professor Merchiston looked more like a patient than a doctor.

Even from the back of the crowd, I could see the scabbed-over cut on his lip, the fading purple around his eyes and the dark stubble on his jaw. He seemed to be favouring his left leg a little, and his movements were jerky, as though the only things keeping him awake were caffeine and adrenaline. Wherever he had spent the night, it certainly wasn't in bed – or at least not his own.

'Hie, you!' He hailed one of the porters. 'Get that thing down this instant.'

His voice was icy as he turned to his audience.

'I highly recommend that the perpetrator comes forward by the end of today. You know where my rooms are.'

He disappeared into the cavernous building and we stood in silence as his footsteps faded away.

'I wouldn't like to be in his lectures today,' one of the men murmured. 'Who has him first?'

I took a deep breath and pushed through the crowd, forcing myself not to turn on my heel and flee.

'We do.'

Merchiston began talking before we had finished filing into the lecture hall, ignoring the few brave students who dawdled by the podium to stare at him, and I frantically scribbled down everything I could catch. Unlike some of the more flamboyant lecturers, who appeared to take the infamous Dr Bell as their role model, he kept the theatrics to a minimum. His voice, whilst not quite a monotone, was level enough that one could miss the dry humour in his words, and I was never entirely sure if he was sharing a joke with us or whether we ourselves were the joke. When roused, his soft burr became a harsh growl, and I had seen students do anything to avoid his ire.

His dark hair was permanently ruffled and unkempt, his black clothes frequently stained and infrequently ironed. He was rarely clean-shaven. Curt and ill-mannered he may have been, but I supposed I could see the attraction. Somehow there was a spark to him, a sort of magnetism that made one want to overlook his shabby appearance and listen to what he had to say.

Today, however, his temper was more brittle than usual. Up close, his clenched fists were white, but his hands too had taken a beating, with skinned knuckles only just starting to heal and yellow-blue bruises on the exposed skin of his wrist. Had this lecture hall been filled with male students, when there were enough bodies to spill out onto the steps between rows of seats, whispers about his appearance would be buzzing. With so few of us, no gossip could go unmissed, but we all stared covertly over our paper and books, trying to diagnose his injuries. He was young enough that a brawl in a public house wasn't out of the question, but surely no man in his thirties would scrap like some callow youth. Perhaps it was a patient from the hospital next door, or a frustrated student. Either way, speculation wouldn't help me survive the onslaught of interrogation that he was known for.

Sleep had done little to refresh me, and I felt even worse than the night before. I shifted impatiently in my seat, craving the distance from my troubling thoughts that only two hours taking notes on the virtues of quinine could provide.

Any hope I had of fading into the background was shattered five minutes into the lecture.

'You,' he called, snapping his fingers impatiently, 'Gilchrist. Administration of quinine.' I had read and reread the chapters in Thomson's *Materia Medica and Therapeutics*, but after a sleepless night, my brain was slow to respond.

'Crystallised sulphate given orally on an empty stomach,' Julia called out.

'I wasn't asking you, Latymer. Gilchrist, if you want to prove that your last essay wasn't an uncharacteristic stroke of luck, then I suggest you answer. How ought this crystallised quinine make its way into the patient?'

'Dissolved in water,' I managed. Julia could snipe at me in the corridors all she wanted, but I'd be damned if I let her best me in a lecture.

Merchiston raised an eyebrow. 'Not in tablet form?'

'Only if the pills are less than fifteen days old or they won't be properly soluble. They should be mixed with tannic acid and cinnamon water to be made palatable and the solution should be kept no longer than three days.' The words spilt out of me and I smiled triumphantly as he nodded, then collapsed back onto the bench with relief.

During the next hour, Merchiston called on the two of us almost constantly. Every time one of us paused for breath, the other would leap in to finish her sentence, and some of the other students began to grumble quietly about getting the chance to talk. He clearly enjoyed pitting us against each other, and strangely enough I found myself enjoying it too. It did nothing to dissolve my pure, undistilled hatred of Julia – nothing could make that palatable – but it made me feel challenged in a way I hadn't been in a long time. At the end of the lecture, he dismissed us with a suggestion that we take any further altercation outside and settle it with fisticuffs like the men. I would have been tempted had the ever-faithful Edith Menzies not swept Julia away with a protective arm that her friend slung off angrily. I contented myself with wishing a particularly bad bout of malaria in her future, with as much unsweetened quinine as she could take.

Merchiston glanced up as I passed by, frowning slightly.

'The perpetrator of this morning's little jape will be punished, I assure you. I'll see to it personally.'

Though his words were meant to soothe, I shivered. Merchiston was a dour, unnerving man at the best of times, but with his thunderous expression, he looked positively menacing.

I smiled awkwardly. 'Thank you, sir,' I managed. Under my breath, I added, 'Just so long as you don't challenge him to a fistfight.'

As the door swung shut behind me, I thought I heard a soft chuckle, like dry leaves in the autumn wind.

I didn't have time to speculate on the cause of his injuries or who was behind the horrible prank this morning. I had an appointment at the morgue.

The draughty dissection room was quiet as I accompanied Professor Williamson in, the only other occupant the shrouded body on the operating table. Our chaperone followed us soundlessly, her eyes sharp and her face expressionless. The thought that we might be engaging in any impropriety in the company of a corpse was distasteful enough to be absurd, but I was grudgingly impressed that a woman who looked like somebody's maiden aunt was willing to watch an autopsy. She moved to sit in a chair in the shadows and brought out her embroidery, as though she were in her own drawing room instead of a chilly medical building.

Williamson had initially refused to conduct seminars with female students 'on grounds of decency', but after the resulting fuss, he had backed down and now watched me with quiet glee as I donned an apron and approached the table, ready to dissect the arm of a corpse who had, by the looks of her, already seen more than her fair share of student's scalpels today.

'Don't be nervous, Gilchrist, it's not like you can do the poor creature any more harm.'

Blocking out his snide commentary, I yanked back the grubby sheet covering my 'patient'. My stomach roiled at the sight, and I gripped the edge of the table so hard my nails made crescent moons in the wood.

The face was blue and bloated, but before rigor mortis had set in, it had been beautiful. It took little imagination to picture how the woman had once looked, because laid out in front of me, with even less dignity in death than she had been afforded in life, was Lucy, the prostitute who had fled the infirmary in tears not four nights ago.

When I was twelve, my paternal grandmother died. She had been chilly and remote, although family history claimed that she had been a social butterfly in her youth. All I knew was a crabbit old woman, clad in musty black even in my earliest memories, as though she meant to outdo the Queen with her lengthy mourning period. I remember standing on my tiptoes to see the prone figure inside the casket, and thinking how much like a waxwork she appeared.

Lucy did not share the suggestion of passive slumber. She barely looked human at all.

'Is there a problem?' Williamson's bored voice jolted me back to the present. I shook my head dumbly. 'Then tell me what you see.'

'I know her.' He looked startled. My words stumbled over themselves. 'From my charitable work at St Giles' Infirmary. I recognised her . . .'

'I see. Yes, very sad business. I'd say she's in a better place now, but given her line of work, I rather doubt it. Laudanum overdose, according to her stomach contents. Strong stuff, too. She must have been earning a pretty penny.' He flushed as he remembered his company.

Bile rose in my throat at his words, and my palms itched to strike him. Struggling to keep my voice calm, I requested a moment alone to pay my respects.

He sighed in irritation at my inconvenient feminine emotions. 'Very well. There's no use getting you to work in this state anyway. Say your prayers and then finish the session in the library.'

He motioned for the porter to leave, then, after gazing at me speculatively for a moment, followed suit. As the heavy wooden doors swung shut behind them, I forced myself to move closer.

Death had not been kind to Lucy, but then neither had life. Although she had given her age at the clinic as nineteen, she looked older now, worn by the ravages of walking the streets. Pox hadn't marred her skin yet – she had been lucky to avoid more serious venereal disease. I remembered how time had stood still for her before I could confirm her pregnancy.

I pulled the sheet back, shuddering at the ugly stitches that marked the place where she had been cut open, ribs cracked open like an egg, to pull out her innards. Tears blurred my vision, safe to shed now that Williamson had gone. She looked angry, somehow, as if her end had not come easily. It should not have come at all, not so soon. I tugged the sheet down and placed my palm on her stomach. Life as a prostitute's child would have been grim, and an orphanage probably worse, but Lucy had been too canny for that.

Surely she must have known a woman who could have taken care of such things, someone with a plentiful stash of gin to hand, or knitting needles that were sterilised if one was lucky or rusted if one was not. Back-street butchery, yes, and far too often fatal – by the hangman's noose if not an incompetent doctor – but better that than the certainty that lay at the bottom of a bottle of laudanum. Perhaps the thought of a bloody, illegal operation scared her when she was little more than a child herself.

I wiped my eyes, allowing the gruesome, sorry scene before me to move back into focus, revealing what I had missed in the first shock of grief. Bruising to the neck – not enough to have killed her, but enough to make me wonder if it was just against life that she had been struggling. I took her cold hand in mine. Her nails were torn, her wrists bruised. She had fought, and against more than simply the injustice of her situation.

I knew what that kind of bruising looked like, the kind

where your wrists were pinned above your head till your arms ached, the fingerprints that took a week to fade. And I knew what restraints looked like too, heavy leather that pressed down on already sore wrists.

But who had done it? A gentleman who got his thrills subjugating women who had nothing left to strip away but the last vestiges of dignity? Or someone who had provided the laudanum and intended to be sure that she drank it?

A scuffle of footsteps and a monosyllabic grunt startled me, and I spun around, my heart pounding.

McVeigh was here and my makeshift vigil was over. She would be left in the dissecting room until there was nothing left to cut or remove, and there was little I could do now but let her go. I fled the room, a sob wrenched from my throat, my head reeling.

Chapter 5

I staggered out into the misty courtyard, where the cold autumn air revived me a little. Nothing could erase the image of Lucy's corpse from my mind, but at least the stench of embalming fluid, laudanum and decomposing flesh was replaced by the sour tang of hops that settled upon Edinburgh like a shroud. The grisly mannequin still dangled from the window, swinging gently in the breeze. My guts clenched, and something hot and sour rose in my throat. I doubled over, vomiting into the gutter. Tears streaked my cheeks as I heaved, kneeling, the damp from rain-slicked cobbles seeping through my skirts.

I remembered the misery in her eyes as her worst fears were confirmed. I remembered the same dread twisting inside me during that cold, bleak period as I waited in the sanatorium for my monthly courses to appear. Whether I escaped my ordeal without conceiving a bastard, or whether my unborn child felt as dreary as I did about life and abandoned any hold on it, I didn't know, but eventually I felt the familiar cramps and could have cried with relief.

Lucy hadn't been so lucky. Life had been cruel to her, but still she had fought for it. She had been stronger than I, but not strong enough. I retched again, but there was nothing left to bring up.

The oblivion laudanum had given her would have been so sweet. Her miserable existence would have fallen away, and she would have slept more soundly than she had in months. I could understand the desire. In that moment, if I could have exchanged every material advantage I had for insensibility – to block out the sight of Lucy's face, first terrified and then blank and bruised; to drive away the memories that crept about the edge of my mind, trying constantly to find a way in – I would have taken it and gladly.

But I had no such drug to hand, and the stones dug into my knees as I knelt there. The chill brought me back to my senses and I welcomed the biting wind. My apron was wet through with rain and stained with vomit. Damp tendrils of hair clung to my skin. I stood shakily, ready to make my way back inside, only to feel the pressure of a hand on my back.

'Miss Gilchrist?'

Professor Merchiston stood before me, the flickering gaslight casting shadows over his face.

'Are you unwell?'

I saw him taking in my dishevelled appearance, my eyes red from crying and my lips speckled with vomit. I knew what 'unwell' meant to a doctor.

'Thank you, Professor, I was merely . . .' I gulped as nausea threatened to overwhelm me again. 'A dissection class – I was overcome. I just needed a little fresh air.'

'You need a pot of tea and a towel,' he commented.

I knew that the chances of getting either were slim.

'The practical joke hasn't been cleared away yet,' I informed him in an effort to distract him from my tear-stained cheeks. I had no fight left in me, but perhaps he could do something.

His expression darkened and his hand fell on my shoulder.

'Don't let them frighten you away.'

I stood frozen in place by the warmth of his skin through my damp blouse.

A door banged somewhere inside the building, and we both started. He pulled his hand back as though I had scalded him.

'I shan't keep you, Miss Gilchrist.'

I fled down the stairs to the morgue.

I found McVeigh slouched and surly in the study adjoining the dissection room. The way he eyed me made me want to flee the room, but I pasted on my best drawing-room smile and stared him down.

'The woman I was supposed to examine. I knew her, and I'd like to arrange a burial. I can pay . . .'

There was an infinitesimal shake of the head. 'Against university regulations, miss. When they're here, they're here. Besides, there'll be no' much left of her by now.'

I shuddered, my nausea returning in waves. 'That's impossible, Mr McVeigh. I saw her less than fifteen minutes ago.'

I shouldn't have been surprised – Lucy was a specimen, a body to be used in death the way she had been in life – but it unsettled me that she would go unmourned to the next student, and the one after that, until there was nothing left for them to use except her skeleton, with no one to care about what had brought her beneath their scalpels.

The thought of the men getting their hands on Lucy – the same men whose hands grabbed and snatched at our skirts as we passed them in the halls, who had strung up that horrid parody of a female student outside the medical school – made my blood run cold.

McVeigh sniffed. 'Aye, well we've a lot of students. It's no' just you lasses.'

'Please,' I said urgently. 'I'll pay you however much

you think is fair.' I ignored the fact that I had no way of getting my hands on the money without asking Aunt Emily, whose generosity was unlikely to stretch to the funeral of a prostitute.

He smiled unpleasantly, sucking his yellow, tobacco-stained teeth, enjoying my discomfort. I could imagine what he might consider a fair price, but it was not one I wanted to pay.

'Rules is rules.'

It was clear that my pleading was futile. Any offer I could make would fall on deaf ears; save something I was not willing to barter. I heard the clock strike the hour, and I had no time to beg.

'What if a friend or relative claimed the body? Then you'd have to let it go, surely?'

He blinked, and then smiled slowly. 'Where d'ye think we gets them from in the first place?'

It didn't bear thinking about. I couldn't imagine the poverty that would mean denying a loved one a decent burial in exchange for a handful of coins.

'But if they did?' I persisted.

He shrugged, clearly eager to be rid of me. 'Aye. I suppose we would.'

I pulled off the brooch at my neck. 'If you keep her . . . intact for another day, you can keep this. Sell it, give it to a sweetheart, I don't care.'

He looked at it impassively, and pocketed it.

'Tomorrow afternoon, then,' I urged.

He gave what I took to be a nod, and I had to content myself with that.

If my uncle found out that I was leaving the confines of the university, he would have me locked up in my room for the rest of my days. But I couldn't go back inside and face the others with my grief. I couldn't hear them dismiss Lucy as just another tart, a whore who deserved everything she got. I fled past clattering trams and taverns, full even before lunchtime, as I stumbled my way down Candlemaker Row. By the time I reached the doors of the infirmary, I was out of breath and sobbing openly.

Fiona broke off from issuing orders when she saw me.

'Sarah! Whatever is the matter? Come inside, girl, and sit down.'

One of the nurses brought me some hot, strong tea and I gulped it down.

'Lucy – the girl who came to us the other day. The . . .'

'The prostitute?' I winced at the blunt way Fiona dismissed her, as though that was all Lucy had been. Not a daughter or a sister or a friend; just another girl who worked the streets.

'I saw her. In the university mortuary. They said she'd killed herself.'

Fiona cursed beneath her breath.

'That poor girl,' she said shakily. 'I wish there was more we could have done for her.' She paused, trying to form her next question as delicately as possible. 'Was she still . . .'

'You think she could have had an abortion?'

'There are back-street butchers all over the city. More than one drunken old sawbones who'll take a girl's money and leave her broken and bleeding and no better off than before.'

'And they say we're not fit to be doctors,' Matilda Campbell grimaced.

'Mr McVeigh said it was probably her family who'd sent her to us. The university, I mean.'

'You spoke to McVeigh?' Fiona looked startled. 'He's hardly the most pleasant of men, Sarah.'

I recalled the way his eyes had dragged across my figure, pinning me in place, and shivered.

'I paid him to keep her so that none of the other students could . . .' I broke off, unable to finish. 'I wanted to arrange a funeral for her.'

She shook her head. 'Sarah, you can't bury every unfortunate soul you come across. You lost your first patient. There will be more; you can't avoid that.'

The thought of a life full of women like Lucy, women I couldn't save any more than I could save myself, weighed impossibly heavy on my conscience.

'Does it get easier?'

She smiled ruefully, the kind that didn't reach her eyes. 'You get harder. In time, you convince yourself it's the same thing.'

I wondered which patient Fiona had failed that had made her look so lost and sad.

'It isn't fair,' I whispered. 'Professor Williamson treated her as though she were nothing. And then when I told him who she was – what she was – he looked at her as though she were so much less than that.'

'Could you do something for me, Sarah?' Fiona asked. 'Don't tell your aunt. We can't afford to lose her patronage, or your help, and if she learns that our patients are the kind of women who seek out illegal procedures, we could be closed down.'

She handed me my coat with an expression that told me our conversation was over.

'Go back to your lecture hall. Save your tears for your examination papers, because they won't do any good here. It may sound harsh, but it's the truth. You can do more for these women with a clear head than you can with a big heart. Your compassion may seem like a good thing now, but if you care too much, it will destroy you.'

'How do I stop caring?'

I looked at Fiona, with her pale, drawn face, the evidence of sleepless nights written across it, and wondered if she took her own advice, or if she was kept awake by a litany of names of women she had lost.

'If I ever find out, I'll let you know.'

The damp mist had broken into a drizzling rain, and I sheltered under the umbrella the infirmary's porter held over my head as we walked in awkward silence. He was hardly the sort of person my aunt would have permitted me to exchange pleasantries with, and in truth I had no idea how one struck up a conversation with a man like that, but all the same our brief walk felt excruciatingly stilted. He escorted me as far as Middle Meadow Walk, sheltering me from the male passers-by as though even brushing their coat-tails would irrevocably damage my reputation, and I took a moment to breathe in the cold autumn air before entering the medical school gates.

That 'kind of woman', Fiona had said. Did she know she was speaking to one? In the weeks following my encounter with Paul Beresford, that horrible purgatory before I knew that I had escaped at least one blot on my character, I had promised myself that I would rather smother my child at birth than live with a permanent reminder of what he had done to me. I hoped that in the rational light of day I would do no such thing, but if I had been pregnant, and had I known someone who would relieve me of my burden, I would have entrusted myself to a hundred drunken sawbones. Fiona knew a lot about medicine but, I thought, very little about desperation.

I staggered through the rest of the day's lectures, barely taking anything in. In biology, I was called upon to answer questions I hadn't heard; in botany, I found myself sketching a diagram on a different page from the rest of the class; and I ended the day by spilling my compound from the chemistry practical all over Moira Owen's apron. Lucy was hardly the first corpse I'd laid eyes on, but she was the first with whom I had felt such kinship, and the sight of her lifeless, battered body had unnerved me. There was only one step I could take that would quell the whisper of doubt in the back of my mind. While the rest of my cohort made for the delights of the university library, I retraced my steps to Forest Road, towards another treasure trove entirely.

The bell jangled loudly as I entered the dim shop, meeting the stern gaze of the man behind the counter with all the bluster I could manage.

'I need to buy a bottle of laudanum.'

Chapter 6

If my dress had not marked me out, then my accent certainly did. I cringed, wishing for the thousandth time that I was back in London, where at least I could open my mouth without drawing attention to myself. Still, if I had expected to be challenged or questioned, I was sorely disappointed. My money was as good as anyone's, it seemed, or perhaps well-brought-up young ladies from England frequented pharmacies alone all the time.

I had seen the bottles in the refuse around the Cowgate; I knew what I was after. I asked for one whose label I recognised – it was by far cheaper than the bottles in the infirmary, but probably watered down so much it was daylight robbery.

Shaking, I left the pharmacy convinced that a fellow student would recognise me. The bottle felt heavy in my reticule and my mind whirled with visions of it breaking, soaking through its brown paper bag and smearing my notes, staining my character. Would they think I was a weak, fragile creature who needed to ward off the vapours, or would they see me for what I truly was – a fallen woman with opiates on her person and the stench of the slums on her skin and hair?

The desire to steal away to the meagre facilities the university offered to women and steady my nerves with a fortifying swig was overwhelming, and I dug my nails into my palms in an effort to stop my hands from fumbling in my bag.

In my first weeks here, I had been overcome daily with the urge to flee, to hide in the stuffy respectability of my aunt's house, far away from the curious eyes of the male students and from Julia Latymer's all-knowing smirk, but then I didn't have the gnawing temptation of release on my person. I wouldn't keep it, I told myself. I would hide the bottle with the rest of the household refuse just as soon as I had ascertained its contents. I forced my steps towards the university and some semblance of respectability.

The lecture theatre was abuzz when I arrived. I caught the tail end of Julia's scornful laugh.

'She should never have tried for a degree at all if she's going to fall at the first hurdle. Some women simply aren't made for it.'

It felt as though my insides were curdling like rotten milk. I faltered in the doorway, wanting to flee but needing to hear what came next.

'Girls like her are ten a penny in London. The only reason they go to scientific talks or philosophy lectures is to meet a man.'

She broke off as Edith elbowed her sharply, nodding towards me. Julia shrugged. 'Like I said, we're different from the others. But sometimes ordinary girls like her just slip through the cracks.'

I perched on the very edge of an aisle seat, not meeting anyone's eye. Where was the girl who had marched up to the front row of the lecture room at St Bart's, daring anyone to send her away?

Alison inched over towards me a little, enough for me to

hear her but far enough away that she could scoot back to the others as soon as Julia saw her.

'A history first-year has left to get married,' she whispered. 'Eleanor Niven – her fiancé said he'd break it off with her if she didn't leave by Christmas. It's such a waste.'

I exhaled a shaky breath. So they hadn't been talking about me after all. I still felt fragile, like a glass ornament rather than a living, breathing woman of flesh and blood, but for once Julia's beastliness had been aimed elsewhere.

Why did we do this to each other? I was as guilty as the next woman, I knew it. I had nodded along like a lapdog when Vanessa Templeton, with her love of chemistry and her heart set on Oxford, had wondered aloud in all seriousness whether our generation had evolved to be brighter than that of our mothers.

'I don't see any of them able to calculate equations in their heads,' she had insisted after we both got into trouble for staying too late at the Museum of Natural History on the day of a ball. 'All they care about is dresses and marrying us off.'

But she had not been so enlightened either, not in the way she had so callously discarded me when news of my ruin began to spread. We had sneered at the way our fellow debutantes competed with each other to be the prettiest, the most charming, swearing we would never fall into such petty rivalries, but in the end had we just exchanged one kind of competition for another?

I stepped into my uncle's carriage with unaccustomed relief, setting my sights on home and a cup of tea. Usually resisting the siren call of another hour in the library or the dissection room would have proved difficult, but I was no longer in the mood to work. My peers would study well into the night, bribing the librarians for just half an hour more in the stacks, but I had been late to dinner too often this past month, and I could not afford to test my relatives' kindness any further. I leant my head against the cracked leather of my seat, and closed my eyes, although I could not drift into sleep.

At home, I unpinned my hair, letting it fall in damp locks down to my waist, and sighed with relief as the girl liberated me from my gown and stays.

The sight of Lucy's bruised, lifeless body haunted me. This wasn't just grief over a woman I had barely known, the very sentimentality that everyone from hospital porters to newspaper editors believed made women unsuited for medicine. Someone had done this to her, and enough people had failed to care that murder had gone unnoticed.

I had no idea what my next step should be, and if I had hoped that the distraction of the after-dinner ritual of dull books and sermonising would distract me, I was left wanting. The hours before I could decently retire to bed seemed to drag, but finally I pressed a dutiful kiss to Aunt Emily's cool cheek and escaped upstairs.

Once in my nightgown and reasonably sure I wouldn't be disturbed, I retrieved my bag and pulled out its contents. I hadn't thought to bring a spoon, so I put the bottle to my lips with shaking hands and let the liquid coat my tongue.

It was the strongest mixture a pharmacist could sell me – costly enough that I would be going without lunch from the refectory for a few days – but from the taste it was weak, diluted with sugar water, with just enough opium to send the first flickering tendrils of pleasure coursing through my veins. A bottle of this would render me insensible, but it wouldn't kill me. Even a mouthful wasn't enough to summon up that drowsy languor it promised. Whatever Lucy had taken, it wasn't this. I had a second gulp, and then a third. And after that, the discrepancies didn't seem terribly important.

As I drifted into unconsciousness, I struggled to place my surroundings. How many times had I woken up to feel the last traces of laudanum leave my system only to submit to the morning round of ice baths and more medication? But the bed was soft, and a fire burnt low in the grate. There were my books, my blue dress strewn on the floor where I had discarded it, my toiletries on the dressing table. I forced back the rising tide of terror. I was in my aunt's house, not the chilly sanatorium in the countryside, a genteel madhouse where girls from good families were taught to behave.

Chapter 7

When I woke, my head pounded and my mouth was unpleasantly dry. I scrabbled around for the small wristwatch I had tossed on my nightstand and squinted at it, frowning. Six thirty in the morning. Once I would have turned over and gone back to sleep, but that was an indulgence no medical student could afford.

One thing was certain – I could have consumed twice as much and been unconscious but alive. If Lucy had committed suicide, she had spent a pretty penny on the tools of her self-destruction, more than I imagined a girl who sold her wares in a Grassmarket brothel could afford.

The sky was still dark when, with my gaze fixed on my boots, I murmured 'Amen' along with the servants. I had missed morning prayers once this month already, and if I was going to prove that I was a reformed character, I had to mend my ways. My aunt smiled at me approvingly, and I felt an unexpected rush of pleasure. It had been a long time since someone had looked at me with such undisguised affection.

Still, I doubted that her delight in my new behaviour would last if she knew that I was headed to one of the rather less salubrious parts of Edinburgh to interview a brothel-keeper.

I believe I was the most diligent student in the faculty that day, until an incident derailed our studies and gave me the opportunity I had been looking for to slip away.

As we wound our way through the corridors to the large, draughty lecture hall – far too spacious for the twelve of us and one professor – I noticed that our peers either studiously avoided our eyes or smirked at us. Doubtless *The Student*, a rag written by undergraduates, had produced yet another flattering caricature of our number. Even *The Scotsman* had carried mocking artwork to accompany its scathing editorials. Well, if all they could criticise was our appearance, I wasn't going to worry about it. My deepest fear was that somehow the ill-kept secret of my disgrace would wind up on the front page, since *The Student* was little better than a scandal sheet most of the time, although its writers fancied it a vehicle for intellectual debate.

We carried on, heads held high, and swept into the lecture hall as though it were the finest drawing room in the country. Our deportment teachers would be proud, I thought to myself with a smile. I could have carried the contents of the Playfair Library on my head without dropping a single volume. Our pride was short-lived, however. Edith was the first to notice, when her arm brushed the wooden seat as she rummaged around in her reticule for pen and paper. She yelped as she saw that her wrist was covered in fine red powder, which, when she moved to brush it off, stained her gloves as well.

'It's all over the seats!' she cried out in dismay. 'A sort of powdery ink.' Leaping to her feet, she discovered that her skirt was similarly ruined. One by one, we stood and examined the damage to our clothing. Ugly red dye marred each and every feminine backside, and no amount of spit and scrubbing would erase it. Our distress was so intense that when Professor Baldwin entered, no one noticed until the loud boom of his voice echoed through the large room.

'And what precisely is the meaning of all this commotion?' he demanded. 'I was under the impression that you were ladies, not common fishwives. Sit down this instant!'

'Look at our skirts!' He stared in horror as Julia turned to show him the damage. 'It's on all of us!'

His voice, when he finally managed to speak, was strangled. 'Miss Latymer, may I ask you to desist from this indelicate display at once. If it is true that you are all somehow . . . indisposed, as I believe to be the case when a number of women are too much in each other's company, then you have no place coming to lectures and displaying your . . . ah . . . condition, let alone flaunting it in this disgusting manner!'

I wondered if perhaps he had gone completely mad, until Moira informed him, in a deathly quiet tone, 'Professor Baldwin, this is red dye.'

I realised with a flush of humiliation what he believed had occurred. Professor Baldwin opened and shut his mouth, in a manner more closely befitting a goldfish than a medical doctor teaching at the university, before saying rather weakly, 'I beg your pardon?'

As though speaking to a person who was somewhat deficient of wit, Moira explained. 'Some of our fellow students – your pupils, Dr Baldwin – have evidently come to the conclusion that it would be a merry jape to cover the seats of our benches in red dye. The colour was presumably chosen to give the impression, to which you have so readily jumped, that we are all menstruating.'

The very word made him look queasy, and I wondered how on earth he coped in his chosen profession if bodily excretions, albeit uniquely feminine ones, horrified him so greatly.

'I cannot imagine,' he said, 'that any of our students – who are, I might add, fine, upstanding young fellows to a man, who have never engaged in the sort of disruptive behaviour to which some of you I am afraid to say are sadly prone – would play such a juvenile and disgusting prank.'

'Really?' Julia demanded. 'Because I can believe it quite readily, Dr Baldwin. In fact, I am only surprised that they have taken so long to carry out a malicious trick of this nature.'

'It is a jape,' Dr Baldwin said. 'A joke, Miss Latymer, friendly roughhousing between fellow students, nothing more. Certainly nothing to get so emotional about.' He spat the word out as if it appalled him as much as our monthly cycles did.

'Oh, so you've chosen to believe us then?' called Moira. 'Well I'll tell you one thing, Dr Baldwin, washing ink stains out of dresses doesn't come cheaply. Shall I send the bill to the university or to you?'

He scowled. 'Don't be ridiculous, young lady. If you cannot bear the occasional silly joke from hard-working students with equilibrium, then I am afraid you have made a grave error in choosing to join those students' ranks. You cannot honestly have been expecting these young gentlemen to accept your presence within their hallowed halls – which until you arrived only admitted women as patients – without a little playful protestation, surely?'

'I can,' Moira said hotly, 'and I do.'

'If you insist on wasting my time with a discussion about domestic affairs, then I hope you will forgive me if I return to my rooms and prepare my next lecture for students who actually have an interest in what I have to teach them.'

Although we gaped open-mouthed at him, it was clear that

we had reached a stalemate. Grudgingly, and with some vociferous complaint, we moved to the third and fourth rows, where the benches were unmarked, and sat seething in silence as he began the lecture.

After Dr Baldwin had left the hall with one final withering comment about our distress at the state of our clothes being further proof that women's brains were too frivolous for matters as weighty as science and medicine, we clamoured to speak.

'It's outrageous!' gasped Alison. 'How dare they do something so . . . so . . .'

'Hateful?' Julia supplied, her dark eyes flashing with fury. 'Quite easily, I imagine. Oh, some of the more enlightened ones might believe in an abstract sort of way in women's access to higher education, but don't let that fool you into thinking that we're accepted here. They've quietened down since the first few weeks, but they were biding their time and we let them lull us into a false sense of security!'

'Then what should we do?' asked Edith. 'If we retaliate, we won't receive anywhere near the leniency they do. We'll be sent down if we cause trouble, and that will be it for lady doctors at Edinburgh. To hell with the law; they'll find a loophole and bar us for good.'

'What choice do we have?' I asked. It was rare that I would involve myself so directly in the concerns of my fellow students, since the majority of them made no bones about the fact that they wished me elsewhere – preferably somewhere very far away – but the prank had made me feel part of the group for once. 'We take the moral high ground, act as though nothing has happened, and in the meantime wear our outdoor coats for the rest of the day.'

'Well of course you'd give in to the first bit of intimidation,' Julia sneered.

'I've had rather a lot of practice lately.' I smiled sweetly. 'And let me remind you, Julia, I'm still here. I won't be frightened off by threats and intimidation, no matter where they come from.'

She backed down, but I saw her flash a look of surprised respect in my direction once no one was looking.

'I agree with Gilchrist,' Alison said. 'I'm not giving a single one of those brutes the satisfaction of knowing that they've ruined my dress or that they've . . .' She trailed off. 'You know, they haven't upset me,' she said with a note of surprise. 'I'm not distressed or weepy or any of the other stupid, girlish words that old windbags like Baldwin use whenever we're frustrated. I'm . . . I'm bloody furious!' she finished, laughing. Moira sent up a cheer, and we all joined in, stamping our feet and banging on the narrow desks in front of us.

'I'll tell you what I'm going to do.' Caroline, normally a little mouse despite her flaming red hair, sounded fierce. 'I'm going to work until I drop, and best every single one of them in the December examinations.'

'You know, most of the seats are still quite heavily powdered,' I mused aloud. 'I don't suppose we have time to clean them before the next lot of students come in, do we?'

'No,' Caroline said, grinning wickedly. 'I don't suppose we do.'

By the end of the day, a piece of paper was tacked to every noticeboard in the medical school informing students that due to an error on the part of the university servants, dye had been left on the benches of one of the lecture halls, and if any students required their clothing laundered, the university would foot the bill. No mention of the culprits was made, but Moira informed us all with glee a few days later that a group of normally rowdy second-years had been seen on hands and knees, scrubbing the dissecting hall with Lysol soap like charwomen. It was a minor victory, but a victory all the same. Most of all, the incident provided the perfect excuse to absent myself on the pretence of going home to change. Instead of hailing a cab, though, my steps took me across the street in the direction of the cramped and dirty Cowgate.

Chapter 8

When I entered Ruby McAllister's brothel, I wasn't sure whether to be relieved or disappointed. I had never really imagined the inside of a house of ill repute before. I was shown into what looked like a terribly ordinary drawing room – provided one didn't examine the features too closely.

I sat down tentatively on an overstuffed horsehair sofa, and tried not to look at the pictures on the walls. Out of the corner of my eye, none of the figures in the paintings looked clothed. I glanced at the bookshelves that lined one wall of the parlour, and decided that the books there were to be similarly avoided. I heard an odd, rhythmic thumping from upstairs, and when it dawned on me exactly what the room's occupants were doing, I blushed to the roots of my hair. The maid brought me a cup of tea, too sweet and milky for my liking, but I sipped it politely whilst trying to reassure myself that not once in my studies had I come across the transmission of syphilis by teacup.

I didn't have to wait long. A portly woman with salt-and-pepper hair entered, giving me a suspicious look.

'There's nae rooms free, if that's what you're after,' she snarled. Her fetid breath told me she had been eating liver and onions recently.

'Not even the one Lucy used?'

She flinched, but didn't break my gaze. I wondered if it had been she who had found the body. 'She's been gone since Friday night, hen. Rooms dinnae stay free for long around here.' She eyed me appraisingly. 'So who is he, then?'

'Who?'

'Your young man. And before you go accusing me of anything, my girls are clean. We have a doctor round here regular, so whatever lover boy's given you, he didnae get it here.'

'I don't have a young man,' I sighed, frustrated. 'Mrs McAllister, Lucy's corpse was delivered to the university for dissection a few days ago. Dr Leadbetter mentioned your . . . establishment as her place of residence, and I thought she might have had some family you could inform.'

'Why d'ye care?' The woman's voice was gruff, but whether from emotion or permanent surliness I couldn't tell. 'What's she to you?'

'A patient,' I said, although it wasn't strictly true. 'She came to the infirmary in a certain type of trouble. I believe she was hoping that one of the doctors would . . . well.'

'Get rid of it?' I was shocked at her matter-of-factness, although I supposed I shouldn't have been. 'Aye, there's few customers for a girl in her condition once she's started to show, and gin and a hot bath dinnae always do the trick.'

'Nevertheless,' I stammered, 'I thought someone should know that she's dead. I asked the porters to keep hold of her body, in case you wanted to arrange a burial.'

She narrowed her eyes. 'Now why would I want to do that?'

'Mrs McAllister, she was in your care! If you don't want to bury her, surely you know someone who does.'

She seemed to falter, then shook her head with a withering

sigh at my obvious naivety. 'Girls who come through my door, they're not the sort with families. Leastways, no family that will spare a ha'penny for them. If they did, d'ye really think they'd be here?'

To my horror, my eyes pricked hotly, and I pinched my lips tightly together to stop myself from crying.

Seeing this, Ruby softened somewhat. 'I'll see what I can do. The university, you say?'

I nodded, then, steeling myself, came to the real reason I had charmed my way into her parlour.

'This is a difficult question, and I appreciate that you might want to protect the confidentiality of your . . . ah . . . customers, but did Lucy have any visitors who might have been, shall we say, less than gentle?' The madam remained impassive. 'Anyone who might have hurt her, even without meaning to?' She shook her head, although I sensed that she was holding something back. 'Lucy's wrists and neck were bruised. That wasn't what killed her, but before she died, she'd put up a fight.'

'My girls can take care of themselves,' Ruby said, but she didn't sound as though she believed it. 'I cannae be every-where at once.' She looked, I thought, a little sad. It was no less than she deserved, I thought angrily.

'You profit from girls like Lucy,' I said coldly, 'and the girl upstairs.' I looked towards the ceiling, where the percussion had increased considerably. 'You have a duty to look after them.'

A lazy smile crawled across her face. 'That's no' a girl, hen.'

I swallowed. 'Oh. Well. My point still stands. Someone hurt Lucy before she died, and I think you know who it was. I won't waste any more of my time or yours, but if you happen to recall anything unusual about Lucy's gentleman callers, this is where you can find me.' I pulled out a notebook from my reticule and scribbled my address, wondering if giving Aunt Emily's address to a brothel-owner was quite the best of ideas. I included a guinea as I passed the page to her, and she glanced at it and nodded.

'If I remember anything,' she said grudgingly. 'You'd best be on your way, lassie, before it gets dark.'

I stepped into the entrance hall, nearly walking into a man who had come downstairs. Given his rumpled appearance and the silence from the room above the parlour, I suspected he had been one of the men I had heard. I tried not to stare after him as he left, wondering what on earth had persuaded him to do what he had recently been doing – not to mention exactly what it was he had been engaged in. A few moments after the door slammed shut behind him, a lithe young man of around eighteen with a shock of black hair and a slightly pinched-looking face slouched downstairs. He glanced at me and smirked.

'Another new girl, Mother McAllister?' he asked. I didn't stay to hear her reply.

I stepped down the street hesitantly, the twilight having given place to lurking darkness. Although the narrow, winding cobbled path was sheltered by tenements from the harsh November winds, it somehow seemed colder down here. Figures shoved past me without a word of apology. I would be lucky to emerge with my purse, not to mention what little was left of my virtue. I couldn't imagine living here, although people clearly did. Lucy had lived here, plied her trade here, and probably died here.

I walked steadily onwards, refusing to turn and flee back to the light, much as I dearly wanted to. There were knots of girls standing on the street, some with male accompaniment, but more without. There was one solitary flower girl, as be-draggled as the violets she was selling – and really, were they even the right colour? Dyed, I supposed, to look more expensive. Had I looked closer, I would probably have seen her palms stained where the damp had leached the dye from the flowers, but this wasn't a place where one could stop and stare in safety. Not for a woman, at least – more than one gentleman, if the term could be so applied, was staring at me with undisguised interest. It was clear they considered any woman walking alone through these streets to be fair game.

Voices behind me made me pick up my pace, as Ruby McAllister turned away a drunkard. I heard his lurching steps in my direction, but before I could run, he had staggered into me. I turned, hoping to fend him off, only to see Professor Merchiston, black eye and all, swaying unsteadily in front of me. He opened his mouth, as if to speak. Instead, he heaved and vomited over me.

I stared at him in horror as the hot, stinking liquid cooled on my skirt and petticoats.

'Madam, I am so sorry,' he slurred, attempting to place a conciliatory hand on my elbow. I backed hastily away, not trusting that his impaired motor function would land his fingers in the right place. He frowned, recognition dawning. 'I know you.' His Scotch-soaked breath was hot against my cheek. 'You're the quiet one.'

'You must be mistaken, sir,' I said, infusing my words with all the ice I could muster. I prayed he would be too drunk to recall our encounter.

'No,' he insisted, 'I do. Gilchrist. Competent, know your poisons. No friends.'

His words stung me. I hadn't realised that my solitary state was quite so obvious.

Before I could protest, he heaved again. Once he had emptied the remaining contents of his stomach on the already foul cobbles, he took a tentative step around it. Before he had taken three paces, he swayed again and collapsed onto the ground.

Reluctant as I was to linger in the dark wynd with my inebriated professor, I knew I couldn't leave him like that. I crouched down next to him. He was unhurt, although there would be a nasty bump on his forehead to match the black eye, and a shard of broken glass had gouged itself into his cheek. Shaking him to something resembling consciousness, I gingerly removed it and pressed my mercifully clean handkerchief against his skin to staunch the trickle of blood.

Somehow he managed to stagger to his feet, looking about him uncertainly.

'If we walk a little further, we can hail you a cab,' I reassured him. The two of us must have made a pretty picture, stumbling through the slums: a tall man of nearly six foot and reeking of alcohol leaning on a slight young woman who looked more like a governess than a prostitute.

I helped him into the carriage and sat opposite him warily. He slumped against the door, eyes fluttering shut. It occurred to me, most inappropriately, that he had extremely thick eyelashes for a man.

'Where to, lassie?'

I realised that I had no idea where Merchiston lived. To return him to the university would result in instant dismissal for him, and probably expulsion and a room in a nearby convent for me.

'Professor,' I said, shaking him gingerly. 'I cannot take you home unless you tell me where you live.'

He slurred an address in a reasonably smart area of town, and I relayed it to the driver. At least it wouldn't take long to get there, I thought, and I could be back at my aunt's house in time for dinner.

We hadn't gone ten yards before Professor Merchiston was

snoring loudly. His black eye had begun to fade a little, and his split lip was almost healed. His injuries lent him a somewhat sinister air, and I began to doubt my wisdom in travelling alone with an inebriated man I barely knew.

We drew up outside a modest but well-kept house and I realised with a sinking feeling that the driver had no intention of helping his passenger out of the vehicle. I prodded Merchiston tentatively in the shoulder and he awoke with a start.

'We're here, Professor.'

He started at me in blank confusion, clearly wondering what on earth he was doing in a hansom cab with one of his female students. Evidently deciding that he was too drunk to care, he opened the carriage door and promptly fell out onto the pavement.

I turned to ask the driver to wait whilst I manoeuvred the Professor into the house, but he was already driving away.

Together we staggered to the front door, which was opened by a mildly scandalised woman with greying red hair barely concealed by her mob cap.

'What on earth is going on here? Professor, what's the matter wi' ye? No, dinnae answer that,' she said without pausing for breath. 'I can smell ye from here. And me having taken the pledge!' Shifting her attention from her recalcitrant employer, she fixed her gimlet gaze on me. 'And just who might you be, lassie?'

'Miss Gilchrist,' Professor Merchiston mumbled. 'Saw her coming out of a brothel.'

'I was only visiting,' I explained hastily. 'I'm a student of Professor Merchiston's, and I do some philanthropic work at St Giles' Infirmary. I was enquiring after a patient.' Well, that was only a partial lie. No need to mention that the patient in question was beyond medical help.

'Hmm. Well you can help me carry the lummox in, then.'

Between the two of us, we managed to drag the lummox in question into the house and up the stairs. At the bedroom door, we paused awkwardly.

'I think it's better if I do this last bit alone, dearie,' she said, not unkindly. 'Wait in the parlour and I'll bring you a pot of tea and get you cleaned up. Oh Professor,' she tutted. Her motherly manner soothed my jangled nerves. 'What on earth have you been doing?'

He slurred something in response. One word, but it was enough to make my blood run cold.

'Lucy.'

Chapter 9

Faced with a looming chemistry practical, I pushed all thoughts of Merchiston and his possible links to Lucy to the back of my mind – in the cold light of day, the idea did seem a little fantastical. He might be charmless and sarcastic, he might frequent brothels, but did that really make him a murderer? There was no reason, I told myself sternly, to be discomfited by his dishevelled appearance this week, or by catching him going into Ruby's. After all, what had I seen? A single gentleman of a certain age outside a house of ill repute wasn't unusual. And if Lucy had been his particular favourite – well, it was hardly unheard of for a man to develop a tendresse for a lady of pleasure.

But the thought refused to leave me.

He might have been an admirable physician and a good lecturer, but he was still flesh and blood, with all the desires that implied. Better, surely, that he slake his lust with a woman he had paid for the privilege than to take advantage of the vulnerable creatures he came into contact with as a doctor – or worse, his female students. Even as I thought that, I knew there was no real difference. Lucy and her sisters were no more complicit in their degradation than I had been in mine – where force and sheer terror had subdued me, so poverty and the threat of the workhouse trapped them.

If the object of his affections had not now been a battered corpse, I could have dismissed it as eccentricity. As it was . . . I shivered, gulping down the last of the hot, sweet coffee, and gathered my things. My uncle's carriage would take me to the university. From there, I was on my own.

In the carriage, I pulled my coat tighter around myself, longing for the comparative warmth of the trams that criss-crossed the city. As I shivered, my uncle glared at me, clearly resenting having to share his morning journey every day with a girl he thought so little of. I wished violently that my relatives would trust me to make my own way to the university. Many of my peers cycled, and I felt a pang of envy every time I saw a woman swish past on her bicycle as I was passed from uncle to driver to chaperone like a parcel. It would have warmed me up, too, I thought bitterly, as I tried to stop my teeth from chattering.

The fact that I was even allowed out of the house surprised me a little – I knew that if Aunt Emily had her way, I wouldn't move from her watchful gaze in the parlour from sun-up to sun-down, in an attempt to protect the tattered remains of my virtue.

We crested the hill of Hanover Street and I couldn't suppress a sigh of pleasure as I saw the city sprawling out beneath me. Beyond the commerce and bustle of Princes Street lay the pleasure gardens, green and lush even as winter crept in. Looming above that were the craggy grey outlines of Castle Rock, with the building itself nestled on top. It was hardly the gothic ruin of my imagination, but its proximity to the modern city was atmospheric, especially shrouded in mist as it was this early in the morning. Nothing more than an attraction for curious visitors these days, its vaults had once been used as a prison, and it was all that separated the wealthy New Town from the poverty and dirt of the Grassmarket and Cowgate.

The horses slowed their pace as they began the ascent of the Mound, the first trains of the day rumbling beneath us through tunnels hewn out of rock. The Bank of Scotland, the last bastion of wealth and privilege before we entered the slums of the Royal Mile, was at the top of the hill, and as we passed it and entered the shabbier Old Town, my uncle lowered his paper and fixed me with a stony glare.

'This is no suitable place for a lady to visit,' he warned me. 'If I hear of you stepping foot outside of the university buildings unaccompanied, you can say goodbye to your studies.'

I felt my cheeks burn, and prayed that my countenance looked innocent. I wondered if he had truly been fooled by the clumsy excuses for my lateness the previous night.

'I promise, Uncle,' I said as meekly as I could. It was not a promise I intended to honour.

'And don't make Calhoun wait for you this evening. We have dinner guests and I expect you to be on your best behaviour.'

I forced my mouth into some approximation of a smile. My relatives had attempted on numerous occasions to reintroduce me into polite society, and each time I had committed some faux pas by mentioning my studies or simply expressing an opinion stronger than complimenting the fish course.

We arrived at the medical school, the grey-stone building surrounding a small courtyard of cobbles lit up by the first rays of silvery morning light, and I dutifully bid my uncle goodbye. Fellow early risers had started to drift in ready to begin the day's work, although as yet I was the only woman. None of the chaperones had arrived, and I was hesitant to push my luck by demanding entry, but it was too cold for protocol.

Burying my freezing hands even further into my fur muff, I shot the porter my most charming smile. He frowned.

'Madam, I'm not sure . . .'

'Oh leave her alone, Donaldson. She's as much right to be here as the rest of them. More, if her last essay is anything to go by.'

I turned, startled to hear Merchiston rising to my defence. Was he hoping to buy my silence with flattery? It stung that he thought so little of me as to assume that would work. But there was no trace of shame or embarrassment in his eyes; just a deep weariness that I recognised. Had he slept as poorly as I had done? Which was he suffering from, I wondered: the after-effects of too much strong drink, or a guilty conscience? He gave me a neutral nod, and ushered me in ahead of him, much to Donaldson's grumbling dismay.

'If they're going to protest that you're too delicate to study medicine, then you're certainly too delicate to stand outside in weather that's a gnat's wing away from freezing,' he commented drily. 'And you can't get into much trouble in the hallway.'

Though I had thought him angular, standing so close to him I realised that he was sinewy, and stronger than he appeared. I thought back to his tight grip on my arm, and wondered anew if those strong hands with their long, slender fingers had been the ones to leave bruises on Lucy's body.

He shifted, looking awkward. 'I believe I have cause to thank you, Miss Gilchrist.'

'It was nothing, Professor, I assure you.'

'I am curious as to one thing, though,' he said in a low voice. 'What in the blazes were you doing in a place like that?'

'Delivering some blankets and food from my aunt,' I said, hoping my lie was a convincing one. 'One of the workers at my uncle's brewery is ill, and she wanted to send them some broth.'

He frowned. 'I find it hard to believe that your aunt sent you to the slums unchaperoned.'

'I was supposed to be accompanied by Fiona Leadbetter, but the infirmary was so busy that I went alone.'

'Dr Leadbetter should take more care of her girls,' he said, and I felt a twinge of guilt at my lie. 'You were lucky you were accosted by me, instead of some drunk who might have . . .' He trailed off. 'If you wish to play Lady Bountiful to Edinburgh's deserving poor, Miss Gilchrist, I suggest you choose your location more wisely. There's nothing deserving about those wretches. Pickpockets, pimps and houses of ill repute, there's not a Christian soul among them.' He lapsed into silence, and I wondered if that was meant to be a warning – or a threat.

There was no escaping the fact that not only was Professor Merchiston on first-name terms with a whore called Lucy, but that I had witnessed him being forcibly ejected from her former establishment. What else could have brought him to that part of the city? It was plausible – more than plausible – that he had simply been on some errand of mercy, plying his trade in one of the city's most deprived areas. Had I been any less cynical and had he been less drunk at the time, I would have privately congratulated him on his philanthropy and banished the event from my mind. But I knew what men were really like. A well-cut suit, a good reputation, even a title – those were no safeguard against immorality. Yes, Professor Merchiston had seemed kind in his dour way. But then so had Paul.

A shiver ran through me that had nothing to do with the cold. I turned my head towards the corridor and saw that he was watching me. He caught my eye, tipped his hat to me and vanished into the lecture hall. I pulled my coat tighter around me and watched as the mist of my breath lingered in the air.

Alison Thornhill arrived soon afterwards, much to my relief.

'Morning, Gilchrist,' she greeted me cheerfully. 'Rotten weather. It's all right for the Scots, they're used to it, but some of us come from warmer climes.'

I smiled. Out of the dozen students, all but three of us – myself, Alison and the hated Julia Latymer – were Scottish. Our dislike of the intemperate weather was the source of much amusement to the others, but I couldn't help noticing that they had still chosen to stay a little longer abed this morning.

Eventually, however, they all drifted in, and we were admitted to Professor Merchiston's lecture. He glanced up as we entered, frowning as though he had been lost in thought and forgotten where he was.

I chose a seat as far away from him as decently possible, and though I trained my eyes on my paper and pen, I felt his gaze bore into me.

'We shall begin, ladies, with our study of laudanum.'

He held in his hand a glass bottle, sloshing the liquid lazily around as he spoke. It was half empty. I shivered. Was this a university prop for lectures, or from his own private collection of narcotics? And if so, who had taken the rest of it?

'Who can recite the properties?'

Edith raised her hand and parroted the textbook's paragraph on the substance, with one or two errors. As he corrected her, I wrote swiftly, my hands trembling so that my writing was jerky and illegible, slanting across the page. I barely lifted my head from my work the entire hour, unable to meet the professor's black gaze. It seemed that whenever I looked up, his eyes would be on me.

But as I feigned concentration, anger coiled inside me. Merchiston had sworn the same oath that I would take when I graduated, and I could not see how he could reconcile purchasing the feigned affections of one of those poor creatures with the promise to restrain himself from indulging in the pleasures of the flesh in any house he entered. The knowledge that one of my professors had the carnal appetites that led to using women like Lucy made me feel ill. I had schooled myself to see them as sexless beings, devoted entirely to their vocation. It was the only way I could feel comfortable with them. Now that I was faced with the reality, I could no longer avoid the spectre of intimacy I had tried so hard to ignore. I wondered if I would ever feel comfortable in his presence if events conspired to leave us alone together; if I would ever be free of the fear that had haunted me for nearly a year.

I thought back to the murders that had ravaged London's East End some years ago. I had only heard whispers, scraps of information gleaned from old newspapers, but when a string of prostitutes were butchered with the most exact precision, the police had thought a doctor responsible. Of course, I didn't suspect Merchiston of being another Ripper, no matter how much he unsettled me. But was it so hard to believe that a man with the power of life and death at his fingertips would choose to exercise it on a defenceless girl whose only crime lay in her inability to escape poverty?

As I walked to join the gaggle of female students waiting for the chaperone to escort them to the Playfair Library to study, I recalled my promise to the porter the day before. Reluctantly I turned away from the courtyard and headed for the stairs that snaked down into the ice-cold cellars of the university buildings. It was time to visit Lucy again.

The dissection room was almost deserted. At the far end of the room, a student was elbow-deep in intestines and spared me no more than a cursory glance.

When I happened upon McVeigh, he glowered at me.

'The girl I saw yesterday – I've spoken to her madam. She says that if you release her, I can pay for a burial.' Not entirely true, but who would contradict me?

'Too late for that,' he informed me curtly. 'She's been taken away.'

'Taken where?' I asked.

'I didnae ask and I didnae care.' He shrugged. 'Woman came claiming she was her landlady' – the tone he used made it clear what he thought of that – 'and said she'd make the arrangements. Name of Ruby McAllister.' He eyed me, smirking. 'Seems she decided she didnae need your help after all, miss.'

He turned on his heel and walked down the corridor, whistling. I stood in the chilly room, looking after him. Had Ruby had a change of heart? Had she informed Lucy's relatives, or taken it upon herself to arrange a funeral out of some sense of guilt at the end Lucy had met? I couldn't imagine that dour, surly woman making any kind of effort to commemorate the life of one of her tarts, let alone one that involved putting her hand in her purse.

McVeigh was lying to me, but not, I thought, on his own behalf. Someone had claimed Lucy since she'd been identified, and from the gleam on his new boots, someone who was generous with their coin. Perhaps the same person who had arranged for her to be sent to the university morgue in the first place, lost among dozens of other anonymous corpses whose identifying features had long since been stripped away. And that meant her killer knew the university very well indeed.

Ignoring all the regulations about not running in the corridors, I dashed after McVeigh as fast as my corset and stays would carry me. He looked unimpressed as I caught up with him.

'Mr McVeigh, where do the bodies we operate on come from?'

'Workhouse mainly. Or the polis, if no one identifies them. And sometimes people cannae afford a burial and offload their dearly departed onto us for a few shillings.'

'And Lucy? Where did she come from?'

'One dead tart among the countless others we get every week? Your guess is as good as mine, miss.'

'But there must be paperwork – a ledger, perhaps?' I persisted. 'Something that tells us who sent her here?'

McVeigh sucked on his teeth. 'Aye,' he admitted. 'But it's confidential.' He gave me a nasty smile, and this time when he moved away I did not follow him.

Chapter 10

There was a fire built up in my bedroom grate when I arrived home. Aunt Emily, in a rare display of humanity, rang for a cup of tea, and hot water for my bath. The day had been long and my head was awhirl. Any thoughts of voicing my suspicions to McVeigh had vanished at the sight of his dour, unsettling countenance. Bad enough that he thought me a sentimental female without seeming like a raving hysteric to boot.

And yet the sight of Lucy's bruised, lifeless body haunted me. I had no idea what my next step should be. I could only hope that the distraction of the dinner party would leave the course clear in my mind when I awoke the next day. I sank into the hot water with an audible murmur of appreciation, feeling warmth creep into my chilled limbs for the first time in hours. The heady scent of lavender soothed me, banishing all thoughts of Lucy and her world far from my mind.

Wrapped in my dressing gown, I towelled off my hair and ordered Agnes to bring out my finest underthings. I needed the feeling of linen and lace against my skin like a suit of armour if I was going to survive tonight's ordeal. Looking dubious but too scared to contradict me, she did so, and the sensation of clean clothes was luxurious.

Standing in front of the mirror in my undergarments, I regarded myself critically. The weight I had lost last year had not returned, and my face still had a pinched, gaunt look to it. The shadows beneath eyes that were once my finest feature marred any appeal they might have had, and my lips were chapped and flaking. I looked more like a patient than a doctor.

The importance to my uncle of tonight's meal was evident in the tightness of my corset. Agnes had to use all her strength to yank the ties that compressed my waist in a futile attempt to give me womanly curves. I thought the overall effect was ridiculous – a parody of the female figure bearing as much resemblance to reality as the gowned mannequin dangling in the university courtyard – but knew that Aunt Emily would approve. So long as I didn't breathe, drink or talk, I could get through the dinner party with minimal pain. To my disappointment, the pale green silk of my nicest gown only added to my pallor, but I hoped that I would pass for delicate and fragile rather than mousy and ill. The last thing I needed was a lecture on the deleterious effect on a woman's health of too much studying. At least, I reminded myself, I possessed neither a moustache nor a masculine countenance, so one ridiculous notion about educated women could be put to rest.

Agnes' attempt to arrange my hair as per Aunt Emily's instructions was, I thought, quite acceptable. The pearl hairpins, a gift from my mother on my twenty-first birthday, were part of a set inherited from my grandmother, and it had taken much pleading for them to remain in my possession at all. Had it not been for Gertie's obstinate refusal to take them, my pretty baubles would have been yet another relic of my past I was forced to discard. Fastening the choker around my neck and arranging the matching ropes of pearls in my décolletage as well as I could, I vowed that I would do everything in my power to mend relations with my immediate family.

Unfortunately, this meant impressing Aunt Emily, and the distant likelihood of that happening depressed my spirits even further. All the more reason to be on my best behaviour tonight – my uncle's old army friend and his wife were likely to be crashing bores, but all that was required of me was silence and a sweet smile. I could bite my tongue for a few hours. The silence might even be soothing after all the arguing and negotiating I was forced to do at the university simply to survive the day. Yes, for once, my aunt and I were in perfect accordance. For once, I wanted to be something other than a medical student, someone other than myself, even if only for one night.

Everyone was already in the drawing room by the time I arrived, sipping aperitifs and making polite conversation, so I couldn't avoid being the centre of attention. I was pronounced 'a charming lassie' by Colonel Greene, and his wife enquired as to the creator of my gown. In reality it was over a year old, but it had been made over sufficiently to pass muster with the current season's trends, and my vanity was mollified by the compliment.

To my mounting concern, Colonel Greene's son, a nervous young man with sweaty palms that left the elbow of my gloves unpleasantly damp, escorted me into dinner. He made no attempt to explain his lofty position at the bank, presumably on the basis that as a mere woman I couldn't possibly understand matters of finance, and for once I was thankful for his assumption. The fragment I followed in the stilted conversation with my uncle was enough to bore me to tears, and instead I listened with something very nearly approaching interest to my aunt's complaint about the latest parlourmaid. I was grateful for the wine that Greene Junior poured for me, although his shaking hands meant that more of it ended up on my napkin than in the glass. I had little taste for alcohol these days, but the cool, crisp liquid was delicious and I realised that I was ravenous. I prayed that my stomach wouldn't rumble before the soup was served.

This was by no means the first dinner party I had attended since my exile to Scotland, but it was easily the most lavish. My apprehension increased with each course, and by the time the pheasant was served, the intentions of my relatives was starkly obvious.

'Good bird, this.' The Colonel nodded with approval through a mouthful of said pheasant. 'One of yours, Hugh?'

My uncle nodded. 'Weekend in the country. Lovely place out by Dunkeld, marvellous shooting. You should join me sometime, Laurence. Miles, I bet you're a crack shot. Steady hand, eh?'

This was so patently not the case that poor Miles could only blush and stammer something about it being the enthusiasm that counted. My uncle's face was a mask of polite agreement, but I knew inside that he was spoiling for a fight. The fact that he didn't correct the younger man, much less call him a lily-livered whippersnapper, was enough to confirm my worst fears.

Finally my family had found someone both desperate enough and wealthy enough to affiance me to. Quite why this seemingly respectable family were willing to welcome a fallen woman and bluestocking into their midst was a mystery to me, and my mind was scrabbling for ways to get out of the situation that wouldn't deepen my disgrace any further.

I wondered if my mother was behind this. I knew my studies were only an excuse to get me away from London society and the gossip that trailed in my wake; I knew this was merely a compromise that helped them far more than it did me. I was still an oddity, the black sheep of the family, but university meant that I was bundled off without the further scandal that disowning me would have caused. It had never occurred to me that it might simply have been a ruse, and that my aunt had been on the lookout for a husband for me ever since I arrived on her doorstep on that rainy August afternoon.

Rage tightened my throat so that I could barely choke down my syllabub. I would not give up the chance I had fought so hard for. I would not be sold off to whatever bidder they could scrounge up for me and live my life somewhere between a well-dressed servant and an unpaid prostitute. Miles seemed harmless enough, but the thought of his touch made me want to vomit. I had submitted myself to a life of spinsterhood, and gladly. I would not give in so easily.

As I exited the dining room with my aunt and Mrs Greene – whose offer to call her Aurora I grudgingly forced myself to accept – I prayed that Miles would say something so inane that even my uncle's goodwill would be tested. What I had initially put down to nerves increasingly resembled a limited intellect. Surely they wouldn't be so cruel as to marry me off to a simpleton? I was the equal of most men of his age as far as education was concerned, whether they liked it or not, but even poor little Agnes could outwit Miles Greene.

Fortunately the drawing room lights were low enough to mask any outward display of the horror I felt, and I hoped my silence would pass for feminine meekness instead of sullenness. As it turned out, Aurora Greene wasn't a bad conversationalist, and played Lady Bountiful for a charity that rescued women from the streets. In a voice that shook with the thrill of the scandal, she recounted the fates of some of the poor unfortunates who entered the doors of the refuge.

'And do you know, it's other women who draw them into

that wretched life in the first place, more often than not,' she informed us.

My aunt demurred that surely no Christian woman would lead another into such a life of vice.

'I can assure you, Emily, I speak the truth. These women get a fee for every poor child they usher to those places. Some of them become quite profitable by it.'

'Ah, but at what cost to their souls, Aurora?'

There was no escaping it – Aunt Emily's eyes were fixed on me, a clear reminder that she considered me little better than the procuresses who provided the brothels with a steady flow of women desperate enough to spread their legs for strangers if it meant a bed for the night and an alternative to the work-house. Luckily if Aurora noticed the subtle admonishment she did not comment on it, and the conversation turned to the fine needlework carried out by the women of her refuge. 'Really, you'd think they were brought up as ladies. And you should see the embroidery on the cushions! Why, some of it is even in the servants' parlour.'

'Perhaps Sarah could accompany you to the reform-atory one afternoon?' Aunt Emily suggested in sugary tones. 'I'm sure her zeal for helping the unfortunate could find a suitable outlet there.' The word *suitable* was aimed squarely at me.

'I'm sure Miss Hartigan would be delighted!' Aurora said. 'The girls are so in need of genteel company to remind them how they ought to behave.'

The thought that I was to be any sort of example was as laughable to me as it was to Aunt Emily. I could hear loud footsteps and louder voices, and as the gentlemen and their accompanying whiff of cigar smoke joined us, I hoped the noise hid my sigh of relief. The port had put Uncle Hugh and Colonel Greene in even higher spirits than before, and Miles was flushed and a tad unsteady on his feet. Perhaps he wasn't used to drinking or simply couldn't hold his liquor – either way, he cringed under the black gaze from his father as he stumbled into a chair, knocking the antimacassar askew. Aunt Emily seamlessly changed the subject from prostitution to the benefits of charity work, and this was where my first misstep occurred.

'You must encounter many sad souls in the course of your studies, Miss Gilchrist,' Miles stammered.

I nodded, unsure of how to proceed. 'I volunteer at an infirmary for the deserving poor. We offer them guidance as much as medical attention, and the bishop has commented on our work on several occasions.' In truth, we offered medical attention to whoever staggered through our doors, and we, like them, were more concerned with their bodies than their souls. Although religious pamphlets were provided for those who chose to take them, that number was minimal, and they generally found their way to the floor of the operating room, soaking up blood and urine. It was at least true that the bishop had commented on our work, although little of what he said had been pleasant. I decided not to mention that he had called us godless harpies with morals no better than the women who walked the street outside the infirmary walls.

'I can't see the gentlemen of the university being happy about this monstrous regiment of women storming their battalions,' chortled Colonel Greene, placing a little too much emphasis on 'monstrous' for my liking.

'They are learning to accommodate us,' I said through gritted teeth, remembering the gangs of fellow students who had shown up on our first day, in protest at our presence. We had not been able to enter the building for a full half-hour, and when we arrived at the lecture hall we were greeted with an empty room and a letter informing us that if we couldn't be bothered to attend on time, Dr Franklin couldn't be bothered to teach us.

'And this work,' Aurora nearly choked on the word, 'you find stimulating?'

'Ladies must have their hobbies,' my uncle chuckled, although his laughter failed to reach his eyes. 'Doubtless she'll tire of it when her attention is diverted to other things, eh, Sarah?'

I feigned ignorance with a vapid smile and silently willed the floor to open up and swallow me whole before I could hurl the dregs of my lukewarm tea at him. The discussion moved to the glorious prospects that apparently awaited Miles at the bank, as well as the glittering political career that the Greenes' elder son was about to embark on. The whole conversation reminded me of the costermongers I passed on my way to the infirmary, but with Miles and myself as the produce being hawked at cut-throat prices. I wondered if he was as bruised and unwanted as I, so difficult to sell that I was all they could get for him. I felt sorry for him after a fashion – this was as humiliating for him as it was for me – and I heard him breathe a soft sigh of relief when the clock struck eleven and his father rose.

I shared his relief. My jaw ached from being clenched in a meek smile, my tongue sore from the many times I had been forced to bite it. Were all women in such pain, I wondered, simply from doing what was expected of them? Laced up so that we could barely breathe or walk, only enough oxygen and energy to agree with the menfolk and sew a few samplers, we hobbled through our days as best we could. What were men so afraid of that they had to confine us like wild animals at the zoo?

As the door banged shut behind them, I turned to go upstairs, glad that this sorry charade was over but dreading the prospect of a second act. My aunt, however, had other ideas.

'Well,' she said, 'that was a charming evening. Miles is certainly growing into a fine young gentleman, don't you think, Sarah?'

'Oh, she was tongue-tied all evening, Emily!' my uncle replied with a roguish grin. 'I believe young Master Greene has quite the new admirer.'

'He is . . .' I struggled to find words to describe Miles other than 'irredeemably stupid'. I settled on 'very nicely dressed'. The inadequacy of my statement drew a gimlet glare from my aunt, but my uncle merely patted me on the shoulder.

'Oh, he caught your eye, then. Charming fellow like that, how could he not? Besides,' he added as his grip tightened, 'we know you aren't exactly a shrinking violet where gentlemen are concerned. I'm sure he'll do very well for you.' I heard Aunt Emily's sharp intake of breath, and found my gaze fixed firmly on my boots, my cheeks scarlet with shame.

'He is a charming young man, Uncle Hugh,' I said, my hands curling into fists in the folds of my skirt. 'I assure you, I am flattered by his attentions. Forgive me, it is late and the excitement of the evening has quite worn me out.'

I fled upstairs before they could see me cry.

I left my pretty dress crumpled on the floor, my pearls dumped unceremoniously on the dressing table to be cleared away by Agnes tomorrow. The effort I had made over my appearance sickened me now that I knew what it had been in aid of, and I vowed to look my plainest tomorrow. I would quote Homer over the dinner table next time the Greenes came to call, and I would dissect my meat as though I were at the operating table. Perhaps I would even join the Rational Dress movement and adopt the bifurcated skirts that Amelia Bloomer had recently pioneered.

And if I did any of that, I would promptly be thrown out

onto the streets or into the nearest madhouse. My options were non-existent – all I could hope for was that another suitable lady would show up and win Miles Greene's dubious affections. I had come so far, only to face the fate I thought I had avoided.

Oh, I had always thought of marriage in favourable terms – I had even considered Paul Beresford a likely candidate once. But in my imagination it had always been a man of my own choosing, and I had thought my future career would guard me against the type who wanted nothing more than a hostess for his parties and a mother for his children. How many gentlemen wanted to marry a woman with a university education, much less one who wielded a scalpel in one hand and a bottle of laudanum in the other?

And now, when the memories of Paul's hands tearing at my skirt and bodice plagued my dreams and the very thought of so much as a kiss on the cheek was enough to make my stomach roil, the whole sordid business made me want to vomit.

The image stirred thoughts I had kept at bay all evening. The memory of skin mottled with bruises contrasted sharply with the woman I had met a few nights ago, angry and frightened but so alive.

Lucy had not died by accident, nor by her own hand, that I was sure of. There was a fierceness to her that made me think she would not have given up so easily. Perhaps she had chosen to forget her troubles, to abandon her grim reality for that soporific state I remembered well. Perhaps she had misjudged the dose, or had just ceased to care what happened to her. Her disgrace had been prolonged; all the more reason for her release to be easy, drifting into an endless, dreamless sleep. Or perhaps someone had forced her mouth open, pinching her nose or clamping her jaw, until she spluttered and choked and swallowing was involuntary. My hand drifted to my own lips, recalling how easy it had been for Dr Waters to force the cold spoonful of medicine between my lips until my struggles subsided. Doctors had many ways of making women take their medicine.

I stared out of my window at the gas lamps that lit the street below. Carriages trundled past, the occasional walker out for an evening stroll. It would be easy to join them, to walk down into the city and become invisible in the evening throng. My aunt's servants wouldn't stop me; they would simply take great delight in reporting my disappearance. And then it would be too late; I would not return. Just swing my legs over the bridge above the railway, a little jump, and it would all be over.

And Paul Beresford would have won a second time, destroying my life as well as my virtue. I fought the temptation for the thousandth time, forced it back into the tiny corner of my mind where I kept it locked away. I had thought I was beyond these wicked thoughts, thought the craving for self-destruction that had taken hold of me in the months following my attack had been banished by hard work and long hours. Now I wondered if that little voice in my mind could ever be quietened. And as I drifted into a fitful, broken sleep, I knew that Lucy had not tried to take her own life.

And I knew that I would not have blamed her if she had.

Chapter 11

'But as for the cowardly, the faithless, the detestable, as for murderers, the sexually immoral, sorcerers, idolaters, and all liars, their portion will be in the lake that burns with fire and sulphur . . .'

As the minister droned on, I struggled to stay awake, regretting the previous night's decision to study until the wee small hours. I at least felt a little closer to understanding Professor Merchiston's subject. *Materia medica*, the study of the properties of drugs, was fascinating, but the pace of study was so fast that I was constantly in fear of getting left behind. It was some small consolation that I was not the only one who felt that way – even the normally unflappable Julia was beginning to look pressured as the intensity of our workload grew.

The men at least had the option of letting off a little steam in their free time. Although they were nowhere near as decadent as their predecessors a decade ago had been, overheard conversations in the corridors always seemed to include discussions of that night at the music hall, or this trip to a particular bawdy house. I suspected that many of them exaggerated their escapades, but although I didn't envy them their pursuits, it rankled that they had an outlet for their energies whilst we only had sewing and paying calls.

Still, although I felt exhausted, I was also exhilarated. I had never worked so hard in my life – not in the schoolroom, where my governess was more concerned about my posture than the date of the Battle of Hastings, and not at school, where my passion for learning was considered rather odd. I might have heartily disliked most of my fellow students, but at least I had something in common with them.

I felt a sharp kick to my ankle – Aunt Emily had noticed my inattention – and tried to focus on the sermon. At home, I had always found staring down at my prayer book to be the easiest option, especially if I had gone to the trouble of secreting a novel in there before the service, but Aunt Emily watched me like a hawk and I knew that I would end up reciting half the service back at her over luncheon, if only to prove that I had been listening.

As we left the church, I caught a glimpse of a familiar face, and, making mumbled excuses to my aunt and uncle that I would be chided for later on, pushed my way through the throng of people as politely as I could until I reached Fiona Leadbetter.

'I didn't expect to see you here,' I said with delight.

'I'm afraid my motives are rather more capitalist than Christian,' she said in a low voice. 'The minister has a substantial fund to aid the deserving poor, and I was hoping he might be persuaded to donate some of it to the infirmary.'

'Do you really think he would approve?'

She sighed with barely concealed irritation, and I realised how wan she looked. 'I have to try, Sarah.'

I bit my lip. 'Is the infirmary really so poor?'

'We're getting by, but barely. Honestly, if it wasn't for your help twice a week, I don't know how we would cope with the influx of patients we see every day. We can't afford to bring on any more nurses, and there certainly isn't enough money for another doctor. I'm dividing my time between seeing patients and charming philanthropists, and most nights I don't see my bed until the clock has chimed one in the morning.'

'Physician, heal thyself,' I warned affectionately. 'If you fall ill, all hell will break loose.'

She flashed me a tired but grateful smile. 'It's nice to see my work appreciated. Heaven knows our patients don't see it that way a lot of the time.'

She was right – days where the doctors were not spat at, cursed, propositioned or threatened with physical violence were few and far between.

I put my hand on her arm. 'Fiona, you're doing such good work. Your patients may not say as much, but if you weren't there, they'd be far worse off.'

'But there are so many people we're not reaching, Sarah.' She sounded defeated, something I wasn't used to hearing from her. I was alarmed.

Before I could reassure her, I saw my aunt making her way over to us with a face hard as iron.

'Sarah, could you please gather your things? Your uncle and I would prefer to have luncheon whilst it's still warm.' Her tone was icy, but I refused to dispense with formalities.

'Aunt Emily, this is Fiona Leadbetter.' I left her title off, knowing that it would only provoke her to use it. 'She runs St Giles' Infirmary, and does all manner of good works. Fiona, Mrs Hugh Fitzherbert, my aunt.'

The two women acknowledged each other with a polite nod, but Fiona was no keener to meet my aunt than my aunt was to meet her. No wonder, given the amount of grumbling I did when I was at the infirmary.

'Aunt Emily is most influential in the Edinburgh Christian Women's Association,' I explained pointedly. 'They support all manner of good causes – why, just last month they helped fund a missionary expedition to the Gold Coast of Africa!'

Fiona's expression thawed as she realised why I was so keen to make the introduction.

'Mrs Fitzherbert, it's a pleasure to meet you. Your niece is quite charming, and practically indispensable. It really is good of her to give her time to help the unfortunate.'

'My niece is far too accommodating for her own good,' Aunt Emily replied. 'I hope you're not getting too used to her, Miss Leadbetter. We do still hold out some hope that she might fulfil her duty as a good Christian woman.'

My cheeks flushed. Fiona, to her credit, did not betray her feelings, but merely nodded her assent. Suddenly I wanted to be anywhere but here. The colliding of my two worlds left my palms sweating through my gloves and my head aching. Luckily, my aunt had no intention of wasting any more time in idle chit-chat with a woman she clearly found undesirable.

In the carriage, she fixed her cold grey gaze on me.

'I do hope, Sarah,' she admonished, 'that you are not mixing with those elements of society that are better left alone.' In Aunt Emily's world, this was practically everybody except the minister, but I was wise enough not to say so.

'I promise, Aunt Emily, the clinic only administers to the most deserving poor.'

'It's not the patients that concern me, Sarah. I know you have this ridiculous notion of becoming a doctor, but I hope you will come to your senses soon enough, and I know that your family feel the same way.'

That got my attention. 'You've heard from Mother?'

'Of course I've heard from her,' she said. 'Do you really think my sister and I don't write to each other?'

I wouldn't know, being banned from writing to mine, but I was wiser than to say so.

'Did she . . . does she ask after me?'

'Of course she does, you silly child. She's your mother. It's not as though she threw you on the streets to starve – although many women would have done just that,' she added. 'She left you in the care of relatives who love you and can be counted on to provide a good Christian example for you.'

'How is she?' I begged, my words stumbling over themselves. 'And Father? How's Gertie? Is she looking forward to her first season?'

There was an awkward pause. 'Under the circumstances, they deemed it wisest not to present Gertrude next May,' Aunt Emily replied. 'She will be staying on at finishing school for another year.'

So not content with ruining my own reputation, I had risked Gertie's future happiness as well. We had been planning her debut for years, and now she would have to wait even longer whilst her friends all took their place in society. How she must hate me.

By the time we had returned home, the rain had once again begun lashing down on the cobbled streets. I was grateful to get inside to the fire, even if the warmth would be accompanied by my aunt's moralising. She was bad enough at the best of times, but Sundays meant her eagle eyes watching me as I prayed for salvation until my throat was raw. As I divested myself of my damp coat and hat, I eyed the parlour anxiously. Initially, I had been confined to my room on Sundays and told to think about my wickedness, but my aunt had quickly realised that leaving me unsupervised surrounded by books had only one effect.

Feeling her eyes on me, I meekly walked into the parlour and deliberately took the most uncomfortable chair. She nodded approvingly, as though physical discomfort and good posture were proof of my commitment to moral rectitude.

Taking the Bible from the bookshelf, she handed it to me.

'Romans 6:13 today, Sarah.'

I didn't even need to look at the page. I had this verse memorised by heart.

'"Do not offer the parts of your body to sin, as instruments of wickedness, but rather offer yourselves to God, as those who have been brought from death to life; and offer the parts of your body to him as instruments of righteousness."'

I wondered if the cause of this wickedness was sitting stiffly in a parlour, choking out the words that denounced him as a sinner. Somehow I doubted it, and the injustice of it twisted inside me. I kept my eyes lowered and my voice level and penitent. I had learnt all too well what fighting against my punishment got me.

As I came to the end of the passage, we were called into luncheon, and I added a silent prayer of thanks for my temporary reprieve. It was the first heartfelt prayer I had offered up all day.

'Dr Radcliffe is coming on Tuesday,' my uncle said. 'I expect you to be home promptly.'

I looked up, startled. 'Are you unwell, Uncle?'

'He isn't here for me,' he replied curtly. When I glanced at Aunt Emily, he sighed irritably. 'It was a condition of your father's that you be . . . kept an eye on. We don't want a repeat of the incident in London, now do we?'

I knew why Dr Radcliffe had been called. I could imagine the questions he would ask, the sensation of his cold, prying fingers against my skin. He would be just like our family doctor, who had birthed me and treated my colic and finally condemned me to life under constant supervision.

It had been Dr Waters who had examined me after the party, confirming my father's fears in hushed tones. 'An act of congress,' he had called it through pursed lips. Had I been lucid enough to speak, I would have used another word entirely, but Father had dosed me with Mother's laudanum after my screams had threatened to wake the entire household, and I had been able to do little else but lie limply on my sheets as a man's hands parted my legs for the second time that night and cold fingers probed sensitive flesh whilst my parents waited outside.

In a way, that examination was worst of all. Dr Waters had never liked me, had been horrified when I announced my intention of becoming a doctor, and had not bothered to be gentle in his ministrations. He had branded me a hysteric, driven to wanton acts by my unhealthy fascination with medicine, and prescribed a stay at a sanatorium in the countryside until the extent of my ruin could be established. I was to have no access to books, and 'this foolish nonsense about doctoring' was to be abandoned permanently. I had the society gossipmongers to thank for escaping the latter fate, at least.

And I was to go through it all again, it seemed, now that I was permitted to leave the constant supervision of my aunt. Just in case I had slipped my chaperones and – what? Spread my legs for one of my professors? Bedded a male student? Or perhaps one of the miscreants who lingered outside the clinic catcalling the female physicians had caught my eye. I schooled my expression into the kind of bland obedience they wanted. 'I won't be late, Uncle. It is very kind of you to be so concerned with my health.'

He grunted and went back to his plate, not noticing the way my grip tightened around my butter knife until my knuckles blanched. If I could, I would have driven it through his heart right there in the dining room, the blunt curve slicing neatly through his left ventricle.

Chapter 12

Medical students swarmed en masse across the courtyard to lectures and tutorials, but I hung back in the shadows until I was sure they had gone. Then, pulling my scarf higher to hide my face, I crossed the street and made for the Grassmarket. It was hard not to feel as though I was Persephone descending into the Underworld, leaving the misty Edinburgh morning behind me. I wondered if I was doing the right thing.

As I came to the Grassmarket, desperately hoping that no one from the infirmary would spy me, I caught sight of a boy of no more than ten slouched against the wall looking uninterested in anything but the bottle in his hand. His eyes flickered lazily over me as I approached, no doubt sizing me up as a possible mark for pickpocketing. He didn't reek of alcohol yet, and when he spoke, his words were not slurred. He'd do for my purpose.

'Wha' d'ye want?' he snarled.

I handed him a folded piece of paper.

'I need you to take this message to one of the porters at the medical school on Bristo Square,' I said. 'I'll give you a shilling if you do – but only,' I added hastily, 'when you've done it. It won't take you ten minutes, a strapping young lad like you.'

He didn't look as though he believed my flattery, and I couldn't blame him – he was scrawny, and if he didn't have rickets, it was only a matter of time. He probably wouldn't survive his fifteenth birthday. Still, off he scampered, giving me time to collect my thoughts before I made my way to Ruby's establishment.

I rapped smartly on the door, unsure if anyone would even be awake to answer – presumably, since so much of their work took place in the evenings, these women would be given to lying in later than one would normally expect. The door was opened by a young girl, who, despite the fact that she was fully dressed, was sleepy-eyed and not entirely coherent. As I enquired after the proprietress – amending my language when I was met with a blank stare – I realised two things. One, that the girl could not be more than fourteen years old, and two, that she was drunk.

'I'm nae meant to let anyone in, miss,' she slurred uncertainly. 'Missus Ruby said so.'

'Oh, but she didn't mean me,' I lied. 'I'm a friend of hers. A doctor.'

It was the last word that gained me entrance, much to my surprise. I had expected disbelief or scorn, but she blithely ushered me in and asked in exaggeratedly polite tones if I would care for some tea. I found myself once again sitting awkwardly in the parlour, trying to find somewhere to rest my gaze other than on the lewd artwork on the wall. I tried crossing to the bookcase, but a brief perusal of one volume left me blushing with embarrassment, if rather better informed about certain acts than I wished to be.

Hurried steps alerted me to Ruby's arrival; she began speaking before she was in the room.

'Doctor, I wasn't expecting to see you so . . .' She trailed off. 'Miss Gilchrist,' she said uncertainly. 'I'm no' sure what it is you're wanting, hen, but I don't think I can help you.'

'The porter at the university said that you collected Lucy's body. I wondered if I might attend the funeral.' She looked at me oddly. I prayed it had not yet taken place. I could, with luck, persuade the police surgeon to pay a visit to the undertaker, but an exhumation would be completely out of the question.

'You're too late,' she snapped, and I felt the last shreds of hope leave me. Lucy's final resting place would be in an unmarked pauper's grave, with no ceremony to reflect on her passing. I wasn't entirely sure what the protocol was for a streetwalker's funeral, but I had wanted it to be attended. I wanted Lucy to be mourned; for her death – natural or not – to be acknowledged in a world that had ignored her in life.

'Then can you at least tell me a little about her,' I pleaded. 'It's foolish, I know, but to meet her so briefly in life and to see her like that . . . I promise I'll never darken your door again.'

This seemed to mollify her, and she nodded slowly. Her hand in the small of my back, she shoved me out into the hall, where the child from earlier stood mouth agape, the promised cup of tea in her hands, spilling the liquid onto the floor.

'If you want to talk, you can pay for the privilege,' she snarled. 'Bessie, we'll be in the Last Drop if anyone calls for me. No' the bailiffs, mind. If they call, what do we say?'

'I've no' heard of ye, and I dinnae ken who y'are,' the girl recited in a monotone.

In the public house, Ruby ordered gin for both of us. She didn't object when I pushed my smeared glass across the table towards her.

'When did Lucy come to you?' I asked, fighting to conceal my eagerness. I didn't want to frighten her off, not before I'd extracted every scrap of information I could from her.

'About six months ago,' she conceded.

'Did she say where she'd been living? Was she at another house?'

'She didnae say and I didnae ask.'

This was worse than making conversation with Aunt Emily's lady's maid. 'Did Lucy have any regular . . . ah . . . callers?' I asked, feeling my cheeks burn. 'Anyone who seemed especially fond of her?'

'They were all fond o' Lucy,' Ruby mused, picking her teeth. They seemed a little too big for her mouth, and I realised they were probably false and designed for someone else. 'She had spirit, ye ken? If she didnae take a fancy to you, you knew it.'

'And did that happen often?'

She snorted. 'Ye cannae afford to be picky in this job, hen. If Lucy wanted a roof over her head, she had to have customers.'

'But was there a particular one?' I pressed. 'Someone who visited her often.'

Suspicion dawned in her rheumy eyes. 'I'm no' sure I like where this conversation is heading, lassie.'

In desperation, I pushed a half-crown across the table. 'Please, Mrs McAllister.'

She ran a grimy thumb across the shiny coin with an unreadable expression, then pushed it back to me firmly.

'My gentlemen pay a lot for me to forget their names, Miss Gilchrist. I'm afraid I cannae be more help.'

She gathered her shawl around her and stood up, nodding me a curt goodbye.

'Not even a gentleman by the name of Merchiston?' I called after her. If Ruby McAllister stumbled a little as she heard that name, it could have been the gin. But somehow I didn't think so. I followed her, determined not to let her go before answering me. 'Did he visit Lucy, Ruby? I swear he'll never find out that you told me.' I wasn't entirely sure

I could keep that promise, but I was desperate.

She turned back, leaning in so close her breath was hot and fetid against my face. 'Get out,' she spat. No mistaking her terror now. 'This is no place for you. What concern is Lucy of yours, eh? She was nae but a body for you to poke and prod and cut up with your knives. What business is that for a woman? If I see you asking questions here again, I'll no' be the one responsible for what happens tae you.'

The door slammed behind her as she stormed into the street, and I sat there for a moment, unnerved by the force of her emotion.

As I gathered my thoughts and stood to leave, I caught the eye of a man at a nearby table. He smiled, revealing fewer teeth than I would have expected in a man his age.

'How much for a little company, hen?'

I stared him down haughtily and swept out with all the dignity I could muster. It wasn't much.

Chapter 13

The rest of the day passed in a blur, and I found I took in little of the wisdom my teachers imparted. At four o'clock, when we were finally released, I made for the entrance.

'Sarah!' Alison called. 'It's Elisabeth Chalmers' at-home today. Aren't you coming?'

I groaned. I was hardly fit for company, especially not that of my peers and the illustrious Mrs Randall Chalmers.

Elisabeth Chalmers had accompanied her sister to Scotland three years before, when the older girl had arrived armed with her sizeable Canadian fortune and looking for a gentleman willing to exchange it for a title. Within six months, she had announced her engagement to the Earl of Speyside. Elisabeth, on the other hand, had met Randall Chalmers, a short, hirsute epidemiologist ten years her senior, at a fund-raising gala for the university and announced her engagement so quickly after her sister's that eyebrows were raised across two continents.

She sat a couple of days a week at the back of the lecture hall, wrapped up against the draughts, either absorbed in a novel or watching the lecture with an expression of mild interest. She was something of a pet to the female students, thanks to her childlike size and physical fragility and it was a fashion among the men to pay court to her in an exaggerated fashion. If their chivalry offended her husband, he never let it show, and though the charming, wry gentleman who doted on a wife whose looks, fortune and youth outstripped him so considerably could easily have been seen as a figure of fun, they treated him with courtesy out of respect for Elisabeth. It was noted, however, that not once had the Chalmerses invited any of the male students for tea.

Although she hid her eyes at the more gruesome aspects of our education, Elisabeth was broadly supportive of our ambitions, if concerned that we were all wasting our youth by spending it in silent contemplation of the practice of medicine. It was this concern that brought about her monthly at-homes: although we spent nearly every waking minute of the day together, Elisabeth was keen for us to socialise as well as discuss our studies, and so for two hours every second Tuesday of the month, we crowded into her drawing room and devoured tea and cake and never once mentioned anatomy, surgery or disease. She could not have failed to notice the tension between our little group, but she never acknowledged it, and for those few hours I could almost be seduced into believing that these women were indeed my closest friends.

So I joined the gaggle of students tramping across the tree-lined Meadows, the walk filled with autumn leaves rimed with frost. The green fields behind the university were popular with strollers and students taking a few gulps of air before being submerged back into the bowels of the lecture halls and the tutors' cramped rooms. With the grey and purple crags looming over the city visible, it was picturesque provided one forgot that the hill was a dormant volcano and the sloping dips of the Meadows were filled-in plague pits from centuries earlier. Still, it felt like glorious freedom, although the company left a little to be desired.

Julia lit a gasper with a flourish I had tried and failed to emulate and therefore dismissed as pretentious, and strolled ahead with Alison on one arm and a sulky Edith on the other. Refusing to be left out, I fell into step with Caroline Carstairs. The youngest of the group, she was gawky and painfully shy, self-conscious of her thick Highlands accent that never disappeared no matter how properly she spoke. She rarely smiled, and when she spoke, she seemed unable to discuss anything other than her studies.

'It's a beautiful day,' I offered awkwardly. I had never been any good at small talk, and these days I so rarely gossiped that when I did, my mouth felt rusty with neglect. She nodded wordlessly, chewing on a damp strand of Titian hair. Any further attempt at conversation was interrupted when a gaggle of young men cycled past, shouting and calling names. One of them threw a stone that caught Edith sharply on the shoulder, and she cried out, as much from alarm as pain.

Town-and-gown riots were rarer than they used to be, but where the sons of the city were now largely left alone by their less-educated neighbours, the vitriol had spread to those of us belonging to the fairer sex.

'How can you stand this so calmly?' asked Alison, exasperated and close to tears after one boy had dogged our steps for ten minutes.

My breath huffed out in a cloud. 'You get used to it. But I must say, one expects it from these brats a little more than from one's own fellow students.'

'Julia's a beast,' Alison said with feeling that would have been more comforting had she not abandoned me in favour of said beast's company so many times before. 'Everyone knows it; they just don't want to be the next target of her cattiness.'

'Well then, she's never going to learn,' I grumbled, wrapping my scarf more tightly around my neck as the breeze gusted around us. 'She'll always be the same, right up until the day we graduate.'

'Was she always that way?' Alison asked. 'I mean, you did know her in London.'

I bit my lip. 'We went to the same parties,' I said. 'That's not quite the same thing.'

I changed the subject, not wanting to dwell on the past. Even here, I still felt the after-effects of that night, like ripples on a pond. When would they end?

The thought that some whiff of the scandal that had sent me from London might had reached the Chalmerses made me feel ill. It wasn't beneath Julia to drop subtle hints about it – she'd managed to alienate the majority of our peers from my company by just that tactic – but if she had said something to Elisabeth, it would inevitably reach the university professors. We were required to have spotless reputations in order to be admitted, and I knew that although gossip and hearsay were hardly admissible in a court of law, it would be more than enough to see me excluded from the one place I had found refuge.

It was with considerable relief that we arrived at the house in Warrender Park Crescent to a warm welcome – the fire burnt in the grate, and tea and crumpets were already laid out in lavish quantities. Elisabeth was pristine in a pale apricot dress that suited her fine colouring well – her hair was verging on red, and in the firelight its warm glow was heightened. She looked radiant and welcoming.

'Girls! How good of you to come. I know how difficult it is for you to take time away from your studies.' She embraced me warmly, and I caught a hint of the powder and scent she used – like everything else about her, it was light and sweet, with the slightest undertone of warm spices. It would be so easy to take her at face value, to see the pretty china doll and to miss the flash of spirit beneath.

'We couldn't resist the invitation, Elisabeth,' Julia dimpled charmingly. 'You know how much we all adore Mrs Flanders' cooking!' Elisabeth had caused something of a scandal by importing her own cook into this fiercely Scottish household, but Mrs Flanders was as popular in her own circle as her mistress was in hers, and her baking was a thing of wonder and joy for girls used to lodging houses and the university refectory.

It was strange to see each other outside of the confines of the university buildings. Women who were perennially hunched over textbooks, ink-stained and wrapped up in shawls to keep out the cold, sat primly on overstuffed armchairs trying to make polite conversation instead of engaging in rigorous academic debate, or bantering with the male students in an effort to show that we weren't intimidated by their hostility.

I watched as Caroline, whom I had seen devour three hot buttered crumpets in as many minutes whilst running between the laboratory and dissecting rooms, nibble daintily on a slice of caraway cake. She looked lost; her home-made dress well-tailored and neat, but hopelessly frumpy next to Elisabeth's restrained elegance. Whilst most of us had come from comfortable homes – and in the case of Julia and myself, rather more so – she and Moira were both working class, fish out of water for more than just their sex among the moneyed second sons or doctors' offspring that made up our male cohorts. But whilst Caroline was overwhelmed, Moira wore her origins proudly. She might not have known which fork to use at a dinner party, but she could wield a scalpel with the best of them, and no ladylike tea party was going to intimidate her.

'What do you think about the vote, Mrs Chalmers?' she asked boldly. I eyed her with reluctant admiration. Whilst I was curious about our chaperone's opinions, I would never have dared express it so openly.

Elisabeth frowned. 'It's so hard to say,' she began. Yes, hard to say indeed that half the country should be forced to abide by its laws yet have no say in its lawmakers. Hard to say that we should continue to be treated as appendages of our husbands and fathers, degree or not. 'Now that women are permitted to study alongside men, now that we – well, you – can enter the professions, surely the franchise can't be too far behind. And yet there is so much resistance – from ladies as much as gentlemen!'

'Aye, ladies,' Moira snapped. 'Easy to think you don't need a voice when you're protected by your husband's money. But go down onto the streets and you won't find such delicate dissembling there. It's all very well being ladylike when you don't have to fight to put a crust on the table. Women work, Mrs Chalmers, women have always worked. We may not have been doctors or scientists or academics, but we've worked. And there's nothing like seeing your mother and father toil just as hard as each other to remind you that the sexes are equal, no matter what the newspapers try to tell us. But it's the ladies of quality who'll slow progress down. And why? Because they've been told for so long that they're weak and silly that they believe it.'

An awkward silence fell.

Julia frowned. 'But Moira, it's women like Emmeline Pankhurst who are fighting for women's suffrage! They reject what they've been raised to believe and they're the ones who can influence the fight for the vote. I don't see how bringing class into it helps matters.'

Julia's mother, I remembered, was renowned for her radical views, and used every dinner party and social gathering to air them in the hope of winning converts to the cause. Like her daughter, she was a natural leader, and she had won over several sceptical politicians merely by persuading their wives to join her for supper. But Moira's eyes burnt, and she was not one to take injustice lightly.

'So we're to stay silent and clean your houses whilst the likes of you and Gilchrist chum up with the men in power, is that it?'

'That's rot, and you know it. We're simply trying to focus our energies where they will be most successful. Although if we were to do that, I'm sure Gilchrist could perform such a duty admirably.'

I jolted back as though she had hit me. Nausea coiled in my stomach, and even Julia blanched slightly, as though she had forgotten where she was.

Smoothly, Elisabeth glided in to calm the waters. 'I don't see why the vote shouldn't be extended to washerwomen as well as heiresses. Even if our brains are weaker than a man's, a lady and her maid are every bit as capable as each other.'

'Except that the washerwoman is likely to be overworked, exhausted and ill,' I pointed out. 'And hardly in a frame of mind to make a decision beyond what to cook for dinner between doing the duchess's laundry, taking in mending and trying to keep the wolf from the door. She might be perfectly capable, but when one is trying to stay off the streets, the workhouse is more important than Parliament.'

'Sarah fancies herself a great philanthropist,' Edith smirked.

'I have no such pretensions,' I said, fighting to keep my temper in check. 'But I'm lucky enough to be allowed to assist at St Giles' Infirmary, and if you spent so much as a day there, you'd understand.'

With the ease of practice that came from years of playing the perfect hostess, Elisabeth turned the subject back to the vote. Her enthusiasm went beyond polite drawing-room conversation, and I was surprised. Most of the female students were agitating for it, of course, as well as the few female academics employed by the university. But aristocratic ladies were supposed to purse their lips and frown in disapproval, rather than confess that they had donated fifty pounds to the Scottish League of Women's Suffrage.

'I shall join them in the long vacation,' Julia announced, to no one's surprise. I wondered cynically how much her passion was inflamed by the thought of political equality, and how much of it was the desire to shock.

'I wish I could go to London and meet the Pankhurst sisters,' Elisabeth sighed. She turned to me, eyes glowing. 'Sarah, you must attend a meeting when you go home for Christmas, and tell us all about it!'

My tight smile did not reach my eyes.

'I will be staying in Edinburgh over Christmas, with my aunt and uncle,' I said.

Elisabeth clapped her hands. 'Well then, you must spend Hogmanay with us! It's such a glorious party; an English New Year is nothing to it.'

'And will your parents be joining you?' Julia asked with syrupy sweetness.

'Of course.' The lie slipped out before I could stop myself, and I relished the startled look in Julia's eyes, before remembering that I would not be seeing my family for some time.

The conversation continued in a similar vein over the afternoon, debating everything from politics to the latest fashions, until, having had their fill of tea and chat, the others drifted back across the darkening Meadows to their lodgings. Soon I was the only one left, and I shifted uncomfortably in my chair, self-conscious about imposing on Elisabeth's kindness.

'Please, Sarah, have some more tea. Or would you prefer

coffee? You look so tired. You all work so hard, I know, but you most of all.'

'That isn't true,' I said. 'Why, Alison Thornhill spends far longer in the library than I do, and Edith is constantly badgering the tutors for extra sessions.'

'In class, perhaps, but what about the infirmary? You do work that the nurses ought to be doing, and you don't even get paid for the privilege!'

'Fiona Leadbetter needs my help, and I give it gladly. They have so little money. It would destroy her if they had to close.'

'That doesn't mean you should let it become your whole life.'

'Oh there's no chance of that,' I said with grim humour. 'Not whilst my aunt is trying to marry me off to Miles Greene.'

At the mention of romance, her face lit up. It was almost comedic, but I had yet to meet anyone capable of resisting her imploring blue gaze.

'I don't like him, so there's no need to look at me like that,' I said. 'Oh, I'm sure he's very sweet, but he's younger than me and, quite frankly, I've met cocker spaniels with more intellect.'

'Is that so important?' Elisabeth asked. 'Surely you're clever enough for both of you!'

I fought back the urge to laugh. It had been a long time since I'd had occasion to consider what I would want from a suitor. Although even the thought of it was discomfiting, I found myself confessing, 'I want someone to discuss things with. Not just little things like household matters, but the state of the world, politics and religion. I want someone who won't talk down to me. And I want someone I don't have to talk down to either. Is that really too much to ask?'

She and I both knew the answer to that.

'It sounds as though you want a debating society, not a husband!'

I sighed. 'Julia's starting one, haven't you heard? She says she's sick of the Women's Debating Society excluding us because they think female doctors are indecent, so she's starting one for the medical students.'

'That should be . . .' Elisabeth trailed off.

'It will be Julia on whatever hobbyhorse is fashionable this week,' I said. 'The vote, bloomers, the right to stay and smoke with the gentlemen after meals instead of retiring to the drawing room to discuss the problem of recruiting decent housemaids.' Seeing her expression, I explained, 'Oh, it's not that I don't want those things, of course I do. But I know Julia well enough to be aware that I won't be welcome there.'

'Why is that? I mean, I've noticed, of course I have, that there's some coolness between the two of you. But why?'

I didn't want to dwell on that, not in this lovely warm room with this sweet, pretty woman who was so innocent of the seedier side of life. I selfishly wanted to keep Elisabeth just as she was, and not tarnish her with my sordid history.

'Julia and I knew each other in London a little. She heard some gossip, and has decided to make up her mind about me.'

An awkward silence fell between us. The company I had kept in London would have laughed to see me so diffident and tongue-tied, but enforced solitude had left me reticent and awkward.

'I do hope I'm not imposing,' I said eventually, in an attempt to change the subject.

Elisabeth shook her head. 'You're not. Truthfully, it's nice to have the company. Randall's at his club,' she added. 'He won't be back till quite late.' Something in the way her smile stretched tautly across her face suggested this wasn't an infrequent occurrence. Could Chalmers really have tired of his pretty young wife so soon? He had not, if his impeccable frock coat was anything to go by, tired of her money.

By the time my uncle's carriage drew up, Elisabeth's sweet candour had melted my shyness and as we talked I felt almost like my old self. I hadn't felt so welcome anywhere in months, and I left with a warm feeling in my stomach that felt a little like friendship.

Chapter 14

If I had hoped that I could spend my evening studying in relative peace, those hopes were dashed before I was ten paces into the hall. Aunt Emily met me with more animation than I had ever seen her show, and the letter she held bore my name on the front in unfamiliar handwriting. It had also been opened, but I made no comment on the fact. I knew I had to choose my battles. As I had suspected, the badly spelt and rather uninspired note was signed by Miles Greene, and I pasted a smile onto my face before meeting Aunt Emily's excited gaze.

'What good manners!' she said. 'And he has such a . . . distinctive hand.' That was one way of putting it. Either his social awkwardness extended to letter-writing, or the trembling in his hands was symptomatic of something. No wonder his parents were so desperate to marry the poor boy off. I would have to pay closer attention to him at our inevitable next encounter – I had no intention of giving up my putative medical career in order to play nursemaid to an ailing husband.

'How delightful,' I smiled weakly.

'You must compose a reply at once,' she ordered. 'Fetch your writing desk and I shall dictate something suitable.

Mona!' She wandered off, calling for the parlourmaid to bring us tea and cake. With a heavy heart I obeyed, and ten minutes later we were ensconced in the parlour with too sweet weak tea and the beginnings of the blandest letter I had ever written.

'You mustn't sound too keen,' Aunt Emily cautioned, as if she wasn't writing the whole thing herself anyway. 'Discretion is the order of the day in matters of the heart. Better he think you cold and uninterested than forward.' Had I formed any sort of attachment to Miles bar some grudging sympathy, I might have disagreed with her advice. As things stood, I felt that the colder, the better.

After an hour of agonising over the perfect phrasing, and consulting everything from etiquette guides to the Bible, the doorbell rang.

I had forgotten that Tuesday was the day Dr Radcliffe was due to call.

'If you'll excuse us, Mrs Fitzherbert . . .'

He followed me upstairs as I made my way to my bedroom, my legs like lead. When he closed the door behind him, I felt the knot of panic tighten. The room with its lit fire felt hot and oppressive. I moved to the window and fumbled with the catch, opening it in the hopes of gasping in some fresh air.

I felt myself yanked back by muscled arms, well used to manhandling unruly patients.

'Might I ask what you were about to do, Miss Gilchrist?'

I could smell coffee on his breath, mixed with the sweat from his skin, and the lingering odour of snuff on yellowed fingertips.

'The room is a little warm, Dr Radcliffe. I simply wanted some air.'

'You'll catch a chill,' he said, as though I were a child or simple-minded. He pushed past me and pulled the window shut. 'We'll have no more of that.'

I realised that he had thought I was going to jump. I tried not to shudder as he moved me to the bed, remembering another cold night and another open window.

And then the medicine and the restraints, the ghastly sanatorium in the countryside where I floated in a haze of laudanum and despair for months. I realised, as I let him manoeuvre me onto the bed, that such thoughts had not plagued me in weeks. True, life in the Fitzherbert household was repressive, and the prospect of trading it for an existence as Mrs Miles Greene was worse, but I felt alive and glad to be so for the first time since I could recall.

'Now remember,' he said as I struggled to remove my undergarments, 'you're the patient here. I suggest you abandon any fanciful notions of doctoring and let me do my job. Please lie still.'

At least his hands were warm, I told myself as he began his examination. He hummed a jaunty tune under his breath as he peeled away my dignity like so many onion skins, and I closed my eyes, trying to imagine myself elsewhere, anywhere. If I resisted, would he call me hysterical? If I did not, would he take it as further proof of my immorality?

The sense of being restrained, if not physically then with fear, was so familiar to me I could taste it. Dr Waters, the staff in the sanatorium, Paul. How could Lucy and girls like her bear it, day after day? The profaning touch of strangers' hands against her skin, clutching and tugging and pushing and pulling?

A sharp pain stabbed me between my thighs, and I fought not to cry out. I refused to let myself associate it with the movements of Radcliffe's hands beneath my skirts. I couldn't think about what he was doing or I would go mad.

Finally satisfied with my current chastity, he asked questions as I dressed behind a screen, a laughable attempt at modesty.

How was I sleeping, what were my bowel movements like, did I have a good appetite? I answered in as much detail as required, waiting for the moment when he would leave to report back to Aunt Emily and I could call for Agnes to run my bath so I could scrub away the memory of his touch. I wondered if his visits would increase now that my relatives had found me an adequate husband.

Agnes came with the hot water and told me that Aunt Emily wanted to see me in the parlour.

To my relief, the good doctor had gone to torment some other poor creature.

'Dr Radcliffe was most pleased by your improvement.' Aunt Emily smiled, as though it had been nothing more than a piano lesson. Dr Radcliffe would say whatever kept him in his rich patron's good graces, but I knew better than to point that out. I loathed his touch, but I needed his approval. 'He says he can't think of a reason why any future husband would need to be . . . ah . . . informed of your condition prior to the wedding night.' In other words, he was satisfied that I was not riddled with venereal disease, as he doubtless believed I deserved to be. 'Still, he is most concerned that your studying is delaying any full recovery.'

I bit back a sigh. 'Aunt Emily, I feel perfectly well.'

'You work far too hard.' It was the second time that day I had heard those words. 'And Dr Radcliffe agrees that your health is still fragile. You must take care not to overexert yourself, especially now that . . . well, now that you're out in society again.' Whose society, I could easily guess.

I smiled weakly. 'I'll do my best.'

I followed Aunt Emily in to dinner, my thoughts tangled and thorny.

Miles was rich, well connected; my guardians approved. He was almost everything I had given up hoping for. And if he wasn't particularly handsome or a witty conversationalist – well, plenty of women married dull men and had a happy life; why should I be any different? This was a chance to escape my disgrace, to be accepted back into my family, to pretend that the past year had never happened.

But it had. And out of all the shame and hurt I had created a new sort of life, one I was not willing to give up so easily.

It was just a letter, I told myself. A polite note that his mother had probably dictated, just as Aunt Emily had crafted my response. It didn't mean the loss of my freedom or abandoning my studies for hearth and home. But I still rubbed the third finger of my left hand as though the wedding band was already tightly around it, permitting no escape.

Chapter 15

The corridors of the Old College were quiet as I strode through, determined to beard the lion in his den. My essay – a rather good one, I thought – was finished a day early, thanks to two hours and a lot of crumpets in a tea house on George IV Bridge. It was my perfect excuse to catch Merchiston off guard. I had little to go on, but he had visited Lucy – that much was certain – and Ruby McAllister, who dealt with rowdy, lust-fuelled men every day, was frightened of him.

'Can I help you, miss?' A white-haired man with a puce complexion peered at me curiously through his spectacles, as though I were an escapee from the zoo that had wandered into the building.

'I'm on my way to meet with Professor Merchiston.' I smiled sweetly. 'Don't worry, I know the way.'

'Are you sure, my dear? He doesn't usually see private patients in his university rooms.'

'I'm not a private patient. I'm one of his students.'

He shook his head. 'I'm terribly sorry, but I can't possibly allow you to meet with him unchaperoned.'

'You were perfectly happy to let me see him alone when

you thought he might be examining me,' I pointed out. His expression clouded.

'Is there a problem, Miss Gilchrist?'

I turned to see the man himself, irritation scrawled across his face.

'I was on my way to see you, Professor. This gentleman was kind enough to show me the way.' I gulped. 'Thank you for your time, sir.'

As the older man stalked off, muttering angrily under his breath, Merchiston turned to me curiously.

'You're a braver man than I, Miss Gilchrist. Professor Herbert has sent down five students this week, and it's only Wednesday.'

When he was amused, I realised, his countenance was quite pleasant. His normally sardonic smile twisted the contours of his face, but now he merely looked pleasantly surprised at my daring. It was almost enough to make both my apprehension and my suspicion melt away.

'Perhaps it would behove him to be a little more polite to the students he hasn't expelled, then,' I muttered sulkily.

Merchiston turned to me with an expression of exaggerated shock. 'Polite? To a student? Miss Gilchrist, you're here to be bullied, harangued, overworked and publicly humiliated in the hope that you might learn something. If you want manners, go back to the drawing room. Failing that . . .' He jerked his head towards his office, and I scurried after him, his black coat-tails flapping in the breeze and making him look even more like Poe's raven than normal.

As the door swung shut behind me, I began to have second thoughts about my plan. I had never been inside Merchiston's office before. It was a small, strange room, a clear indication of his place in the pecking order here. His height meant that he dominated the space, looming over his desk until he sat in his chair, motioning carelessly for me to follow suit.

'What can I do for you, Miss Gilchrist? Or are you here purely to frighten septuagenarian professors and cause chaos wherever you go?'

'My essay on the history and administration of chloroform,' I said, handing over my spurious excuse for visiting him.

'Early,' he commented. 'To what do I owe the honour?'

'I didn't want it to get lost in the pile tomorrow,' I replied innocently. The answer wasn't as glib as it seemed – more than one female student had been forced to redo her work after the original was 'misplaced' – usually at the hands of one of the male students, but occasionally a deliberate act on the part of an unsympathetic faculty member.

Luckily he accepted my answer without argument. I paused, reluctant to leave now that I had gained a private interview with him.

'Was there something else you wanted?'

I blushed. There was nothing feigned about it; as the moment came to confront him, I could barely get the words out.

'It is of a rather delicate nature. That is, I . . .'

He sighed heavily. 'Miss Gilchrist, I am a physician. If you anticipate being indisposed for tomorrow's lecture, simply say so. Unlike some of my colleagues, I do not consider your natural monthly courses to be any barrier to your fitness as a doctor. Drink some beef tea, ensure that you are fully rested and I will expect you in my lecture on Monday, having made up any work you were forced to miss.'

It would never cease to amaze me the mystical properties otherwise sensible, educated men ascribed to a perfectly natural function. If all women were really laid low every month as men seemed to think, the world would grind to a halt.

'Actually, it pertains to a patient I attended at St Giles' Infirmary. A patient who later turned up in the university dissecting rooms.'

He nodded. 'These things happen. Unfortunate, true, but not every family can afford a burial.'

'I believe she was murdered.'

He went very still, and in a quiet voice I told him what I had seen, watching him carefully for any flicker of guilt. When I had finished, I saw that his fists were clenched so hard his knuckles were white.

He was silent for a long time, as though he were trying to suppress what he wanted to say. Finally he spoke, and I realised that his voice was trembling with anger.

'Miss Gilchrist, that may be the most fantastical story I have ever heard. Perhaps you should stick to your textbooks and leave those sensational novels alone. Are your studies really so dull that you have to find excitement everywhere? For God's sake, woman, you're not even qualified to perform a proper autopsy, and yet here you are, shouting murder to all and sundry!' His jaw spasmed. 'That poor girl probably saw more violence in a day than you've encountered in a lifetime. Of course she had bruises. I'm sorry to admit it, but there are plenty of men out there who enjoy inflicting pain on women, the more downtrodden the better. And if you'd suffered what she did, then perhaps you would have found comfort in a laudanum bottle as well. Don't romanticise this. You're talking about a girl's life. It may not have been worth much to you, but please don't turn it into something out of the worst kind of novel.'

'Her name was Lucy.' The mask slipped – just for a moment, but long enough to see the shocked recognition in his eyes. There was something familiar about those eyes, something I couldn't place. Even the colour was hard to pin down, somewhere between blue and grey, like the Scottish summer sky. 'I believe you knew her.'

He turned from me, busying himself with some papers on his desk. 'I am afraid you have been misinformed.' His voice was little more than a whisper.

'There's a madam down in the Cowgate who would say differently, Professor.' I laced the word with all the venom I could muster. 'And before you say you've never met her, I should point out that I saw you leaving her establishment!'

He whirled to face me, rigid with anger. 'And your plan is to . . . what? Blackmail me? If this is some underhanded attempt to ensure your academic success, you're wasting your time. Overactive imagination aside, you're intelligent and dedicated. I suggest you stop wasting both your time and mine and return to the library.'

I reeled at the implication that I would stoop so low as to use a woman's death to secure my own future. 'My plan, Professor, is to find out who murdered her and why no one reported it to the relevant authorities. Since Ruby McAllister has been less than forthcoming about her former employee's acquaintances, you were simply the next on my list.'

Merchiston's eyes were cold as ice, and the smile into which he shaped his lips looked more like a grimace.

'Did you know that she was pregnant?' I asked, forcing the words out from between gritted teeth.

There was no disguising the look of horror that came over him, and he fought to take command of his emotions. How often, I wondered, did he lose that battle?

'You do realise that I could have you committed for these ramblings?' he said in a low, steady voice. 'With your reputation, Miss Gilchrist, no one would bat an eyelid. Perhaps another rest cure in the country is called for – isn't that how your family physician treated your last lot of wild accusations?'

He might as well have hit me for the effect his words caused.

'Get out of my office. If you attempt to speak with me privately again, I shall inform the Dean that you made improper advances towards me and have you expelled from the university.'

I was shaking as I left Merchiston's office. I had expected denial, surprise, but not this vehement anger. I walked quickly down the corridor, mind racing, praying that I wouldn't run into the irascible Professor Herbert. If I did, I knew that what little resolve I had would crumble, and I would be left a sobbing mess.

It would have been too much to ask for my reputation not to have preceded me, and the gossip started by Julia Latymer had plagued me ever since she recognised me in our first lecture. Until now, though, the faculty had made no mention of it. The discovery that Merchiston knew not only the rumours that had swirled around after that fateful night but the punishment that followed made me want to vomit. He saw me as nothing but a hysterical little girl, making up stories to garner attention.

Or perhaps I had hit too close to home when I had all but accused him of murder. I wondered with a shudder just how hollow those threats were. It seemed that my fate as Mrs Miles Green might be more inescapable than I had feared.

I emerged into the courtyard, the watery late-afternoon sun bathing the streets a few hundred yards in front of me. In the square, however, I was standing in chilly shadow, the gothic architecture of the buildings looming over me. I had always loved this place, but now I wanted to be far from it, and far away from Gregory Merchiston's accusations. I broke into a run as I left the Old College, no longer caring who saw me. I needed air and solitude, and there was only one place for me to get it.

I was out of breath by the time I reached the foot of Arthur's Seat. In pleasanter weather, it was a nice spot for a picnic, but even in the grey drizzle I found it soothing. Up here, far enough away from the breweries and factories that the air was crisp and clear, I could finally breathe. My tears dried in the chilly breeze, but for once I didn't mind the cold. The air was still tangy with hops and the traces of factory smoke, but the wind was bracing and the rain cool against my overheated skin. My cheeks were burning with shame, but shock and hurt had been eclipsed by rage.

I sat on a patch of damp grass, gazing out across the city as I mulled over what had just happened. Merchiston knew Lucy; there was no denying that. But he hadn't known that she was pregnant. There had been pain in his eyes – just a flicker, just for a moment – and it was more than just empathy for the dead girl. If he had suspected that the child was his, however slim the chance was given her occupation, I could not imagine how he must be feeling now. Was there remorse at the unforeseen consequences of his actions? Or was he pragmatic about the whole thing, relieved to be rid of the burden not only of a troublesome lover but an illegitimate child as well?

I cursed myself for showing my hand too soon. He would be watching me now, like the hawk he so closely resembled. And he knew my weaknesses. One false step could get me thrown out of medical school. I would either have to tread very carefully, or abandon any hope of discovering the truth behind Lucy's death. What was she to me, after all? Just a vulnerable girl stuck in a vile profession as so many others were. I had recognised something of myself in her, true, but why take on her problems as well as my own? I tried to block out the murmurings of my conscience, scolding myself for letting my emotions get the better of me.

A couple walked past, clearly sweethearts, and the sight made a smile rise unbidden to my lips. I could give in. I could marry Miles Greene or hope for someone better. I could somehow convince my aunt for a stay of execution, an engagement long enough to finish my studies. I could move on with my life instead of trying to avenge past injustices by championing the cause of every wronged woman who crossed my path.

Was Professor Merchiston right? Had I let my imagination run away with me again, when my studies should have provided enough fascination? What a foolish little girl. I had fought for this. I had begged and pleaded and finally threatened my parents to let me come here, reminding them that university was at least better than lingering in the asylum that posed as a rest cure. If I was condemned to live my life as a disreputable spinster, I had pointed out, better that I at least have an occupation. And now, instead of embracing that vocation, I was seeing mystery where there was none to be had, playing out my strange fantasies in the hope of what? Redemption? The chance to save a woman whose life had been blighted, much as my own had, by the needs and actions of unscrupulous men?

Merchiston's threat rang in my ears. I didn't doubt that he'd see it through if he had to. And another fear lurked in the recesses of my mind – if he had killed Lucy, what was to stop him disposing of me as well? I had no friends here, he'd said so himself. Who would really miss me if I disappeared?

A clock chimed in the distance, and I realised I was missing another lecture. At this rate, it wouldn't only be Merchiston baying for me to be sent down. Still, I couldn't face the thought of returning to the university, of battling Julia's sneers, the men's taunts and Merchiston's accusing gaze. But there was somewhere I thought I might receive a warm welcome.

Chapter 16

'Sarah, how delightful to see you again!' If Elisabeth Chalmers was surprised at my arriving in her parlour, damp and dishevelled, she had the good grace not to show it. She ordered some tea to be brought to us as if I had been paying a prearranged social call, but as soon as the maid left us she turned to me, her eyes bright with curiosity, pushing me down into a chair by the fire.

'Sarah! What on earth is the matter?'

'That man,' I hissed through gritted teeth. 'That bloody man! How dare he? Threatening me with expulsion when I've done nothing wrong – what the hell is he so afraid of?'

Elisabeth stared at me in mounting horror. 'Who wants to expel you? Sarah, what have you done?'

'Nothing!' I almost shouted, months of pent-up rage exploding out of me. 'I have done nothing wrong except challenge a man – who is supposed to be a gentleman – on his actions, which are, quite frankly, dubious to say the least. And he said he'd have me sent down if I kept asking questions. How dare he? How bloody *dare* he?'

Elisabeth put a soothing hand on my elbow. 'Catch your breath for a moment. Who are you talking about?'

'Professor Merchiston,' I said sullenly.

There was a sharp intake of breath. 'Gregory? He threatened you?'

I took a deep breath. Elisabeth was the closest thing I had to a friend in Edinburgh, and if I could confide in anyone, it would be her. Lucy's story tumbled out of me, and I found myself weeping openly over her death for the first time.

By the time I was finished, my voice was hoarse and I felt exhausted from my torrent of emotion. 'She was bruised, Elisabeth. It might have been a laudanum overdose, but she didn't take it willingly.'

'Oh good Lord.' Elisabeth slumped in her seat, her face drained of the little colour it possessed.

'So I started asking questions, and that's when I found Merchiston at her – ah – former residence.'

'Sarah, Gregory is a doctor! He's perfectly entitled to ask questions if he suspects that a death may be suspicious.'

'Perhaps,' I conceded, 'but that doesn't explain why he was looking for Lucy and then denied knowing her. I found him stumbling out of her brothel in a drunken stupor, and helped him home only to hear him mumbling about her to his housekeeper.'

Elisabeth drew a ragged breath. 'You're sure? It couldn't have been some other girl?'

I shook my head. 'He knew her, even if he says he didn't. The girl's madam all but confessed it. I'm as confused as you are, Elisabeth. But what he didn't know – not until I told him today – was that Lucy was pregnant. I've never seen a man go so pale. I thought he was going to fall into a swoon – I was about to get out my smelling salts! And when he recovered, he was angrier than I've ever seen him before. He told me to stop asking questions, and that if I persisted, he would speak to the Dean of the School of Medicine and have me sent down.' The reality of the situation crashed over me, and I felt choked with panic. 'Elisabeth, I can't lose my place here! It's all I have left.'

'Then you must cease this investigation at once.' My friend's voice was firm, her countenance unwavering. 'Sarah, whatever romantic notions you may have about this poor girl, put them out of your mind. You can't help her now. I cannot sit here and watch you sacrifice your future on a whim!'

I closed my eyes. Elisabeth was right – and, in his own way, so was Professor Merchiston. 'But if I don't do it, no one else will. Someone stole her body from the dissecting rooms. One of the porters said her madam had taken it, but I spoke to her and she was lying, I'm sure of it. I just don't know why. This is no accident, and someone doesn't want the truth to be told. It's murder, I'd bet my life on it.'

'That's precisely what you *are* doing!'

I shook my head. 'I can't let Lucy's death go unpunished. It would be immoral. No one else will speak up for her, no one else cares. They just dismiss her because she was no better than she ought to be, because she was a whore . . .'

'And she reminds you of yourself,' Elisabeth finished softly. I stared at her, sick to my stomach. 'I may choose to stay above rumour and malicious gossip, Sarah, but that doesn't mean I don't hear it.'

'Is there anyone in Edinburgh who hasn't heard of my misfortune?' I asked bitterly. 'Merchiston knew. He told me that my reputation preceded me, and that it would take very little convincing for the Dean to have me sent down.'

To my surprise, Elisabeth cursed quietly. 'That's cold. I can't believe Gregory would say something like that.'

'Well obviously you don't know him as well as you think,' I snapped.

'Of course, one knows these things go on,' she murmured,

'but one never expects it of one's friends. And not someone like Merchiston. He's so upstanding, so . . .'

'Respectable?' I finished bitterly. 'Oh Elisabeth. Respectability means nothing when it comes to women. You're sheltered by Professor Chalmers; he's a good man, but many men lack his moral rectitude. Women are there to be used, and if they are willing, then it's a bonus.'

I turned my face to the fire so that she couldn't see my tears fall. When I had mastered my emotions, I returned my focus to the one person who needed it most.

'So what do I do about Lucy?'

'Nothing,' she told me firmly. 'You can't risk your future like that, not after . . . Well, you have had enough disappointments for a lifetime.' I opened my mouth to disagree with her angrily. 'But,' she added, 'you're not the only one who can make enquiries.' She pressed my hand. 'Take it to the police. If they won't do anything, come back. We're two intelligent women; I'm sure we can ask the right questions.'

I smiled for the first time in days. I was beginning to get the distinct feeling I had underestimated her. Whatever my next steps were, I was not going to take them alone.

Chapter 17

I had never seen the inside of a police station; I doubted that many women of my position had. Though I had practised my statement about Paul for hours, scribbled the vile words down on paper, composed myself as far as I could in anticipation of questions that never came, my father, who would have reported a theft of one of his priceless bloody bibelots in a heartbeat, had been content to spare his daughter's violator the trouble of answering for his actions.

The courtyard was jammed with carriages, and I stepped gingerly across the cobbles to avoid the manure the horses had left in their wake. Inside, I stood at the back of a queue of people, some of whom were obstreperous and others merely drunk. A harassed young man with ginger hair and a frustrated expression was dealing with the torrent of people, although whether they were victims, criminals, witnesses or merely voyeurs was beyond my deductive capabilities.

Finally I reached the desk and smiled as confidently as I could at the policeman.

'I'm terribly sorry to bother you, Officer, but would it be possible to speak with your medical examiner? I'm from St Giles' Infirmary, and I have a question about one of our former patients.'

Clearly relieved that I wasn't protesting my innocence or impugning anyone else's, the officer opened the door behind him and bellowed, 'There's a lassie here says she's a nurse from the infirmary, wants tae speak to the doctor. Has he shown up yet?'

There was a mumbled reply that I couldn't make out, and then my officer reappeared.

'He's due in any moment, miss. If you come this way, we'll find you somewhere to sit where you won't be disturbed.'

I flashed him my most charming smile. 'Thank you, you're very kind.'

'So you're a nurse, are you?'

'Actually, I'm a medical student.' My response provoked a gale of laughter.

'Aye, that's a good one, lassie.' Little more than I had expected. 'McLean, this wee thing says she's a doctor.'

'Naw, they're all bearded ladies from up Newington way,' his colleague argued. 'They're no' pretty faces like hers.'

I shifted in my seat with discomfort, painfully aware that I was alone in a room with four strange men.

'I assure you, gentlemen,' I informed them in my frostiest tone, 'I am enrolled at the University of Edinburgh.'

'Aye, I heard about that,' one mused. 'They let lasses in now. Shocking.'

'How do we know this isn't a wind-up? Coming in here, wasting our time with your nonsense?'

'What happened – someone steal your stethoscope?'

I was rapidly reaching boiling point, unsure how much longer I could remain here without throwing something. The thought of a night in the cells did not appeal.

'I assure you I have a perfectly legitimate enquiry. I—'

'Someone get that bloody woman out of here!'

The room fell silent and I swivelled to see the newcomer.

Standing in front of me, cheeks reddened with anger and the late autumn wind, was Professor Merchiston.

'It's not enough to harass me at the university; you have to follow me here? Well, young lady, these gentlemen won't be as tolerant of your nonsense as I was. They're ruffians, the lot of them, and the ones in the cells are little better. If you value what little is left of your reputation, I suggest that you leave. Immediately.'

'Lovers' tiff, is it?' one of the policemen called out, to the amusement of his brethren. 'Give your sweetheart a kiss, Doctor!'

Merchiston turned his scowl towards them. He didn't flinch.

'She is not my sweetheart. She is a bloody nuisance. What half-baked tales has she been telling you, eh? Too many novels, that's your problem, Gilchrist. Perhaps if you concentrated a little more on your studies and a little less on your flights of fancy, I might have been able to mark your last essay higher.'

'That essay was more than adequate,' I argued, barely aware of the fact that I had risen to my feet. 'If you've failed me for it, then I'll take it to the Dean. You have no right to take out your petty grievances against me on my work.'

'Petty grievances?' he stormed. 'You accused me of murder!'

The room fell silent and the officers stared at us both.

'I . . . I didn't accuse . . .'

'As near as damn it. For the love of God, Gilchrist, a girl of your obvious brains shouldn't be wasting her time playing detective. Leave the solving of crimes to this sorry lot, and get back to your studies.'

'Do this "sorry lot" know about your association with Lucy?' I turned to them. 'Gentlemen, a young woman was murdered not two weeks ago, and yet her death has been treated as a common suicide.'

'Let me assure you,' Merchiston said, leaning close enough that I could feel his warm breath tickle my hair, 'Lucy did not arrive here, dead or alive. I give you my word on that, as the police medical examiner.'

I stared at him coldly. 'What a coincidence.'

'Why don't you try asking Ruby McAllister? If that bitch sent Lucy's body directly to the university morgue, it wasn't with my consent.'

'I . . .'

'It wasn't with my bloody consent!' he roared. There was pain in his voice, and I was half tempted to believe him. But there were too many questions that lacked answers, and the violence seeping from every pore terrified me. Murderer or not, Gregory Merchiston was a dangerous man, and I had made an enemy out of him.

'I believe you,' I gasped. 'I do. Please, just let me go. I promise I won't ask any more questions. I'll let the matter drop. Just let me go, and I'll forget I ever met her.' With the shadows playing across his face, I couldn't ascertain his expression, and this made me even more uneasy.

'Well,' he said finally, after a long silence. 'Make sure that you do.'

As I turned and left, I heard him explaining my behaviour to his colleagues – the words 'hysterical female' were used. I walked out into the darkening streets wondering if I had just made a terrible mistake. The chill I felt now had little to do with the late-afternoon wind, or the heavy drops of rain that stained my skirt. I stood there in the darkness for a long time, wondering how it was that I felt my answer had disappointed him in some way.

Chapter 18

It was early enough when I arrived at the university that only a few keen students were up and about. A solitary runner was making his chilly circumference of the Meadows, much to my admiration. I stood and watched him until a few cyclists swooped past me. There had been snow on the ground when I left the house, and it unnerved me to realise that the year had circled round again. And yet so much had happened. 1892 had been a hellish year and I would not be sad to see the back of it, yet now I had what I had wanted for so long. No longer was I simply sitting in medical lectures at the London School of Medicine for Women, wishing passionately that I could be allowed to really study, not just be a dilettante who scribbled useless notes that she was never going to need. My circumstances might be restrictive, but how much more intellectual freedom did I have!

Turning back up Middle Meadow Walk to begin my day in earnest, I caught sight of a familiar figure striding away from the medical buildings with a grim expression. The desire to follow Professor Merchiston was overwhelming, and a quick glance at my wristwatch showed me that I had plenty of time before my biology lecture. I remained a good few feet behind him, ready to dart away if he realised he was being shadowed.

He maintained a brisk pace, and I was forced to scuttle along to avoid losing him in the throng of people that grew steadily thicker as we drew closer to the Royal Mile. I was out of breath and felt the beginnings of a stitch in my side – being treated like an invalid or a mental deficient for so long had had a detrimental effect on my physical health – but I managed to keep up as he turned onto Cockburn Street. If he had been heading to Princes Street, he could have caught an omnibus or hailed a cab – but if he had been going somewhere so innocuous, he would hardly have turned so sharply I almost missed it and slunk like an alleycat down Fleshmarket Close.

The stench of raw meat had presaged my tentative arrival at the entrance of the close, and I was deeply thankful for my medical training as I took a few hesitant steps down the narrow alley beloved of the city butchers because the chilly stone walls to each side kept their wares fresh. I suppressed a sigh of disappointment – had I risked my reputation for nothing more than catching Gregory Merchiston in the act of buying a few pounds of beef mince? But it was not into one of the butcher's that he disappeared; rather through the doorway of one of the tenements.

After a few moments, ensuring that he would not emerge again immediately, I made for the occupier of the butcher's shop that faced the doorway.

'Excuse me, sir, but can you tell me who lives in the building opposite?'

The man's initial friendliness turned to outright disapproval.

'Dinnae waste your time, hen. If you've any sense, you'll go straight home. This is nae place for the likes of you.'

'What kind of place is it, then?'

'During the day, it's quiet enough. It's at night their trade picks up.'

'It's a brothel?'

If Merchiston was a frequenter of such places, it made sense that he didn't limit himself to one house – or perhaps he had found another girl to his taste now that Lucy was gone. I remembered the warmth of his hand on my shoulder in the courtyard. The thought of that same hand caressing Lucy or some other poor wretch, of dropping a coin or two onto the table beside her bed, made bile well up in my throat and my face grow hot.

The butcher snorted. 'Nae, hen. It's worse than that.' He leant closer, and his fetid breath gusted against my face. '*Opium.*'

Opium dens promised a sort of Eastern exoticism that was markedly absent when I actually ventured inside one. It was the Orient via Orkney, as far as I could tell – a faded tartan curtain obscuring whatever secrets the room beyond held, and a woman barring my way who had clearly never been further east than Musselburgh.

'Can I help you?' she asked coldly.

'I . . .' This was where I trailed off. I had not anticipated such a cheerless reception, assuming in my naivety that they would welcome my custom, such as it was. It was time to dust off the mistaken assumption that had gained me entrance into Ruby McAllister's home. 'The gentleman who just entered, he's my . . . um . . . my husband. Tell me, does he frequent this place often?'

The proprietress' smile did not meet her eyes.

'Gregory Merchiston is a bachelor, as I'm sure you're aware if you make a habit of following him down dark alleyways.'

'Well he's not my husband yet, more my fiancé . . .' I stammered.

'Tell me, young lady, what is your purpose here? Blackmail? I'd advise against it. He is not an enemy any sensible woman would care to make.'

'What do you mean?' I asked in a low voice.

She smirked 'What exactly do you suspect him of? What could be worse than a doctor falling prey to such a shameful addiction?'

'Murder,' I whispered. The word hung between us. Our silence was broken by one of her customers, a stumbling, bleary-eyed man with what looked like a rather bad case of delirium tremens. All of a sudden I remembered what this woman did and how Lucy had died. Anger rose up inside me, and as soon as the poor fellow had begun his shaky descent down the stairs, I turned to her.

'What do you know about a girl – a prostitute – named Lucy?' Her eyes betrayed a flicker of recognition, but she said nothing. 'Was she a customer of yours?'

Her eyes narrowed. 'Do you really expect me to answer that?'

'Why not? You've already told me that Merchiston is. You know his name, his profession, his marital status – what more do you know?'

She shrugged. 'The good professor is a medical man, as you doubtless know. Is it so strange that he should attend those customers who are, on occasion, taken ill here?'

'Is that what he was doing with Lucy?' I demanded. 'Caring for her? Is that how she ended up dead with a stomach full of laudanum?'

'That is how people end up unless they're careful.' She moved closer to me, and although I was taller than she, I felt distinctly uncomfortable. 'Especially if they come here asking questions.'

I backed away. 'I'm sorry to have bothered you. Good day.'

'One more thing, Miss Gilchrist?' I froze in my tracks. I had not given her my name. 'If you enter these premises again, I will call a policeman. My clientele is quite varied. Let me assure you that should a man of the law find you here, it is not me that would be going to prison.'

I stumbled blindly down the staircase and exited the opium den into the dim light and putrid air of Fleshmarket Close.

I didn't stop running until the university was in sight.

Chapter 19

The sweet smell of opium smoke lingered in my nostrils despite my dash through the drizzling streets back to the university. Physiology was the last thing on my mind as I paced the corridor, waiting for the tutor to arrive.

Brothels were one thing, but an opium den? The man was a chemist, for God's sake – he knew how dangerous the stuff was. Laudanum was harmless in comparison, but I knew how seductive even that could be. Two men walked past, joking about a patient they had treated, and I watched them go, realising how little I knew about any of the people I spent my days cloistered with.

A woman's footsteps rang out and I looked up – a foolish impulse, since it wasn't as though they were any friendlier than the men. Edith met my eyes before looking down at the floor from a pointed distance. I wondered if Julia had forbidden her from speaking to me.

My chest felt tight when I thought of how far the reality was from what I had envisaged when I came here. I had watched students at the London School of Medicine for Women gad about together arm in arm or cycle through Regent's Park with their shared jokes and camaraderie. I had expected something more than this ragtag handful of girls – some like Caroline barely out of the schoolroom, some like Julia and myself inching slowly towards the limits of marriageable age. Put simply, we had nothing in common but an interest in our studies, and that was something none of us were used to sharing. We were still the same oddities that we were at home; if there was strength in numbers, we had yet to exercise it.

Loneliness stabbed at my gut and I turned to Edith, desperate for even a snatched moment of companionship.

'How did you find the Latin translation? I thought it was a bit of a slog.'

'Well you can't copy mine,' she said sullenly.

'I hadn't been planning to,' I said, stung. 'Maybe Julia cribs off you, but some of us prefer to do our own work.'

I regretted ever striking up the conversation. I had breezed through the damn Latin, but I hadn't thought boasting would endear me to her.

'I'm not her servant!' Her cheeks were red, clashing horribly with hair that could only be called strawberry blonde by someone feeling very charitable.

Another social misstep. At this rate I would graduate as friendless as I had begun.

'I only meant—'

'This is a new world,' Edith said in a rush. 'An English aristocrat can be friends with a doctor's daughter from Stirling. We share the same lodging, eat the same food, attend the same lectures. You have no idea what we have in common.'

I laughed, but there was no mirth in it. 'You aren't out of her shadow long enough for anyone to find out!'

'How would you know? You spend all your time with your rich relations. The only other person you speak to is Thornhill, and everyone knows her people have money.'

My blood boiled. 'In case you haven't noticed, I can't go where I'm not invited. The only place anyone talks to me is an infirmary in the slums! You think you've made your mind up about me, but Julia made it up for you the moment she set eyes on me here. Tell your bosom friend to please decide if I'm a snob or a slut, because it's getting exhausting being both.'

I moved to the noticeboard and read an advertisement for a rugby game twenty times over. By the time we were called into the tutorial, my eyes were dry.

After a pointless hour in which I was no more enlightened as to the skeletal system of the common horse than before, I made for the library. I wasn't going to make Edith like me and I was even less likely to correctly identify an equine patella, but an idea had occurred to me. I found a spare desk and rummaged around in my reticule for a blank sheet of paper and a pencil. The Viennese art tutor my mother had engaged for Gertie and myself one tedious autumn had, I thought, not been a complete waste. After two hours of ripped paper, some quiet swearing that almost saw me ejected from the premises, and a detailed consideration of the sharply angled planes of Professor Merchiston's face, I had a reasonable likeness of both him and Lucy. If either were regular visitors to that miserable dwelling off Cockburn Street, then someone would recognise them.

'Good Lord, Gilchrist!' Alison gawped at me, ignoring the shushes her distinctly-not-a-whisper provoked. 'Don't tell me you're pie-eyed over that tyrant!'

A groan sounded from a nearby table. 'Oh God. *Women*. I told you this would happen.'

I felt my forehead prickle with sweat and my cheeks flush. There was no way I could tell Alison the truth, but I knew what this looked like.

Grabbing my things, I dragged her out of the reading room and into the stairwell.

'I'm, ah, doing a study of the male facial structure, and since Professor Merchiston's is so . . . distinctive, I thought he'd be a good subject,' I gabbled, hoping I sounded close to convincing. 'I mean, his face is so bony, he's practically a skeleton. I'm going to start on his muscles next.'

Alison snorted.

'On his face, Thornhill! I'm going to diagram the zygomaticus major and minor and the procerus muscle and the occipito . . . occip . . .'

'Occipitofrontalis?' she asked sweetly, with a wicked gleam in her eye.

'The very one,' I said through gritted teeth. 'I swear on my life, Thornhill, I'm not some silly schoolgirl with a pash. I know what you all think of me, but I'm not like that.' Somehow it felt very important that Alison not think I had romantic feelings for the man. I turned the paper over to Lucy's portrait. 'See?'

She examined it. 'Oh, a female version as well. How clever. You'd make quite the good portrait artist if you ever abandoned medicine.'

'Not on your life.'

'You might not be destined for a future as an artist starving in a garret, but you did miss lunch.' She was right, I realised; I was famished. 'Here, I took some extra boiled potatoes. I'm always ravenous by three o'clock otherwise.' She handed me a greasy paper bag filled with warm, buttery potatoes, and I could have kissed her.

As we made our way to the solitary cloakroom the medical school allotted for female students – facilities that the professors had been too embarrassed to even mention in our first weeks, much to our discomfort and the annoyance of the proprietress of a nearby coffee house – Edith's earlier words returned to me.

'Do you think I'm a snob?'

Alison blinked. 'You're a little aloof, perhaps. Maybe if you tried harder to get on Julia's good side, things wouldn't be so difficult. But you're not a snob.' She gave an embarrassed laugh. 'I sometimes wonder if I am, though. Oh, not intentionally. But I don't know how to talk to someone like Caroline, and frankly, Moira terrifies me. I feel like she blames me for all the world's ills just because I was born into money. Julia's just . . . easier, somehow. Like we're speaking the same language. Literally, sometimes – when Caroline breaks out into Scots, she may as well be talking in Chinese. I knew medical school would be difficult, but I thought it would be the work, not the other students.'

It felt like she was speaking my thoughts aloud. It hadn't occurred to me that even someone as comfortable in her social standing, as reassuringly normal as Alison, would feel out of place here.

'You should join us for dinner one night,' I offered tentatively. 'I'm sure my aunt and uncle wouldn't mind.'

The idea of Uncle Hugh being on his best behaviour around what he termed 'book-learned termagants' delighted me – and if I could persuade them to invite her on a night when the Greenes were visiting, her incessant cheeriness might prove a useful buffer. Not only that – another socially acceptable friend meant more chances to escape the stuffy confines of their house, something that would prove useful if I wanted to find out more about the connection between Merchiston and Lucy.

The portraits rested safely in my reticule as we made our way to the afternoon lecture. Somehow it felt like his gaze was burning through the leather of my bag, silently watching me.

Chapter 20

The anatomy theatre was a grand room for grand men to display their mastery over the human body. Decades ago, this would have been a brutal affair – a fully conscious patient, dirty instruments, blood-soaked sawdust coating the floor. Tonight, it was sanitised and tidy, if no less bloody.

Tonight, it was a performance.

Julia shifted impatiently and tapped her foot. I felt no such anticipation. Whilst I was grateful to be there, and curious to see for myself how the esteemed Professor Mackay, Fellow of the Royal College of Surgeons, worked, I felt uneasy. Surely the other women had some qualms about the procedure. Surely they felt some kinship with the wretched figure on the table. For all her pride, even Julia Latymer couldn't think she was invincible.

As the great man himself, a legend in the wards of the Royal Infirmary of Edinburgh for his prowess with a scalpel and in the whisky-soaked environs of the New Club for his tales of medical derring-do, strode into the room, we stood en masse to applaud him. I was beginning to feel nauseous.

'Hysteria,' he announced. 'The modern woman's greatest curse.' His words were met with raucous laughter. 'A variety of remedies have been invented to tackle such an affliction – laudanum, stimulation of the lower regions, even this new fad, psychology.' He smiled, but there was little humour in it. 'As if any problem could be solved by a woman talking more!'

Cloistered at the front, we felt every eye in the room upon us. Edith had stiffened and was staring fixedly in front of her, lips pinched. Julia looked as though she wanted to take a swing at someone. I wondered if that was why we had been given such a choice position. Not as a sop to our gentler sex, but as a warning.

Holding up his hand to silence the laughter – having finally decided our humiliation was at an end – Mackay continued, 'But there is one remedy whose supremacy remains unchallenged. Through one simple procedure, we can restore this woman's equilibrium, making her a fit wife and mother once more.' Applause. He looked at us, stony-faced and silent on the front row. 'You disagree, ladies? Perhaps you feel she should remain as she is – melancholic, aggressive, in danger of taking her own life?'

'And what about leaving her scarred and infertile from completely unnecessary surgery?' I asked, shaking. 'How enthusiastic do you imagine she'll feel about her husband and children then, Professor?'

The room was deathly silent.

'If you have a better suggestion,' he said slowly, 'then perhaps you, not I, should be standing up here, Miss . . .'

'Gilchrist,' Julia supplied. Hateful beast.

I shook my head, not trusting myself to speak. As much as what we were about to witness filled me with anger, I was not going to let him ban me from the operating theatre. He had railed against admitting women as it was – if I fuelled the fire and he returned to his previous position, then the chilly indifference with which my peers treated me would turn to hatred.

He gave me a thin-lipped smile, unblinking, reminding me of the snakes at the Zoological Gardens.

'It will calm her nerves,' he continued, 'and leave her better able to look after her husband and children. With the added benefit, of course, of preventing any further progeny.'

How kind of him. Of course, there were far less brutal ways of ensuring that a woman didn't fall pregnant, or at least carry the child to term. But as Fiona had so amply illustrated, no respectable doctor would collude in such a practice. At least the infirmary offered advice about contraception, unreliable though it was. And whilst I could see why vinegar-soaked sponges might not appeal to the husbands, surely the wives had the right to ensure they avoided unwanted pregnancy? But as we were witnessing, it was men who controlled our reproductive futures.

'When she wakes, there will be discomfort at first, of course, but she will find that her melancholia is gone, and that the nightly fits of rage that caused her to attack her husband have subsided entirely.'

I could hazard a guess at what had caused her anger, and I didn't think removal of her reproductive organs would solve the problem.

I felt overwhelmed by the futility of my presence. First Lucy, now this. There was nothing I could do but observe and offer what little comfort I was able. Even when I was a qualified doctor, I could only look after them whilst they were in my care. The world outside was beyond my control, a cesspit of violence no matter what one's social circle.

Silence fell as Mackay turned to his patient. Tears stung the corners of my eyes and I hated every single person in the room with a white-hot fury for treating this butchery as entertainment.

Still, I would not leave. The poor wretch deserved to have at least one person present who saw her as a human being, not just a canvas for Mackay's bloody artistry.

In the harsh electric light – nothing but the best, the most modern inventions, for Edinburgh's surgeons – the tray of instruments sparkled and shone. Mackay selected a scalpel with solemnity and, forever playing to his audience, pressed it with a flourish against the woman's flesh.

The lights flickered and the room went dark.

'For Christ's sake!' Mackay roared. 'McVeigh, get the porters and find out what the hell is going on. If that had happened a second later, I'd have made the incision and she'd be bleeding out.'

There was something unnerving about the darkened room and its unconscious occupant. The men were laughing and jostling one another, calling out to us with offers to soothe our fears that implied the opposite. Wordlessly we huddled closer together, less afraid of the nameless horrors of the dark than of what our male counterparts might do under its cover. I felt a presence pass by me, and although the room was stifling, I shivered.

McVeigh returned, with lamps that threw eerie shadows across the room. Alison breathed a sigh of relief, and even Julia and Edith moved away from each other. I hadn't thought Edith to be the skittish type. When a beam of oily light fell on the woman on the table, the room went into uproar.

The sheets that had protected what little modesty she had been afforded were lying in a heap on the floor. Whoever had removed them had also arranged her limbs, unresisting and pliant from the chloroform, in such a manner that one hand was resting limply on her breast and the other lay suggestively on the tangle of dark curls at the juncture of her legs.

The anaesthetist cursed and jolted back, the patient's chloroform mask slipping. To my horror, she murmured before he collected himself and submerged her in blessed unconsciousness again.

'Quieten down, gentlemen,' Mackay roared above the din. 'There are ladies present. May I remind you that the operating theatre is not the place for foolish japes. Keep the horseplay to the cadavers if you must. Oh for God's sake, McVeigh, I cannot operate by lamplight! The surgery will have to wait. Take her away.'

My palms were slick with sweat.

'It's disgusting,' Julia called out. 'And I bet he won't even punish the culprit!'

'He doesn't know who it was,' Edith pointed out reasonably.

'He doesn't care,' I corrected her. 'It could have been any of them. It could have been him. They weren't bothered about her dignity before they assaulted her.'

The others drifted away, back to their cosy digs and an evening of unexpected freedom by the fireside. Too proud to ask even for Alison Thornhill's company, I was left alone in the shadows.

Eager to escape the taunts of the male students, I made for the back staircase, pausing as the sound of murmuring voices reached me. Had both speakers not been unmistakably female, I would have thought I had stumbled across an assignation. A few more steps revealed the two people I least wanted to see at that moment. Julia's expression was grim, her lips pinched together so tightly they had gone white. In contrast, Edith was red-eyed and flushed – a striking contrast from the mousy girl I was used to.

They looked up as they heard me approach – Edith defiantly, Julia with something that looked a lot like guilt.

'Spying, Gilchrist?' she asked coldly.

'I didn't realise there was anyone here.'

Julia tossed her head. 'Well go on then. It isn't as though you were interrupting anything important.' She flounced back up the stairs, rejoining the throng and leaving her friend looking lost and abandoned. She was a bully. True, Edith was bad-tempered and snappish, and in other circumstances I would have had little time for her, but her woeful expression tugged at my heart.

'She's a beast,' I said with feeling. Edith's eyes flashed as though she wanted to contradict me, but she stayed silent. 'If this is how she treats her friends,' I continued, 'then I'm glad I'm her enemy.' This at least provoked a smile, or at least a wry quirk of the lips.

'She's not so bad,' Edith sighed. 'The worst thing is, she's right.'

'Right or not, she shouldn't speak to you like that.'

'Whereas you stand up to her every time, don't you, Gilchrist?' Her words might have been sarcastic, but for once, her tone wasn't. When she followed Julia, I made no attempt to stop her.

I stood in the freezing evening air, watching my breath hang like mist.

'You shouldn't be out here alone, Miss Gilchrist.'

I turned to see Professor Merchiston standing there.

'I was just going to send a note to my uncle,' I told him, my posture stiff and unwelcoming.

'Don't be ridiculous, you can't wait outside on a night like this. I'll call a cab and escort you home.'

'I hardly think that would be proper. Perhaps if we can find a chaperone . . .'

'I won't set foot outside the cab, so no need to worry about what your aunt might say. Besides,' he added with a wry grin, 'it isn't as though you haven't been in a cab unaccompanied with me before.'

'You were drunk,' I replied tartly. 'The only thing you could have managed was an assault on my reputation – and it's a little late for that, don't you think?'

We stood in awkward silence for a moment.

'Miss Gilchrist, when you came to my rooms, I said something unforgivable. I will not pain you further by mentioning it again, but please believe it was said in the heat of anger, and I have regretted it ever since. At least let me do the service of escorting you home.'

His words touched me. I wanted more than anything to reply in kind. I looked at him, half cloaked in shadows, his face tired and sad, and wondered if he was really capable of murder.

'That is a very kind offer, Professor Merchiston, but I couldn't possibly accept.'

In the dim light, his expression was unreadable, but I felt a strange stab of guilt.

'I'll hail you a cab,' he said stiffly. 'But I shan't accompany you. I'm sorry for any offence caused.'

Within moments I was ushered into a waiting hansom cab. Alone with my thoughts, I found my hand creeping towards my belly, where, beneath the layers of fabric, a pale, jagged scar marred my skin.

Chapter 21

A cure for hysterical, melancholic women indeed.

The doctors at the sanatorium had promised my father that it would put an end to my ramblings about Paul Beresford, about education and becoming a doctor. When cutting had failed, restraints and the sweet release of opiates had dulled me into submission, but the legacy of the surgery lingered. If my aunt's plans came to fruition, I would be a barren wife, a woman whose belly, forever traced with the scars from surgery, would never swell, never fulfil the one task society asked of me.

I had still been hazy with laudanum when my mother had bundled me into the carriage. She and Father had sat opposite me, purse-lipped and silent, refusing to tell me where we were going until we were alighting at a large house an hour outside London. 'A rest', they had called it; I was 'over-wrought'. This was what came of indulging my foolish notions of an education. They had not lingered; satisfied that my temporary retreat from the world was as civilised as Dr Waters had been promised, my mother gave me a chilly kiss on the cheek and bid me farewell. My father did not look at me. I was shown to a room – airy, light, comfortable, but a prison nonetheless, with a door that locked behind me.

It was to be a chance to reflect. I was not to read, or to dwell on the events of recent days. I was to pray, sleep, refocus my mind towards healthier topics than medicine. I could sew, but only in the company of one of the nurses. I was too frightened and confused at first to appreciate the harm I could do to myself even with an embroidery needle, but their fears would be justified and I had the scars on more than just my stomach to prove it.

Three months it took for them to return. Three months without so much as a letter, until I thought I had been abandoned there forever. Then my father arrived to take me home, to tell me that a solution had been found: that I was going to Scotland to study if that was what I wanted, but I was not to come home again. That my relatives would care for me, but I would be left to make my own way in the world and should expect nothing from him or my mother but the kindness they had already shown me. I had heaped too much shame on the family – first by my hoydenish ways, my suffragist leanings, my obsession with a university education, and now by this. A reputation in ruins and our family name dragged through the dirt. I was lucky, he told me, to be allowed to keep it. As far as he was concerned, he now only had one daughter.

Compared to that, Aunt Emily was positively maternal.

'Sarah! What a pleasant surprise to see you home at a reasonable hour.'

If I looked as bad as I felt, she made no comment.

'The lecture finished earlier than I expected.' I forced a weak smile. 'I didn't want to trouble you by sending for Calhoun, so I had the porter call me a cab.'

'Your uncle is still at his club,' my aunt replied, a trace of disapproval in her tone. 'Shall I ring for some supper?'

My stomach roiled at the thought of food, the smell of sweat and antiseptic clinging to my nostrils and the bloody gash on the patient's stomach still fresh in my mind.

'Perhaps just a pot of tea, then,' she said as I grimaced. 'I'm writing to Margaret – I'll send your regards.'

Mother. After tonight's debacle and the memories it had prompted, I didn't know if the thought of her was soothing or heartbreaking. I knew that I wanted her – her presence, her comfort – but just as the daughter she had loved no longer existed, the mother I craved was gone forever. I looked over at Aunt Emily, seeing echoes of her sister in the set of her mouth, the firmness of her chin, and I suddenly felt more homesick than I ever had.

'Give her my love,' I said softly. 'Forgive me, Aunt Emily, I'm very tired. I think an early night may be in order.'

In the months I had been apart from my family, the emotional wounds had begun to close. I suspected they would never fully heal, not even if I redeemed myself by marrying Miles and being brought back into the familial fold. As for the woman I had become – a student, a bluestocking, a woman who associated with prostitutes and policemen and accused her professors of murder – they would have me locked up and this time no one would come to my aid.

If Aunt Emily discovered that my interest in Edinburgh's unfortunates went beyond the infirmary doors, I did not know what she would do. Would it be better to be thrown out onto the streets or to be confined to my room until some suitable marital transaction could take place? It wasn't a choice I cared to make.

When I was qualified, I told myself as Agnes slipped the nightgown over my head. When I was out from my aunt's protection. When I could do as I pleased. Then I could champion the rights of girls like Lucy; then I could right a dozen wrongs. I simply had to bide my time.

The maid bobbed a curtsey, dimmed the lights and left me to my thoughts. My conscience shifted and stirred, uneasy. There would be other helpless girls crossing my path in the future; the world had no shortage of them. But Lucy had come into my life now, and powerless as I felt, trapped as I was, I had to act. Justice had to be done, at least once, at least for her. How many people had turned from me with a flicker of guilt, believing me but absolving themselves of responsibility? As Julia Latymer reminded me on a daily basis, I was not like the others. I knew how the world worked, I knew it could be cruel, and I was not content to let it remain so.

My sleep was fitful and full of disturbing images, the way sleep always was now. After the incident at the ball – and how was it that even I could not refer to it by its proper name? – I had stayed awake for three nights, terrified that if I closed my eyes for even a moment, all the memories I was fighting back would come flooding over me. And on the fourth night, they did. I think it was the screaming that first alerted my mother to the fact that something seriously untoward had occurred, that it was more than a cheap seduction at a dance. I remember my bedroom door opening, and her figure silhouetted in the doorway. She stood there silently, and never came in even when I called for her. I remember her hushing Gertie and sending her back to bed, and dismissing the servants in their turn. I spent that night, and so many subsequent ones, alone, too frightened to go back to sleep because I knew that if the nightmares came, once again no one would rescue me.

Was that how Lucy had felt? I wondered. When had she first taken to the streets? Had she been protected until then, or was that the only life she had ever known? I suspected not, because she still looked young and fresh, still a bloom of health on her cheeks, unlike the wretched whores who prowled the slums with wigs and false teeth and diseases beyond cure. So she must have known comfort once. How did she survive the degradation, knowing that there was no one there to care for her, to rescue her when she cried out? Even if Ruby McAllister protected her girls like a lioness with her cubs, I knew that profit would win out. Fear of poverty was a powerful motivator, I could understand that, but to allow such wicked things to occur and merely stand by and pocket the money was insupportable. But then, who was I to judge Ruby, when I knew so little of her life?

This strange new world I had stumbled into had rules I could barely comprehend. Heaven knows, the regulations of polite society were beyond me half the time, and I was raised to them. But the connections, the unspoken arrangements that would have helped me make sense of Lucy's life, and perhaps her death as well, were barred to me. I knew what Ruby and women like her thought of me. I saw the way they looked at Fiona and her colleagues – sad spinsters on errands of mercy, swooping in and telling them how to live their lives. I couldn't blame them. And how they saw me must be far worse. At best, I was a foolish girl playing in the slums, like Marie Antoinette and her shepherdess games in the dying days of Versailles. At worst . . . what? Did they think I found some kind of depraved enjoyment, some illicit thrill in all this?

Perhaps they were right. Advocating for Lucy had made me feel better about my own predicament – in my way, wasn't I using her just as the fine gentlemen from the New Town did, as an escape from my dull, privileged life? My problems, though they seemed insurmountable at times, were nothing in comparison to the lives of these women. Worn out before they were thirty from too many children and too little money to feed all those hungry mouths, turning to prostitution to make the week's rent when work at the factories or taking in mending was hard to come by. And in an overcrowded city like Edinburgh, it was always hard to come by. The salubrious air of the New Town was far away from that stinking hellhole. I had little to complain about. I had a roof over my head, food in my belly, and I was training for a profession that, although it might not have welcomed me with open arms, would eventually ensure that I was able to keep myself with a measure of independence unknown to women like Lucy and Ruby.

I had told myself I would put away these thoughts, but I had entered that world and it wasn't willing to let me go that easily. And even if I abandoned my investigations entirely, gave myself up to my studies and the promise of marriage to a man who bored me to tears, I would only ever be pretending. The scars from the months I had spent locked away had all but faded, but I still felt the wounds as fresh and painful as ever.

Chapter 22

The sheets of paper lay on every desk, positioned precisely. I groaned aloud at the thought of an unexpected test for which I was in no way prepared, but as I read it, I realised it had nothing to do with the skeletal system.

'The Edinburgh Women Students' Morality Union?' Whatever it was it sounded dire. Worse than that – it sounded compulsory.

'Julia's latest hobbyhorse,' Alison grimaced. 'It's a temperance movement, of sorts.'

'Oh, it isn't just a temperance league!' Julia Latymer's eyes glittered with missionary zeal and not a little bit of malice. 'The Women's Morality Union is dedicated to not only upholding standards here at the medical school, but improving the lives of women throughout Edinburgh. After all, as doctors, moral well-being must be as important to us as the physical health of our patients. I hope you'll consider joining us, Sarah. They do say that charity begins at home.'

With her hand on my shoulder and a mock-sympathetic look on my face, she sounded exactly like nearly every doctor I had ever met, more interested in judging me than in any diagnosis. I was only surprised she wasn't puffing on a cigar and reading the racing papers in the University Club.

'Are you so desperate to ingratiate yourself with the gentlemen that you're willing to act like one?'

Julia's lips thinned and she stepped back with a scowl, as though my very presence was infectious.

'I'm doing you a favour,' she sneered. 'The whole university whispers about you. Parading yourself around all high and mighty when you're no better than the whores in that ramshackle infirmary that calls itself a hospital. One more fallen woman who couldn't make respectability stick.'

My fingers itched to slap her, and I twisted them in the fabric of my skirt in an effort not to strike.

'Direct your morality lecture to the men, Julia. They can drink and carouse until morning while we have to be paragons of virtue, and you don't think it the littlest bit unfair?'

'It doesn't matter what I think! It doesn't matter what any of us think. If we want to study medicine, we have to be above reproach. Do you think I give a damn about your hurt feelings, Gilchrist? The only reason I care what they say about you is because it makes it easier for them to say it about the rest of us. I have fought tooth and nail for this, and you're ruining it. You'll ruin us all. One bad apple in the barrel and suddenly the whole damned experiment is over, we're back in the drawing room hoping some man takes a fancy to us! I won't lose this chance because a spoilt society slut couldn't keep her legs closed.'

Any retort I could have made was interrupted by the entrance of Moira Owen and Caroline Carstairs, who roomed together off the Royal Mile.

I looked at Julia's smug, superior face and swore that I would not attend a single meeting of her damned Morality Union. Like so many of my promises, it was another one I would be unable to keep.

I was rendering the optic nerve in precise pencil strokes when Alison leant over.

'You've been to the slums,' she whispered. 'How bad are they really?'

I grimaced. 'About as bad as you'd imagine. Families sleeping eight to a room, children with bellies distended from malnutrition, and damp that seeps into your bones and doesn't leave.'

'And hardly a mile away, we live in comfort,' Alison sighed in wonderment. 'Well, relative comfort. I'm sure our landlady is gulling us with the amount of coal we're allowed in our rooms.'

Hard as life in the Cowgate was, I wasn't sure that even the most unrepentant wretch deserved Alison at her most well-meaning.

'If you want to take up philanthropy, you might start somewhere a little less bleak. Just until you get used to it,' I offered awkwardly.

'It's the Morality Union,' she whispered. 'We're going on a rescue mission.'

The apprehension I felt for my friend was quickly replaced by a sinking feeling at the pit of my stomach.

'Who are you rescuing?' I had a horrible feeling I already knew the answer.

'Julia wants us to take some pamphlets about sexual immorality and hand them out outside brothels, to stop the men going in. We're taking donations so we can give the women money for a bed for the night.'

'They already have a bed. You'll be giving temperance society money to women who'll spend it on gin. And frankly, I can't blame them – even listening to Julia makes me want to take to the bottle.'

She frowned. 'You can't be saying you approve of such degradation?'

'Of course not! But causing a public disturbance in the slums is hardly the way to prevent it. For one thing, it isn't safe. Tell me you're bringing a chaperone with you.'

'Reverend Spinks is accompanying us.'

I wasn't sure how that pious old milquetoast would be of any protection, unless it was letting him get pickpocketed first.

'When?'

'Tomorrow night, after lectures.'

'Is six o'clock a time traditionally known for vice and perversions of all natures?'

Alison blushed. 'Reverend Spinks refused to accompany us any later. He said it's too dangerous.'

For once, I agreed with him.

'I'm going with you. No, don't argue – and I don't care what Latymer says. She doesn't have the monopoly on standing in the freezing cold making a fool of herself, and while I couldn't give a tinker's damn about her, you may as well have someone who knows her way out.'

The night was bitter as we made our way from the medical school down Forrest Road, towards a part of the city that only I was familiar with. I hoped at the very least that Julia had brought a map, although I doubted the building we were seeking would be located on one.

In the distance, a tram clattered past, and we stepped gingerly over the rain-slicked cobbles. Greyfriars Kirk, unassuming in daylight or seen from the window of a safe, warm carriage, was gothic and eerie in the lamplight behind heavy iron gates that looked even more ominous than the graveyard they were protecting.

'James MacFarlane says it's haunted,' whispered Caroline Carstairs, and even I couldn't resist a shiver.

'It's a graveyard, of course it's haunted!' Alison squeaked in mounting hysteria.

'Oh don't be so feeble, both of you!' Julia snapped. 'You see dead bodies and severed limbs practically every day. The only difference here is six feet of loam and the level of decomposition. And James MacFarlane is sitting his second-year examinations for the third time, so I wouldn't hold him up as the fount of all knowledge.'

I wondered who had been the unkind soul who had first leeched the romance out of Julia's soul. God help the poor man who eventually married her.

Remembering that he was supposed to be our protector, Reverend Spinks pulled himself up to his full gawky height in what I assumed was an attempt to look manly and reassuring.

'Ladies, rest assured that there is nothing to fear. The kirkyard is sacred ground where no ghost would dare to tread. If, ah, in fact the dead walked, which they most assuredly do not. The only spirits you need fear are the ones served in that godless establishment.' He nodded at the public house that backed onto the kirk, rowdy already. As a gaggle of patrons entered, I caught a strong whiff of tobacco and stale beer. A few jeered mild obscenities, but one, a man in a green gabardine coat, merely stared at us. I shuddered.

'Perhaps we should hand out some pamphlets here?' Edith suggested.

'I hardly think that appropriate,' Reverend Spinks stammered, as though he were not leading us directly towards vice and depredation as it was.

'Might not be appropriate, but it would be warm,' Alison grumbled.

'We have to make sacrifices for the cause, Thornhill,' Julia replied crisply, burrowing her hands in Edith's muff nonetheless.

Candlemaker Row seemed twice as long when one was on foot in the dark, and we found ourselves lapsing into uncharacteristic silence, huddled close together and walking briskly, our breath ghosting into the frigid air. Feeble or not, even Julia practically scurried past the other kirkyard entrance until we reached the Grassmarket. When she turned purposefully away from the Cowgate and into a familiar wynd, my heart sank.

We were going to Ruby McAllister's.

Chapter 23

A man stood silhouetted at the mouth of the wynd, a top hat casting a long shadow in the dim light, his coat fluttering in the breeze.

'What d'we have here, then? It's a dreich night to be standing outside – why don't you lassies come inside and I'll see if I can warm you up?'

'Excuse me, sir, do you realise what sort of establishment this is?' Julia demanded, in a voice that sounded painfully unsuited to her surroundings.

He laughed. 'Well I was hoping it was a bawdy house, aye. I'm sure there are lassies in there can explain it to you, miss.'

'Sir, the women within those walls are desperate. They're starving, addicted to laudanum or worse; some of them have many other mouths to feed. They deserve better than to be degraded by you! Have mercy on them and leave for the night.'

'Out of my way, lassie. I came here looking for female company friendlier than yours.'

He pushed past, brushing off the pamphlet that Julia thrust at him and trampling it underfoot.

'These women are living in poverty, and you have corrupted them!' The door slammed behind him, and Julia muffled a scream of frustration with her glove. I was unsettled to realise that I recognised the feeling. Perhaps she and I were not as dissimilar as we both wanted to believe.

'They're no' living in poverty, hen, and those kind gentlemen are the reason why.'

Ruby McAllister, dressed top to toe in cheap finery, stood in the doorway with a thunderous expression. Candle-light glinted off diamonds that were about as real as her teeth, and inside we heard music and laughter. It sounded like a raucous dinner party rather than a den of iniquity, and my companions were all craning their necks, eager to get a glimpse of sin.

'Are you the proprietress of this establishment, madam?' Reverend Spinks asked.

'It's mah house, if that's what y'mean.'

Julia pushed in front of the hapless cleric. 'We are the Edinburgh Women Students' Morality Union, and—'

Ruby jerked her thumb up the wynd. 'University's that way, hen.'

'Oh we know exactly where we are, madam. And we'd like to speak to your girls.'

'They're a little busy, I'm afraid.'

'We want to help them, to assist them out of the depths to which they have fallen,' Julia said, sounding a little less sure of herself.

'Oh aye? Did you bring blankets? Food? Medicine? Anything they could actually use? You cannae feed a bairn on morals.'

'I said we should have brought something,' I muttered to Alison.

Ruby McAllister must have had ears like a bat, because she

looked straight in my direction and her eyes hardened.

'Well, if it isn't the crusading Miss Gilchrist. I should ha' ken you'd be behind this. So quick to blame everyone else for the world's ills, but you never look closer to home, do you? Just because someone has a fine coat and a full purse doesn't mean they can be trusted.'

'You don't seem to have a problem relieving them of their purses,' Julia said, her confidence returning. 'How much do you make off these poor wretches?'

Ruby looked at her coldly.

'I ken your type, miss. You're no' interested in saving my girls, you're only interested in protecting your own reputation.'

'If one gentleman heard us and thought better of his actions . . .'

'You won't change their minds; all you'll do is lose us a night's takings and put my girls one day closer to the streets. Never mind, lass. Shoo one man away, but maybe later they'll get lucky and have two men at once. It all balances out in the end.'

In the stunned silence that followed, a figure came and stood behind Ruby. I recognised the slim young man from my first visit – the one I had heard 'entertaining' another gentleman.

'Shame on you!' Julia shouted at him. 'Using women to sate your base desires! You're no better than an animal! Those women have families; do you ever think about that?'

I tugged at her sleeve. 'Julia, he isn't visiting any of the girls. He works there.'

Her breath huffed out into the icy air as she laughed. 'Since when did brothels have footmen?'

'The more exclusive establishments do,' the young man smirked. 'But this isnae one of them and I'm no' a footman, hen. Dinnae worry, your virtue is safe wi' me. You've got more to fear from some of the drabs upstairs – they'll take anyone who can pay, and you look like you've got money.' He slammed the door in her face

Julia stumbled back, open-mouthed with shock and anger.

'How dare he?' she snarled. 'That filthy sodomite. I should call a policeman.'

'We'd better go,' Edith suggested, looking miserable.

Julia shook off her friend's arm. 'I won't be frightened off. Let him see that some of us have standards.'

She straightened up, gathering what was left of her pamphlets. I had seen that smile before, on a stuffed shark in the National History Museum. She banged on the window with her fist so hard I thought she would smash the glass.

The red velvet curtains twitched, and the painted face of a woman no older than us peered out.

Julia held up a pamphlet and called to her, 'You don't have to do this! We can get you a bed for the night! If your madam won't let you leave, we'll call a policeman.'

The woman let out a cry and vanished behind the curtain.

Julia turned back to us triumphantly.

'You terrified her!' I snapped. 'If the police come, they'll arrest everyone.'

'At least it will spare her one night of this.'

'As if she'll get treated any better in a prison cell!'

She glared back mulishly. 'Maybe I taught her the error of her ways.'

The door opened again, and we were confronted by a furious Ruby.

'That did the trick, hen. We've all repented and we'll spend the evening in quiet contemplation, with maybe a wee bit of backgammon. Now piss off before some of these gents take a fancy to you.'

Defeated, we trudged back to the bridge and civilisation. Some of the men had spilt out of the public house and were making their inebriated way down to the brothels. The man who had been watching us earlier was among them, leaning against the wall in a casual pose. I wondered how long he had been standing there.

'Tell me, Gilchrist, are you acquainted with every madam in the city?' Julia asked nastily.

I sighed. 'She brings her girls to the infirmary sometimes. More to the point, how did you know how to find a brothel in the first place?'

'I heard some of the men talking when I was waiting to go into the lecture theatre.'

'The lecturers?' I asked. Had Merchiston been boasting of his conquests to his colleagues?

'Of course not.' Julia sounded appalled. 'As though any respectable member of the medical establishment would be seen in such a place!' For all her progressive leanings, sometimes my nemesis could be bewilderingly naive. 'It was some of the third-year students. Anthony Hardy and his unevolved cronies.'

Reverend Spinks cleared his throat awkwardly, clearly uncomfortable with the mention of evolution. Personally, I struggled to imagine Hardy as being part of any divine plan.

In our humiliation, the whole mission seemed so tawdry – the patronising efforts of rich women who wanted to save lives but tithed only what society dictated to charity. It was the same everywhere – the Salvationists in their uniforms with shiny buttons only marched singing down the poorest streets; the Temperance League published scathing articles about the demon drink that parted working men from their wages; and I had been taught from birth that female desire was aberrant and restricted to the slums, whose inhabitants lived more like beasts than men, while ladies submitted to their husbands' attentions only as a duty. Why were we so desperate to believe that anything more than sheer luck separated the people in drawing rooms from those in the slums?

I followed the others back to the medical school, where the Reverend chose the opportunity to give us a sermon. When my carriage arrived, it was a blessed relief.

When I alighted at my uncle's house, bright electric light spilling onto the pavement as the butler opened the door, I felt the tug of guilt catch at my throat. I was no better than the wretches huddled under the Cowgate's arches, and neither was Julia. But while fortune might not have smiled on me lately, at least it hadn't abandoned me completely.

As the housemaid took my coat, I forced a smile onto my face, ready to spin my relatives a yarn about the wholesome evening I had spent. Fire crackled in the grate, the tea from the pot was scalding, but as I played the role of virtuous niece, I felt the evening's damp and desperation settle in my bones.

The others were probably sound asleep, I thought as I peeled off my undergarments in the privacy of my room, safe in the knowledge that they had fought the good fight, imagining vainly that their protests might have planted a seed of lingering doubt in the mind of gentleman or whore. They were so innocent. They were so lucky. They hadn't turned away a frightened, desperate girl. They didn't have a woman's death on their conscience, her blood on their hands. They were little girls dressed in their teacher's clothes, playing with women's lives as they'd once played with their dolls, unaware that all the sermonising in the world wouldn't save the soul of someone with a malnourished body.

Prostitution was the final resting place for a girl of unclean virtue, the place that lay in wait for anyone who fell through the cracks of civilised society. I knew that was why my uncle permitted me to assist at the infirmary, to remind me weekly of the fate that have would befallen me had they not consented to take me in. And the gas lamps on the streets illuminated other unfortunates, ones who didn't have a bed for the night, who might have gone gladly to Ruby McAllister's house of ill repute rather than shiver under rags before the Scottish winter claimed them. It was a choice I never wanted to make, a choice no one should have to.

The last trickle of laudanum hidden away behind my books would have soothed my battered nerves and sore muscles, left me docile and malleable just like everyone wanted, ready to pour into whatever mould they chose. My relatives could shape me into the perfect wife and mother, Julia into another soldier for her army – even Fiona wanted to keep my attention firmly inside the clinic walls, like blinkers on a horse.

But as I looked at its hiding place, I forced myself to think about Lucy's body on the dissecting table and all the steps that had led her there. The distance between us had never seemed so precarious. If I wanted to rectify the damage I had done, I needed my wits about me.

We were a subdued group the next morning. Julia sat silent and sullen, glaring at her botany textbook during a chemistry lab, and on the other side of the room, Edith's eyes were red and swollen. Probably she had been blamed for the night's debacle through her bosom friend's convoluted logic.

'I don't know how you do it,' Alison murmured as our test tube frothed over dangerously. 'That place was ghastly. Will you think me awful if I stick to general practice when I graduate, instead of ministering to the great unwashed with you?'

I smiled fondly, having never once imagined the comfort-loving Alison Thornhill as an angel of mercy in the slums. 'The problem with the great unwashed is – well, you can imagine. And frankly, I'll be surprised if I make it through this term, let alone graduate. I didn't even look at my *materia medica* notes last night, and you know how Merchiston likes picking on me.'

I dabbed fruitlessly at the spilt chemicals with my handkerchief, wondering if the fabric was supposed to dissolve like that.

'Oh, he's like that with everyone – he always looks as though you've spoilt his favourite pen. I much prefer Professor Chalmers, he's far more jolly.'

That was Alison in a nutshell – so keen to think well of everyone that she could only conceive of the smallest of slights. As I watched in horror as the solution – which had, I was forced to admit, contained a little too much sulphuric acid – ate away at the bench, I decided against mentioning that his grievance was because I had accused him of murder.

It was with considerable relief that I exited the laboratory, Professor McClory's admonishments still ringing in my ears. Any hope I had of a moment to wolf down a sandwich and treat the small burn on my left index finger evaporated when Julia and Moira shepherded us all into a deserted side corridor.

'Ladies, our mission last night was less than successful,' Julia began. There was muffled laughter from the ranks. 'But one thing is clear – if we want to challenge the immorality on our streets, we need to take our crusade to the hallowed halls of academia.' We stared blankly, sleep-deprived to a woman and at least one of us having inhaled noxious gas not ten minutes earlier. 'Anthony Hardy, the one who was boasting about visiting brothels! I saved some pamphlets and I think it's about time we paid him and his reprobate gang of chums a visit. He had a cadaver dissection this morning and he normally spends luncheon in the common room, so if we follow this corridor, we should meet him coming up the back staircase.'

'I don't see why you're expecting this to work when last night was such a disaster,' I grumbled.

'That's because you don't possess my moral rectitude, Gilchrist,' Julia said. 'Perhaps if you listened more and criticised the Morality Union less, you might learn something.'

Luckily, the object of our hunt arrived at that point, whistling a jaunty music-hall song.

'Our pioneering would-be doctoresses! What a charming sight. Well,' he grinned, 'most of you, anyway.'

Rolling her eyes, Julia blocked his path. 'There's nothing charming about your behaviour, Hardy. While we spent last night in the freezing cold, trying to save the souls of the poor girls in the Grassmarket bawdy houses, I hear you have been leading them further into degradation.'

Hardy, who barely possessed the sense God gave a flea and whose presence at the university could be put down to his father's seat on the board of the Royal College of Surgeons, paused for a moment to parse Julia's argument. Eventually his face lit up with comprehension.

'Oh, you mean visiting tarts? Well, all work and no play makes a gent terribly dull, you know. I've always wondered, how do you girls blow off a little steam?' His sentence trailed off into an anguished squawk as Julia stamped on his foot.

'Do dignity and honour mean nothing to you? You took an oath to save lives, not to endanger souls!'

'Now steady on there – I haven't technically taken any oaths yet. You don't do that until you graduate, see. If you graduate.'

Any sympathy I had felt for Hardy being press-ganged by a

marauding Morality Union vanished at his implication.

'So you don't deny visiting Ruby McAllister's establishment on Mackenzie's Wynd?' I demanded.

'Not you too,' he groaned. 'Merchiston has already hauled me over the coals and threatened to have me sent down. As though that miserable scarecrow was some beacon of morality!' He snorted. 'At least I've never been tried for murder.'

Chapter 24

It felt as though all the air had escaped from the room.

'Didn't know about that, did you, Little Miss Know-It-All?' he smirked. 'Just ask Andrew Blair – his fiancée's father is a QC in Aberdeen, and he says there was the most frightful scandal when Merchiston came to work here.'

'But surely if he was acquitted . . .' Julia stammered.

'But that's the thing – he wasn't. The best they could do was Not Proven.' At my blank expression he explained, 'Oh, it's some Scots legal nonsense. When they can't find the evidence to make the crime stick but they're pretty sure you've done it, they judge it Not Proven. The Scotch verdict, they call it – probably because no other country would be so petty-minded as to clear you while still implying you're guilty.'

He paused, realising that he was outnumbered by Scots-women. Out of the corner of my eye, I saw Moira's fingers tighten around her scalpel in patriotic offence.

'Who was he supposed to have murdered?'

Hardy shrugged, as if that wasn't of the faintest importance. 'I haven't a clue. There was a woman involved, I think. Isn't there always when a chap finds himself in trouble? Anyway, there's no use looking at me like I've desecrated a village of virgins. I didn't get past the parlour – the old cat who runs the place threw us out as soon as she heard we were students. I told her our money was as good as anyone's, but she was having none of it. So it's back to Mrs Palm and her five friendly daughters for me.' He adopted a hangdog expression. 'I'm practically a eunuch.'

'You're a disgusting pig,' Julia said sweetly.

He snorted. 'Christ, you'll have to toughen up if you want to practise medicine. If you're going to act like men, Miss Latymer, you'd better develop some balls.' He winked at me. 'Don't worry, I'm sure there's a diagram in your textbook.'

Had he not sauntered off when he did, there might have been another murder blighting the hallowed reputation of the University of Edinburgh. As it was, Moira was left hissing like an angry cat and Julia swore profusely under her breath.

'I can't believe we missed lunch for some ridiculous gossip,' Alison grumbled.

I shook my head. The thought of what Hardy had done after being evicted from Ruby's establishment was far too vivid in my mind. 'I'm never eating again.'

'Perhaps we should stand outside Mrs Palm's next,' Caroline Carstairs offered helpfully.

A strangled yelp came from Alison's direction, and even Julia was blushing.

'That isn't a real place,' I explained gently.

'Well then, what did he mean?'

'Don't,' I groaned. 'Don't ask questions you don't want to know the answers to. Please, just live in blessed ignorance.'

'Can we return to the original point?' Julia whispered. 'Professor Merchiston was tried for murder! I'd say that was a little more disturbing than Hardy's onanism. Oh for God's sake, buy a dictionary, Carstairs!'

'At least he wasn't guilty,' Edith said, not sounding terribly reassured.

'Everything but!' Moira barked. 'I read about a woman who was found Not Proven and she went on to poison her next three husbands!'

'Don't underestimate how a reputation will protect a man,' I said grimly. 'The innocence of men like Merchiston rests on their good name, not on what they have or haven't done. If a man like that causes you harm, you'd better hope you're wealthy, titled and male, or the law will cast you aside like rubbish.'

Moira blinked. 'A bit bleak, Gilchrist.'

'It's the truth,' Edith said quietly. 'A man like Professor Merchiston can shrug off a little scandal, but for a woman . . .'

'We all know what scandal does to women,' Alison finished, pointedly. Everyone tried very hard not to look at me.

'Murderer or not, he's still teaching here,' Moira said firmly. She glanced at her wristwatch. 'In fact, he's probably waiting for us now. Under the circumstances, I don't ever want to be late for one of his lectures again.'

With a murmur of agreement, we began to move as one through the corridors. Julia turned to me as though she wanted to say something. Not wanting to hear whatever new taunts she had thought up, I hurried away.

It was not, of course, the first time I had sat in one of Professor Merchiston's lectures and examined him for any trace or hint of unreasonable violence. But as I glanced around, I felt an odd sense of camaraderie seeing my fellow students doing so as well. That I was not alone in my suspicions should have soothed me – instead, my thoughts were jangled and confusing.

If he noticed our inattention – which surely he did, his lips pressed thinner than usual and his manner even brusquer – he overlooked our muffled yawns and the occasional wrong answer. His lecture was pitched lower than normal, as though his thoughts too were elsewhere, and together we all plodded on until our hour was up.

'For an alternative description, I recommend you search out Raybourn's *Notes on Pharmacology* ahead of your examinations. You can find it at James Thin the bookseller's, or in the library if you prefer your copies dog-eared and ink-splattered . . .' He broke off mid-sentence. 'Miss Carstairs, is there a problem? Or are you telling fortunes like a gipsy at the country fair? Because if so, I was under the impression that you're supposed to read other people's palms.'

Caroline was staring at her hand with revulsion. Experimentally, she flexed her fingers into a circle and shuddered.

She caught my gaze with an expression of horror, and I nodded apologetically. Innocence didn't last long here for any of us, it seemed.

The Chalmerses' house was a cocoon of warmth banishing the late-afternoon chill from my bones, and I gulped the coffee Elisabeth had poured for me gratefully. A plate of her cook's very best biscuits lay on the table, a fire roared in the grate, and best of all, my fingers no longer smelt of formaldehyde despite an hour and a half spent with a scalpel and a deceased frog.

It would have been a lovely scene – 'The Bluestocking and Her Companion', an artist would call it – had I not once again turned the conversation to darker matters and Gregory Merchiston's role in them.

Elisabeth's exasperation was becoming evident. 'Sarah, this is becoming quite the vendetta! Suspect the man by all means, but if it gets out that you're blackening his character to the wife of one of his colleagues, you'll be sent down. I agree that his behaviour has been . . . well, somewhat unorthodox, but I know the man and I simply don't think—'

'Did you know he was accused of murder?' I interrupted. Elisabeth flinched. 'Oh God, you did! And you never said anything. Why?'

'It was a mistake,' she said firmly. 'His sister had got herself into some trouble and the man responsible was found dead. Gregory had been seen arguing with him a few days before, and the police jumped to conclusions. He was acquitted, Sarah! I know you have little faith in the law, but even you have to respect that.'

'He wasn't acquitted,' I bit out.

Elisabeth looked confused. 'He was found not guilty.'

'The verdict was Not Proven,' I corrected. 'A slap on the wrist from a judge who couldn't or wouldn't convict him. You're so eager to believe him innocent, to trust a man simply because he's dined with you, that you're blind to the facts.'

'Randall told me about it, it's true,' Elisabeth confessed. 'He didn't want me to hear it from a student or another faculty member spreading malicious gossip.' She looked at me pointedly and I sank further down into my chair. 'But he told me that Gregory was found innocent.'

'He probably thought that explaining the detail of Scots law would be too much for your feeble female mind,' I muttered.

My friend glared at me. 'I may not be studying for a medical degree, Sarah, but I'm not a complete fool. And may I remind you that it is Randall you women have to thank for being here at all? He has championed your cause, defended you to your detractors and made sure the miscreants who played that ghastly prank on you all with the red ink were found and punished. He deserves better than that, and if you want to ask him about it—'

'Ask who what?' the subject of our conversation asked amiably, if not grammatically, as he entered the room. 'Miss

Gilchrist, a pleasure as always. Darling, tell me that we're eating early. I've been arguing with the Bursar all afternoon and I'm absolutely famished.'

'It seems that rumours about Gregory and that dreadful court case have reached the first-year students,' his wife said grimly.

'Well, it was only a matter of time,' Chalmers said ruefully. 'Although I was hoping that the female students might be spared the gossip. Bad enough that half the lecturers don't want you here at all without hearing that one of them was once questioned in connection with a murder.'

'A little more than questioned, I believe,' I prompted. Elisabeth sighed audibly.

'It was five years ago. The girl, his sister, was barely more than fourteen, Gregory recently widowed from the cholera epidemic and paralysed with guilt over not having been able to save his wife and son. The girl had run off with her school-master, who abandoned her as soon as he realised that Gregory wouldn't pay for their upkeep. There were some unpleasant words, enough that when the bast— ahem, the blackguard was found dead, his acquaintances all pointed the finger at Gregory. The judge knew that it was a fool's errand from the start, but there was no denying that Gregory had the motive and the strength to crush the man's windpipe like that.' Elisabeth gave a cry of horror. 'My love, I'm sorry. I forgot myself. Anyway, no one believed he could have done it, and after a little grumbling from the higher-ups, he was hired by the university. You can't hang a man on no evidence, and Merchiston's reputation spoke for itself.'

'And his sister?' Elisabeth asked, her eyes wide with concern. 'He never mentions her.'

A spasm of pain flashed over Chalmers' face. 'Not every story has a happy ending, my dear.'

We were all silent for a moment, the only sound the pop and crackle of the logs in the grate.

'I've asked Sarah to stay for dinner. We're having something light this evening – the poor girl has just come from a dissection.'

'No frogs' legs then?' he chuckled.

I winced, remembering the poor amphibian specimen and the mess I had made of him.

The housemaid entered with a swift curtsey, and informed us that dinner was being served in the dining room. I followed my friends in with a heavy heart and a troubled conscience. I had details, I realised, but I was no closer than before to an answer about Gregory Merchiston's aptitude for murder.

Chapter 25

The infirmary was in turmoil when I arrived. An overturned omnibus that afternoon had resulted in an influx of patients, and Fiona and her colleagues were struggling to keep up. I had barely deposited my coat in the cramped office when I was set to work carrying bedpans and sterilising instruments and any other task that the rest of the staff had no time for. An hour after I arrived, I was cleaning a particularly ugly suppurating wound when I heard a commotion in the makeshift reception area. It wasn't unusual for a patient to turn violent, whether through drink or fear or just frustration at their miserable lives, so I continued dabbing disinfectant on the pus-filled sore until a sharp cry startled me.

Fiona was pressed up against the wall, the tip of a kitchen knife at the hollow of her throat.

'You bitch,' a girl of no more than fifteen gasped out through her tears. 'You said you'd take care of it. You said you'd get rid of it.'

'I said I'd help you,' Fiona said, fighting to keep her voice calm. 'A family, perhaps, to foster the child whilst you find a more suitable occupation. But I won't perform an illegal operation.'

The knife stayed dangerously in place, but the girl's voice softened. 'Lucy said . . .'

My breath hitched in my throat.

Fiona spoke firmly. 'Lucy said the same thing as you, and received the same response. God has sent you this child as a way out of your wickedness. Your time would be better spent planning for its arrival than arguing with me trying to prevent it.'

Matilda Campbell, the clinic's anaesthetist, pulled the sobbing girl away from Fiona, and the knife clattered to the floor. She cradled the child, murmuring soothing words and escorting her with the minimum of fuss to one of the examining rooms.

Fiona stooped to pick up the knife, and I rushed to her side. 'Thank God for Tillie,' she laughed shakily. 'I swear she doesn't need ether – she could just talk her patients into blissful unconsciousness.'

I shuddered at her clinical tone, wondering if I would ever be able to see the clinic's patients as mere tools for scientific discovery, rather than the people they were.

Her shoulders slumped. 'I'm feeling rather unwell after my recent experience, Sarah. I think you'd better escort me home.'

Fiona's lodgings were cramped but cosy, little more luxurious than those occupied by my fellow students. Still, next to the fire with a pot of strong tea on the table and muffins pierced precariously on toasting forks, it felt like heaven.

'Thank you for inviting me,' I said shyly. 'I know how busy you are.'

'Nonsense,' Fiona said. 'It's the least I can do to thank you. You've been invaluable these past weeks. I do hope you'll consider staying on in a professional capacity once you're qualified. If we last that long.'

My heart leapt at the suggestion. I had whiled away many nights in London imagining what life as a doctor would be like. Sometimes my fantasies included ministering to the poor as Fiona suggested, or travelling to Africa with the missionaries; a bustling hospital where I was recognised as a competent surgeon, or even simply a quiet practice where women could avoid the uncomfortable ministrations of a male doctor. The thought of a real future, independent of disapproving relatives or an unwanted husband, made me giddy with joy. But that possibility only lasted a moment.

'Assuming I even graduate. My aunt has found me a prospective husband.' I laughed bitterly. 'All this time I thought they were at least tolerating my studies, and it turns out they were just waiting for a suitable candidate.'

'Might he be sympathetic to your cause?'

'I barely know him! That's not the way the Gilchrists do things. He could be a staunch traditionalist or a male suffragist – all I know is his family has a lengthy entry in Debrett's.'

Fiona squeezed my hand. 'I hope for your sake you can find a way out of it. There are some women who can combine medicine and a family life, but they're the exceptions. Men can have a wife, five children and a string of mistresses, but if you're a woman, then you have to choose.'

'Is that why you never married?' I asked tentatively.

She smiled tightly. 'Even the kindest of men can disappoint you.'

I voiced a thought that had been nagging at me since our unruly patient had been carted off. 'That girl. Was there nowhere else that could help her? I know they exist. Doctors who help girls who are . . . in trouble, like she was. Like Lucy was.'

Fiona paled. 'Sarah, what are you trying to tell me?'

I felt a hot wave of shame wash over me and shrank from

her doctor's gaze. I had nothing to worry about, but that sick feeling of guilt prickled at my skin all the same. This was how it would be from now on, the first conclusion anyone would jump to. Fiona didn't know about my sordid history, but others did. Every time I looked tired or plump, every time I fought down a rising tide of vomit at the dissection table, the assumption would be the same – I had fallen back into my old ways and paid the price. It didn't matter how impossible it was with my scarred stomach and butchered reproductive system; the accusation was as bad as the crime.

'I'm not . . .' I managed to say. 'I didn't . . . I didn't mean me. But these girls must go somewhere, surely?'

'Old witches with gin and rusty knitting needles, you mean? That's what it looks like, Sarah. I've treated women who gave themselves lead poisoning, or broken limbs from a fall. Women who contract septicaemia because their fee only covered a sharp knife, not a clean one. Put aside any thoughts of kindly wise women with pennyroyal tea. You could be struck off for even talking about it in front of the wrong person. For God's sake, we could lose the few benefactors we still have!'

I thought back to a staircase and the bruises that followed, the sight of my mother watching immobile from a doorway, and I knew there were some things I could never share.

She paused, hand hovering over the teapot. 'If you do ever find yourself in a situation you can't get out of, promise me you'll let me know? That's not something anyone should have to go through alone.'

I wished I had known her in London. What it would have been to have her on my side when everyone from my parents to my doctors was trying to scrub the events of that night from my body and my mind. The rawness was fading, but her presence was a balm.

'Your patients are very lucky to have you,' I whispered.

She was silent for a long moment before I asked the question that had been preying on my mind every time I saw her frowning over the accounts or trying to charm some new donor.

'Is the infirmary really in so much trouble?'

Fiona grimaced. 'If it weren't for your uncle's good nature—'

'You mean his money,' I interrupted.

'Quite. Without that help, we'd be bankrupt by now. We're going to have to raise our fees as it is, even if it means sending away the people who need us most. The problem is,' she sighed, rubbing her eyes, 'there are so many of them.'

'Like Lucy,' I said quietly.

Fiona laughed. 'Oh, if it weren't for Ruby McAllister and women like her, we would have had to close our doors long ago. Whoremongers may cause as many problems as they solve, but at least they pay their bills.' She caught my shocked expression in the flickering firelight. 'I'm sorry, Sarah. I'd forgotten that you aren't quite as cynical as the rest of us.' She sipped her tea, eyeing me over the rim of the cup. 'Don't worry, you will be.'

I couldn't imagine seeing prostitution in such pragmatic terms.

'Is there nothing we can do to help them?'

'Help them? Do you really think that if you rescue a girl from that life she'll vanish from our doorstep? At least with Ruby she'll have a roof over her head, decent food and as much gin as she needs to forget how dreadful her life is. How many of our other patients can say the same?'

'Is that really the best they're supposed to hope for?' I burst out. 'Trading their bodies for security? I suppose they should be grateful to women like Ruby. After all, it isn't as though girls like Lucy have feelings.'

Fiona leant forward and covered my hand with hers.

'Don't dwell on the fate of one girl, Sarah. We see women like her every day. Ruby will have found a replacement by now, some girl who was walking the streets or in another madam's employ. She'll take Lucy's place in her bed, with her callers, and soon even Ruby will forget she ever existed. I suggest you do the same.'

I snatched my hand away and pressed it to my mouth, trying to force back the sob that fought its way out of my throat. Fiona sighed. 'For God's sake, Sarah! Ruby sold her corpse to the university for dissection. She can't afford finer feelings about another dead whore, and neither can you.'

My breath caught in my throat. 'Ruby sold her? But she told me—'

Fiona blanched. 'You went to speak to her? Alone? Sarah, you bloody little fool! Do you have any idea how dangerous that was? You're lucky to have made it out of there alive. Women like Ruby wait all their wretched careers for silly untouched girls like you to stumble through their doors. A cup of tea laced with opium and you'd never have left. The perfect girl for men who like their whores with a little refinement.'

I shuddered. I might not be as untarnished as Fiona assumed, but the thought that Ruby might have trapped me there had never occurred to me. I saw myself through Fiona's world-weary eyes – a naive young lady wandering the slums like a tourist along the streets of Paris, protected only by the false sense of invulnerability that wealth and privilege afforded.

'Promise me you won't go back there,' she said. 'Give me your word, Sarah. If anything happened to you, I'd never forgive myself.'

I swallowed and made a promise I didn't know if I could keep.

We returned to the clinic in time for my uncle's carriage, and I gazed out of the window lost in thought. Women whose gowns offered little protection against the elements and even less against passers-by stood shivering in huddles, waiting for a man to like the look of them enough for a quick tumble. Even in this freezing weather, a few customers approached, and they disappeared in pairs to a more private location. I watched idly, numbed now to the shock of seeing this trade in flesh take place before my eyes. As the carriage drove through a puddle of yellow gaslight, I saw the glint of coins being exchanged, and a familiar set of features was illuminated briefly in the artificial light.

It was Randall Chalmers.

Chapter 26

I barely listened during Professor Chalmers' epidemiology lecture. I didn't want to hear a word the man said, to be forced to take him as a mentor, an exemplar of medical ability, when I knew him for the hypocrite he was. My driver had not lingered, the horses trotting briskly out of the slums as Chalmers and the woman he had bought left to conclude their transaction, and I was glad of it. I didn't want to see where he went next.

I was tired, so tired, of following men through their endless maze of degradation – first Paul, then Merchiston, and now the husband of the closest thing I had to a friend. I was sick with anger and disappointment. How dare he? He was using some of the most fragile women in the city for his idle gratification, with no thought about his wife, whose heart this would break, or the diseases to which he was exposing a woman he had vowed to love and to cherish. I wondered if there was any honour in men anymore; if there ever had been.

He called on me, and I answered mechanically, my thoughts not in the lecture hall with him but in the warm comfort of his wife's drawing room.

How would I tell Elisabeth? My heart ached at the thought,

but she had a right to know, to refuse him entry to her bed unless he could prove he was healthy and faithful, unless he swore to cease these illicit visits to the most degraded of Edinburgh's women. And yet the thought of tearing her world asunder, of dragging even more filth into her life, made me ill. What right had I to ruin her happiness? But I wasn't ruining it, I reminded myself. Randall Chalmers was. And if he was too much of a coward and a hypocrite to let his wife know about his secret life, then I most certainly was not.

I sat through the morning's lectures, resolved to focus on my work. By the time the clock in the square tolled midday, I was thinking like a medical student again. It was a relief to break for luncheon – I hadn't eaten much of the toast Agnes had brought me, and I had gone directly to the library before the rest of the house had risen, so had been denied a decent breakfast. I caught Alison Thornhill's eye as we left the lecture theatre.

'I'll stand you a cup of coffee and a sticky bun if you'll distract me from thinking about our *materia medica* essays,' I offered.

She grimaced. 'I think I need something stronger if I don't want to cry over mine.'

'Our reputations are in enough trouble as it is,' I laughed. 'If we start drinking alcohol with luncheon, they might never recover.'

Ten minutes later saw us at a cramped table in a tea room on the South Bridge, where, just as Alison had promised, the coffee was strong and the food cheap.

'The first month, I was so homesick I cried myself to sleep every night,' she confessed. 'I even packed my bags twice. The last time I made it halfway to Waverley station!'

'What made you turn back?' I asked curiously.

She was silent for a moment. 'I imagined what my life

would be like if I got on the train and went home, tail between my legs, to settle down with the man Mama had picked out for me when I was still in pigtails. No university, no profession, just suffocating slowly for the rest of my life.'

It was a grim image, and not one I was sure I had avoided.

Alison looked at me expectantly. I pasted on a smile.

'I don't get homesick,' I lied.

'At least you're with family.'

I snorted. 'Aunt Emily and Uncle Hugh? I've had more fun at funerals. They're desperate for me to give up my studies, but at least they haven't tried to stop me.'

We carefully avoided my strained relationship with our classmates and the reason for it. I could have told her the truth then and there – something in her countenance gave me the idea that she would be sympathetic – but words failed me, and I let her assume the stories were true. It was, I knew, very difficult not to listen when scurrilous rumours were being passed from student to student. Still, although I appreciated Alison's lack of interest, I didn't entirely believe in it.

The hour passed pleasantly, but soon it was time to return to the draughty lecture hall and await our collective fate. My stomach was in my boots, and the similarly grim expressions on the faces of my fellow students did little to reassure me. All they had to worry about was the quality of their work. I had made the error of turning the arbiter of my academic fate into an adversary.

Never one to spare a student public humiliation, Merchiston chose to read out our marks and call us up to receive our dissected papers. It was a mixed bag, and for once I couldn't even enjoy the *Schadenfreude* of seeing Edith receive an appallingly low mark and an essay correspondingly scribbled all over in blood-red ink.

'Miss Sarah Gilchrist,' he announced, his voice as free of any inflection as it had been when he had read out the names of my fellows. 'Ninety-seven per cent.' So I wasn't to be punished for my investigations after all. Somehow I managed to make my way back to my seat, where I read the few comments scribbled in the margins. *Overall a good attempt, but I get the distinct impression your mind was elsewhere when you wrote this. Don't let it happen again – G. M.*

It wasn't an explicit threat. After our previous encounters, it didn't have to be.

I let the crowd of students surge past me, wanting to speak to the professor alone. As I passed him on my way out, I paused. He tensed, clearly expecting a row.

'Thank you, sir.' I meant it. 'I'll do better next time.' I left it to him to decide if I meant my academic work or my investigation.

His smile as I exited the room was tinged with something akin to amusement, but his eyes remained cold. I was not sorry to leave, but as I moved out into the corridor, I glanced back to see his gaze still fixed on me.

I threw myself into work that afternoon, desperate for a reprieve from the complications that had wormed their way into my life. I took notes until my hand cramped, my skin blotchy with ink, and even as we walked between classrooms, I endeavoured to keep my mind off Lucy by reciting the periodic table to myself. My studies had always been my refuge; I didn't know how I would cope if they were taken away from me. I barely spoke a word except to answer questions, and my arm ached with the amount of times I had raised it.

My attempts at distraction didn't stop at the lecture theatre. I had hit upon the cleverest scheme in my attempts to win over Aunt Emily and Uncle Hugh, one that did not involve an eligible bachelor to redeem me. I had joined the Edinburgh University Women's Christian Union and was to attend a dinner tonight with Reverend Spinks at the home of Aileen Ferguson, the history department's only female lecturer.

Over a parsimonious meal Reverend Spinks frowned as he tried to understand my presence. 'But surely the medical lassies have their own society? Why, I spoke to them just last week.' I groaned inwardly. It was true that Jessie McBride, a daughter of the manse from Inverclyde studying mathematics, had set up just such a society a month earlier in protest at the 'medical lassies'' exclusion from the EUWCU committee, but she had made it abundantly clear that I would not be welcome as a member. Although no great fan of Julia Latymer's, finding the other girl too radical for her more conservative liking, she had nevertheless eaten up every detail of the tale Julia had spun of my disgrace, and felt that my presence there imperilled the other female students – and possibly some of the men as well.

There was only one thing to do to avoid any reference to the scandal that tainted me. I pasted on the charming smile I had been using on Aunt Emily to little avail these past few months and lied through my teeth.

'But it is such a small group, Reverend, and we are in each other's pockets constantly as it is. I had hoped to extend my circle of Christian acquaintances here.'

My remarks passed muster, for he simply shrugged and turned his attention to what had doubtless been his keynote speech at the meeting last week.

'If there was ever a group of young ladies more in need of guidance,' he sighed, shaking his head. 'No good can come of this fad for lady doctors. Such intimate knowledge of . . . of the human form,' he was blushing madly, and I would have felt sorry for him if I hadn't felt so angry, 'is neither healthy nor moral. It can only end in disaster and ruin, I warn you now!'

'But surely,' I argued, 'it is far more proper for a lady to be administered to by one of her own sex?'

'Nonsense.' Reverend Spinks frowned. 'Why, medical men are above such things.'

'Then the same must apply to medical women!' I pointed out.

Seeing that I was not to be argued with, he reverted back to condescension as a means of silencing me.

'My dear girl,' he informed me, blithely ignoring the way I bridled at the unwanted endearment, 'you should consider it your duty to stay above the venal concerns of the body and instead pay attention to improving the condition of the human soul.'

'But we are not above the concerns of the body,' a red-headed girl argued, leaning her elbows on the table to the thin-lipped horror of Reverend Spinks. 'Why, if we must produce another generation of good Christian souls, we can hardly avoid it.'

I thought the good Reverend was about to faint with shock. I wondered idly in what his disgust of the human body was rooted. Mostly I was grateful that his opprobrium was diverted from me, at least temporarily.

When we retired to the drawing room, leaving the Reverend and Mr Ferguson to their cigars and piety, conversation descended into a free-for-all. Although the majority of my companions seemed a trifle hazy, to say the least, about what went on in the marital bed, they were nonetheless opinionated on the matter to a degree that would have horrified the Reverend.

I hung back, not wanting to risk drawing attention to myself lest rumours of my past had circulated around the whole damn university, but a historian by the name of Clara Hamilton dragged me into the debate with a determined expression and I found myself explaining the damage that ignorance could do and telling them about the girls little more than children who arrived at the infirmary with no understanding of how they came to be pregnant.

Cloistered as I was in the medical school, which had little to do with the rest of the university barring shared science lectures, my exposure to the other women newly admitted had been minimal. Away from the hothouse that I had found less than welcoming, I found a certain morbid fascination with my studies amongst even the more prim and proper members of the group. Mired in essay after lecture after experiment after dissection I had developed an immunity to the work we were doing, although it thrilled me no less for that. I realised I was building up the mental calluses needed for my chosen path, and I felt a little surge of pride.

The whole evening cheered me so much that, although I doubted Reverend Spinks would have me back, I began to feel part of the fabric of the university in a way I had hoped I would before my past was raked up again. Guilt pricked me as I realised that I hadn't thought of Lucy all evening. Perhaps Merchiston was right; perhaps this was a matter best left alone.

Drinking tea with Aunt Emily in her parlour, I was able to answer with total honesty her questions about the day's activities. Without the fear that I would let something slip, we talked with relative ease. She pointedly ignored all explicit references to my studies, but at least she wasn't criticising them outright. I wondered how much that had to do with acceptance, and how much with the fact that the Greenes had asked if we would accompany them to church on Sunday, an invitation Aunt Emily issued like a military command over breakfast. I suspected that I would not like the answer. In any case, there was a hurdle to be overcome before I was reunited with my would-be suitor, one that would require holding my tongue on matters more delicate than fending off an unwanted proposal. The Chalmerses had invited us to take a walk around the pleasure gardens on Saturday afternoon, and Aunt Emily had accepted with relish.

Princes Street Gardens were crowded with people taking in the crisp autumn air, although it was still tinged with the ever-present hops from the brewery. The leaves had fallen from the trees in beautiful red and gold piles, sometimes gusting across the path in the breeze, and in the distance, an orchestra was playing in the bandstand. Above us, the castle loomed dark and grey, like something out of an Ann Radcliffe novel, but the paths were busy with people enjoying the rare day of sunshine.

My aunt engaged Elisabeth in conversation about Canada – which she appeared to have simultaneously confused with America, Australia and the North Pole – and my uncle walked alongside Professor Chalmers in comparative silence interspersed with occasional grunts. I was desperate to get Elisabeth alone, but instead I walked obediently next to Aunt Emily, who had launched into a spirited account of the shooting party she had attended in the Highlands the previous year. I realised that my arrival in August had meant they had had to forgo the weekend shooting parties during grouse season, and for once I felt sorry for my relatives. My entrance into their life had disrupted it, and I had never properly apologised. Still, the thought of being dragged to a country house for the weekend to admire the feathery corpses resulting from my uncle's expeditions with his friends didn't exactly appeal, and I was glad to have missed it.

I was wearing my new walking dress for the occasion – now that I had a suitor and tenuous connections via Elisabeth with an earl, my aunt had taken me to her dressmaker, and I was clad in striped silk with a parasol to match. My lace fichu might have been a little itchy, and the corset tighter than I would have liked, but I knew that my teal and chocolate concoction was striking. It had been a long time since I had enjoyed turning heads. I revelled in the late-afternoon sun and the admiring glances – even my aunt's tedious conversation was tolerable on such a day, although I was required to do little more than nod my head in agreement any time she or Elisabeth said anything that sounded like a definitive statement. In my aunt's case, deferring as she did to the sister of a countess, that was rarely, and I found it hard to believe that Elisabeth could have an opinion on a matter over which I would ever radically disagree.

'You must join my sister and her husband when they host their next party,' Elisabeth was saying. 'Their cook is wonderful, and I'm sure you'd find it most delightful.'

'Do they know the Greenes?' Aunt Emily asked. My heart sank to my boots. Elisabeth feigned ignorance. 'The Greenes? Oh yes, the banking family.' Something in her voice made it clear that the Greenes were considered not quite the thing in her sister's set. 'Mm, I believe they are distantly acquainted.' Her tone implied that her sister, at least, was very happy about that distance.

Clever girl! I could have hugged her there and then. I might not have been able to produce a single good reason why I should not be pushed into a betrothal with Miles – 'I don't like him' and 'he slurps his soup' not being considered acceptable reasons to refuse a proposal – but Elisabeth had, with one arched eyebrow and a few well-chosen words, loosened the bonds of potential matrimony a little.

Aunt Emily nodded, clearly unsure of how to proceed now that her attempt at name-dropping had failed. Luckily, at that point she spied a friend of hers and we were joined by another chattering matron eager to hear all about Canada and – more importantly – Elisabeth's sister and brother-in-law. I hoped that society gossip would never tarnish Elisabeth's charmed life – if anyone so much as cut her in public, I would slap them. Something about her made me feel terribly protective, and I realised that we were becoming fast friends.

Ahead of us, the gentlemen paused, allowing us to catch up. As I watched Elisabeth smile radiantly at her husband, ignorant of his infidelities, I could barely swallow. Professor Chalmers was hardly of the calibre my aunt preferred in her acquaintances, but his wife's lineage gained him entrance to any dining room in Edinburgh. Had he married Elisabeth for her fortune and connections? I wondered. Up until recently, I had thought theirs truly a love match, but could love die so very quickly? I supposed it must, or half the brothels in the city would close down overnight. And yet he looked as devoted as before, though I thought I detected the merest suggestion of trouble in his eyes as he conversed. He was a charming man, if neither the handsomest nor the youngest Elisabeth could have attracted. Despite their initial misgivings, my aunt and uncle hung on his every word, and he was witty enough to quite make them forget how they knew him.

'What do you think of this new influx of lassies in your lecture halls then, Chalmers?' Uncle Hugh asked.

'I would hardly be here if I disapproved, Mr Fitzherbert,' Randall said. 'As your niece has proved, women have just the same capacity for learning as men.'

'Nonsense!' Uncle Hugh snorted. His temper, I noticed drily, was not quite roused enough for him to lose the semblance of jocularity. It seemed Aunt Emily was not the only one entranced by the prospect of meeting the nobility. 'Hasn't it been proved that women's brains are weaker?'

Randall gave a pained smile. 'Not conclusively, Mr Fitzherbert.'

Uncle Hugh looked put out. 'Could have sworn I read it somewhere,' he mumbled.

'Perhaps you were thinking of horses,' I suggested acidly, knowing full well that Uncle Hugh never read so much as a postcard unless it mentioned racing. He glared at me, and I regretted my sudden bravery. They wouldn't thank me if I embarrassed them in public as well as private. Elisabeth looked the picture of propriety, but I could tell from her sparkling eyes and pinched lips that she was longing to laugh. This was, I realised, the most fun I had ever had at one of my aunt's social outings. I hoped she would consider making the Chalmerses a permanent fixture in our lives.

'No, this is a new age,' Randall said. 'Women are independent now; they're getting a chance to spread their wings.'

'Well I for one don't hold with it,' Aunt Emily said crisply, her friend nodding approval.

Randall frowned. 'And yet you allow your niece to study medicine?'

I caught my breath. I wasn't sure how much, if anything, Elisabeth knew about my past.

'Sarah's parents were . . . persuaded,' Aunt Emily said. 'Luckily, they felt that if she were going to persist in such a modern notion, she should at least do it with adequate supervision. Did you know that in some universities' – she said the word as though she meant gambling den or brothel, which in all probability she did – 'they allow women to live entirely unsupervised?'

Like most of Aunt Emily's remarks about women pursuing higher education, this was nonsense.

'The residence halls are very well chaperoned,' I offered

timidly, not seeking to annoy her any further.

'But hardly comparable to being at home with their families, which is where they belong.'

'Sarah is fortunate that she has the two of you to keep her on the path of righteousness,' Elisabeth said sweetly.

Had she been any closer, I would have kicked her, but I contented myself with shooting daggers at her with my eyes.

Eventually Elisabeth and I managed to separate ourselves from the group and speak in lowered tones.

'I'm afraid Randall hasn't been terribly forthcoming about Professor Merchiston,' she murmured, raising a gloved hand in acknowledgement of yet another acquaintance, but angling her parasol to act as a buffer between them. 'We saw him at a faculty dinner the other night, and you're right, something is wrong. He looks terribly tired, and older somehow. I wish I could help him.'

'Well I don't!' I snapped. My voice must have been louder than I intended, and Aunt Emily shot me a sharp look, reminding me to act like a lady. 'You may defend him all you like, Elisabeth; he's mixed up in all this somehow and I intend to find out how.'

'As do I,' she said soothingly. 'But you'll find that you'll catch far more flies with honey than with vinegar.'

'I'm not going to charm him,' I muttered obstinately. 'Even if I wanted to, he wouldn't be seen within a yard of me without a chaperone.'

'And nor should you!' she chided laughingly. 'But be serious for a moment. Whatever we do now, you must be careful of your reputation above all things. I can't afford to lose you as a friend, should you get sent away.'

I was touched. 'Elisabeth, you have the widest circle of friends of anyone I know. Everyone simply adores you!'

'They adore me, yes,' she said, 'but they don't see me. They think I'm pretty and perfect and fragile, they indulge my every whim, but they don't stop to wonder what I think about things. Only you – and, of course, Randall.' She blushed, and I was struck again by how thoroughly besotted she was with her husband. 'My sister might have longed for a title, but I came over to Scotland because I wanted adventure. I thought I was going to have to content myself with charity work and living through you girls, but this – now this is living.' She frowned. 'Is it terrible to think that way? I don't mean I'm glad that that poor girl was murdered, but it feels so damned good to be doing something useful for once!' She laughed at my shocked expression. 'Oh Sarah. I'm not so prim and proper, you know.'

I realised that I didn't just have a friend, I had a co-conspirator. The thought warmed me considerably. I had made the mistake of only seeing her surface and not the witty woman beneath the good manners and pretty dresses. I only hoped that she would be strong enough to withstand what I had to tell her.

The next day – a cold, sunny Sunday – marked my first public appearance with Miles Greene on my arm. The church was by no means the closest to our house, but its location in the finest part of the New Town meant that the crème de la crème of Edinburgh society crammed in there once a week in their Sunday best, coming more to show off than to bow their heads in solemn worship.

We had contrived to sit in the row across from the Greene family, so it was natural that we should all walk out together. The first bite of winter hung in the air as we exited the church, but the cold was not yet unpleasant. Since the day was sunny, if crisp, it was inevitable that we should promenade in the beautiful gardens beneath the craggy outcrop that housed the castle, and even more so that Miles should smile awkwardly and take my arm.

The fact that both sets of adults were a good few feet behind us did not escape my attention, and I dragged my heels as discreetly as I could in order to minimise the privacy he clearly hoped for. I prayed silently that a proposal would not come today, not before I had come up with a way to refuse that made it sound like it wasn't my idea.

He had returned from his tour of Europe little over a year ago, and I greedily listened to his descriptions of Italy and France. I had never been to the Louvre or the canals of Venice, and his description of the Eiffel Tower, the architectural marvel erected a decade earlier, made me sigh with envy. I hoped my interest in his travels would not be confused with interest in the man himself. I would not give up my liberty for anything, not even the chance to see the world if it meant that I must do so on my honeymoon.

And I had to admit to myself, my feelings were not unmixed with bitterness. For while Miles was gallivanting across the Continent, mixing with princes and poets, I had been in Dorset under the dubious care of the sanatorium staff. A beautiful part of England, but although the country air had been intended to revive me, in the end I had tasted little of it. I shivered as the memory of the sterile white rooms and probing cold hands of the physicians assailed me.

'Are you cold, Miss Gilchrist?'

'A little,' I confessed, although telling him that I had spent the spring in what was little more than a genteel madhouse for ladies of good breeding and unstable temperament would doubtless have cooled his ardour. I wondered how much longer we would be out, and if I could plead a headache or some other ladylike complaint in order to escape. I knew that such a ploy would result in my being confined to my bed the next day, however, and I had no intention of sinking further in Professor Merchiston's esteem.

Just the thought of the surly doctor made me scowl. I did not like the man. Nor, for that matter, did I trust him. And yet my fate was bound inextricably to his – he had made it crystal clear that any besmirching of his reputation regarding Lucy would be met with the complete and final dismantling of mine. Seeing my only other option smile down next to me, unaware of the blob of egg on his cravat or the clamminess of his palm pressed against mine, I knew that I had little choice in the matter. What had happened to Lucy was regrettable, but I could not allow the loss of a stranger's life to ruin my only chance of happiness.

Guilt tightened inside me, acrid and inescapable, but I forced myself to ignore it. Instead, I prattled gaily about my studies and described the dissection of the liver in such precise detail that my companion turned quite green. I asked him, although the closeness of our heads implied that our conversation was far more intimate, what he thought of the talk of women's suffrage. At this he blanched and asked if I really believed that ladies had any aptitude for politics. I replied, in tones that were they overheard could pass as coquettish, that if we could handle surgery, then matters of state could not be so far beyond our reach.

I couldn't suppress a gleeful smile as Miles handed me into the carriage with considerably less enthusiasm than he had shown taking my arm an hour earlier. From the conspiratorial – and not remotely subtle – smile my aunt gave me, it was clear that she thought the morning had been a success. It had, but not in the way she had imagined.

Over luncheon, I was subjected to a post-mortem more intense than anything my tutors could throw at me – what did he say, did I speak too much or too little, did he look at me with admiration? Seeking only a quiet life and the chance to escape the usual afternoon of religious contemplation and self-flagellation in favour of a good hour or two with my physiology textbook, I played to the hilt the role of demure young lady being wooed. It must have been successful, because I was to be left to my own devices that afternoon. As I was leaving the table, Aunt Emily pressed my hand.

'I'm writing to your mother this afternoon. Margaret will be so proud.'

My throat felt thick and I managed a watery smile before closing the door behind me. I had no intention of accepting a proposal from Miles Greene, even supposing he offered, though the idea of disappointing my parents again hurt more than I could bear. But it was more than just the thought of my mother's reaction. Aunt Emily was radiant, delighted that her wayward charge was being invited back into the fold, and by such an illustrious shepherd. She looked more than pleased that her plan was coming to fruition – she looked genuinely happy for me.

I sank down on my bed, lost in thought, my longed-for hours of study forgotten. Aunt Emily was concerned about my welfare, my immediate physical needs and the state of my immortal soul, but it had never before occurred to me that she might love me. Rather than acting on my mother's instructions, she genuinely believed that marriage to Miles was the best way of securing my future happiness.

I couldn't imagine anyone who was married to Uncle Hugh being so convinced that marriage was a fairy-tale ending. I had seen Aunt Emily look at him with lips pinched so thin they barely had any colour but stay faithfully silent. I had never wondered before about her feelings for him. I suppose if I had thought about it at all, I had taken it for granted that she loved him, in that romantic way children have when they assume their parents married for love rather than social position, money or respectability. It had never occurred to me that there were times when she simply did not like him. Was he her choice? I wondered. I doubted my grandparents had arranged it.

From my mother's disapproving mien whenever Uncle Hugh's name entered the conversation, it sounded as though Aunt Emily had rebelled to marry him. He had been a wealthy if partly self-made gentleman from Aberdeen whose canny investment in the brewing industry rather than his lineage accounted for his position in Edinburgh society. Despite his professional connections to the demon drink – or perhaps because of them – he was staunchly religious, and my aunt had undergone some sort of conversion when he had come to London in search of a bride with sufficient breeding to compensate for his lack of the same. I had a faint suspicion that whilst they had not actually eloped – I had seen their wedding portrait displayed in the parlour, although neither of them looked particularly happy in it – they had come perilously close. I could not imagine Uncle Hugh doing anything so scandalous, nor Aunt Emily something so spontaneous, but family lore was not to be argued with.

I wondered what the letter would say. The thought of making my mother proud, of seeing something other than shame and disgust in her eyes, made my heart leap. Until that fateful night in the library, I could not have imagined anything that would bring me so low in her estimation, despite her disapproval of my modern ideas and radical sensibilities. Then again, Aunt Emily's ideas of what was best for any of her nieces and nephews had always differed from Mother's. It was a measure of the extent of my disgrace that Mother thought her puritanical younger sister a beneficial influence.

I felt unnervingly as though I were a gift for my mother – Aunt Emily was returning her tarnished daughter tidied up and polished. My disgrace would become a mysterious history from before I married, only to be discussed in hushed tones whenever I was out of earshot. My fanciful ideas of practising medicine would be an amusing anecdote for dinner parties and I would join the ranks of the respectable married ladies who had turned heads in their wilder younger days. I shuddered at the thought. I had burnt my bridges as far as respectability was concerned – it would be hypocrisy of the tallest order to return to that world now, after I had rejected everything I had been raised with.

Sighing, I opened my books and settled down to my studies. Everything else could wait until tomorrow, I told myself firmly. My family, Miles, the constant nagging guilt whenever I thought of Lucy. I had a future of my own to secure.

Chapter 27

Uncle Hugh was late down for breakfast. I had finished my eggs and was jiggling my foot anxiously before Aunt Emily scolded me for unladylike behaviour. Channelling my nervous energies into an extra portion of toast and marmalade – equally unladylike, in Aunt Emily's extensive and exacting book, but on the basis that it stopped me from talking, she let the infraction slide – I kept glancing anxiously at the dining room door. Eventually he slumped into the room, bleary-eyed and scowling, and grunted at the parlourmaid to bring him coffee and the rapidly cooling bacon. He ate torturously slowly, lingering over every mouthful, and I wondered if he was genuinely enjoying the fact that I would be late.

Eventually he swigged down the last of his coffee and indicated in gruff monosyllables that we should be off, as though I were the reason for our tardiness in leaving the house. The traffic on Princes Street was inevitably chaotic, and it took us nearly half an hour to reach Bristo Place. I could have arrived there sooner by walking, even in a corset and boots that pinched. I raced through the gothic arches of the entrance, to the tutting and irritated shouts of the pedestrians I passed, coming into perilously close contact with more than one bicycle, and clattered into the square of the medical school.

To my surprise, my fellow students were still standing outside. There were raised voices, and a crowd had gathered.

I inched my way through, wondering what on earth could be detaining them.

'At least this one has the decency to dress like a woman,' laughed one man to his friend, noting my appearance. I understood the meaning of his words as I made my way to the front of the crowd.

'I have been given the strictest instructions not to admit any student wearing inappropriate dress,' the porter announced firmly for what was clearly the hundredth time, as he stood in the doorway barring the way.

'What utter nonsense,' scoffed a trouser-clad Julia. Some of her coterie agreed, but most looked uneasy or simply tired of the whole charade and impatient to enter and begin the day's work. For once, I felt sorry for her. 'I am no more improperly dressed than these fine gentlemen,' she said, waving her arm in the direction of her audience.

'But you aren't a gentleman, are you?' the porter said wearily. 'And the rules strictly state that ladies' – he uttered the word with heavy irony – 'are only to be admitted on the proviso that they are wearing correct dress – that is, a *dress*.'

'Oh give it up, Julia,' Alison grumbled. 'It's freezing out here, and you're making us miss our first lecture. I swear, if I plough the December examinations because of you, I won't be held responsible for my actions! Look here,' she appealed to the porter, 'can't those of us who did bother to finish putting on our clothes this morning go in? It isn't fair that we should all suffer because of Latymer's sartorial principles.'

A few of the other girls agreed with her, but Moira Owen whirled around in a blaze of fury.

'Do you not see what they're doing?' she snarled. 'Trying

to halt the wheels of progress! Why shouldn't we dress for comfort as men do?'

'There's nothing comfortable about a morning suit,' one of our watchers called out merrily. 'And should you care to try out a top hat, be my guest – the things are damned heavy!'

Moira shot him a withering glance and sniffed contemptuously.

'Given all the fuss you people make about "doctors in petticoats", I'd have thought you'd be delighted to have one of us show up in trousers!'

'And yet I don't see you making the effort for the cause, Owen,' I muttered. She turned to me with a nasty smirk.

'Oh, I wouldn't expect you to sacrifice your vanity for political freedom, Gilchrist. You'd wither and die without male attention!'

There were whoops and cheers from the male students, and the odd chuckle from at least one lecturer, and I wished passionately that I could either sink down through the cobblestones through an act of providence, or dash her brains out on them.

Realising that the commotion risked getting out of control, the porter raised his voice above the crowd.

'Those ladies who have arrived in proper attire may enter the building. Those of you who are wearing . . .' He trailed off, not sure what to call the garment clothing Julia below the waist.

'Bloomers,' she supplied crisply. 'After Amelia Bloomer bicyclist, champion of women's rights and erstwhile leader of the Rational Dress movement.'

'Aye, well,' he said, clearly too embarrassed to attempt the term himself. 'Anyone wearing those is not permitted to come inside, d'ye ken?'

Moira raised a fist in the air, in a gesture clearly intended to look political rather than a little bit ridiculous. 'Friends and sisters!' she cried out in tones that rang off the stone walls encircling us. 'If you value freedom of expression and champion equal rights for women, then you will stand outside with us and make a statement to the university authorities that we will not accept this treatment!'

To her credit, Julia looked annoyed and more than a little embarrassed at her friend's enthusiasm. I suspected that given half the chance she would have walked home and changed into something more universally acceptable before continuing her day's classes. But since she could hardly back down in front of what appeared to be half the medical school, she called out in a slightly weaker voice:

'For those of you who agree with us that women have a right to dress in clothes that are comfortable and modest, rather than in corsets designed to exaggerate the feminine figure to attract the attention of the opposite sex' – here she shot me a nasty look – 'I am calling an emergency meeting of the Women's Morality Society tonight at seven o'clock in the tea rooms on Nicholson Street!'

'Be that as it may,' the porter shouted over the noise, clearly wishing he had not started the fracas, 'those of you not in breach of university regulations had better go in at once before you miss any more time.'

Politics and solidarity was one thing; missing precious hours of lecture time was something else entirely, and much to Julia and Moira's irritation, only Edith lingered outside with them.

As we slunk into the lecture theatre, Professor Merchiston was standing in the empty room with a thunderous expression.

'And what bloody time do you call this, ladies?' he demanded.

'I'm sorry, Professor,' Alison stammered, 'but the porter

refused to let Julia in, and . . . well, it all got a little out of hand.'

'Did he indeed?' Merchiston looked curious. 'And was he within his rights?'

'Technically,' Caroline said reluctantly. 'But he could at least have let the rest of us in!'

'Well I won't penalise those of you who are here,' he said. 'I presume Miss Menzies and Miss Owen fell foul of his rulebook as well?'

'They're standing outside in solidarity,' I informed him, fighting to keep the smirk out of my voice. I might have disliked him, but that wasn't going to stop me getting Moira into trouble after the way she had singled me out in the quad.

His beetling brows drew together – an action that required little movement at the best of times.

'Be that as it may, I now have forty minutes in which to impart an hour's worth of information. I shall speak quickly, and I expect you all to keep up with me.'

He kept his side of the bargain and we barely kept ours. By the time we exited the hall, my hands had cramped in agony.

'I have a dissection tutorial with Dr Turner now,' I groaned to Alison. 'I don't think I can hold the scalpel!'

'I may never use this hand again,' she replied in tones of equal despair, massaging her hand with a wince. 'I might have to become ambidextrous!'

'I can teach you,' Caroline offered awkwardly. 'I wrote with my left hand until my governess beat it out of me. All I'll need is a ruler and some bandages to strap your other hand to your shoulder.'

We stared in mute horror for a moment, before collapsing into a fit of giggles. The morning's incident, coupled with the fierce intensity of our abbreviated lecture, had created an atmosphere of near hysteria that took very little to push it into the real thing.

'Women,' one of the older students said in disgusted tones as he passed us in the hallway. 'They're constitutionally incapable of intellectual thought. Look, they're half mad already!'

The morning's events had shattered our usual ability to concentrate. Normally we were twice as solemn as the men – and yet still seen as three times more frivolous – but for once we were relaxed to the point of giddiness, passing notes and whispers until more than one professor threatened to walk out. Professor Chalmers' lecture was even more of a struggle for me than the others, but for very different reasons. Despite his usual jocular demeanour and the way he had welcomed me as his wife's friend, I couldn't forget what I had seen. It was worse, in a way, than my discovery of Merchiston's indiscretions. I had respected the dour professor, but I had genuinely liked Randall Chalmers. Reconciling the man who hung on his wife's every word with an adulterer and buyer of women was an uncomfortable task. But how much worse, I thought, would it be for Elisabeth?

'Miss Gilchrist,' he called as we trailed out. 'Elisabeth wanted to pass on her regards, to tell you how much she enjoyed meeting your aunt and uncle and to say that you must come to dinner one night next week.'

I smiled queasily, wondering if that invitation would still be issued once I had revealed her husband's nocturnal activities.

In the hallway, my tormentor awaited me in fine form.

'My, my, aren't we the favourite,' Julia sneered. 'Are you sure that invitation was from Mrs Chalmers? Or is it Professor Chalmers you're interested in?'

'How dare you?' I hissed. 'You may think you can insult me, Julia Latymer, but don't you dare bring Professor Chalmers or Elisabeth into this! They have extended to me nothing but friendship – which, quite frankly, is more than any of you have done. I won't have you dragging their names through the mud, you spiteful bitch!'

She flinched, but her cruel smirk never slipped. 'I've seen the way Professor Merchiston looks at you, Gilchrist. I won't have the reputation of every other female student smeared by your behaviour.'

She turned on her heel and stalked away, the others trailing after her.

In our next lecture, I took a seat a row behind her, now more appropriately clad. It was far enough away that I wouldn't be tempted to stab her with my fountain pen, and I spent the hour seething silently. Somewhere a bell chimed, and I realised that not only was it time for lunch, but that I was ravenous.

'You were impressive earlier,' a voice said behind me. It was Alison Thornhill, looking considerably sheepish. 'You do realise that the reason she hates you so much is because you're the only one here capable of beating her to the top of the class?'

'That's not the reason, Alison, and you know it.'

'No, it is,' she insisted. 'Why, Julia fancies herself such a modern woman, she wouldn't care if a girl took a dozen lovers.' It was on the tip of my tongue to protest that I hadn't taken a damned lover at all, but Alison swept on. 'She knows you're a challenge, and she'd love to get rid of you, but whatever she says she doesn't think you're a . . .'

'Whore?' I finished. Alison blushed. 'She may not, but the rest of you do. You think I'm tarnishing your precious reputations by even daring to show my face here. You claim to want to advance the cause of women's rights, but you're hypocrites, the lot of you. I know what the men say about all of us behind our backs, and sometimes not even that. Having a woman say it doesn't make it any truer. Are we to be nothing more than gossips, Alison? I thought we were trying to break away from those poison-filled drawing rooms, and those small lives that are only enlivened by inventing some scandal or other. Don't we have better things to do? No wonder the men hate us, no wonder they think we're only capable of trivial thought. When have we ever proved them wrong?'

I was as surprised as Alison by my outburst, but oh, it felt good to say it!

'You're right, of course,' she said slowly. 'And I've been as rotten as the rest of them – worse, even, because I never believed what they said about you, not once. But I still avoided you, because I didn't want Julia to turn on me next.'

'We've exchanged a tyranny of men for a tyranny of Julia Latymer,' I said lightly, trying to accept the apology she so tentatively offered without admitting how much her avoidance of me had caused me pain. 'I think it's time to end it.'

'Friends?' she said softly, offering me her hand.

'Friends,' I said, taking it. 'Now please can we go and have some lunch? I think I've done enough shouting in public spaces on an empty stomach, don't you?'

As we left the building, I tugged my coat tighter around me. The sky was heavy and slate grey, and the wind was even colder than before.

'Our landlady said it's going to snow this afternoon,' Alison commented.

I shuddered. 'I wonder if the infirmary would miss me if I just went straight home to the fireside.'

'Probably,' Alison laughed. 'Dr Leadbetter sounds like a martinet; I wouldn't get on her bad side for the world! She seems to have taken a liking to you, though.'

'Well, you know how she champions the fallen women of the world,' I said lightly, trying to inject some humour into my grim social standing.

Alison looked all consternation, clearly not sure if this was something she was allowed to laugh at or not.

'You know, for all their supposed progressive beliefs, Latymer and her crew do behave like frightful old biddies,' she said finally. 'George Eliot – why, she lived with a married man as if she were his wife, and society frowned on it but she got through it. So really, one oughtn't to be too censorious.'

I had found that people accepted behaviour from writers and poets that was less welcome in a physician, but it was an apology of sorts and I squeezed her arm in silent thanks.

'Will you start dressing in trousers next?' ' I asked curiously.

Alison snorted. 'Hardly!' At my look, she added, 'I don't see why, just because we want to enter a male-dominated profession, we have to start dressing like them as well. I mean, really. Can you imagine me in a frock coat?'

The image of Alison, who was considerably heavier than the rake-thin Moira Owen or even the pulchritudinous Julia, in a frock coat and top hat was incongruous, to say the least.

'I'd be tempted, if only my aunt wouldn't have a conniption at the very thought.'

Alison grimaced sympathetically. 'Are they so terribly strict?'

'They've given me a freer rein of late,' I admitted. 'But only because the prospect of some poor fool considering my hand in marriage means I need new dresses. I hope my parents are sending them a decent allowance for me,' I added, 'because Aunt Emily has spent an absolute fortune at the dressmaker's. Not,' I glanced down ruefully, 'that it was on anything I can wear to lectures.'

'I think it's better to look a little dowdy,' Alison argued. 'I think it makes the gentlemen respect us more if we don't look like fashion plates.'

'You see, this is where I agree with Julia,' I frowned. 'Why should it matter what the gentlemen think, provided we are comfortable and happy with the way we look? I can just as easily dissect something in trousers as I can in skirts, and it would be a damn sight less restrictive.'

Alison giggled. 'Then you'll be joining her society?'

I raised an eyebrow. 'I doubt they'd have me. It's bad enough my bringing shame on the entire university and the medical school in particular by my very presence; I suspect that polluting the environment of the University of Edinburgh Rational Dress Society might be a step too far for our self-appointed guardian of morality.'

Alison leant over confidentially. 'I don't think we're missing much,' she whispered.

Chapter 28

The fire crackled in the grate and I breathed in the scent of woodsmoke, tea and toast. Of home. Elisabeth added a few idle stitches to her embroidery, humming to herself, whilst my anatomy textbook lay on my lap, open but unread. I had been freezing when I arrived, soaked to the skin from the few moments I had spent in the inclement weather between university and carriage, carriage and the house I had come to think of as my refuge. Now I was warm and dry, lounging in companionable silence and preparing myself to destroy Elisabeth's safe, lazy comfort.

'Is Professor Chalmers joining us for dinner tonight?' I asked finally.

Elisabeth glanced up from her sewing. 'I don't think so. He told Cook he'd probably eat at his club.' She resumed the neat, perfect stitches on the hem of a gown for one of her fellow chaperone's grandchildren. I could leave it there, let her enjoy her kind gesture, pretend I hadn't seen her husband buying the favours of some poor wretch two nights ago.

'Which club is it?'

She frowned. 'The New Club. Why the curiosity?' She grinned impishly. 'Is Mr Greene a member?'

I groaned. 'Why did you have to mention him? I was having such a lovely afternoon.' I knew that I could only ignore his existence for so long when it was my aunt's chief topic of conversation, but I relished the respite when I was out of the house. Before I had spoken to Alison, only Elisabeth knew of my unwanted suitor's attentions, and despite all evidence to the contrary, she held out hope that if a match was to be made it would be a happy one. I wished I did not have to crush her romantic fantasies for my future or her own, but hearth and home could only protect a woman from the harsh realities of the world for so long.

Plucking up all my courage, I spoke. 'Elisabeth, how much do you know of where the Professor goes in the evening?'

She blinked. 'He spends a great deal of time in his rooms at the university and in the laboratory. I've had to send one of the servants to collect him from the library because he's forgotten a dinner engagement on more than one occasion. Sometimes he goes to the music hall and refuses to take me no matter how often I beg, but if he doesn't come home, it's because he works long into the night and stays at his club. I miss him greatly when he does, but it's hardly unusual.'

'And his health. It is . . . robust? In . . . um . . . all areas?'

She laughed. 'You're starting to sound more and more like a doctor every day! He could do with drinking a little less claret and not filling his plate quite so abundantly, but otherwise he appears to be in perfect health. Why do you ask?'

'And yours?' I persisted. 'No discomfort? No infection?'

She stared at me in confusion. 'I cannot make you out at all. What on earth are you getting at?'

My carefully considered words spilt out in a rush. 'Elisabeth, your husband doesn't spend all his time at the club or the library. He visits women, prostitutes, in the slums. I've seen him.'

Silence hung heavy between us, and I wished more than anything I could take my words back.

'I'm afraid you are mistaken,' she said coldly.

'I'm telling you this because you have a right to know,' I pressed on. 'If he shares your bed, he's putting you at risk of all sorts of diseases.'

'Whether or not my husband shares my bed is no concern of yours,' she said, and I felt lower than a worm. 'I regret, Sarah, that your experience of men has been so disagreeable. But to come into my house and make such accusations . . . Yours is a very ugly view of the world. I will not share it, and I will not have it under my roof. Get out.'

I had expected tears, disbelief, perhaps anger at Randall. I had not expected this. I stood, trembling, and left her by the fireside. As the door closed behind me, I heard her begin to sob. Although I longed to turn back to comfort her, I knew I would not be welcome.

Stepping out into the bitter winter night, I felt my last connection to the woman I had once been fall away. The friendship, the endless hours gossiping by the fireside, none of that could exist in my new life. I was a pariah everywhere I turned, a fallen woman or a freak of nature. As I shivered through the streets, watching carriages deposit men, women and families home for the evening, I decided to make my way to the one place I still belonged.

The usually crowded Cowgate was quiet tonight, the streets only lined with those who, like me, had nowhere else to go. As I stepped into the infirmary, Matilda Campbell greeted me warmly.

'Sarah! We weren't expecting you tonight, were we? It's Fiona's evening off. Poor child, you're a positive icicle!'

She pulled off my cloak and led me through to the small office, draping my wet coat before the fire.

'I'm sorry to show up unannounced,' I said through chattering teeth. 'I found myself unexpectedly free tonight, and I thought you could use some help.'

'We can always use that,' she smiled, unpinning my hair and rubbing it vigorously with a towel. She reminded me a little of the nursemaid I had as a child. 'Still, I'm surprised your aunt and uncle agreed.'

'I haven't exactly told them,' I admitted. 'I was supposed to be taking tea with Mrs Chalmers, but then she had a headache and I thought I might as well make use of my evening.'

Dr Campbell frowned. 'You know we can't afford to anger your uncle, Sarah. Perhaps it would be best if you just went straight home.'

My heart sank. 'And spend the evening reading conduct books and listening to my aunt extol the virtues of marriage and motherhood that an overeducated spinster will forever be deprived of? I'd rather empty bedpans. I mean it!'

She laughed. 'You're a strange one. But no stranger than the rest of us, and if it's bedpans you want, girl, then it's bedpans you'll get.'

On my knees, clearing up the pungent mess made by a woman crying out in pain from the after-effects of a tumour removal, I wondered if I should regret my offer. But the work, unpleasant though it was, kept my mind off the look in Elisabeth's eyes when she had ordered me out of her house. There was a girl in the bed opposite, little more than fifteen, whose stillborn child, six weeks premature, would have likely been severely disabled if he had lived, thanks to his mother's syphilis. The thought of that happening to Elisabeth when I could prevent it was unthinkable. Far better that I lose her by revealing the truth than stay silent and wait for some virus or other to take hold and ruin her life.

For the next two hours I stitched up wounds, helped set

broken legs and watched, fascinated, as Dr Bourne removed a laundrywoman's inflamed appendix. I scrubbed my hands clean with carbolic soap whilst every part of my body ached, surrounded by people whose lives were so unimaginably wretched that my troubles paled in comparison. Beggars and streetwalkers, guttersnipes, honest working women and pickpockets – they couldn't have cared less about my morality. Perhaps the women I worked alongside would have, had they known. Perhaps they would have taken a more enlightened view. All I knew was that they shared my anger at what this world reduced women to, and I was grateful to do what I could to help.

Dr Campbell entered the sluice, worry written all over her face. 'Sarah, you didn't move any of the laudanum bottles from the cupboard, did you?'

I shook my head. 'I helped Dr Bourne administer some to a few of the patients, but that's all. I don't think I've even seen the key all evening.'

She sighed. 'Then our thief strikes again. I've just counted, and there are two missing.'

'You have a thief?'

'Drugs do go missing from time to time – no matter how careful we are, some of our patients are canny. And those who are addicted can be very clever indeed.'

'Is it just laudanum?'

'Not always. The strangest things. Soap, bandages – things we'd give away freely, if we could afford to – but it's usually medicine. Normally anaesthetic, something to dull the pain when the gin stops working. I honestly can't say I blame the people who take it, but it's hardly something we can afford. Especially not when they steal instruments. I sometimes wonder how often we mend the injuries caused by our own supplies.'

I had seen the streets outside the infirmary doors, and I didn't like the thought of some of our patients wandering around wielding scalpels.

'Poverty,' Dr Campbell continued. 'That's what's to blame. If you've got a sick child at home, or an infection that's gone septic, and you see something that will help just lying around, in seemingly unlimited supply, why not take it? We can't help everyone, and our patients know that.'

I closed my eyes, hating the picture of the world that she presented, but knowing that communities like the Cowgate were rife across Edinburgh, lives being eked out on a few mouthfuls of stale bread a day, families living in one filthy room they could barely afford. Perhaps Fiona had been right. Perhaps girls like Lucy were the lucky ones.

'You need to go home,' Dr Campbell told me firmly. 'Lie to your aunt and uncle all you will; if you're late and they find out where you were, it'll be our heads on the block, not yours.'

She looked around for the porter, but he had his hands full restraining a drunk woman threatening violence to everyone around her.

'I'll walk up and hail a cab by myself,' I told her. 'I'll be perfectly safe.'

It was against her better judgement, but she relented. 'At least go up by the Royal Mile, then, not the kirkyard,' she said tiredly. 'Otherwise you won't make it out in one piece.'

I gathered my things, promising to be careful, and exited into the cold, but no less malodorous, night air.

I kept my head down and walked briskly through the streets, wanting to be home and warm as much as anything else. Now that the sleet had eased off, the streets were more crowded and I had to move swiftly to avoid being jostled, or worse. As I reached the mouth of the Cowgate, where

Candlemaker Row became the Grassmarket, I caught sight of a tall, familiar figure making his way down from the civilised world of the streets above to the noise and violence of the stews, and I found myself following Gregory Merchiston for the second time.

Chapter 29

This time, he did nothing more than glance at the narrow wynd that housed Ruby's dwelling, his attention clearly on a more pressing engagement. I wondered if he was going to meet Randall Chalmers, and I found myself treading quietly a few yards behind him, all thoughts of home forgotten.

He joined a throng of men standing outside an unmarked building, one of whom greeted him by name, slapped his back and let him pass. Seeing that it was not only men who entered made me gather my courage and edge closer to the crowd, praying that I didn't look as out of place as I felt. The men who had greeted Merchiston eyed me, but didn't move out of my way. Gingerly, and with considerable reluctance, I squeezed between them, trying not to inhale the scent of stale beer and tobacco mixed with rank sweat.

'That'll be a shilling, hen,' the woman at the door said, sucking what remained of her teeth. I handed the coin over, still no clearer as to what I was paying for. The fact that they admitted me at all ruled out at least one sort of entertainment – or I hoped it did – but when I entered the dark, dank corridor, my heart pounded at what lay at the end of it.

A rush of hot air, light and noise assaulted my senses, and I found myself stumbling into a large, crowded room. Drunks, prostitutes and hawkers jostled one another, and buxom women with tankards of ale competed with florid men selling hot meat pies for a penny each. At the centre of the room was a square, cordoned off from the throng by a length of dirty, fraying rope.

'Who's on tonight?' I heard the man next to me ask, through a mouthful of gristle and flaking pastry.

Before he could answer, a man entered the ring and the crowd calmed enough for him to be heard.

'Good evening, ladies and gentlemen,' he called out, although I highly doubted his audience included either. 'Place your bets and dinnae be stingy, because tonight we've got a real beauty. Back in the ring after a wee spell at Her Majesty's pleasure, Herbert Reid. And his opponent, seeing if he can repeat last week's victory, Gregory Merchiston.'

To the roar of the assembled throng, the two pugilists entered the ring. The room swam in front of me, the only thing remaining in focus the figure of Gregory Merchiston. A figure lacking not only the greatcoat and hat he had been wearing when I lost him in the crowd, but also his shirt.

The room seemed unbearably warm. My corset felt too tight, and I fought for air. Blood thrummed in my veins and I felt my cheeks burn. There was something undeniably indecent about seeing my professor this way, stripped to the waist. If ever I had doubted his physical strength before, I didn't now.

His everyday garb, I was forced to acknowledge, didn't do him justice. Tailcoats, top hats and academic gowns made him look gaunt, but it was clear to me now that he was wiry rather than lanky. In the light from the flickering gas lamps I could see the ridges of his muscles, the coarse dark hair on his chest making his skin look even paler, the starburst of scar tissue that scattered his torso and back like constellations.

As his fist swung to make the first punch, bone connecting with bone in a strangely balletic movement, I forced my thoughts along more scientific lines, imagining the sweat-slicked skin stripped away and the taut muscle beneath exposed to my gaze. I recited the name of each muscle under my breath, and mentally splinted every bone that cracked. It didn't work. Already, my clothes stuck to my skin with perspiration, and I was sure I was blushing. My mouth was dry, as though all the liquid in my body had pooled somewhere else entirely.

With a sudden surge of the crowd I found myself at the front, so close I could see every inch of the two men. A shove from his opponent sent Merchiston reeling in my direction, and as he hit the floor with a sickening thump, our eyes locked. While the crowd cheered Reid's victory and goaded the loser, Merchiston sat up, wincing in agony, and spat phlegm and blood onto the floor. His lips were dotted with blood, and bruises were starting to blossom across his ribcage. With a last long, searching look at me, he scrambled to his feet and shook his opponent's hand with a dignity that surprised me – if Reid had given me the thrashing Merchiston had received, I would have spat in his eye. I shrank back into the crowd, praying his gaze wouldn't find me, and when he turned to mop his brow, I fled.

Chapter 30

Outside, the cold air hit me like a slap, taking my breath away. My legs felt decidedly wobbly. I had no other thought in my mind except to get away, and I broke into a run that left me breathless as I scrambled to the top of Candlemaker Row.

I hailed the first cab that passed and spent my journey home in a daze. Claiming a headache, I sank gratefully into the hot bath Agnes ran for me, closing my eyes.

I wondered how I had ended up here. Once a respected, if rebellious, daughter of a financier, now I was a fallen woman in the eyes of society, a moral degenerate who aped men by studying medicine, and the kind of woman who followed a man through the slums and watched, open-mouthed and wide-eyed, as he fought half-naked in a room full of whores and criminals. I shook my head. I should study, and go to church more. Take my aunt's advice before I lost what was left of my reputation.

And yet I could not pretend. I was no longer part of my aunt's world, no matter how much she tried to rehabilitate me. Even if I married Miles Greene, I would only be a pale imitator of the women in his circle, and I knew I could not keep it up for long. Like Fiona Leadbetter, I was more at home in the Cowgate slums than in a New Town drawing room. I could not enjoy the life I used to live, not now I knew what it was based on – the exploitation of women. I saw how the factory workers lived so that the fabric of my bonnet and coat were made to society's satisfaction; I knew how easy it was for a woman to slip through the cracks of the civilised world and end up like Lucy.

Had she seen Merchiston as I had, fierce and animalistic, every last shred of his respectable daylight self discarded? Had she been frightened or drawn to him?

It did not matter how striking he was, I told myself sternly. He had been accused of one murder and I suspected him of a second, so his physical appearance mattered not a jot. But the more I tried to put the image of his shirtless figure from my mind, the more it tormented me. He had been, I was forced to admit, devastatingly handsome. The warmth that suffused me was not entirely an unfamiliar sensation, which was why it bothered me all the more. I knew where these feelings led – to ruin and shame. And surely that pointed even more to Merchiston's guilt? If he could overwhelm me with his presence, then what could he have done with a look, a word, or a touch?

My dangerously seductive train of thought was broken by the scalding sensation of hot tea against my hand. I cursed, and decided to blame Merchiston for that as well. Dratted man, I wished I had never met him. I pitied his late wife with a passion – I could only imagine how she must have been in thrall to him. And if my suspicions about the nature of his dalliances with poor Lucy were indeed accurate, who knew what horrifying perversions she had submitted to behind the bedroom door?

It was rapidly becoming clear that I read too many novels

– I was beginning to entertain thoughts that would have made Catherine Morland blush. At least part of the blame, I thought, lay with the puritanical faculty, who, for reasons of their own, linked female study of medicine with a predisposition for amorality. Either they were right – which was manifestly nonsense – or they had given me ideas I was better off not having.

My dreams, such as they were, were fractured and strange. Memories of Lucy's corpse resurfaced, and I dreamt that Merchiston's breath was warm against my neck as I sliced into her torso. He ran his hand tenderly across her breasts as I cut, and somehow I could feel his touch as though it were my body his hands were caressing. And then it was – his lips hard against mine, the stench of formaldehyde mingling with his cologne. I felt every inch of him straining against me, and I kissed him back with a fervour that unnerved me even in my drugged sleep. As I lay back on the bed, urging him to take his pleasure with me, part of me realised that it was still Lucy's body he was touching, but now very much alive. The memory of his naked body assailed me – because I had looked, of course I had looked – and I ached with a longing that even Paul, in the weeks before he had followed me to the library, had never provoked.

The next day was purgatory. The man who spoke from the lectern at the front of the room was almost unrecognisable as the feral fighter from the previous night. I found my eyes tracing the way his clothes draped across his frame, remembering the taut muscle beneath. I felt my cheeks flame, and when he caught my eye, my breath stuttered. Afterwards, I stood to leave on legs as wobbly as they had been last night, but he stopped me.

'Miss Gilchrist? A word.'

His tone chilled me, and I wanted nothing more than to

follow my classmates out. I lingered reluctantly by the lectern as he gathered his things.

'You are skating on very thin ice,' he said in a low voice. I felt dizzy with fear that he would tell someone – the Dean, my family, anyone – about my whereabouts the night before; that he knew the thoughts that plagued me. But he continued, and his next words fell like cold water over me. 'Professor Chalmers would be more than within his rights to ask for your immediate removal from the university, as would I.'

I stared at him dumbly. I had forgotten that he and Chalmers were friends. Clearly, I thought bitterly, they had a lot in common.

'I merely reported what I saw,' I said quietly, refusing to break his gaze.

'You see an awful lot of things, don't you, Miss Gilchrist?' he murmured, and I knew in that moment that he had felt the heat of my gaze on him in the boxing ring, seen me watching him with thoughts that had nothing whatsoever to do with my studies, or the crime I had accused him of.

He pulled back, and the spell was broken.

'I suggest that you reflect on your recent behaviour and tell Mrs Chalmers that you were mistaken, apologising profusely for the upset you have caused. However, if you prefer, I can go to the Dean right now and inform him of every detail of your history and your activities since matriculating here, including your whereabouts last night. And if that isn't enough to get you expelled, please do not think I am above inventing a few new ones.'

'Don't you dare throw my past back in my face,' I spat. 'Elisabeth Chalmers has a right to know where her husband goes at night. You know the dangers he's exposing her to!'

'I know a damn sight more than you do about where Randall Chalmers goes of an evening,' he growled. 'The evidence of one's own eyes can be misinterpreted, whether the scene is a back alley or a library in a town house.'

I felt my cheeks flame as the meaning of his words hit home.

'You have no idea what you're dealing with here. You play doctor a few nights a week in the slums and you think you know what that life is like. You have no idea to what evils poverty and desperation can lead a person.'

'I know that they are not confined to the slums,' I choked out. 'I know that vice and depravity can lurk beneath even the most sophisticated of facades. And I know how men band together to protect one another, no matter their class.'

His expression softened to something not unlike sympathy. 'I know. And for what it's worth, Miss Gilchrist, I wish you did not. I appreciate that I have given you no cause to do so, but I'm asking you to trust me.'

Perhaps it was the pity in his eyes or the repeat of his earlier threat, but in that moment I hated him.

'I will not lie about what I saw, Professor,' I said, fighting for composure. 'I won't dare mention it again, but I won't apologise for telling the truth. Elisabeth will thank me for it.'

'Elisabeth won't leave her room!' he burst out. 'Randall says she won't admit him, and the servants keep bringing her food that she won't touch. She's in danger of making herself ill, and all because you had to rush to tell her the latest sordid scandal you think you've uncovered.' He sighed. 'You've a vivid imagination, I'll give you that, Miss Gilchrist. But perhaps fewer penny dreadfuls and a little more common sense wouldn't go amiss. You're here to study medicine, not to save the world's women from the clutches of mustachio-twirling villains in top hats.'

'This is all a joke to you, isn't it?' I ground out. 'And you're right – it's ridiculous. To think that a woman deserves to know that her husband is intimate with streetwalkers; that another woman's life is worth enough for her death to be investigated. And that I should delude myself into thinking that I put the past behind me when I left London, only for you to keep dragging it before my eyes every time I threaten to step out of line! I'll keep my mouth shut, Professor. You haven't left me with much choice. But do not think for one moment that I will ever trust you.'

I turned on my heel and strode out into the corridor, taking great pleasure in slamming the door behind me.

Chapter 31

The absence of Elisabeth from my life gnawed away at me. She wasn't the first friend I'd lost this past year, but her loss hit the hardest. I had meant to protect her, but in the end I had pushed her further away. I hoped fervently that she would at least heed my advice and stay out of Randall's bed – and that he would let her. University life was miserable – neither he nor Merchiston would so much as look at me, and without the will to fight Julia's *froideur*, I found myself spending days barely speaking a word, even to Alison. When I arrived home, my throat felt rusty with lack of use, and even Aunt Emily's sermonising was welcome. Society, it seemed, was as harsh on those who sympathised with fallen women as on those who fell. With Fiona's warning ringing in my ears and Merchiston's repeated threats of expulsion hanging over me, I was forced to put my investigations on hold.

Although my aunt made enquiries after Elisabeth that I rebuffed with clumsy excuses, she did not attempt to hide her delight at having me home every evening, barring those I spent at the infirmary. She made a point of telling me that she had mentioned Miles in a letter to my mother, and that the response had been approving. Should a happy event come to pass, she pointed out, my parents would have to come to Scotland to meet my betrothed. I smiled sweetly at him all through dinner the next night, feeling myself blossom under my aunt's warm gaze, but in bed that night I felt disgusted with myself, with my craven desire to win the respect of people who not six months ago had labelled me wicked. I was like a cur, I thought, slinking back to the man who'd kicked it just because he threw it a few scraps and scratched behind its ears on occasion.

I no longer ventured outside the permitted areas of home, university and infirmary. Weeks went by without my speaking Lucy's name aloud, and I forced thoughts of her to the back of my mind during waking hours, only to have her resurface in my dreams. Although Randall Chalmers never called on me now, I prepared obsessively before every lecture in order that I might impress him if he did. Merchiston's grudging respect for my abilities continued, and even Williamson was forced to compliment me after a particularly exact dissection.

The threat of ending my first term in failure and ignominy receded, and as I made my way to the infirmary on another damp and freezing night, my blood was singing, and I practically bounded out of the carriage and into the clinic. In rooms packed to the rafters with the sick, the inebriated and the clearly unwashed, I found the stuff of my studies take shape, word made flesh, and as I was set to work, I realised I was smiling.

Despite my surroundings, despite the unfeminine labour of intellectual exertion, what would really have appalled Aunt Emily was how physical the business of doctoring was. I heaved a large woman onto a bed, held a scrawny but aggressive girl of ten or so still as Fiona cleaned her cuts and scrapes, and helped her set a broken bone with a crack I wasn't sure I would ever get used to. I dashed from room to room, carrying bottles and bandages and bedpans – moving considerably more carefully when the latter were full – and even though the fire in the waiting room grate was as sickly as some of the patients, I felt myself sweating through my undergarments.

At last the clinic was quiet for the first time all evening. Matilda Campbell sat by the fire knitting as a nurse darned some sheets. There was a pot of tea on Fiona's desk along with some biscuits, and the whole thing was touchingly domestic.

Fiona reached for the tea with a sigh of relief.

'Help yourself to milk and sugar, and as many of Tillie's biscuits as you can manage. You've earned them.'

I glowed at the praise and accepted the offering. Perched on an upturned crate and drinking stewed tea from a chipped mug – 'Like a navvy,' I could hear my mother saying – I enjoyed the companionable silence as Fiona frowned over some papers and Matilda's needles clacked. Better this than a drawing room full of whatever my family would call polite company. Better this than anything I could imagine. I could take Julia's sniping and my aunt's disapproval if I knew my life would one day always be like this.

'How many years before you graduate, Sarah?' Matilda asked.

'She wants to steal you away from general practice,' Fiona laughed. 'Don't let her – sometimes I wonder why I ever gave it up!'

'Because you're a masochist, same as the rest of us. I can't picture you in a nice study treating well-bred ladies for their anaemia. Thank God for us you saw sense.'

'You had a private practice?' Somehow I had never thought of Fiona having a life away from the clinic, or the clinic without Fiona.

'For a few years. Only a handful of patients deigned to be

treated by a woman, so I closed up shop and moved somewhere more enlightened.'

'Somewhere less picky, you mean.'

Fiona shrugged. 'Once you see the conditions people live in, how do you go back? I had a little money and the ground floor of this building was for sale. God knows it doesn't feel like it some days, but we've done some good here.'

'What Fiona isn't saying is that she renovated everything herself,' Matilda interjected. 'Painted the walls, cleared out the rubble and the rats – she even tried to install the gas lamps!'

'In retrospect, that wasn't my cleverest idea.' Fiona held up a finger with a scar I had never noticed before. 'I barely passed chemistry by the skin of my teeth, but even then I should have known not to stand quite so close to a lamp with an open flame. Singed a perfectly good apron as well.'

I had never lit a gas lamp in my life, nor had I worn an apron until I set foot in the clinic. The idea of marching into the slums armed only with a medical degree and gumption felt like something out of a fairy tale. But I knew how it felt to have your eyes opened to the ugliness of some people's lives, and I wondered if I could ever be content with rich patients and a comfortable life.

It felt like the past four years had been spent trying to get to where I was – studying medicine, with all the wonders of the human body unfolding with every textbook page. Then for a while, all I had cared about was escaping the looks and muffled laughter that had surrounded me like a fog. I had wished so hard for this moment that I had barely considered what would come next. For the first time in so long, I felt that I had a future.

'I hadn't thought,' I said. 'I wanted to be a doctor, but I'm wondering if I ever really knew what that meant. There are so many options – surgery, general practice, epidemiology, obstetrics . . .'

'I recommend anaesthesia,' Matilda said, stretching. 'The patients are far less bother.'

'Only if you get the mask on in time,' Fiona added sweetly. 'Otherwise you wind up with a black eye, chloroform everywhere and a patient limping halfway out of the door.'

Matilda scowled. Revenge for the gas-lamp story, I imagined. 'Once, Fiona. That happened once. And I personally thought my black eye made me look rather rakish, even though my poor husband did get a scolding from the neighbours.'

'You're married?' I was intrigued. 'All my aunt ever says is that no man would marry a lady doctor and that I'm ruining my prospects for good.'

'You'd be wise to listen,' Fiona said. 'Euan Campbell is one in a million – even the ones that like a bit of spark in their women grow tired of empty beds and cold mutton for dinner every time there's an emergency.'

She splashed some more tea into her cup angrily, and Matilda caught my eye, a quick shake of the head warning me not to ask any questions.

'I promise I'll stay a spinster and come and work here as soon as I'm qualified,' I said lightly, trying to hide how badly I wanted it. Here was the camaraderie I had hoped to find with my fellow students; here was medicine in all its messy, urgent glory.

'Maybe by then we'll be able to afford to pay you,' Matilda grinned. 'God knows we've enough work for three more doctors.'

'Which is why we should get the niece of our benefactor cleaned up and home in time for supper.' Fiona handed me a damp cloth, and I dabbed ineffectually at hands covered in another person's grime. By the time Calhoun arrived, I was sitting demurely in the waiting room, playing the part of a perfect lady.

I hugged Fiona impulsively. 'He didn't deserve you, whoever he was,' I whispered. She blushed, taken aback by my fierce affection. I wondered who had been the last person to show her any genuine kindness, and why it was that someone who gave everything she had to strangers got so little in return from her friends.

As the horses trotted out of the Cowgate, I looked back to see Fiona standing half in shadows and lost in thought.

Chapter 32

In the end, it took Aurora Greene and her refuge for penitent fallen women to jolt me out of the rut I had fallen into.

The reformatory, a looming building not far from the Queen's palace at Holyrood, stood behind high walls that looked as though they belonged outside a prison. I wanted nothing more than to linger in the relative safety of the carriage, but my aunt scowled at my slowness and prodded my foot with the ferrule of her umbrella.

'Don't dawdle, Sarah!'

Reluctantly, I stepped out into the grey afternoon, a light drizzle of rain misting the air. I doubted the place looked welcoming even at the height of summer and felt a flicker of annoyance at my own sense of foreboding. That far-off rumble of thunder was the Scottish weather in all its inclemency, not some ominous harbinger of what I would find behind those walls.

Professor Merchiston was right: I was acting like the heroine of a gothic novel.

I traced my finger over the engraved plaque as Aunt Emily rang the visitor's bell with vigour.

'Don't dirty your gloves,' she snapped, yanking my hand back.

I mumbled my apologies as the heavy wooden door creaked open, revealing a sullen-looking girl of about sixteen in a housemaid's uniform.

'We have an appointment with Miss Hartigan,' Aunt Emily informed her crisply. She turned wordlessly and walked across the courtyard to the house, leaving us to scurry after her. From the way she eyed me, I could tell she assumed I was the latest inhabitant of St Catherine's Home for Girls.

Inside, the hallway was dark and musty, gas lamps illuminating samplers with religious messages and dire warnings. The maid led us through poky passages and paused before a door marked 'Miss Caroline Hartigan, Matron'.

Miss Hartigan was a woman of middling height whose fading golden hair was scraped back into a bun of impressive severity. She looked as though she might have been almost pretty once, but when she smiled to greet us, it didn't reach her eyes.

'Mrs Fitzherbert,' she nodded, 'thank you for taking an interest in our refuge.' Her gaze flickered to me, and I felt her appraise me as she must have done countless other ruined girls. 'And this must be Miss Gilchrist.'

I nodded mutely, suddenly scared that if I opened my mouth, she would detect the stain of sin in my speech and I would find myself an inmate rather than a visitor.

'It is so kind of you to devote your time to the less fortunate. I'm sure you will be a most beneficial influence on my charges.'

Aunt Emily's expression conveyed doubt that I would ever be a beneficial influence on anyone, but she remained silent.

'I hope I can be of some comfort,' I said weakly.

Miss Hartigan arched an eyebrow. 'Comfort? Miss

Gilchrist, comfort is the last thing these girls need. Hard work, plain food and sermons will help put them back on the path.'

Beside me, Aunt Emily was nodding vigorously in agreement, and I wondered if I was going to be subjected to gruel for supper from now on.

I pulled out my Bible from my reticule. 'I should have said that I hope I can be of service, Miss Hartigan,' I apologised.

'We'll see,' was all the dragon had to say to that. 'I must warn you, though, these are not the type of girls you are used to associating with. Despite all our best efforts, some of them can be rather coarse.'

'I volunteer my time at St Giles' Infirmary on the Cowgate,' I offered. 'I doubt they can be worse.'

Her eyes widened and her polite smile tensed. 'I see,' she said, giving me a searching look. 'Well then, I'm sure you know what you're about. Dr Leadbetter has been most generous with her medical attention. I had no idea we were to have another doctor in our midst.' She didn't seem happy about it. 'Now, I must give you the tour of our little establishment.' She swept ahead of us, mistress of her domain, and we were forced to scurry after her.

I was reminded, incongruously, of Ruby McAllister's lodgings. Although the paintings on the wall showed Biblical scenes rather than lewd drawings and the walls were whitewashed instead of covered in damask drapes, something about the mixture of fear and resentment in the girls' eyes as Miss Hartigan swept past, the proprietorial way she pointed out this or that inmate's defects, reminded me of the way the brothel-keeper had reduced her girls to a charming smile or an ample bosom. I wondered how many of them had escaped a place like Ruby's, and if they had noticed the parallels too.

For all Miss Hartigan's sermonising, I knew that some of the girls at least would end up there or somewhere like it, or on the streets if they were even less fortunate. In their position, would I have chosen sin and a pretty dress over salvation and a shapeless grey pinafore? We passed a scared-looking child blacking the grate, who trembled when we drew too close, and I wondered what on earth such a young thing had done to warrant confinement here. As she turned to drop a shaky curtsey, I saw that she had a board around her neck with *Liar* written in copperplate letters.

'May is an orphan,' Miss Hartigan informed us, not bothering to lower her voice. 'She was taken in by some distant cousins, but they were compelled to send her to me after she told scurrilous tales about her adoptive father. We are trying to instil honesty into her, but she persists in repeating the stories and frightening the other girls. She wears that sign to remind others not to heed her.'

I shivered, both at the implication of her words and the bland harshness of her tone. How many other girls had been sent here to keep them quiet? As my aunt and Miss Hartigan moved on, I hung back. I touched May's arm and she let out a little shriek that she muffled with her hand. In the gloom, I could see the whites of her eyes. She looked like a trapped animal.

'I'm sorry to have frightened you,' I said as gently as possible. 'I just wanted to tell you I believe you. And that what he did was wrong and it wasn't your fault, no matter what he said. I know Miss Hartigan isn't exactly kind, but at least you're safe here.'

She gave me a look that was older than her years. 'Aye,' she said tonelessly. 'That's what Lucy said.'

My heart hammered in my chest so loudly that I thought May must have been able to hear it.

'Lucy?' I whispered.

'She lived here for a while, but she ran away.' She bit her

lip, looking frightened. 'Miss Hartigan said she were a wicked girl, and we weren't to talk about her again.'

'I won't tell her,' I promised. 'What did Lucy look like?'

'Dark hair,' May said, looking confused. 'It was long. Miss Hartigan didn't make her cut it like some of the others because she was nearly old enough to leave. And her eyes were a sort of greyish green. D'ye ken her, miss?'

'I think I have seen her,' I said carefully, not wanting to tell May of the fate that had met her friend. I rummaged in my bag and withdrew her portrait. 'Is this her?'

It had become so creased that I had been forced to redraw it. Although this second version was as close to the original as I could make it, it seemed still further from Lucy's true likeness, as if her memory was being eroded even as her flesh began to degrade in some unknown plot.

The girl nodded, wiping her nose on her sleeve. 'Aye, that's Lucy.' She took the picture from me and turned it over thoughtfully, then pointed at the picture of Merchiston on the other side.

'And that's the man that took her away.'

Chapter 33

If Aurora Greene was anything less than delighted to see me, she hid it very well. Dressed in a rich teal that brought out the blue of her eyes, as Aunt Emily effusively informed her, she was on sparkling form. I tried to imagine life as her daughter-in-law, forever in her shadow, and failed. Sitting opposite her, in a light green dress that had looked charmingly delicate in my looking glass that morning, I felt like a faded imitation, a pale watercolour of a girl next to Rossetti's finest.

She clasped my hands, and I wondered if she was imagining a ring on one.

'Emily tells me that you got on famously at the reformatory yesterday! I'm sure you did Miss Hartigan's girls a world of good.'

'I hope so,' I said, shrinking under her effusiveness.

'And it must make a pleasant change from all those sick people.' She shuddered. Half the girls there had had rickets, most were malnourished to a degree that all the plain food in the world wasn't going to cure, and from the unpleasant itching on my scalp, at least one of them had had lice.

'Yes.' I smiled weakly. 'Although that is rewarding too, in its own way.'

'Hmm.' Aurora looked politely unconvinced and I muffled a yelp when the heel of Aunt Emily's shoe connected with my ankle.

'Tell me,' I pressed, 'where does Miss Hartigan find these girls? Are they all orphans or . . . um . . .' I trailed off, unable to find a euphemism for 'prostitute' suitable for the parlour.

She nodded sadly. 'Most. Although some have families who simply despair of them, and find that the unadorned environment of the reformatory calms their wild spirits.' Unadorned was one word for it; the place was practically a prison.

'What an excellent idea,' Aunt Emily replied pointedly. 'They say boys can be troublesome, but girls these days have all manner of strange ideas in their heads – and this fad for female emancipation is only making matters worse.'

Aurora nodded sagely, and the two lapsed into discussion of the sad state of affairs that all this political agitating and foolish nonsense about education – 'begging your pardon, Sarah' – had led to.

'And where do they go afterwards?' I interrupted. 'Miss Hartigan's girls? Do they all go into service?'

'Some stay on as teachers, like Miss Dawson, the deputy Matron. One or two get married immediately – I know of a curate who found a most submissive and obliging wife in one of the reformatory's successes. He was most pleased with her modesty and penitence, and they now reside in Kirkcaldy, I believe.'

I shuddered inwardly at the thought. I doubt the curate's bride had been given much choice, and the thought of him picking out a suitable wife from the miserable girls I had met, as though he were choosing a new surplice, turned my stomach. But I knew better than to say so.

'It just shows that even the most ungovernable girls can be made to turn their back on their former ways and accept a life of wifely servitude,' Aunt Emily agreed, her eyes hard and glittering as she looked at me for concurrence.

'Do they all turn their backs on sin?' I questioned. 'It would be a rare success indeed if every one of them went on to live a life of moral rectitude.'

Aunt Emily glared at me. 'I'm sure there are one or two incurable cases,' she said tartly. 'Some girls are simply born wicked and don't appreciate the help they're given to become upstanding Christian women.'

Subtlety, thy name is Emily Fitzherbert.

I allowed the conversation to drift to more pressing matters, such as the weather and the health of Aurora's new lady's maid, but before we left, I expressed a carefully worded interest in Mrs Greene's own visits to the reformatory – had she met any girls who had caught her attention particularly; did Miss Hartigan discuss their progress with her? To my disappointment, she only seemed to remember the dullest girls, the remorseful, quiet ones who all blurred into one for her anyway.

The thing that stood out most clearly in Aurora Greene's mind was her own generosity of spirit and pocket in helping these girls onto a better path. I wondered if she was doing the same for me; if I was simply another charity case to be redeemed. 'This is my daughter-in-law,' I imagined her telling her friends in hushed tones. 'Her family thought she was a hopeless case, with a ruined reputation and,' she would shudder, 'a *university education*. But here she is, a wife and mother, the paragon of Christian virtue.' Aunt Emily would be delighted, my mother would forgive me and I would die of boredom within a week.

'She has taken a fancy to you,' my aunt gloated in the

privacy of her carriage. 'I think she is impressed by your good works, even in that dreadful place.'

'Would she be as impressed with a doctor for a daughter-in-law?' I snapped. Aunt Emily was silent, her lips pinched and her face pale. We had never openly acknowledged where this whole business was leading, but now it was unavoidable.

'You'll find marriage needs your sharp mind just as much as medicine,' she warned.

She sounded exactly like her sister. 'Being a wife and mother is as hard as any university degree,' Mother had told me once when I had flown into yet another fury at the prospect of being forced into marriage and motherhood. 'Save your brains for your husband.'

My mother was clever, cultured, able to hold her own in conversation. I should have liked to see her go up against any one of the professors at the university. But her cleverness was cloaked in yards of lace and hats with exotic plumage, and although she spoke French and German with a fluency I myself lacked, her preferred language was that of conduct books and etiquette manuals. My father was lauded for his brains, but he had never rescued a trading agreement simply by altering a seating arrangement.

Men like Uncle Hugh and my father could pretend they wanted a dimwit for a wife all they liked, but when it came to running a household and a family, what use was an imbecile with as many feathers in her head as on her Parisian-trimmed hat? If I submitted to the fate my family were plotting over dinner parties and social calls, I would be bored but I would never be idle.

'For all that men crow over their accomplishments, we wives work just as hard,' Aunt Emily coaxed. 'Use your mathematics for balancing a household budget and then tell me you don't have an occupation.'

'And I suppose other duties are pure biology,' I suggested tartly.

'Don't be so vulgar, Sarah! Surely,' she added, a pleading note in her voice, 'if you were offered the option of a better life, a normal life, you would take it? Under present circumstances, I quite understand your need for a distraction—'

'A profession,' I interrupted. 'It isn't a profanity, Aunt Emily, you can say the word.'

'It's no substitute for a husband, and you know it!' The words echoed in the air like a gunshot.

'I don't want a husband,' I replied through gritted teeth.

'I can understand that you might be tentative about certain . . . aspects of marriage,' she said quietly. I stared at her in mute shock. 'But the protection offered by a husband, a home . . . Surely you must see that all this gallivanting around, aping the men, is just throwing yourself in the path of similar trouble?'

It was as good as admitting what had really happened to me that night. Of all the people to have listened to my protestations, had Aunt Emily been the one to believe me all this time?

'You were so unwell,' she continued diffidently. I wondered just how much my mother had told her; if she had even the faintest inkling that any marriage she consigned me to would be barren even if I could suffer Miles' clammy attentions. 'All those hours you spend reading textbooks won't get colour back into your cheeks. I know you think me harsh, but you cannot want to become a pariah! If you would just unbend a little, you might find real happiness.'

It was the kindest thing I could ever remember her saying to me, and unwanted tears pricked at the corners of my eyes. I blinked them back sulkily and stared out of the window. I couldn't afford to dwell on this softening of my stern aunt.

Despite all Merchiston's warnings, I finally had new information about Lucy, and I knew just where to find more.

Against all the odds, my acquaintance with the Greenes looked as though it would prove useful after all.

Chapter 34

As Mrs Effie Muir, my aunt's best friend, explained in minute detail the problems she was having with her new parlourmaid, I smiled sympathetically and scanned the crowds for Caroline Hartigan. She was being paraded around the room by Aunt Emily, keen to show off the beneficiary of her generosity. Miss Hartigan recited her thanks again and again, while intimating to each new acquaintance just how welcome further donations to the refuge would be. Beneath her smile, she looked out of place in what was clearly her best dress – a sober oyster-grey affair that did little for her complexion and made her look more like a governess who had temporarily mislaid her charges than the proprietress of a reformatory. By the time Aunt Emily approached us, the other woman was clearly flagging, and after the rote introductions had been made, I turned to my aunt.

'You must allow me to take over – you've barely sat down all night, and I know that Mrs Muir wants to tell you all about the difficulties she's having with her servants. Do take a seat and enjoy the party – I'll introduce Miss Hartigan to the minister.'

For all her love of showing off, at the prospect of a chance to complain about the terrible standards in service these days,

Aunt Emily handed Miss Hartigan over to me like a parcel. I quickly ushered her away, eager to get her on her own.

'You must be thirsty,' I twittered, hoping to disarm her. 'Please, let me get you a drink.'

She gave me a tight smile. 'I'm afraid I never touch alcohol.' Of course – a more sanctimonious woman I had yet to meet; God forbid one drop of the demon drink should pass her lips. So much for my hope that she might become a little too relaxed and find herself saying more than she should.

'Some lemonade, then,' I pressed, taking her by the arm. Once we were both suitably refreshed, I steered her to a quiet corner of the room where we were unlikely to be interrupted.

'Your aunt's donation was most kind,' she began, repeating the sentiment she must have recited a dozen times already this evening. 'The work we do couldn't possibly continue without such generous benefactors.'

I seized on the first area of common ground I had come across.

'Why, St Giles' Infirmary has a similar problem!' I gushed. 'But I must say, you have far better luck in securing funding. How on earth do you manage it?' Miss Hartigan's eyes widened. 'Of course,' I rushed on before she had a chance to respond, 'we must meet some of the same unfortunate women.'

'I believe that some of the wretched souls we seek to guide onto a better path originate from the slums,' she concurred, unsure if I was leading her into some trap that would see Aunt Emily's promise of funds dissolve before her eyes.

'And do many return?' I asked, fighting to keep my tone light. 'Only I believe I know a girl who stayed at your establishment. Her name was Lucy, and she left with a man named Gregory Merchiston.'

Miss Hartigan swallowed convulsively, and she seemed even paler than before. Although her next words were spoken in a firm voice that brooked no disagreement, I knew I had hit my mark. 'I'm afraid some women appear to be past redemption,' she said pointedly.

I fought the urge to slap her. 'Not terribly Christian of you,' I replied coolly. 'I know my aunt was most impressed by your commitment to saving the souls of *all* the girls who enter your doors.' A note of warning crept into my voice. 'In fact, I believe that was the deciding factor in choosing to bestow what I am certain is only the first of many generous gifts on your reformatory.'

Understanding dawned in her eyes. 'Of course, some of our girls have to be sent to us several times before God's message finally sinks in. Perhaps this Lucy is one of them. Your aunt is presenting the donation in front of the whole refuge tomorrow – if you attend, I'll look through my records and see if I recall anyone by that name.'

I smiled at my first piece of good news in weeks. 'I look forward to it, Miss Hartigan.'

My triumph, although justified, was not without its consequences. If ever I had envied the male students their freedom, it was not the next morning. Getting up had never been harder, and it was only through the concerted efforts of Agnes – who eventually resorted to pinching me awake – that I made it out of the door in time to catch my first lecture. I had gulped down a cup of strong black coffee, and was luckily feeling the effects by the time Dr Williamson called on me to dissect an arm. Disembodied limbs and a pounding head was hardly the most pleasant combination. I resolved firmly to take the pledge and never drink again, as I made a slightly shakier than normal incision in the firm, cool flesh. Focusing all my efforts on my work proved helpful, even if the smell turned my stomach, and I returned to my seat feeling almost thoroughly rejuvenated.

Early that evening, Aunt Emily and I alighted from our carriage into the reformatory courtyard. Aunt Emily was dressed as every inch the Lady Bountiful in a plum coat and dramatically large hat trimmed with more feathers than I had ever seen in one place, including on a bird. Next to her, the building looked even darker and dingier than before.

'Well,' she tutted, 'at least now they can afford a few more gas lamps.' I cringed, wondering how much of the bequest Miss Hartigan would have to sacrifice to lighting. How unsurprising that my aunt was more concerned with the building's exterior rather than the lives of the girls locked inside. Doubtless they would soon be attired in smart new pinafores and neat little straw boaters that would be of no use when they left Miss Hartigan's care with rickets and precious few skills to allow them to survive in the harsh world outside.

Rather than say any of this aloud, I meekly followed her across the yard, where five girls paused their game of hopscotch to stare at us. Their expressions were unreadable, schooled to impassiveness just as their wealthier counterparts across the city were. Society lady or scullery maid – no matter what our future held, we were expected to go about it looking as though we had never even conceived of having an opinion about anything.

As we were led through the gloomy corridors, Aunt Emily expounding on her visions of architectural improvement all the while, I scoured the rooms we passed for a glimpse of May, the girl I had spoken to before. As we neared Miss Hartigan's study, I fought to calm the pounding of my heart. She could be at her lessons, or working in the laundry. There were any number of reasons why I had not seen her, but the thought that she had run off in search of Lucy would not abandon me.

Aunt Emily shifted impatiently from foot to foot as our guide's hesitant knock was met with silence. When another rap on the door was similarly ignored, she pushed past, muttering crossly under her breath. She paused in the doorway, and I craned my neck to see what had stopped her mid-sentence.

Caroline Hartigan lay slumped on the floor. Behind us, the girl started to scream, and I winced as I heard the crack of my aunt's palm against her cheek.

'Hush, child,' she said firmly. 'You're hysterical. Sarah, what on earth are you doing?'

I pressed my fingers against the cool skin of Miss Hartigan's wrist. There was no pulse, nor from her pallor did I really expect to find one. There was a horrible bluish tinge to her complexion, and a dark trickle of dried blood crusted her nostril.

'Someone should call the police,' I said grimly.

'It is all in hand,' Aunt Emily informed me. 'I have sent Jessie to find a grown-up and a policeman in that order.' She paused. 'I don't suppose you can . . . do anything, can you?'

'I'm a first-year medical student, Aunt Emily. We don't study resurrection until our final year.'

'Well there's no call for blasphemy,' she sniffed. 'I wonder if we can get a cup of tea. Do let me know if you see any of the girls loitering. I'm absolutely parched.'

I gazed at her in amazement. She could fall into a swoon if you used the wrong knife at dinner, but here she was standing over a corpse, ordering a pot of Darjeeling as though she were at home in the parlour.

I leant against the wall, feeling suddenly dizzy. My heart pounded, my palms were clammy and I stared at the second suspicious death to cross my path. Was this how Lucy had looked when she died? Or was her body bundled off to the morgue whilst she was still warm? But Lucy had been frail and malnourished, while Caroline Hartigan was tall and well built. Subduing her would have been no easy task.

I realised for the first time that the room was in a state of disarray. The inkwell had been turned over, dripping a dark pool onto the floor, the desk drawers had been left hanging open, and the lamp was crooked, as though it had been knocked in a struggle. She had fought back, and hard. I looked down at the woman at my feet. I hadn't particularly liked her in life, but I had to admire her courage.

The clatter of feet made me turn. Miss Hartigan's deputy, a Miss Dawson, hovered in the corridor, wringing her hands anxiously.

'Is it true?' she asked tremulously. 'That Miss Hartigan is . . . is . . . indisposed?'

'She's a little more than that,' Aunt Emily said.

The local constabulary were nothing if not prompt, and by the time Aunt Emily and I had soothed Miss Dawson's paroxysms of hysteria and shooed away half a dozen morbid girls, Jessie puffed up to us, seemingly recovered from her shock, announcing that 'The polis is here, ma'am.'

'It's Sergeant Lester, who came when Kitty Ross tried to set fire to the schoolroom,' another girl announced breathlessly. It seemed that looking after a house full of mob-capped delinquents had its fair share of problems.

Sergeant Lester and Miss Dawson were clearly acquainted, although quite how closely, her blush only allowed me to speculate. He assured us that the doctor was on his way, and once he had asked the requisite questions, we stood in awkward silence. It was clear that he was discomfited by Aunt Emily's unflappable demeanour and my medical knowledge, and couldn't wait to be away from us, in less intimidating company. A gang of thieves, perhaps, or a nice murderer.

'He'll be here in a moment,' he said, as much to reassure

himself as us. 'He'll only want to ask a few questions and then he'll take care of . . . Ah, here he is now.'

'Don't move anything, Lester,' called a voice. 'I'll need to examine the body *in situ*. Ladies, thank you for waiting, I'm sure this must have been a terrible . . .' He trailed off, staring at me. 'Shock.'

'Aunt Emily,' I sighed, 'this is Professor Merchiston. He lectures at the university. Professor, Mrs Hugh Fitzherbert, my guardian.'

He bowed deeply, but I caught something glinting darkly in his eyes.

'Mrs Fitzherbert, it's a pleasure. I'm sorry that we're meeting under such unfortunate circumstances.'

It was unnerving. I had seen Merchiston drunk, stern, stripped to the waist and cold with fury. I had never seen him charming.

'Professor,' Aunt Emily said coolly, inclining her head in acknowledgement. 'I had no idea that the University of Edinburgh selected their tutors from the local constabulary.' Her tone implied that the city's policemen were little better than the criminals they caught.

'This is a charitable effort on Professor Merchiston's part.' He raised his eyebrows as I interjected. I had no idea which one of us was more surprised at the speed with which I rushed to his defence. 'Many of the faculty engage in philanthropic efforts as well as their teaching and research.'

'Quite so,' he agreed smoothly. 'Much as Miss Gilchrist here likes to involve herself in all manner of good causes. Quite the angel of mercy, your niece.'

I watched with trepidation as he knelt down next to Miss Hartigan's body with an unreadable expression on his face.

'Ladies,' he said after a moment, with a smile that failed to reach his eyes, 'I don't want to keep you longer than necessary at such an upsetting scene.' He'd be lucky, I thought. Aunt Emily would be dining out on this for weeks; she wasn't going to miss a second of potential gossip. 'Is the body exactly as you found it?' He glared at me. 'No extracurricular examinations, Miss Gilchrist?'

'I wouldn't dream of it,' I replied sweetly. 'But since you ask, might I be of some assistance, Professor?' Despite his protestations, I had not entirely dismissed the possibility of Merchiston as a killer. I wasn't letting him have unfettered access to yet another murder victim, if I could possibly avoid it, no matter how much it offended Aunt Emily's sense of propriety.

'I hardly think—' she choked out.

'What an excellent idea, Miss Gilchrist,' he replied. I gazed at him in dumb wonderment. His smile did not reach his eyes, but it did show plenty of teeth. I gulped. 'Do forgive me, Mrs Fitzherbert, but I would find your niece's excellent observation skills most useful if you can possibly spare her. Provided,' he added drily, 'that she keeps her imagination in check.'

'Well,' Aunt Emily fluttered, caught between respectability and morbid curiosity, 'if you're sure she can be of use . . .' She allowed herself to be led away by Sergeant Lester, glancing over her shoulder at me with a mixture of apprehension and envy. I had never guessed that beneath the prim propriety lurked a woman with a taste for death.

Merchiston ran a hand through already unruly hair and stared at me.

'Why is it, Miss Gilchrist, that whenever there is a hint of trouble lately, I seem to find you at the centre of it?'

'I'm sure I don't know what you mean,' I replied frostily.

He stood and took a step towards me, and I found myself inching backwards instinctively. No. I would hold my ground against this man, no matter what I thought him capable of.

'Don't play the proper young lady with me, Gilchrist. First I find you wandering the slums entirely unchaperoned. Then you accuse me of murder. And if that wasn't enough, I am called to the scene of a crime only to find you standing calmly over a dead body!'

'My aunt and I were visiting Miss Hartigan,' I said coldly.

'Well I'm afraid she isn't receiving callers at present.'

'You callous, unfeeling bastard,' I whispered. 'Does a woman's life really mean so little to you?'

His eyes darkened. 'I can assure you, madam, that it means a great deal to me. And at least I am here on official police business rather than skulking around playing lady detective.'

'Miss Hartigan should be grateful that you show such an interest,' I snarled. 'It's more than Lucy ever got. Or perhaps your interest waned and you needed to dispose of her.'

Had I been a man, I think Gregory Merchiston would have hit me. His whole body shuddered with an emotion I could not identify.

'One more word out of you, Gilchrist,' he said in a low voice. 'One more word, and I swear I won't be held responsible for my actions.'

'You never are, are you?' I said quietly. 'Men like you. You hide behind your position, your title, claiming morality. And then if you go too far ... well then, it was her fault. She tempted you. She asked for it. And you walk away blameless whilst her life is in ruins.'

His eyes softened with understanding. I looked away. I could live with his anger, his self-righteous fury, but I couldn't bear to see his pity.

'I'm sorry,' he said quietly. 'For goading you and for ... Well. No woman deserves to go through what you have. And no man should ever escape justice because he has a spotless reputation and a position in society.'

'What about Lucy?' I asked. I was shaking, I realised, and I didn't know if it was from fear, the unwanted memories, or his closeness. He was unnerving in anger but his sympathy was positively terrifying. How did he know so much about me? Gossip was one thing, but how could he know the truth?

'I didn't kill her.'

I wanted to believe him, I realised. More than anything, in this moment I wanted Merchiston to be innocent.

'But you knew her. What was she to you? Your mistress, or just another whore you bought for your pleasure?'

'Don't you dare call Lucy a whore!' His spittle hit my face. I didn't move, not even to wipe it off. I wouldn't budge an inch until I got my answer.

'Then tell me what she was,' I insisted.

He ran his hand over his stubbled jaw, looking tired and defeated.

'Lucy is . . .' His voice broke. 'She was my sister.'

Chapter 35

'My father died when Lucy was just a wean,' he explained, his voice raw. 'She was an accident; they thought my mother was long past childbearing age, and my father wasn't in the best of health. He worked in the cotton mills and they had sent stronger men than him to an early grave. I was in Glasgow by then, trying to carve out a life for myself. Really, I was just living by my wits and my fists, but I got by, and some months I even had enough money to send home. But after my father died, I knew Ma couldn't handle things by herself, not with Lucy to look after. So I moved back home, became the man of the house. I had some brains and my father was well loved by our neighbours, so when I was looking for work, the village doctor took me on as an apprentice. He was an old sawbones, but he cared about his patients and he taught me well. He was the one who encouraged me to go to university, even lent me some money to get me started.

'Lucy was in school by that point, and Ma was taking in extra sewing work. I wish I could say I came home every chance I got, but that wouldn't be true. Some weeks I didn't even write. I was lost in my studies, in the freedom I'd tasted once before and then sacrificed. I tell you something, if you think the young men at the medical school are bad now, you'd have had a shock if you'd seen us.' He shook his head ruefully. 'I wasn't as wild as some of the others – perhaps if I hadn't met Isobel when I did, I might have sown a few more wild oats. But we were married as soon as I graduated, and then William came along soon afterwards.' He shot me a sidelong glance, and I understood that his son's arrival had taken something less than the nine months one would have reasonably expected. So he had retained some of his former ways, then.

'I stayed in Edinburgh, doing a little teaching of my own but mostly building up a small private practice in Newington. I was a long way from the country bumpkin that had come to Glasgow at nineteen, and further still from the rough bastard that left it. I was so pleased with myself, with my shiny silver pocket watch and my long list of patients. I had a beautiful wife, a bonny boy and money in the bank. I still sent some of it home every month, but it never occurred to me that they might have needed more than money until Lucy showed up on my doorstep one night, soaked to the skin. It turned out this wasn't the first time she'd run away from home – she'd been living with her schoolmaster for six months, but when she told him she was pregnant, he turned her out onto the streets and went back to his wife. She was fourteen.' His voice cracked. 'She wanted me to take her in and do something about it, and damn near smashed up the parlour when I refused. But she was malnourished and she'd walked for miles and hitched the rest, paying her way God knows how. A few days later and the problem took care of itself.'

I covered his hand with mine. The coroner's carriage juddered over the cobbles, and I tried to block out the thuds as the body of Caroline Hartigan was jolted from side to side. Merchiston was so lost in his memories that I doubted he even noticed.

'Our mother wanted her to start at the mill, but she refused. She wanted to live with me and move in society – she didn't realise that a doctor was little better than a tradesman in the eyes of the gentry. Isobel had the idea of sending her into service, but she didn't make it through the year. I tried her as a nurse in the hospital, but there was easy access to alcohol and opium and more than a few young men, and eventually she lost that job as well.

'Then cholera ripped through the city, and I had my hands full. There was barely time to see my family, let alone a sister who wanted nothing to do with me. I didn't even notice Isobel's symptoms until it was too late, and by that time . . . William didn't have a chance. There's a saying, isn't there, that cobblers' wives always go barefoot and doctors' wives die young. Perhaps if I hadn't been so obsessed with bolstering my own reputation, single-handedly rescuing the poor and downtrodden of Edinburgh, I might have been able to save them.'

I shook my head. 'How could you? So little was known about cholera – so little still is – you couldn't have done anything.'

'Tell that to Lucy,' he said quietly, before continuing. 'It seemed best to send her to school, but she was so wayward . . . Hartigan's prison was the only place that would take her. In the end, she begged me to let her leave but ran away before she'd been home a week.'

'And ended up in Ruby's employ,' I finished.

'She wasn't the only one,' he said. 'I recognised a few of the girls when I called on Lucy. I assumed they'd run away together, but then another girl arrived a month later . . .'

'You mean Miss Hartigan had some sort of . . . of . . . arrangement with Ruby?'

'A trade in girls no one would miss,' he said in a leaden

tone. 'Before she ran away, I hadn't visited Lucy in two months. I'd been in London, presenting a paper, and then in the Highlands for a few weeks on a walking tour. Lucy could be difficult; she was never going to be one of the reformatory's successes. Perhaps Miss Hartigan thought it was the lesser of two evils – remove a troublemaker and say she ran away of her own accord. And I believed her, until my own bloody sister showed up in the cells for offering what they politely term "criminal conversations" before Ruby bailed her out.'

'But why would she stay there? Once you returned to Edinburgh, once you found her – why not just come home?'

'Ruby keeps her girls well medicated.' He grimaced. 'Gin, laudanum . . . God knows where she gets it from; she had an entire chemist's worth last time I checked. Addicts, every one of them, and she's their chief supplier.'

I frowned. 'So that's why you went to the opium den? To find out where Ruby was getting the stuff from?'

He sighed. 'Madame Lily told me about that. Is there anywhere you haven't followed me, Miss Gilchrist?'

Remembering the bare-knuckle fight I had witnessed, I blushed to the roots of my hair.

'Randall was making some enquiries on my behalf,' he continued. Shame engulfed me and I couldn't meet his gaze. One more in a long line of foolish assumptions, then. 'He was the only one who knew about Lucy – bad enough that I don't come from a distinguished family like my colleagues; having a prostitute for a sister would have finished my career. I asked him not to tell Elisabeth.' He swallowed. 'I was too ashamed. I know what people say about me. The Scotch verdict. The murderer who escaped with his life and whatever shabby reputation he had. I was lucky to get this position; do you think I would find another if they discovered that Lucy was . . .'

'The police employ you, knowing about your past,' I said
curiously. 'Why do they do that?'

He looked almost embarrassed. 'I have certain . . . contacts.
They know of my methods. Let's just say that doctors with
deductive training will always be in demand.' My interest was
piqued, but after the day's revelations, I felt he deserved to
keep some secrets. 'I didn't do it,' he said, and I found that
I believed him. 'They couldn't prove it was me, but they
couldn't prove it wasn't either, and so they left me hanging
metaphorically rather than literally. For which I suppose I
should count myself lucky.' He didn't sound as though he did.

'With your detective work, I'm surprised you couldn't clear
your own name,' I said with an attempt at levity.

'I had my reasons,' he said quietly. 'Maybe I'll tell you
about it one day. For now, can we stick to the murder in front
of us?'

We lapsed into silence, and he drummed his fingers on the
leather upholstery, lost in thought.

'Miss Hartigan was suffocated by someone who wanted it
to look like a burglary,' he said slowly. 'Early this morning, by
the looks of it. But why not in the middle of the night, when
everyone was asleep?'

'They could have been looking for money,' I suggested, 'or
perhaps it was a relative of one of the girls. It could even have
been one of them.'

'It was an adult,' he said thoughtfully. 'An adult, but not
necessarily a man. Someone her own height, and if the scratch
beneath her ear was anything to go by, a woman.'

'Rather detailed for someone who hasn't had a chance to
examine her properly yet.'

He shrugged. 'I had a good teacher.'

A thought occurred to me. 'Ruby is about Miss Hartigan's
height.'

Before I could finish, he was on his feet, banging the carriage roof with his fist.

'Driver! Mackenzie's Wynd, as fast as you can!'

The carriage swung into the Grassmarket and pulled up outside the wynd where Ruby's brothel was located.

Merchiston turned to me. 'Don't even think about getting out. You've spent more than enough time in pits like this. In any case, the Dean frowns upon professors taking their male students into dens of iniquity – I dread to think what he'd say if he knew I was accompanying a woman.'

'In that case,' I smiled sweetly, 'you'd better not tell him.'

Grumbling but not explicitly forbidding me to follow him, he strode off into the darkness and I ran after him like a dog at the heels of her master, wondering if I had really been so wrong about him.

We waited in the parlour, both studiously ignoring the artwork adorning the walls and the noises from the rooms upstairs as we waited for the girl to return.

'She says you're barred. Both of you. She disnae want you coming around upsetting the girls, no' after the stooshie the other night.'

Merchiston looked curiously at me, and I wished I could sink into the ground. Damn Julia Latymer and her proselytising.

'I keep Ruby McAllister in gin and clean bedsheets; the least she can do is tell me that to my face.'

He went to push past the girl, who kicked him sharply in the shins and yelled as though all the demons of hell were attacking her.

'It can wait,' I told him. 'We can come back when she's calmed down, but if Caroline Hartigan has any answers to give us, then we'd better hurry.'

'And to think I worried you were too emotional to make a

good doctor,' Merchiston said as he followed me back out onto the street.

If the men at the police station were surprised to see Professor Merchiston accompanied by two women, one living and one dead, they had the sense not to say anything. I expected him to shoo me away as two porters placed the body on the table, but instead he looked at me with a challenge in his eyes.

'I'm going to need another pair of hands. Would you care to assist?'

Had Caroline Hartigan been in any position to disapprove, she surely would have found my delight distasteful. 'There's nothing I'd like more, Professor.'

The room that Merchiston was allocated to perform his autopsies was freezing cold. I shivered, and my companion glanced at me.

'You'll soon warm up once we get to work. Take my coat for now, and sterilise those instruments.'

Gingerly I slipped his heavy black greatcoat about my shoulders and moved to the table where his knives were kept. I couldn't help but be impressed – I knew some doctors who didn't sterilise their instruments when the patient was alive, and the fact that Merchiston did so when he was operating on a body beyond infection put him higher in my esteem. I undressed Miss Hartigan, remembering the upright woman I had encountered and how horrified she would have been to see herself so degraded. When I had pulled away the last of her undergarments, Merchiston leant on her chest and a sickening splintering crack sounded as he fractured her ribcage with a grunt. To my astonishment, he then handed me the scalpel.

'Go on,' he said, smirking. 'Show me what you're capable of.' With a brief defiant glare, I sliced confidently into Miss Hartigan's torso with a clean, neat line. I glanced up. He nodded meditatively, his eyes on my work. 'Carry on.' I widened the cut until I could see the purplish blue of the lungs. He made a noise that seemed to indicate I should continue, so I reached into the chest cavity and scooped out the left lung. I was aware of his presence behind me, perfectly still and silent but reassuring nonetheless. My hand faltered, distracted by his nearness. 'Keep going, lass. Breathe.'

'You make it sound as though I'm the patient, not the doctor.'

'Please accept my apologies, Doctor-in-training Gilchrist,' he murmured, and without turning, I could tell that he was smiling again.

I pressed the tip of the scalpel to the tissue and cut firmly.

'Suffocation: that was how Burke and Hare murdered their victims. Barely leaves a trace, unless you know exactly what you're looking for. They sold countless bodies to the university for dissection and no one was any the wiser.' His voice was raspy with emotion, and I could tell that he remembered how I had come to find Lucy's body in the first place. 'It happened just up the road from Ruby's house, you know,' he continued. 'People still tell stories about the demon doctors, on dreich, dark nights. Maybe that was what gave our murderer the idea.'

The grandfather clock in the hall chimed eight o'clock and I froze in horror.

Merchiston glanced at me. 'Your aunt will be wondering where you are.'

I cursed softly. It would take me an hour to get home, and I wouldn't have time to dress for dinner. I prayed that this was one night when my uncle had chosen to stay at his club.

'You go,' he said, with a wave of his hand. 'I'll deal with Miss Hartigan. Did she have any family we need to notify?'

I shook my head. 'I've no idea. Someone at the reformatory

must know, or maybe Fiona Leadbetter – apparently the infirmary doctors helped them out from time to time.'

I was at the door when he spoke again.

'I'd been waiting for years for Lucy to show up on my slab. Then she died, and I didn't even get that. A grotesque thing to be jealous of, Miss Gilchrist, but there we are.'

The door I closed was heavy and thick, but I knew that behind it, Gregory Merchiston was crying.

Chapter 36

I arrived early at the university the next morning, and immediately went in search of Merchiston. Luckily, Professor Chalmers was nowhere to be seen, but neither was my unexpected ally.

Returning to the courtyard, I saw a couple pressed together in the shadows, murmuring urgently. I could only hear the woman's voice, low and passionate. Above us, a door opened and a shaft of light illuminated the woman. I gasped in shock as I recognised the chartreuse wool of Julia Latymer's dress. Without thinking, I stepped closer, straining to hear the voice of her lover. I hoped to catch her out, humiliate her the way she had humiliated me, or at least have a little leverage to make her cease her campaign against me. As I edged closer, the murmuring continued, and I realised with a queer sort of feeling that the reason I couldn't make out a man's voice was because there was no man present.

Pressed against the wall, her hair in disarray and her neck being covered in hungry kisses, was Edith.

I stepped back with a gasp, and Julia's head whipped around. I had seen her angry, I had seen her gloating, but I had never before seen her frightened. She pulled back from Edith as if the other girl had burnt her.

'Gilchrist,' she choked out. 'I . . . we . . .'

'Don't tell anyone,' Edith interrupted, her voice raw. 'You might not like us, you might have every reason in the world to run to the Dean right now and get us sent down for immoral conduct, but please don't. I'm begging you.'

'Why not?' It took a moment before I recognised the cold voice as my own.

'Because,' Julia said with a bitter smile, 'you're better than we are.'

I looked at her silently, unable to speak for a moment. Then, without thinking, I raised my hand and slapped her soundly across the cheek.

'You hypocritical bitch,' I said in a low voice. 'How dare you flatter me when for months – for months, Julia! – you have been spreading lies about me to every single person who crosses our path. I have lost friends because of you. I can't count the times I left lectures nearly in tears, vowing I'd never come back. And now you tell me I'm better than you. Well for once, Julia Latymer, I agree.'

Julia and I had taken great care not to be alone since the first week we had met in Edinburgh. For my part, it was a deliberate effort to stop me clawing her eyes out. What her reasoning was, I did not know. In fact, her behaviour was a complete mystery to me, since I had done nothing to make her hate me.

Now we met each other's gaze, Edith all but forgotten.

'You aren't the only one who left London to escape gossip, Sarah. I was going to the London School of Medicine for Women. I had a friend, we were going to take rooms together.' Her breath hitched, and in the dim light I saw her already pale skin take on an ashen hue. 'I misinterpreted our friendship. She was disgusted, she threatened to tell everyone . . .' She broke off, and for the first time I felt sorry for her. 'You might have been reckless, but at least everyone understood that. What would they have said if they'd found out about me?'

'So why turn on me?' I asked, exasperated. 'We both had secrets; why persecute the one person who was in the same position?'

Julia laughed bitterly. 'The same position? Sarah, men who love other men are thrown into prison. I'd be lucky if I escaped the madhouse. You've heard what the men say about us – if we respond to their flirting we're immoral, if we don't then we're unnatural. Better to be a prig than an invert.' She spat the last word, shaking. 'And you know how fast rumour travels. I couldn't risk you finding out about me and telling everyone.'

'So instead you made sure no one would speak to me, much less believe me,' I finished. 'That's hardly sisterhood, Julia.'

'That's society,' she replied, and we both knew it was true. 'Anyway, it didn't work.'

We both turned to look at Edith. Blushing and awkward, she kept her eyes fixed on Julia, and I wondered how I had ever mistaken her affection for blind admiration. 'I knew. I knew from the way she looked at me.' She flashed me a wry smile. 'It's exactly the way Professor Merchiston looks at you.'

'That's not true!' I protested hotly, my cheeks flaming. 'After everything you've just told me, how dare you imply—'

'I didn't say you looked back,' Edith said innocently.

'Anyway,' Julia pressed on. 'Now you know the truth. It's up to you what to do next.'

What was one more secret in the mass of knowledge I had gained these past few weeks?

'Nothing,' I told her, firmly. 'You have my word. I don't care that the two of you are close. I know what it's like to keep secrets. I won't tell a soul, I swear, but for God's sake, Julia, try to show the same compassion to me. We don't have to be friends, but I'm tired of having enemies.'

She nodded, and the sound of footsteps echoed on the stone flags. 'Shall we join the others?' She looped her arm through Edith's, shooting me a defiant glare that faded into the beginnings of a real smile when I merely shrugged. Together we moved out of the chilly shadows and into the morning sunlight.

I spent the morning trying not to stare at them, wondering how such an unlikely relationship had blossomed. The day dragged, and my impatience to seek out Merchiston and discover what Miss Hartigan's post-mortem had revealed warred with Edith's earlier words. I wondered how I could possibly face him.

One other person I had to face was Professor Chalmers. The apology I owed him would not be an easy one, and I doubted that my friendship with Elisabeth would ever fully recover.

Any thoughts I had had about delivering that apology in person were diverted when McVeigh interrupted our lecture. He lingered in Randall's eyeline, reluctant to even step over the threshold into our presence until he was ushered forward.

He handed him something and Randall frowned.

'Miss Gilchrist? A note for you.'

The note was scrawled, misspelt, the paper stained with blotches of ink and other things I preferred not to think about. It instructed me very clearly that should I wish to learn more about Lucy's death, I should attend the mortuary after my last lecture.

I prayed that the hastily dashed-off missive to my uncle would halt the carriage's arrival at four o'clock. My good behaviour had earned me a loosening of the reins of late, and I

hoped that my claim of an extended session in the library
would result in nothing more than a lecture on the dangers of
too much reading on the delicate female brain.

My heart thumped as I descended the staircase to the
dissection rooms. Voices echoed as a pair of students joked
over their macabre work, and I realised that I had never been
down here in the presence of the male students. The university,
with its quixotic notions of propriety, preferred its lady
students not to dissect their corpses in the presence of the
opposite sex, presumably because the known aphrodisiac
effects of decomposing would send us all into paroxysms of
ecstatic immorality.

Silence fell, and I felt their eyes upon me, a lone woman
wandering the halls without a chaperone.

'Can I be of assistance?' I recognised the speaker as a man
named Anderson. His tone dripped with concern, but his
smile made my skin crawl.

'I have a meeting with Mr McVeigh,' I stammered.

'The porter?' An eyebrow rose. 'Without your chaperone?
Isn't that a little . . . against the rules, Walker?'

His friend furrowed his brow. 'I'm sure the Dean would be
very interested to hear how one of the female students is
meeting a man alone on university grounds.'

'You might not want me here,' I spat, 'but here I am. Now
will you kindly direct me to McVeigh, or would you prefer it
if I just screamed for help?'

I turned to leave, and froze as I felt something caress my
back, and move lower. I turned to face my molester and found
myself mere inches from the bobbing, grinning face of a
skeleton. On instinct, my hand had grabbed the wrist, and I
felt the dry, stick-like ulna crack between my fingers. I jolted
back, but not before I realised that the body was not entirely
decomposed.

'He's just being friendly, Doctor,' Walker leered from behind his cadaver. 'We're all very friendly here. Especially McVeigh. You know, he normally has to pay for his company, but it seems now that he's getting it for free. Tell me, is this in exchange for your tuition, or do you just want your pick of the fresh bodies?'

'I'm sure we can help with that,' Anderson smirked. 'You must get tired of examining corpses – wouldn't you like to practise on a patient who's a little warmer?'

He was close enough that I could feel his breath on my cheek. I stumbled backwards until I met the wall and closed my eyes in desperation.

'Now you can't possibly examine someone dressed like that,' he murmured. 'At least take your coat off.'

'It's a little cold for that, don't you think?' I asked through chattering teeth that had very little to do with the cold. My shaking hands reached up to remove my hat.

'That's it,' he praised encouragingly, as though I were a child that had performed a clever trick. A moment later, the smug satisfaction on his face crumpled into pain.

'You fucking bitch,' he hissed, lapping the blood from his hand where my hatpin had pierced the flesh. 'You'll pay for that.' He lunged forward again, only for my knee to meet a part of his anatomy my education to date had taught me was on the sensitive side. He collapsed, grunting in pain. His companion looked less than eager to confront me.

'Unless you'd like to find out just how good I am with a scalpel, I suggest you go back to manhandling your corpses,' I spat.

'You're all the same,' Anderson wheezed after me. 'Frigid bloody spinsters who can't take a joke.'

With the door safely closed between myself and the anatomists, I leant against the cold stone wall, breathing heavily. My legs were shaking and I felt sick. The memory of Paul's hands on my skin, pushing up my skirts, pinning my arms against the bookcase, threatened to overwhelm me.

His words rang in my ears. *Don't struggle, Sarah, I'm just being friendly. I thought you wanted to be a doctor. You can't be such a prude with your patients.*

Chapter 37

I forced myself to stand up. I wanted nothing more than to run up the stairs, into the comparative light and warmth, far away from Walker and Anderson and their little 'jokes'.

But McVeigh's note had my interest piqued. He certainly hadn't shown any inclination to help me the other day, but clearly something had happened to change his mind. With a shiver, I recalled Walker's comment about McVeigh paying for his company. Had the information he wanted to relay been found at a brothel?

It didn't matter, I told myself. I couldn't afford to choose who assisted me in this endeavour. And if McVeigh had a preference for tarts, he might be persuaded to show a little sympathy for Lucy. Still, it didn't make me any happier about visiting him alone, and I wondered if I should have found some flimsy pretext to lure a chaperone along with me. If Merchiston had known what I was about, he would have gone in my place, and perhaps I should have let him. I had walked blithely to my own destruction once before, thanks to Paul Beresford and that blasted deserted library, and with my new-found knowledge of the horrors of the world, I should have turned back.

Like a fool, I didn't.

Moving along the corridor with its flickering gas lamps, I heard the low murmur of a voice and hastened my steps towards it.

'Mr McVeigh?' I called out. 'It's Miss Gilchrist. You said you wanted to see me.'

I turned the corner only to find the corridor deserted. There was no voice now, and yet I had the unshakable feeling that someone had stood here only moments before.

A noise from behind me made me jump, and I turned, hair standing on end, before I realised it had come from one of the dissection rooms. Turning back, I saw a flash of red and a pair of large hands grabbed me; then, before I could cry out, something damp covered my nose and mouth and everything else faded away.

When I opened my eyes, I found myself sprawled in a heap on the stone floor. It was cold, and the sour tang of day-old sweat hung in the air. My mind felt cloudy and my head throbbed. As memory returned, I felt my blood turn to ice. Heart hammering in my chest, I remembered the men in the dissection room. Had they followed me, over-powered me, taken what I would not freely give? I didn't think so – I felt sore but not violated, and a cursory glance at my watch revealed it was little over ten minutes since my last lecture had ended. They had meant to scare me then, not hurt me.

Wincing, I stood and noticed the instrument of my assault at my feet. A handkerchief, soaked in chloroform. Feeling shaky, I forced myself to turn back the way I had come and return to Walker and Anderson what they had mislaid.

Neither so much as glanced up when I entered the room, so absorbed were they in their respective tasks: Walker elbow-deep in some poor fellow's sternum, Anderson preoccupied with the skeleton with which I had become so unpleasantly familiar.

'I believe one of you dropped this,' I said, forcing any emotion out of my voice. 'I came to return it.'

Walker glanced up. 'Not mine. But if you were missing our company . . .'

'I wasn't,' I snapped. 'Tell me, gentlemen, do you have to drug all your women?'

'What's the harpy on about now?' Anderson growled.

'Wants to return a handkerchief. Soaked in chloroform, by the smell of it.'

Anderson glared, the memory of my self-defence still rankling. 'This might be too much for your delicate little brain to comprehend, but none of the patients down here require anaesthesia.'

Looking at the exposed chest cavity on Walker's table, I had to concede his point, however crudely made.

Shrugging, he returned his attention to the corpse. 'Could be anyone's. Give it to your sweetheart when you find him. Now leave us in peace, you bloody virago.'

I walked out, still clutching the fabric. Much as I disliked the men, I didn't think they had left the dissection room.

McVeigh was nowhere to be seen, and I decided to abandon my search, eager to return to the land of the living.

I looked at the note crumpled in my hand. I hadn't questioned it, just stumbled down here in blind naivety, convinced that the porter had decided to help me out of the goodness of his heart. McVeigh, who knew where Lucy's body had come from; McVeigh, who had told me she had been taken away to be buried. Who, if rumour was to be believed, had more than a professional acquaintance with the local brothels. How easy it would have been to conceal his crime in a place where one more corpse would go unnoticed. And who was to say that she was the first? I had walked into his trap like a lamb to the slaughter, when I had every reason in the world not to trust him. Had he only meant to frighten me, or did he mean to return, to see me on the slab the way he had seen Lucy?

Unable to bear being trapped in this chilly, morbid place for a moment longer, I broke into a run, desperate to get into the fresh air and light, where I could think . . .

I rounded the corner and collided with someone, finding myself sprawled on the floor for the second time that day.

'For God's sake, look where you're going, you blasted woman!'

No mistaking those surly tones. I felt my cheeks burn at the memory of the body I had just slammed into stripped to the waist and glistening with a sheen of sweat.

Merchiston sighed. 'Gilchrist. I might have known. Are you incapable of staying out of trouble for more than five minutes?' He helped me to my feet and I shivered, remembering the same hands covering mine, warm and reassuring, as we worked together in the police mortuary. 'And might I remind you,' he added in a stern tone, 'that running in the corridors is strictly forbidden?'

Despite my recent ordeal, I found myself smiling. 'I assure you, Professor, it won't happen again. Unless,' I grimaced, 'someone else tries to attack me.'

He reached out as if to comfort me, but caught himself. 'Attack you? Sarah, what happened? Are you all right?'

Scared and still shaking though I was, his inadvertent use of my Christian name warmed me.

'McVeigh, I think,' I said softly. I prayed that my suspicions were correct, otherwise I would be implicating yet another innocent man.

He frowned. 'The porter? I'll thrash his hide and have him

dismissed. Then I'll frogmarch him to the polis myself and have him thrown in the cells for having the sheer bloody temerity to—'

I stopped him. 'He didn't interfere with me, if that's what you think. But he did give me one hell of a fright.' Merchiston nodded, struggling to stay silent and let me speak. His eyes were dark with fury, and his breathing came in harsh, angry snorts like a mad bull. I remembered suddenly why I had been so afraid of him. 'He sent me this note,' I explained, handing it to him, 'but when I came down here, I couldn't find him.' I paused, recalling the other unpleasant incident I had faced. 'If you're looking to thrash someone, might I suggest Walker and Anderson? They weren't exactly welcoming.'

Merchiston's countenance darkened further. 'Aye, I know who you mean,' he muttered, and I almost felt sorry for them. Almost.

'Then, when I went to look for McVeigh, someone grabbed me from behind and covered my nose and mouth with this.' I fished the chloroform-soaked handkerchief out of my reticule. His eyes widened. 'Professor, I think McVeigh lured me down here to frighten me. Walker said that he visits prostitutes, and I know that he's responsible for collecting the corpses donated for dissection. He even prepared Lucy, for God's sake!'

Merchiston held a hand up, looking ill. I mentally chastised myself for reminding him of the gruesome end his beloved sister had come to.

'If he didn't murder Lucy himself, then he knows who did. McVeigh intended for you to abandon your investigation, makeshift and foolish as it is. I suggest you do so, and leave me to take care of him.'

Keen as I was to see this through to the end, I couldn't stand another moment down there.

'You will let me know?'

'I will. And Sarah – thank you. You've been a thorn in my side these past few weeks, but you have helped me more than I can possibly say. If ever I can find a way to thank you—'

I cut him off. 'Just don't fail me in the Christmas examinations.'

Chapter 38

Students scurried past Teviot House from one lecture to the next, and the strains of Saint-Saëns echoed from the Reid Concert Hall, where the music students were practising. That fleeting sense of reassurance that I had felt standing with Merchiston outside the dissection rooms had vanished. My head still throbbed with the after-effects of the chloroform, and I felt horribly tired. In the past few days, I had come to trust the dour professor, even to like him. But I could no longer be certain that he was telling the truth. I had stumbled down so many blind alleyways in the course of my 'makeshift and foolish' attempt to find Lucy's murderer, but weeks later, I still felt no closer to any answer.

It was a relief to leave the claustrophobic environs of the university for the rookeries, and I arrived for my shift at the infirmary eager to lose myself in the work. By the end, I was swaying on my feet. Although the doctors and nurses around me had worked far harder and accomplished far more, most on considerably less sleep, I felt bone weary. I wondered in a flash of exhausted terror how I would ever survive as a doctor with so little stamina. I knew that days and nights like this and far worse would become my normal routine, with meals and sleep snatched here and there in rare quiet moments, but I was still soft and weak; my life as a lady, albeit an educated one, had not prepared me for hard work. I realised with a sinking feeling in my stomach that our end-of-term examinations were only a few weeks away and my marks in chemistry were still not what they should be. I was, if not excelling myself, at least not heaping shame down upon my head in every other subject, but chemistry had been my cross to bear for years now, and it didn't seem to be getting any easier.

At least tomorrow was Saturday, and I could spend the day in the warm, even if I was paying calls and being dragged from one house to the next with exactly the same conversation taking place and only the quality of the cakes being any different. I also knew that the following day meant spending two hours in church trying not to fall asleep as the Reverend droned on and on about hellfire and damnation. It should not have been possible to make eternal torment sound quite so dull, but if the minister were to be believed, the devil wanted nothing more than to bore us all to death.

As I removed my apron, noting with annoyance that the blood and vomit I had spent the afternoon clearing up had soaked through to my dress, Fiona came in looking haggard.

'Off already? You lucky thing! I still have house calls to make this afternoon,' she groaned.

'Dr Thomas is worried about overworking me,' I smiled. Mairead Thomas was easily the most kind-hearted of the staff at the infirmary, and one of the youngest – as she had pointed out earlier, she remembered a little more vividly than her colleagues the days of balancing her studies with whatever clinical work she could get.

'She's too soft on you,' Fiona chuckled. 'I thought you young ones were supposed to be full of energy. Look at you, you're stooping like an old woman!'

'I am not!' I replied, outraged and standing up straight. 'I'll have you know I could have carried on for hours if Dr Thomas hadn't relieved me.'

'Then you won't object to accompanying me on my rounds,' Fiona smiled wickedly. I laughed, realising how readily I had walked into her trap.

'Just promise that we'll be finished by eight,' I told her. 'I'm supposed to be having supper with Elisabeth Chalmers.' If nothing else, my truce with Merchiston had returned my friend to me, and I was looking forward to seeing her even if it meant apologising to both her and Randall in person.

Fiona frowned, and I realised that she did not entirely approve of Elisabeth. Perhaps she thought that mixing in such rarefied circles was frivolous for a woman who was supposed to be dedicating her life to helping the less fortunate. Still, she accepted my request readily enough, and I followed her out into the streets, where I was surprised to see that she intended to walk rather than take the tram, an omnibus or a carriage.

'It's not far,' she assured me. 'Only three or four houses. You can apply some dressings, but I'm afraid it won't be anything terribly complicated. Most of these poor souls are too old to make it down to the clinic easily, or too afraid of hospitals to venture through our doors. At least we can make them comfortable in their own homes, such as they are.'

The light was fading rapidly, not helped by the fact that we were walking through narrow alleyways that could barely be called streets, where the buildings loomed and leant and blocked out even the tiniest scrap of sky. I could not imagine what it would be like to grow up in such an environment, and not for the first time I found myself empathising with the drunks and addicts who found their way to the infirmary in search of help we could not give them, though their need was none the less for not being physical.

In the dim light, Fiona looked grim and exhausted, and I wondered what toll it took on her, working in these conditions every day. She could do with a holiday, I thought, or at least a good meal. She had lost weight in the past few weeks, and tonight she wore a sad, resigned expression. I wished that she would open up to me and share her troubles, but I knew that asking would only result in a gruff refusal of my offer of friendship. She had been even more isolated from her colleagues of late, and Tillie Campbell had commented in low tones that she was working even harder than usual, and took every death of a patient to heart as though it personally grieved her. Well, if all I could do was assist her in her rounds in these run-down tenements and slums, then I would do it gladly.

After the first house call, where we eased what suffering we could in a family who had to contend with whooping cough on top of rickets and malnutrition, I resolved to count my blessings. Had I been born into the world I was visiting, I would likely not have survived to my present age, much less gained any sort of education. If infant disease hadn't killed me, childbirth combined with the unsanitary conditions in which these people lived almost certainly would have.

Although the houses we visited were dingy and their occupants poor, Fiona had the knack of acting like an honoured guest as much as a physician. After we had departed from one house, leaving an elderly woman in as much comfort as we could – which was to say not very much at all – I asked her why she was so willing to accept the stale cake or bread and butter that her patients and their families pressed on us.

'Surely it would be better to let them eat it themselves, rather than drain what little resources they have?' I questioned, confused by her constant acceptance.

My mentor shrugged. 'It's a point of pride for them. If I

refused, it would insult them, casting aspersions on their kitchen or their purse.'

This part of the city was so run-down and ignored that no one had thought to install electricity in any of the buildings, much less the street lamps.

'It's not far,' Fiona said, squinting into the darkness. 'Here, this will warm you up.' She pressed a flask into my hand, and as I gulped the coffee greedily, I felt the medicinal tang of whisky burn my throat.

Eventually we paused as Fiona fumbled with matches and a lamp to illuminate the gloom, and mounted the stairs of a dingy building that looked uninhabited.

'Are you sure this is the place?' I asked nervously.

'Oh, quite sure,' she called back, and I followed her with trepidation.

On the second floor, she pushed open a door and I heard her voice soothing the room's inhabitants.

As I stepped into the room, the door slammed behind me and a key turned in the lock.

Chapter 39

The room was small and cramped, with a long table taking up most of the space. It looked like an operating table, and I realised with confusion that there was another, smaller table with surgical implements on it. A glass-fronted cupboard was filled with bottles, and as I moved closer, I recognised ether and chloroform.

I turned to Fiona in confusion. She was pale, but there was a determined cast to her expression.

'I'm sorry, Sarah,' she said in a voice that shook only slightly. 'If there was any other way, believe me, I'd let you leave here unharmed. But you kept asking questions.' Her voice broke, and she pressed her hand to her mouth, unable to speak for a moment. 'First Lucy, now you. Am I to have no peace?'

A sick sort of dread filled me.

'I told you to leave well alone.' Fiona's voice was cold as she mastered herself. 'I did all I could. What happens now is your own fault. You haven't left me with a choice.'

'You killed Lucy. Fiona, why?'

She shook her head. 'It doesn't matter.'

'It matters to me! You killed a woman; you at least owe me

an explanation. What is this room? Some sort of makeshift operating theatre?'

She nodded, her lips pressed tightly together.

'I help women. When they're . . . in trouble.'

'You carry out abortions?' I asked. 'Fiona, that's illegal! I know you're helping these girls, but you could be hanged!'

'Do you think I don't know that?' she snarled. 'Lucy did too. Oh, she was very clever. Cleverer than her brother – she knew that if I didn't want her to talk, there was no end to what she could extort from me.'

'She was blackmailing you?'

'Money, laudanum . . . even morphine once. I came so close to getting caught.'

'You stole from the infirmary?' It was ridiculous really, but even after everything I had learned since walking in here, that shocked me the most.

'I replaced everything I could,' she said angrily. 'But if she had gone to the police like she threatened, we would have been closed down. I would have gone to prison! Everything we worked for would have been ruined, just because some silly slut died on my operating table.'

So Lucy hadn't been the first.

'It was an accident,' she whispered. 'Things go wrong in operations, you know that. Especially when you're forced to work in a tiny room with no natural light and no running water. And I was tired, so tired, Sarah.' She was tired now, leaning against the table with a look of wretched exhaustion etched on her face. 'I think the scalpel must have slipped, because suddenly there was so much blood everywhere. I knew something had gone wrong – I'd done something wrong – and it all happened so fast.' She stopped, gulping in air, and I realised she was crying. 'She was dead before I could do anything.'

'And Lucy found out?'

'Amelia was another of Ruby's girls. When she didn't return, Lucy came to me. She knew who I was – there had been girls at the reformatory; I did quite the brisk business there. That bloody curate who had them on their knees five times a day couldn't keep his hands off Caroline's chits, and she could hardly show her funders a refuge full of pregnant tarts. Lucy said she knew that Amelia was going to see me, and when I tried to deny it, she realised what had happened.'

'What did you do to Lucy?' I asked.

She laughed harshly. 'Thank God for McVeigh. That lecherous drunk has been thrown out of every brothel in the city, but it didn't take much for me to convince Ruby to open her doors to him again. Not if she wanted my help getting her sluts out of trouble. It was simple enough to get him to take Lucy's body to the dissection room along with the other unfortunates.'

It was shocking, it was illegal, but I could have understood it. Could have. Only . . .

'Lucy didn't die from a botched operation, Fiona,' I said softly.

She looked up as though she had forgotten I was there. 'Oh. No, it wouldn't have done any good. She'd have blabbed to her bloody brother whether I got rid of her brat or not.' She smiled at my expression, but there was no warmth in it. 'Oh, you worked that one out as well? Clever girl. Professor high-and-mighty Merchiston, who wouldn't sully his hands helping the likes of us down here, has a sister on the game.'

'Had,' I corrected.

'She laughed at me,' Fiona said quietly. 'Cheeks red with rouge and her belly swollen with some stranger's brat, and she laughed at me. How are we supposed to do good in the world when men call us witches or madwomen and even whores hold us in contempt? They come to us, thighs still sticky from the last man they lay with, and expect us to be able to help. We tell ourselves they wouldn't survive without us, but the truth is we can't survive without them. Nice girls don't see women like us.' She stroked my hair softly, and I found myself leaning into her touch. 'But then it's been a long time since you've been a nice girl, isn't it, Sarah?' A maternal kiss pressed against my forehead. 'I saw you, watching him at that brawl. You didn't care if he might be a murderer then, did you? Do you really think Merchiston doesn't take his fill like the rest of them? My wards are full of the women he's come in, cried over, called by his dead wife's name. Just because he gives them pleasure first and doesn't beat them afterwards doesn't make him a hero; you'd see that if you'd been thinking with your brain instead of your cunt. Instead, you're no better than they are, a silly tart who thinks a man will see past her sins and love her just the same. But they never do.' She shrugged. 'It was risky, putting her under the same roof as Merchiston, but it was all I could think of.'

'How did you know she was his sister?' I asked hoarsely.

Fiona smiled as though this was terribly funny. 'You never noticed the resemblance? Strange, I spotted it straight away. It's the eyes. They've haunted me ever since. In any case, she told me. So proud, she was, boasting about her brother over at the university who would ensure I got what I deserved. She didn't like me pointing out that he wasn't at all proud of his whore of a sister.'

'Don't call her that,' I snarled, tears pricking at the corners of my eyes. 'After everything you've done, how dare you call her that? Still, better a whore than a murderer.'

The slap took me by surprise, and I realised then just how

strong Fiona was. It wouldn't have taken much for her to overpower a slip of a thing like Lucy, malnourished as she was.

'As though you're any better,' she sneered. I felt as though someone had emptied cold water down my back. 'Oh, I know all about you, Sarah Gilchrist. I know exactly why you were sent away, why you came to Edinburgh. The gossip, the scandal, the asylum for rich young ladies who can't be controlled. What other hospital would offer a job to a woman like that?

'I'd have thought you of all people would have noticed the laudanum. You do seem to have developed quite a taste for it. Which makes my task so much easier . . .'

She picked up a bottle, and my blood ran cold. She would not let me go now, not after I had learnt every sordid little secret about her double life.

I hadn't realised until now just how very much I wanted to live. Even without a medical career, even stranded in this city away from my family. I'd marry Miles Greene if it meant getting out of this room alive. I was going to fight.

I had fought Paul Beresford. I'd scratched his face, and his friends had laughed about it afterwards, but at the time he'd called me a vicious little bitch and ripped at the neckline of my gown, and all my struggling had done me no good.

I was stronger now.

I opened my mouth to scream, but she lunged forward, forcing me to the operating bed. She fastened one wrist to the table with a thick leather strap, but I managed to scratch her cheek with my free hand. She yanked my arm so hard I felt it come loose from its socket. When she let go of me and moved to the makeshift medicine cupboard, I was almost relieved. The pain was excruciating.

She glanced at me. 'It's just enough to calm you down,

Sarah. I have plans for you.' I stared dumbly, and she showed me another bottle. Opium. 'I'm quite prepared to swear I saw you taking it from the store cupboard at the infirmary, when they finally find you. Your aunt won't be surprised, will she? I know she thinks you're no better than you ought to be. First sex, now opiates . . . she'll wonder why she ever wasted her time with you. Even if you survive, I'll make sure you have no chance of redemption. I won't have a girl like you destroying everything I've done, all the women I've tried to help. You don't deserve it, but then neither do I.'

My ankles were next, secured so tightly they hurt. I squirmed, trying to kick her, but every movement sent red-hot shards of pain shooting through my shoulder. I cried out, but she carried on talking as if we were having a pot of tea at the infirmary.

'And do men thank us? No, they spit at us in the street and turn from us when we come to ask for funding, when all we do is make their lives easier. We clear up their mess. The diseases, the pregnancies, the bruises and the botched abortions – we sweep them away and then turn the girls back out onto the street for the next man to spill his seed into. I treat girls from their first dose of the clap at twelve to the final strains of syphilis at twenty-five, and then I move on to their daughters. Don't look so shocked, Sarah – the men do the same. If you want something fresh and unsullied in this world, you'd better get them young. Innocence doesn't last long, not on the streets and not in the drawing room. And this is the life you would choose?' She shook her head. 'Don't tell me this isn't a release. Don't tell me you haven't thought of this. I can make it swift, Sarah, and I can make it painless. That's more than most people get.'

'It's more than Lucy got,' I said through clenched teeth. 'I saw the bruises, Fiona, I know she fought you.'

'Till the bitter end.' Fiona smiled sadly. 'She had some spirit in her, that one. They all do, at the start. That's what makes it so hard to watch. Every man takes a little more of a girl's fight away; you should know that by now.'

I thought of Lucy. The reformatory girls, ground down by endless penance for the smallest of sins. I thought of Ruby, bold as brass and twice as brazen, and imagined her at their age. I thought of the part of me that died a little more with every one of Julia Latymer's taunts or my aunt's frowns. Paul had hurt me, given me a vile mockery of my own desires, left me dry-mouthed and shaking at every imagined threat. But no matter what my family said, he hadn't ruined me.

'I won't end up like Lucy,' I whispered softly. 'And I won't end up like you.'

Her hand cracked against my jaw, and I felt the metallic tang of blood in my mouth. She pinched my nose roughly, and I found myself gasping for air.

'Lie still and take your medicine, like a good girl.'

The laudanum splashed onto my mouth and chin, and I choked, trying to spit it out. When she was quite sure I had failed, she forced the thick leather strap into my mouth.

It had been the favourite tool of the doctors in the sanatorium. Laudanum, chloroform, gags – why was so much of medicine devoted to shutting women up? I had been swallowing my screams for the best part of a year.

I struggled to spit out the leather, trying to speak.

'Oh, your aunt will think the worst of you, my dear. As everyone does. Do you think anyone you've blabbed to will take you seriously when you're found slumped in an opium den?'

I thought of the foul-smelling room in Fleshmarket Close, and the shame it would bring on my family if I was discovered there. 'Is there anyone in this wretched city who isn't in your pay?' I asked bitterly.

'I'm the only one who'll help them. I've saved Madame Lily's clientele from the ignominy of overdosing in a slum, the customers of half the brothels in the city from more doses of the clap than you've had hot dinners, and that deviant McVeigh from the sack, the noose or worse.'

'And Caroline Hartigan?' I asked, although I suspected the answer.

'Oh Sarah. Where did you think Ruby's girls came from? I told you they hadn't lived blameless lives. Thanks to me, the troublesome ones do a midnight flit and Miss Hartigan preserves her reputation as the rehabilitator of wayward girls.'

'While you line your pockets,' I spat. 'You call yourself a doctor? You're nothing but a procuress and a butcher!'

'Do you know what butchery looks like?' she asked quietly, her voice trembling with menace and an emotion I could not name. 'Butchery looks like waking up in skirts soaked with your own blood and piss and paying half your week's salary for the desperate hope that you might have spared the workhouse another illegitimate child.

'At least Lucy had a swift death. Who wouldn't prefer that?' She smiled bitterly. 'I know I would have.' She wiped a tear away angrily. 'I got engaged only a few years after I finished my studies. We were so in love, but I didn't want a child. I was working in a clinic in Leeds, and one of the nurses told me about a doctor who helped women in my predicament. I don't think he'd been near a medical lecture in his life, but by the time I realised that, I was half-unconscious. When I came to, I was bloody and sore, but at least it was over. I didn't have to give up my life, my career. Or so I thought.' She shook her head angrily. 'I'd picked up an infection. My fiancé accused me of taking a lover, but better that than he find out the truth and have me arrested. My family threw me out onto the streets, and if it hadn't been for the kindness of some friends, I might well have stayed there. I got away as quickly as I could and came here to start over again. But that man ruined my life. I couldn't let it happen to another girl, and so the first time someone came to me, begging me to help her . . . how could I turn her away?'

I hadn't thought I could feel sorry for Fiona. The missionary zeal I so admired had soured, and the desperation I had only ever glimpsed beneath the surface was in full force. I had thought her uncaring, but it seemed as though I had been wrong about that as well. Yet though I couldn't fault her for the choices she had made, nothing justified what she had done to Lucy.

'I leased this room, and until August, everything worked perfectly. I was helping these women in a way I never could at the clinic, not without risking exposure. But one mistake and everything I'd worked for would have been stripped from me! How could that be fair? How could I let one stupid, greedy girl take away everything I had built here? The infirmary is only running because I can bring in the money to keep it open. If I weren't here, the place would tumble to the ground. They need me, Sarah, you know that.'

'Then let me leave here and I won't say a word. I promise, Fiona. Let me help you. You're tired. You're not thinking clearly.'

'I've been tired for years, but I'm thinking perfectly clearly.' She sighed. 'Sometimes I think I'm the only one who is.'

'I won't tell a soul, Fiona, I swear,' I whispered hoarsely, trembling so hard my lips could barely form the words. 'But why kill Miss Hartigan?'

'Your aunt saw to that,' she spat. 'With her bloody money,

there was no need to pay Ruby for her more troublesome charges to disappear. She was terrified that she'd be discovered, so when a rich benefactress came along, she was more than willing to sever ties. She even replaced me as their physician! Let that be a lesson, Sarah – every time you think life can't possibly get more unfair, it does.'

She smiled suddenly, and that echo of the woman I thought I knew was somehow more terrifying than her fury.

'You know, Hartigan thought you were there because of me. When she heard you were studying to be a doctor, she thought I'd sent you to blackmail her. She would have said something eventually. A pity, really. I made quite a profit from her and Ruby.' She shook her head sadly. 'That stupid bitch. I should never have involved Ruby in the first place. But she paid me such a good price for the morphine I delivered to keep her sluts docile, far more than it was worth. What does it matter if the clinic was a few bottles lighter than it should have been?' She smiled bitterly. 'Morphine and whores, Sarah. That's what my precious infirmary is built on. Still feel virtuous?'

'Then let me help,' I begged. 'Let me leave, and I'll do what I can. I'll make it a condition of my bloody engagement if I have to – he's a rich man. We can keep the infirmary open without all this, I promise.'

She stroked my hair gently, and that one small kindness told me that nothing I said now would save me.

'I thought when you came along, with your bleeding heart and your rich relatives, that you might save us. I really did. But you're dangerous, Sarah. You could ruin everything.'

There was a sound outside the door. Indicating threateningly that I was to keep silent, she edged towards it just as the wood splintered and a figure came crashing into the room.

From my vantage point, what happened next was a blur. All

I was aware of was the glint of a blade, the spurt of crimson blood against the wall and the body of Fiona Leadbetter collapsing into the arms of Gregory Merchiston, and then everything went black.

Chapter 40

The smell of carbolic soap revived me better than any smelling salts, and as I regained consciousness for the second time that day, I opened my eyes to see Professor Merchiston on his hands and knees, scrubbing the floor, frothy pink foam covering his large hands as he washed away Fiona Leadbetter's blood. With consciousness came the tearing pain from my shoulder. I retched, but little came out besides bile. It was enough to draw Merchiston's attention, however, and he looked up.

'Thank God,' he sighed heavily.

He sat on the bed next to me, the perfect image of the concerned physician, and unbuckled the straps around my wrists and ankles, massaging my wrists tenderly before taking my pulse. His fingers were cold and wet, but the human contact reassured me that this was no delirium.

'Your shoulder is dislocated – subclavicular anterior dislocation, to be precise. Fiona?'

I nodded.

'At least she kept the place stocked with drugs. Here,' he said, passing me a bottle of morphine.

I shrank back. 'Not that. I'd rather have the pain. She tried to . . . I'd rather be conscious, if it's all the same to you. I won't scream,' I added dully. Now that my pulse was returning to normal, I realised how sore my throat was, how sore every part of me was. Fiona had prevailed in the end – I had no voice, no fight left.

'You're a braver woman than I, Miss Gilchrist. I dislocated mine in the ring ten years ago and cried for my mother.' Moving his attention to my shoulder, he ran his hand over it lightly. I whimpered in pain. 'This may hurt a little,' he said apologetically.

'Remember I'm a medical student, Professor,' I said. 'I know what that mea— *Oh dear sweet Christ!*'

It hurt a lot more than a little. I continued to curse like a navvy as Merchiston fashioned some muslin from the cupboard into a makeshift sling, biting back another scream as he eased my arm into it. I let out a ragged breath. It hurt like hell, but at least I could move.

We sat in silence for a moment as the events of the past hour caught up with me. I was so tired that when the tears came, I couldn't have held them back if I had wanted to.

'She murdered Lucy,' I whispered.

'I never saw it,' he said, voice roughened with grief and lack of sleep. 'Not until . . .'

'How did you realise I was here?' I asked blearily.

'McVeigh,' he sighed. 'He wasn't so bloody brave when I was interrogating him. By the time he'd told me where Fiona kept her room, you'd already left. I thought I was too late. Here, drink this. It might help with the pain.'

He handed me a flask, and I gulped, only to choke as it burnt my throat.

'Are you trying to poison me?' I spluttered. 'What was that?'

'A Speyside single malt older than you are,' he grumbled. 'Remind me not to waste good Scotch on you again.'

I tried to look suitably shamefaced, especially since the jumble of words he had responded with made it sound as though the noxious liquid had probably been expensive, but given that I felt like I had swallowed something out of the university chemistry labs, it probably wasn't very convincing.

'I thought it might be good for shock,' he explained.

'Isn't that brandy?'

'I was in a hurry!' he exploded. 'Tillie Campbell had informed me that you, fool that you are, had gone off to the slums with a woman I'd just realised was a murderess. I'm sorry if I didn't stop to choose something more appropriate!'

I nodded shakily. 'I never thought I'd be grateful to McVeigh.'

'I had to swear he wouldn't lose his position over it – a promise, I'm sorry to say, I'll have to keep if I don't want the whole university to know what my sister was. I'd gladly have seen him sacked if it wouldn't doom me into the bargain. And I'd see Fiona swinging from the gallows if I hadn't had to . . .'

It was only a fraction of a second, but I saw his eyes dart to a corner of the room. I followed his gaze, and stared uncomprehendingly at the object covered by a rough blanket. When reality dawned on me, I began to scream. He pressed his fingers against my mouth in a desperate attempt to hush me, and I struggled as best I could despite the hazy effects of the chloroform.

'It was self-defence,' he said when I quieted enough for him to remove his hand. 'I don't know if you realise,' he added grimly, 'but Dr Leadbetter was bloody strong.' I noticed a scratch on his face, and that his torn shirt was sticking to him in damp red patches.

I felt my own bruises gingerly. 'She was,' I conceded quietly. Was. I stared at the lumpen shape, unable to take my eyes away from the body of the woman I had thought was my friend. I didn't know what was harder to believe: that she had been deceiving me all along, that she had been the one to kill Lucy – or that she was dead. Suddenly my throat filled with acid vomit, and I emptied the paltry contents of my stomach all over the floor.

Merchiston handed me a relatively clean rag, and I wiped my face and dress as best I could. He was lost in thought.

'Lucy was blackmailing her.' I didn't want to tell him, but there was nothing to be gained by keeping it a secret, and he deserved to know why his sister had died.

'She needed the money,' Merchiston sighed. 'I gave her what I could, but my salary isn't exactly . . .' He trailed off. 'Perhaps if I'd been more generous, she wouldn't have threatened Fiona. Christ, she should never have fallen into Ruby's clutches in the first place but she was so bloody stubborn.'

'You did everything you could,' I told him, although I had no way of knowing whether or not it was true.

'She should never have had to go to Fiona to get rid of the child. I'd have done it for her; how could she not have known that?' His voice was raw with pain, but his words shocked me. 'Oh, don't look at me like that. The women in these slums can barely afford to feed the children they have. If they want to end a pregnancy, there are countless ways to do it. I'd rather they be seen by a doctor, especially a woman doctor, than by some of the back-street butchers around here.'

'You could be struck off for saying that,' I said, appalled.

'I had no idea she was even pregnant,' he said brokenly. 'I'm sorry to say it, but it did occur to me that you were just trying to get a reaction out of me.'

'It worked,' I pointed out. 'Would you really have had me expelled?'

He looked affronted. 'Of course not. You have a lot of

potential, Sarah. I'd hate to see that go to waste. But I couldn't risk you getting caught up in this. I was in danger enough, but a woman, alone?'

'I think Fiona Leadbetter proved just how resourceful one woman can be,' I said grimly. 'What are you – we – going to do with . . . ?' I waved my hand in the general direction of her body.

'We can't dispose of her here. There's a gentleman with a fishing trawler who owes me a favour. He can see to it.'

Not for the first time, it occurred to me that Gregory Merchiston had a number of unsavoury acquaintances.

'She has no family to speak of,' he continued. 'I believe there is a great-aunt somewhere, Carlisle perhaps, but no one close. She had very few friends and those she had, she kept at arm's length.' He looked at me. 'I think you might have been the closest person to her.'

Despite what Fiona had done, and what she had tried to do to me, his words made me unbearably sad. I remembered the look in her eyes as she had locked the door. If there had been another way to silence me, I think she would have taken it. But mixed with the remorse, there had been something else, a queer sort of excitement. In the end, she had killed for the sake of killing, deliberately blind to all her other options. She had played games with the lives of vulnerable people as though they were chess pieces, and for all her kindness to me, I would never truly be able to forgive her.

'We should leave,' Merchiston sighed. 'I'll hire a cart and call my friendly fisherman once I've delivered you safely home. You need half-decent medical attention, and I can't give it to you here.'

'No,' I murmured. 'Not my aunt's. Anywhere but there. Take me to the infirmary.' I was aware that my words were slurring, but I couldn't bring myself to care.

He shook his head. 'Too many questions. Especially with . . .' He stared at Fiona's corpse with an expression I couldn't identify. Regret, perhaps. Not something I would have expected from him. Then again, I recalled Fiona's tortured, desperate expression as she had stood over me.

He pulled me to my feet, but it became quickly apparent that I couldn't stand unaided. With his arm around my waist to support me, I partly stumbled and was partly dragged across the floor. By the time we got to the stairs, it was clear he was going to have to carry me. When he scooped me up, I was too tired to object.

The lamplighter had been down here, I realised. The street was bathed in flickering light, and somehow the shadows were more threatening than the darkness had been.

I was dimly aware of being bundled into a carriage, but I was so tired that I couldn't bring myself to care. As we jolted down the poorly paved street, the pain invaded my consciousness and I mumbled a curse.

'You're awake,' Merchiston said. 'Good.'

I grunted, although whether it was out of pain or at his lack of sympathy, even I wasn't sure.

'Sarah, you need to stay awake. You have a concussion, and you know what that means.' My eyes drooped. 'Sarah! Tell me the symptoms of a concussion.'

I did so reluctantly, wanting nothing more than to close my eyes.

'Very good,' he said soothingly. 'Now, how would you treat it?'

I told him, stumbling over the words.

We carried on like this, him quizzing me about basic diagnoses, me providing the answers through a haze of pain. The part of me that was awake enough to respond wondered if this would count toward my end-of-term examinations.

Chapter 41

It was dark outside, and I had no idea where we were. I tried to retrace the path Fiona had led me in my mind, but my brain kept flitting from memory to memory, like stones skimming across a pond. Eventually I realised that we were heading through the Meadows, the moon hovering over the castle and bathing it in eerie light. Despite Merchiston's best efforts, I faded in and out of consciousness as we travelled; the smoother road meant the jolting of the carriage bothered my injuries less, although my head still throbbed. As we clattered to a halt, and he lifted me gently out of the cab, I realised he was carrying me towards an open front door, light and voices spilling out into the street.

'Merchiston, thank God. We've been worried out of our minds. You should have let me come with you, man, not sent a bloody note!'

'Is Sarah safe?' I recognised that voice, but when my brain scrabbled for a name, I drew a blank. I just knew it meant safety, friendship, tea and honeyed crumpets by the fire as we talked. *Elisabeth*. She clutched my hand as we went inside the house, talking frantically. 'Gregory, is she all right? Lord, she's black and blue. What did that bitch do to her?' I had never heard her so angry.

I felt an odd juddering against my cheek, and realised that Merchiston was laughing as he lowered me to a sofa.

'He's hysterical,' I heard Professor Chalmers say. 'Gregory, for God's sake, get hold of yourself! Eilidh, can you fetch Professor Merchiston a pot of coffee? Black and sweet, as strong as you can make it.'

I felt a cold, damp cloth against my forehead, and gingerly opened my eyes. Although the light hurt at first, as my eyes adjusted I realised that the lamps were turned down low and the grate was glowing with the beginnings of a fire.

Elisabeth sat by my side, her eyes red with weeping.

'You're awake.' She sighed with relief. 'My dear, we were so worried about you. Gregory made us promise not to send a policeman. He knew you couldn't be dragged into another scandal.'

'What on earth possessed you to go off with that madwoman?' Merchiston growled.

'Come now, Gregory, Fiona Leadbetter fooled everyone,' Randall chided. 'I wouldn't have believed it myself if Sarah hadn't gone missing.'

'How long has it been?' I asked. Hours could have passed, or days; I had no idea.

Randall glanced at the clock on the mantelpiece. 'It's nearly one in the morning.'

'Aunt Emily,' I murmured. 'She's going to be furious.' The reality of the situation settled on me, and I struggled to sit up. 'My God, she'll throw me out! I have to go home. No, Elisabeth, leave me alone, I have to get back to the house.'

'It's all right,' Elisabeth soothed. 'When we realised where you had gone, I sent a message saying that you were spending the night with me because I had been taken ill.' She grimaced.

'Of course, now your aunt thinks I'm in a certain condition. She sent the most effusively euphemistic reply I've ever read. Why you British can't learn to speak plainly, I have no idea.'

I heard Randall and Merchiston talking in low voices as Elisabeth tried to distract me by telling me how brave I was. I caught words here and there.

'Fiona,' I said. 'We left her there. We can't just leave her there, we can't.' Tears choked me, running hot down my cheeks. I convulsed, shuddering with sobs, crying for the friend I had lost, who had found herself in a situation that had spiralled so quickly out of her limited control.

'We didn't leave her there,' Merchiston corrected.

Randall whirled around, staring at him in amazement.

'You brought her here? What the hell did you think you were doing?'

'I couldn't risk the body being discovered,' he said. 'And believe me, the cabbie won't talk. I know him of old, and he has a great deal more to lose by talking than I do.' He ran a hand through his hair. 'I'm sorry, I'll send him away. My housekeeper won't ask questions.'

Beneath the horror and exhaustion of the evening, I felt terribly sad. Whilst Lucy at least had people to mourn her, there would be nowhere to go for Fiona's friends and colleagues. What would we even tell them?

'She did a lot of good,' I whispered. 'She deserves to be remembered for that, at least.'

'Would you have been so bloody magnanimous if it had been me after all?' Merchiston said. 'I don't deny that Fiona helped a great number of people, but why the hell should she get a memorial?'

I shrugged, wincing at the nagging ache in my shoulder. We were sitting in Elisabeth's parlour, discussing the best way to dispose of a body. I wasn't in the mood to argue morality.

'If we leave her to be discovered, there's a chance the trail will lead back to us.'

'The river?' Elisabeth's voice shook. I squeezed her hand, grateful beyond words that she was staying so calm in a crisis that must have horrified her.

Merchiston shook his head. 'It won't wash. I'm afraid that her body . . . well, the way she died is obvious. I know someone taking his boat out on the Forth this morning, he owes me enough favours not to ask questions.'

I remembered that sickening sound of knife entering flesh, and the shocked look on her face before her eyes had rolled back. I heaved again, spluttering and dribbling bile on Elisabeth and myself. True to form, she simply mopped it up with the damp cloth, although she did look faintly disgusted as she did it.

'Lucky you've got a good nurse there, eh, Sarah?' Randall smiled gently. I tried to smile back, but all I could manage was a grimace.

'Perhaps I've found my calling,' Elisabeth said with forced lightness. 'Can she sleep yet?'

The doctors shook their heads in unison.

'I wouldn't risk it. Perhaps coffee?' Merchiston suggested.

His sallow skin was even paler than usual, and there were dark shadows under his eyes. Fiona had clearly landed a few good punches – there was a shiner on his cheekbone, and his jaw had been clawed where a five o'clock shadow crept across his face. He looked drained, and I couldn't blame him. No matter how horrible my ordeal, his was much worse. He had come face to face with his sister's murderer and killed her all in the same night. It was a miracle he wasn't in pieces, and I didn't know whether to be impressed or frightened by his resilience. He turned and caught me staring, and I couldn't account for the blush that crept across my cheeks. Before I could look away, his eyes locked onto mine, and for a moment I found myself unable to breathe. Then, with what looked like an act of will, he tore his gaze away and rose.

'But first a bath,' Elisabeth said firmly. 'And some fresh clothes. For both of you.'

'And then breakfast,' I pleaded. All of a sudden I was starving. Elisabeth rang the bell, and I realised that she was turning the household upside down for us without a second thought.

She helped me upstairs, and summoned her lady's maid, hastily dressed and fuzzy with sleep, to pour me a bath and help me undress. The water was hot and scented with roses and lavender, too relaxing really for my fragile state. Elisabeth prevented me from dozing off by splashing me repeatedly every time I looked as though I were closing my eyes, and before long we were giggling like schoolgirls. She washed my hair for me, and I revelled in her touch. After Fiona's assault and the odd, lingering sensations Merchiston's hands had left, it was a relief just to be cared for. I thought of the way I had hurt her, with the best of intentions and the worst of results.

'I'm sorry, Elisabeth – for what I said about Randall. I jumped to conclusions. He's a good man, and a devoted husband. I know he'd never hurt you.'

She hugged me tightly. 'You were just trying to help. Plenty of people would have said nothing, or laughed at me behind my back. You just wanted to protect me.'

She wrapped me in a towel, the way my nursemaid used to do when I was a child, and found me some clean clothes.

I was surprised to discover that one of Elisabeth's old dresses fitted me, and said as much.

'I put on a little weight last autumn,' she said in an odd, tight voice. 'It didn't last.' She turned away, but I divined her meaning and crushed her into a hug.

'Don't tell anyone,' she whispered. 'I couldn't bear the pity.'

'I think you know enough of my secrets for me to share the burden for once,' I murmured into her hair, stroking rhythmic circles on her back as I felt silent tears soak through the fabric.

Chapter 42

Considerably cleaner, I made my way downstairs to discover an impressive breakfast laid out on the dining room table. Tucking into a plate of kippers and black pudding – not a combination I would have chosen, but it looked delicious just then – with the sleeves of a fresh shirt pushed up to his elbows, was Merchiston. Realising we were alone in the room, I found myself tongue-tied.

'Would you care for some coffee, Miss Gilchrist?' he asked through a mouthful of kipper.

So we were back on formal terms. The thought made me feel something akin to sadness.

I nodded. 'Please, Professor.' He looked as though he were going to object to my use of his title, but whatever he was going to say he forced back, and handed me my coffee in silence.

'Try the devilled kidneys,' he offered. 'They're very good.' From the state of his plate and the platters left by the servants, I realised he was on his second helping, at least.

'I shouldn't have spent so long in the bath,' I apologised, helping myself to toast, bacon, eggs and the devilled kidneys, which smelt as good as Merchiston had promised. 'But Lord, it feels wonderful to be clean again!'

He was focusing on his breakfast very intently, and the slightest flush of colour mingled with the bruises on his face. The realisation that I had embarrassed him made my cheeks burn, but I was somehow secretly pleased. I took a gulp of the scalding coffee to find it just as sweet as I liked it, and tucked into my own plate with gusto.

At length I noticed that he had finished and was resting on his elbows, watching me curiously. It was on the tip of my tongue to scold him and tell him to remove his elbows from the table, but I fought the impulse. I remembered Fiona, and the swift, practised way he had dispatched her. It wouldn't do, I warned myself, to get too friendly with him.

'What?' I scowled.

'I wanted . . .' He trailed off, looking as though he wished he hadn't spoken. He opened his mouth again, but then shook his head and sipped his coffee. I suddenly wanted very much to hear what he had to say.

'Professor Merchiston?' I asked tentatively. 'What is it?'

'I wanted to tell you about Lucy,' he said in a rush. I was touched at how willing he was to confide in me, and yet somehow disappointed, although I could not have put into words exactly what it was I had wanted him to say.

I nodded slowly. This, I realised, was what I had needed all along. Not just to find her killer and bring him – *her*, I reminded myself, with an odd, aching pain I suspected would never leave me – to justice. I had wanted to know Lucy, not just for what she did, but also for who she was.

'Please,' I said softly. 'I think I would like that very much.'

He talked about the little girl she had been, and the rebellious woman she had grown into. Of the plans she had had for her life and the existence she had eked out in the slums, too stubbornly proud to accept more than the occasional coin from her brother. He talked about the mother she could have been, about how they could have raised her child together.

He laid his head on his arms and sobbed quietly. I marvelled at his lack of self-consciousness, but he was beyond embarrassment or even anger now. This was raw pain, a pain I suspected he had not allowed himself to feel until now. He had been fuelled by anger, as I had been, I realised. I stood, and went to him, putting my arms around him tenderly. After a while, the gasping sobs subsided, but I carried on stroking his back the way I had soothed Elisabeth, enjoying the heat of his body against mine.

I must have come to the same realisation of what we were doing as he did, and at the same time. It was as though we had both suddenly woken from a dream, and as I pulled my hand back, he lifted his head to look at me. His eyes were wet, and darker than I had ever seen them, but for a moment I thought he was no longer heartbroken.

His gaze lingered on my mouth, and I felt it almost like a touch. I felt his breath on my lips and I opened them, acting on some primal instinct. His head moved closer, or maybe mine did. I couldn't tell, wasn't thinking; I just knew that I needed him closer to me but that somehow he would never be close enough.

'Sarah, I—'

We pulled back so quickly it was almost comical. Elisabeth stood in the doorway, blushing so deeply that it clashed with her hair.

She looked flummoxed, but it was gone in a moment and the facade of the perfect hostess descended, although her eyes sparkled.

'Do you have quite enough coffee there, Gregory?' she asked sweetly, as if he had not been so close to her unmarried friend that he was practically kissing me. I banished the thought from my mind, and moved back to my own seat on shaky legs that had little, I suspected, to do with the previous night's ordeal.

He cleared his throat, looking everywhere except at either Elisabeth or myself.

'Plenty, thank you, Elisabeth.' He lifted his coffee cup as if to illustrate his point, making a face when he saw it was empty. He looked comical in his flustered embarrassment, and I realised that however frightened I had been of him before, he was ten times more dangerous like this, rumpled and vulnerable. Elisabeth's eyes caught mine, making it clear in that indefinable way that women have when they communicate with one another without words that very soon we were going to have a conversation about the scene she had just witnessed. I sipped my own coffee, only to realise that I had left it to go stone cold as I had listened to Gregory – to Professor Merchiston – talk.

'I told your aunt you would be back for luncheon,' Elisabeth said. 'Randall says you can rest now – do you think you can sleep for a few hours?'

I was tired, more tired than I had ever been in my entire life, but more than that, I wanted to get away from Gregory Merchiston in the hope that I could leave the emotions he stirred in me in the dining room as well. I think I knew even then that it would not be that easy.

I followed Elisabeth upstairs.

'I think I might have to invite you both over for afternoon tea this week,' she said, a note of teasing warning in her voice.

I just shrugged, beyond caring about the promised interrogation, and pulled the cool, crisp sheets over me, asleep before she had even quit the room.

When I awoke, birds were singing. I went downstairs

only to be met with the sight of Merchiston pulling on his greatcoat.

'I apologise,' he said in a low voice, 'if it appeared earlier that I was about to take advantage of your weakened state. I can assure you that nothing was further from my mind.'

I wanted to tell him that he was wrong, that I had been neither weak nor taken advantage of, but I sensed he knew that perfectly well, and his subterfuge was as much for him as it was for me. There was, however, one last thing I needed to say to him.

'Professor, I am afraid I have judged you very harshly these past weeks. I believed you guilty of some of the worst crimes imaginable, and I never once allowed you to defend yourself to me. I know what it's like to be convicted in public opinion when you know there is more to the story than is being discussed over afternoon tea across the city.' I smiled bitterly, and he covered my hand with his own gloved one. 'I owe you my life, Professor Merchiston, but more than that, I owe you my forgiveness. Please accept it along with my friendship.'

I had seen him smile before, but it had never reached his eyes. I felt this was not an offer he was accustomed to getting, and was all the more precious for it.

'Miss Gilchrist,' he said formally, taking my hand and shaking it firmly. 'I would be honoured to consider you a friend. But I must warn you' – he looked at me with an echo of his former sternness – 'that I did not save your life only to have you fail your winter-term examinations. May I have your word that you will stay out of trouble – for the rest of this term at least?'

I found myself smiling more broadly than I remembered smiling in a very long time. Despite the nightmarish events of the night before, I was somehow very happy.

I held out my hand once more, trying to push to the back

of my mind just how eager I was to have this contact.

'I promise,' I vowed with a smile. 'In fact, I can safely say that my days of investigating are firmly behind me.'

He raised an eyebrow quizzically, but took my hand all the same.

'You will forgive me, Miss Gilchrist, if I do not entirely believe that. In fact, I distinctly remember myself saying the same thing to Dr Bell once.'

I stared at him as realisation dawned.

'Dr Bell? Dr Joseph Bell? The man who inspired Conan Doyle to create . . .'

He cleared his throat awkwardly. 'Sherlock Holmes, yes. Bell had some unusual ideas about the detection of crime, and as a student with an interest in pharmacology and poisons, our paths crossed. He provided some much-needed assistance early on in my career. In fact, he was the one who suggested I work with the local constabulary; he thought I had a flair for it.'

I gasped. 'You investigated a crime with Sherlock Holmes?'

'I asked Dr Bell's advice on a particularly tricky strangulation case,' he replied sharply. 'I assure you, Miss Gilchrist, no pipes, violins or hounds were involved.'

The carriage drew up on the street outside.

I raised an eyebrow. 'After you, my dear Watson.'

Above the grey stone buildings, the morning mist was starting to lift. The heavy grey clouds began to pinken with the morning sun, and I could see how the events of the night had aged Gregory Merchiston's tired face.

'We should go home,' I whispered softly, taking his arm. He looked surprised at the touch, but not displeased. He nodded wearily, and tucked my elbow beneath his. Careful of my shoulder, which was still throbbing with pain, he helped me into the carriage, and for one microscopic moment, I thought he was going to kiss me. But the moment passed, as these moments tend to do, and he simply climbed in after me. I wasn't disappointed, but I wasn't frightened either. I knew that the look in his eyes had less to do with lust and more to do with a kind of respect I had never known before.

'What will your aunt and uncle say?' he asked as we jolted forwards.

I shrugged helplessly. 'I wish I knew. It's doubtful they'll want me to leave the house again, let alone practise medicine. Or perhaps they'll throw me out onto the streets.'

'They might surprise you,' he said softly.

I smiled. 'Perhaps. I haven't exactly proved myself to be a perfect judge of character lately.'

'I'll speak for you.'

'They'll assume you're my lover.' I sighed tiredly. 'If it gets out that we've spent any time together outside of the lecture theatre, most people will.'

His fists clenched, but his voice was even. 'And that doesn't bother you?'

'Of course it does. But I can't control how people see me, and I'm tired of living my life as though I'm ashamed of things that aren't my fault.'

'I'll still speak for you,' he repeated. His words, and the uncompromising tone in which he said them, brought a smile to my face. He was damning his own reputation by standing by me, but he didn't care. Perhaps I reminded him of Lucy, or perhaps he would have been a man of principle either way. Perhaps there was something else, something neither of us was ready to name, and might never be.

Whatever the reason, I was grateful for his support, and as we passed through the slums of the Cowgate towards the New Town, where life was less hard and vastly more complicated, I felt a renewed surge of confidence.

Whatever the future held, of one thing I was certain – I was going to become a doctor, no matter what it took. I could only pray that when I succeeded, I had even a fraction of the courage of the man sitting next to me.

I had no idea then of quite how much courage I was going to need.

Acknowledgements

This book would not have been possible without the support and input of some very wonderful people:

Lola, whose support, enthusiasm and faith in me has kept me going through difficult times and been a source of continued delight through the good – writing this book is only the second best decision I've ever made. My father without whose medical advice, motivation and good Scotch this book may never have been written. The all-powerful Newby matriarchy (and David) are the dictionary definition of family, and probably a few other more colourful words as well. Thanks to Ruth, Lis, Karen and Cathryn for all the advice, passionfruit daquiris, corsets and *Dr Quinn, Medicine Woman* marathons; to my writing coven, Lucy Ribchester, Lynsey May and Kirsty Logan and to Cat Valente, Deanna Raybourn and Lilit Marcus for providing excellent writing role models. And thank you to my unofficial sister-in-law Lande, for all her support.

I owe a huge debt of thanks to Laura Macdougall, agent extraordinaire, to my terrific editor Imogen Taylor and to Sarah Savitt for falling in love with Sarah. Thanks to everyone at Headline for making this such a wonderful experience.

Above all, this book is about sisterhood – if I know anything about that it's thanks to Clare, who has always had my back.

THE WAGES of SIN

Bonus Material

The Character of Edinburgh

Q&A with Kaite Welsh

The Wages of Sin began as my love letter to Edinburgh, long before I thought I'd live there again. It's a strange sort of love letter, blood-spattered and angry, and at the start my narrator, Sarah Gilchrist, doesn't even like it very much. Sarah is not in Edinburgh by choice – she's been exiled by her rich family following a scandal that leaves her free to pursue the medical degree she's always wanted – and the dreich weather and grey stone buildings reflect her state of mind at the start of the book.

As a student I had Classics lectures in a wing of the old medical school and every day I passed two plaques, one to Sophia Jex-Blake, the first woman to study medicine at Edinburgh, and one to Arthur Conan Doyle who found his own literary inspiration there. Feminist history and Victorian crime – it was clear that the Venn diagram of my interests overlapped at the University of Edinburgh. The idea of a female medical student who investigated murders, bound by a corset and restrictive gender roles, began to take root.

I began the novel when I was living in London and missing Edinburgh like a lost lover – the kind you technically can live without, you'd just rather not. I crammed the book into the nooks and crannies of my life, writing on the Tube, at lunch, at night, and as I went about my life in 21st century London,

I felt the constant thrum of Victorian Edinburgh like an engine. It wasn't until I was packing my things and signing the rental agreement on a flat in Leith that my soon-to-be-agent got in touch, proof if I needed it that moving home was the right thing to do. Once I lived here the book began to change subtly, my surroundings infusing my writing the way the smell of hops seep into my hair and clothes (and, confusingly, sofa cushions).

Wandering the Old Town in search for inspiration, I often find myself tugged down a particular wynd or side street where a plot point starts to develop. Oscar de Muriel, whose novels also take place in Victorian Edinburgh, once told me a story about successfully navigating the city armed only with a map from the 1880s. I've been known to give directions using landmarks that no longer exist and I've found myself purposefully striding to the clinic where Sarah meets Lucy, the woman whose death – and unhappy life – she finds herself avenging, only to remember that it doesn't exist and I wouldn't be qualified to work there if it did. As it happens, the place where I located the clinic is now a restaurant and looking around and saying excitedly 'I've killed someone in here!' will result in the waiter avoiding you for the whole evening. Sometimes, when I'm stuck or (more likely) procrastinating, I find myself avoiding entire areas of the city because I feel guilty that I'm not writing. Conversely, the best spaces for me to write are the places where I used to write my essays as a student. I have a specific table at Elephants and Bagels where I wrote 13,000 words one day – and got through an entire loyalty card thanks to a lot of coffee – and then there's the National Library of Scotland's archives that let me slice into the seedy underbelly of the city and dissect its contents. It's easier to write near the university, it tricks my mind into forgetting what era I'm in.

I have three Edinburghs in my head – Sarah's, with its

carriages and slums, the Edinburgh of my student days seen through a haze of lectures, alcohol and ill-advised kisses, and my present life. There are places where these worlds intersect and places I go to escape, where the veil between the living and the fictional dead are stronger, but I always find myself coming back through the Cowgate or over George IV Bridge to the shadowed, solemn courtyard of the medical school, hunting out Sarah's next mystery.

Q & A

Your protagonist, Sarah Gilchrist, lives at a time when being a female medical student was deeply controversial, and it makes for a brilliant premise. How did you come up with this idea?

I've always been fascinated by the entrance of women into the professions. I devoured Philip Pullman's 'Sally Lockhart' series as a teenager, and the intersection of that with the gothic and frequently gory world of Victorian medicine was irresistible. I read textbooks for fun, because that's the kind of super-cool teenage girl I was, and ended up knowing far more about 19th century medical advances and legal cases than any 15-year-old should. Then I discovered grunge and riot grrrl (which I still love) and boys (that phase didn't stick) and only came back to my first loves when I was studying at the University of Edinburgh and found two plaques in the old medical school – one to Sophia Jex-Blake, the first woman to be admitted as a medical student, and one to Arthur Conan Doyle, creator of Sherlock Holmes.

So have you known for some time that you wanted to write historical fiction?

Yes, it's always been historical for me. That's probably 50–60% of what I read for pleasure – either historical fiction, chunky Victorian novels or biographies.

My aunt runs education and engagement programmes in museums, so there were always opportunities as a child to dress up as a bedraggled apprentice in a cotton mill or as one of the Brontë sisters. Writing historical fiction lets me slip into another time period without the pressure of having to give the mob-cap or jar of leeches back at the end of the day.

If I hadn't been a writer, I'd have liked to be an historian or a time traveller. I always keep an eye out for the TARDIS, just in case.

The Wages of Sin has been described as a 'feminist historical crime novel'. Was it important to you that it was a feminist novel, or did that just come from the story itself?

I don't think I could write a book that wasn't feminist. I can't switch that part of my brain off, and frankly I don't want to. It's not as though I'm going to run out of material any time soon, sadly.

You brilliantly evoke Victorian Edinburgh. What were your key resources? What helped you to immerse yourself in the era?

It helps that a lot of Edinburgh hasn't physically changed that much! If I need to absorb myself in Sarah's time period I just wander around the old medical school building, or the Old

Quad where the law library is, and find scenes coming to life in my imagination. The Cowgate, where a lot of the action takes place, is now full of clubs and student accommodation rather than slum dwellings and brothels, but it's somehow still dark and unsettling even on the brightest day.

In terms of research, Elaine Thomson's brilliant PhD thesis on Victorian women doctors in Edinburgh was invaluable. I remember reading it and just being delighted that someone else shared my weird obsession. A few years later, I was having lunch with the wonderful historical novelist E.S. Thomson and she mentioned the PhD she'd written. Thankfully, although we cover similar topics we have different time periods – she has 1840s apothecary Jem Flockhart, a woman who has to live as a man in order to pursue her profession.

I also found the 1892 *Edinburgh Student Songbook* in a second-hand bookshop in Yorkshire, quite by chance. It's full of bizarre in-jokes and song parodies about the professors and gave me a real flavour of what student life was like. I've written a full-length parody of *A Very Modern Major General* called *A Very Modern-Minded Graduette*, which may or may not make it into a later book (but which I can, given enough gin, be persuaded to sing).

What was your favourite nugget of research that you came across (a fact, an anecdote, a picture, a story), and did it make it into the book?

There's a scene fairly early on where some of the male students spread red ink powder on the lecture theatre benches, so it covers the women's skirts and makes it look like they've been menstruating. It's so horrible but so vivid. I remember reading it in the archives of the National Library of Scotland, then turning my phone back on when I left, to see that someone had tweeted in response to an opinion piece I'd written in the *Telegraph*: 'Oh, she must be on her period.' Nothing changes.

I'm currently working on a piece about the history of trolling for BBC Scotland's The Social, and it's fascinating but infuriating.

What other parallels do you see between Sarah's world and the modern world? How far have we come?

Every time we take a step forward for women's rights, it seems like we take two steps back. Sarah spends her life fighting for the right to be taken seriously in her profession. Before November 2016, I thought women had won that battle. But every woman who aims for success makes cracks in the glass ceiling, whether it's a plucky Victorian medical student or a Presidential candidate.

Tell us about your path to publication: was it a rocky road or a smooth slide?

Suspiciously smooth – I'm still waiting for the other shoe to drop! I'd queried a few agents and was implementing their editorial suggestions when the wonderful Laura Macdougall, then a commissioning editor at Hodder and Stoughton, dropped me a line. She'd seen the opening chapters on my website and wondered if I had an agent. I explained I was still querying and she explained she was looking to make the move from editor to agent, but in the meantime she'd love to see the full manuscript. A month or so later, the postman delivered a hand-annotated copy of my book full of lovely compliments and useful amendments, and a box of chocolate biscuits to help with the editorial process. We then ended up judging the

Green Carnation Prize together and realised we had similar taste in books. Once she joined Tibor Jones & Associates, there was no looking back.

How do you go about structuring your novels? Do you plan tightly, or plunge right it? And has it changed for your second novel?

Plunge right into it, get around 20,000 words in and wish I'd planned. That gives me enough time to have gotten a sense of what kind of story I'm trying to tell without having gone so far that if I'm going off-course. The next 10,000 words are sheer torture but after that, I can see the way ahead.

I like being surprised when I write, seeing what bubbles to the surface. I started *Wages* with a vague idea of who Lucy's murderer was, only to realise halfway through that I was wrong. With the second book, which I've just turned in, I was writing a confession scene only for the supposed murderer to implicate someone else entirely!

And what's been the hardest part of the writing process so far?

Definitely battling self-doubt. I thought that would evaporate after I got a book deal, but no chance!

***The Wages of Sin* is the first in a series. Can you tell us anything about what Sarah will be up to next, or are you keeping your cards close to your chest?**

Sarah's view of the world is pretty black and white at the start of *Wages*. Over the second book, she's figuring out the direction of her own moral compass while trying to extricate herself from a tricky situation and solve a murder that's much closer to home. Also, there's haggis.

I actually have about five or six more books in the series loosely outlined that I'm desperate to write. I'm starting Book 3 at the moment and I'm nowhere near done playing in Sarah's world.

If you do ever tire of the 19th century, which other historical eras would you like to explore?

I'd love to tackle Renaissance France during Catherine de Medici's regency. I have an outline for another series about the group of noble women she called her 'Flying Squad': well-born courtesans who acted as spies. As well as Sarah Gilchrist, there are two Victorian standalone novels I want to write and I'd like to have a go at the Regency period as well. Oh, and the French Revolution. Basically, I have a very long list of things I want to write and not enough time to write them in. Maybe one day I'll even write something contemporary. Who knows.

And now, my most important question: how many buttered crumpets did you eat while writing *The Wages of Sin*? I ask this because I seem to have eaten rather a lot while reading it. And what are your essential writing snacks?

Buttered crumpets are one of my major food groups, but they're actually quite tricky to write with because the melted butter gets into the keyboard and then my butter-obsessed cat Franklin tries to eat it. My ultimate writing food is goats' cheese slathered on cherry scones. I cannot recommend that highly enough. Preferably consumed with a large pot of Lapsang Souchong while listening to Chopin and the sounds of a rainstorm in the background. That's my idea of perfect happiness.

This interview first appeared on Historiamag.com. Questions by Anna Mazzola.

SEE
WHAT
I
HAVE
DONE

SARAH
SCHMIDT

*I yelled 'Someone's killed father.' I breathed in kerosene air,
licked the thickness from my teeth.*

Just after 11am on 4th August 1892, the bodies of Andrew and
Abby Borden are discovered. He's found on the sitting room sofa,
she upstairs on the bedroom floor, both murdered with an axe.

It is younger daughter Lizzie who is first on the scene, so it is Lizzie
who the police first question, but there are others in the household
with stories to tell: older sister Emma, Irish maid Bridget, the girls'
Uncle John, and a boy who knows more than anyone realises.

In a dazzlingly original and chilling reimagining of this most
notorious of unsolved mysteries, Sarah Schmidt opens the door to
the Borden home and leads us into its murkiest corners, where
jealousies, slow-brewed rivalries and the darkest of thoughts reside.

The clock on the mantel ticked ticked.

'[A] seminal voice of the future . . . a dark, dense visceral ride that
proves that this former librarian could be on course to become one
of the breakout writers of the decade' *Stylist*

'[A] gory and gripping debut' *Observer*

ISBN 978 1 4722 4087 3

TINDER
PRESS

A
PLACE
CALLED
WINTER

PATRICK
GALE

Harry Cane has followed tradition at every step, until an illicit affair forces him to abandon the golden suburbs of Edwardian England and travel to the town of Winter in the newly colonised Canadian prairies. There, isolated in a beautiful but harsh landscape, Harry embarks on an extraordinary journey, not only of physical hardship, but also of acute self-discovery.

'Gale's confident, supple prose expresses the labour and hardship that toughen Harry's body as they calm his mind . . . Harry Cane is one of many, the disappeared who were not wanted by their families or their societies and whose stories were long shrouded with shame. This fascinating novel is their elegy' *Guardian*

'Gale's novels are imbued with clear-eyed psychological truths navigating the emotional landscape of characters it is impossible not to care about deeply. Sensitive and compelling' *Irish Times*

'A mesmerising storyteller; this novel is written with intelligence and warmth' *The Times*

ISBN 978 1 4722 0531 5

TINDER
PRESS

Mussolini's ISLAND

SARAH DAY

Non mollare. Never give up.

Italy, 1939. Francesco has been imprisoned on the tiny island of San Domino, among a group of men that include his lovers, friends and enemies. Certain one of their number has betrayed them all to the fascist police, they are determined to find out who.

Before long Francesco meets Elena, a young island girl desperate to escape her cloistered existence. Dazzled by the beautiful young man, she cannot help but pin all her hopes on him. When Elena discovers the truth about the prisoners, the fine line between love and hate pulls her towards an act that can only have terrible consequences for all.

'Impressive . . . Day handles her plot with great dexterity'
The Sunday Times

'A fascinating debut . . . Day is a talent to watch' *The Times*

'A genuine standout amongst literary debuts. This complex, brave and powerful novel, both tender and hard-hitting, features fine writing and a transporting sense of place'
Isabel Costello

ISBN 978 1 4722 3820 7

TINDER
PRESS

You are invited to join us behind the scenes at Tinder Press

TINDER PRESS

To meet our authors, browse our books
and discover exclusive content on our
blog visit us at

www.tinderpress.co.uk

For the latest news and views from the team
Follow us on Twitter

@TinderPress